AMANDA PELLEGRINO

Smile and Look Pretty

PARK
ROW
BOOKS

PARK™
ROW
BOOKS™

Recycling programs for this product may not exist in your area.

ISBN-13: 978-0-7783-1112-6

Smile and Look Pretty

Copyright © 2022 by Amanda Pellegrino

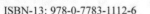

This is a work of fiction. Names, characters, places and incidents are either the product of the author's imagination or are used fictitiously. Any resemblance to actual persons, living or dead, businesses, companies, events or locales is entirely coincidental.

Park Row Books
22 Adelaide St. West, 41st Floor
Toronto, Ontario M5H 4E3, Canada
ParkRowBooks.com
BookClubbish.com

Printed in Italy by Grafica Veneta

To all the assistants I've met along the way.

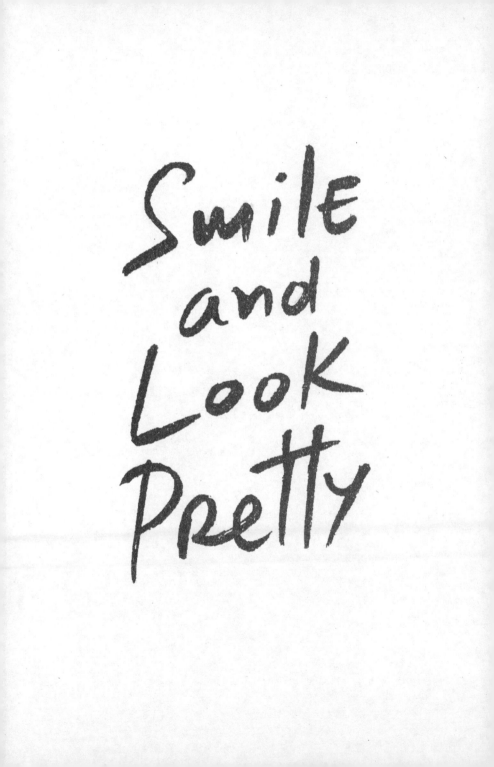

1

The signs were always there. He was late to a few meetings. He started happy hour at 2:00 p.m. He promoted from within.

The signs weren't noticeable at first. Until they were.

He was late to Marjorie's meetings, not Ben's. He offered scotch on the rocks to the guys. Most of his former male assistants were now editors.

It took years of working with him for Cate to learn those things. To realize they were signs.

But he had a reputation. *That* she knew from the beginning.

"You'll need a thick skin," he'd said on her first day. A warning.

She didn't extend him the same courtesy.

CATE COULD TELL YOU every book Larcey Publishing had ever released in its twenty-year history, and how old she had been when she first read it. The red LP stood out on all the spines in her dad's "home office," which was really the walk-in closet of her parents' bedroom converted into a small library lined with bookshelves, the clothing rails outfitted with a plank of painted wood to form a desk. When she got home from school, she'd sneak into her parents' room and read whatever book was on her dad's nightstand that week—no matter how age inappropriate the title. By the time she was ten, she knew she wanted to spend her life helping people tell stories. Important stories that no one would hear otherwise.

Matthew Larcey was a literary prodigy, not just to her dad, but to the world. Before he was thirty, he was known as the next Maxwell Perkins and by thirty-five he used that acclaim to start his own publishing house. Jobs there were the only ones Cate applied to during her senior year of college. She started as a production assistant ten days after graduation, and when the position of Matt's executive assistant opened a year later, she was the first to apply.

Matt's assistant at the time was a lovely girl from Texas named Eleanor, who tried and failed to suppress her Southern accent. (Cate later learned Matt forbid *y'all* from conversations. *Sigh.*) She interviewed Cate in a conference room with dull gray walls and two suicide-proof windows that looked out onto Sixth Avenue, forty-nine flights below. Cate wore her go-to black dress with a leather trim and had prepped in the bathroom a few minutes before: whispering her elevator pitch while applying more mascara; detailing her current responsibilities as an assistant while running some Moroccan oil through her frizzy hair; listing her favorite books while swapping out flats and a cardigan for heels and a blazer.

Twenty minutes into the interview, Matt Larcey walked in, wearing jeans and an AC/DC T-shirt with a small hole in the neck. Eyes wide, Cate and Eleanor watched him slowly sit down at the opposite side of the long conference table, typing on his phone. Despite having worked there for a year, Cate had never met the company's founder. He wasn't good-looking in the traditional sense—he was far too old for Cate anyway—but his salt-and-pepper hair paired with his tailored jeans emitted a kind of effortless power that Cate found enigmatic. She felt reassured knowing he had smile lines. Maybe it meant he wasn't as difficult as his reputation implied.

Eleanor's gaze darted to Matt and then back to Cate. "Um, as I was saying—"

"Did you tell her why you're being replaced?" he interrupted, looking up at them. His phone buzzed against the table four times while Eleanor went as red as the LP on the company's logo.

"I wasn't available enough," she said quietly.

"Be specific."

Eleanor took a long breath and offered Cate a tight-lipped smile. "I was on vacation and missed an urgent email."

Cate wanted to crawl under the table and come back when the tension was gone.

"If I'm working, you're working," Matt said. "That's the deal."

Seems logical, Cate thought. *Sign*.

"I know why you're here." He looked at Cate with an arched brow. "You're a *reader*. Right? That's what your Twitter bio says? You want to publish something that matters. The next great American novel, a book that will change the course of literature forever."

Eleanor seemed to be shrinking in front of them, getting smaller and smaller with every word.

"If that's what gets you through the day, great," Matt continued. "By all means, try to find the next Zadie Smith. If you play by the rules, maybe you will. But there are a lot of others out there who would kill for this job. So don't think you'll get any favors. If you earn the book, you'll get the book. Otherwise it will be you here picking out your own successor."

When Eleanor appeared at Cate's cubicle a few weeks later,

offering her the job, Cate immediately accepted. Because she *was* a reader. She *did* want to find the next great American novel. And, despite its founder's reputation, Larcey Publishing was the best place to do that.

EXACTLY TWO YEARS LATER, Cate sat at her desk in the forty-ninth floor bullpen, moving her eyes slowly across the floor-to-ceiling color-coded bookshelves packed with LP titles, thinking about how she was officially the longest lasting assistant in Larcey's history. When she had first started, each day she would look up from her desk at the wall of books in awe, like a tourist admiring the Chrysler Building, and dream about the day books she discovered and edited would join those shelves. Now, she had trouble remembering why she wanted to work there so badly in the first place.

She let out a deep breath. A wall of color-coded bookshelves was pretty to look at until you realized how painful it was to put together.

The executive assistants' desks were located in the EAB, or Elusive Assistant Beau monde, as Cate called it before she got the job with Matt. It actually stood for Executive Assistant Bullpen, but hardly anyone knew that. To Finance they were Evil Annoying Babies; to editors, Eager Ass-kissing Brown-nosers; and to Marketing, Expendable Agenda Builders. Whatever they were called, she was one of them. In the center of the rectangular room were two circular velvet couches around a glass coffee table with a bouquet of flowers Cate was somehow in charge of buying and maintaining each week. Lining the perimeter of the room were seven desks, perfectly positioned outside each boss's glass office so that each assistant was always being watched. Like fish in a bowl.

Cate glanced over her shoulder toward the shadows behind the now-curtained glass wall of Matt's office, listening to the mumbles of the third editor in two months getting fired, and wondered—as they all did at that point—when *she* should expect the email from HR inviting her to meet them in Matt's office at 6:30 p.m. on a Thursday.

Lucy, the CFO's assistant, wheeled her chair toward Cate. "Maggie, huh?" she said, folding her long blond hair behind her ears as if that would help her gossip better.

"Seems that way," Cate responded.

"Do you know what happened? I thought the self-help category was doing well."

Cate shrugged. "I'm not sure." She tried to look busy, maximizing and minimizing documents, opening and closing her calendar. Lucy was a great work wife, but she only got the job because her third cousin twice removed was Stephen King's neighbor or something. This made her a "must hire," thus untouchable. And Lucy knew it. She was more often found scooting across the bullpen in her white wheelie chair spreading rumors than actually working.

"Of course you know, Cate. You're probably on the HR email."

As Matt's assistant, Cate was on all his emails. About the rounds of golf he planned next week. About every book that each editor wanted to acquire this season. About all the firings. She knew that Maggie, a self-help editor, was being fired for considering a position at Peacock Press. Not only were they Larcey's main competitor, but Cate once heard a rumor that Matt dated its publisher in college, and she broke up with him in favor of his rugby-playing roommate. Either way, the rivalry seemed personal. They had offered Maggie $10K more and a nearly unlimited budget to acquire all the self-help books she could get her hands on. Cate knew everything. And that power was not something she was about to give up for Lucy. It was all she had.

"I guess self-help isn't doing as well as we thought," Cate said.

Before Lucy could reply, Maggie threw open Matt's door. The entire room started furiously typing as Maggie stomped past the EAB, two suited HR reps scurrying behind her. Lucy picked up the first paper she could find on Cate's desk and examined it so closely you'd think she'd just discovered the Rosetta Stone.

As soon as Maggie was out of earshot, Lucy said, "God, that was awkward." She lowered her voice to a conspiratorial whisper. "I heard she's going to Peacock."

"Do you really think it's Peacock?" Spencer Park whispered from his desk. "What, are they trying to poach everyone?"

"Poaching the people you want is more cost-effective than buying a company and paying for all the people you don't," Lucy responded. Cate could have sworn Lucy's head cocked toward Matt's office for the latter part of that statement.

Lucy returned to her desk and everyone went back to normal until a few moments later, when the heavy glass door behind her opened again. Cate didn't need to turn around to know it was Matt leaving. Her back might be facing his office all day, but she knew his movements by heart. In the same way, she imagined, he probably knew hers.

Matt moseyed to the front of her desk, moving his worn, expensive leather briefcase from his right hand to his left. He'd been kayaking that weekend, and he always got blisters on his dominant hand when he kayaked. Cate hated that she knew that. "Why are you still here?" he asked, as if his *I'm working, you're working, that's the deal* speech didn't play on a loop in her head 24/7. As if that wasn't why she kept her phone on loud all the time, why she woke up panicking in the middle of the night about missing an email, and why she was that girl who showed up to bars on Saturdays hiding her laptop in her purse.

"Just finishing up some work." Cate glanced at her nearly

empty inbox. She was supposed to be on her way to The Shit List, a much-needed weekly vent session with her friends. Instead, she was going to be late. Not that that was unusual for her. If Matt was there, Cate was there, after all.

He looked at Cate, then at the other assistants, all furiously typing again to seem occupied. "Looks like everyone else is working a lot harder than you are right now."

Well, I'm talking to you, Cate wanted to say. *I stopped typing to talk to you.*

What actually came out of her mouth was, "Have a good night."

She watched him walk across the EAB and offer a wave and a smile to three executive assistants standing at the bookshelf, peeling some titles off the wall. "You all work too hard. This place would be in shambles without you," he said to them before turning the corner toward the elevator bank.

After answering a few more emails, Cate poured some whiskey into her Bitches Get Stuff Done mug, grabbed her Board Meeting Makeup Kit out of the bottom drawer of her desk and walked into the bathroom. She was already going to be fifteen minutes late to The Shit List; what was another fifteen to look presentable and rub some slightly off-colored concealer on the under-eye circles that seemed to grow darker throughout the day?

She had discovered the necessity of a makeup kit on her second day as Matt's assistant. He had a board meeting, which was one of the only times she saw him in a suit.

"At exactly four fifteen, I need you to come into the meeting and bring me a cup of coffee," he said. "Just put it in front of me and walk out. Don't look at me. Don't look at anyone. Just in and out. And, you know—" he looked her up and down "—look…*presentable.*"

Cate could feel her cheeks flame as he walked away. She

didn't wear a lot of makeup, but she did always at least look *presentable* for work.

"Here," said the CMO's assistant at the time. She dropped a small pink-and-white Lilly Pulitzer bag on Cate's desk. "That's code for *put on some makeup.*"

"I have makeup on." Cate rubbed her cheek as if the pressure from her fingers could force blush to suddenly appear.

She nudged the bag forward. "Not the kind men notice."

Reluctantly, Cate unzipped it and inside found one of everything: powder foundation, mascara, eyeliner, eye shadow, blush, red lipstick. No variety. Bare minimum to look like the maximum.

"Put it on my desk when you're done. You should keep a board meeting kit here, too. This won't be the only time you'll need it."

After two years of board, author, and literary agent meetings, dropping things off at home for his kid, picking his wife up in the lobby, and countless other occasions for which Cate was told to "look presentable," getting ready for margaritas with her friends was the only time she used the kit to show herself off, rather than be shown off.

Happy two-year-work-aversary, Cate thought to herself as she put her makeup bag back in her desk. She took another look at the bookshelf on her way out. *Two years too many.*

THE WEEKLY CALENDAR invite for The Shit List pinged on Cate's phone as she darted up the Union Square subway staircase. The late May humidity combined with 6-train rush hour crowd left small beads of sweat on her upper lip and made her curls wild and frizzy. She passed the produce market closing up shop for the night and the men playing chess under the streetlights.

When Cate arrived at Sobremesa, she waved at the hostess

and then at their favorite bartender as she beelined past the crowded bar to join everyone at their usual booth in the back. Sobremesa was a strange place: corporate but lowbrow. That was strategic. Find a bar where they were the only group under forty so no one around would recognize their bosses' names when Lauren said Pete, an Emmy-winning screenwriter, had been avoiding her all day; or Max complained that Richard, a morning news anchor, had stared at her butt for the entire live shoot; or Olivia yelled about Nate, a washed-up actor who refused to realize he was no long relevant. They didn't need their work gossip on Page Six.

Cate stopped when she saw the three of them in their usual spot, laughing at something Olivia said, a half-empty pitcher of spicy margaritas moving between them. Lauren was squinting through her black-rimmed glasses, always refusing to consider a new prescription until she got promoted and could afford the co-pay. Olivia's topknot bounced side to side on her head as she spoke enthusiastically with her hands, one of her dramatic tendencies as a budding actress. Max sat in the corner, plucking salt crystals off the rim of her glass and licking them off her pointer finger.

"Wow," Lauren said when she spotted Cate.

"What?" Cate sank into the booth next to her. Lauren was making too much eye contact, the way she did when she was annoyed. Max poured the remainder of the pitcher into a fourth glass and pushed it toward Cate.

Lauren took a long sip from the tiny straw before saying, "Nice shirt."

Shit. Cate was wearing Lauren's top. The black T-shirt she told Lauren she'd wash and return to her closet three wears before. The one that now had semipermanent white deodorant circles under the armpits and was ever so slightly stretched out around the chest to fit Cate's larger cup size. "Sorry," she said to Lauren, who would hold a grudge until the freshly cleaned and folded shirt was back in her dresser. It would be at least a month before Cate could borrow anything from Lauren again, which was a bummer because she'd had her eye on a black pleated midiskirt for a date next week.

"Whatever," Lauren said with a sigh. "Should we just start?" She motioned toward the waitress and, when she arrived, ordered another pitcher of margaritas in Spanish.

In the center of the table was a small stack of cash to which Cate added her five-dollar contribution. She ripped a napkin into quarters and handed them out, scribbling onto the thin paper, the words bleeding together. *I booked Matt's $37,000 first-class tickets for his family's Kenyan safari an hour after realizing that unless I get a raise or my student loans disappear into the ether, I can't afford to go home to Illinois for Thanksgiving for the fourth year in a row.* Then she crossed out the latter half. No one she knew could ever afford to leave New York then, which was why the four of them always ended up doing Friendsgiving instead. It wasn't the same as cooking with her mom and then watching her dad unbutton his pants to fall asleep in his La-Z-Boy in front of the football game, but it was something.

After everyone finished scribbling on their napkins, the storytelling began.

Lauren complained about wheeling an industrial printer covered in blue tarp from the writers' trailer to Pete's trailer parked four long city avenues away during a thunderstorm. Then, upon showing up to work drenched, was asked by one of the writers to get coffee for everyone since "she was already wet."

Olivia had spent an entire day this week trying to sneak into the W Hotel Residences by schmoozing a young security guard so that she could do Nate's laundry there because he liked the smell of their detergent. "It's The Laundress," Olivia said, rubbing her temples as if the mere mention of the brand's name gave her a headache. "It's what he uses too. Bought it for him myself. But he *insists* it's different."

Max had to pretend Sheena's five-year-old son was hers so she could pick up his ADD medication before the anchor's weekend getaway to a resort in New Mexico. The pharmacist had seemed skeptical, but Max couldn't return to the newsroom without it. "I made a comment questioning how we still live in a world where young motherhood is challenged," Max said. The pharmacist had stopped asking questions.

The best part about their four-year friendship, Cate found, was the lack of explanations. They didn't have to preface names in their stories with "my boss" or "my friend" or "the cashier at my bodega." They never needed to fill anyone in on what they missed. Because they didn't miss anything. They knew everything about each other's lives. Cate knew that Lauren hadn't brought a guy home in at least a year and hadn't had sex in at least that long as well. She knew that Olivia rolled her eyes at her Southern Peachtree roots but would secretly perk up whenever a familiar accent was within earshot, reminding her of home. And Cate knew that Max's parents wielded enough old money power and privilege to get her promoted anywhere, but Max insisted on earning it herself.

Knowing everything about her friends also meant knowing everything about their bosses. Lauren's boss kept bottles of tequila, whiskey, and gin underneath the couch in his trailer. Cate could tell by looking at a paparazzi photo of Olivia's boss in *People* Magazine whether it was a coincidental shot or he had Olivia tip them off about his whereabouts. Cate could recognize by Max's outfit whether she expected Richard, the handsy morning anchor, to be in the office that day.

Once all the stories were told and the napkin scraps circled the tea light on the table like a strange sacrificial ceremony,

Lauren said, "Can I make the executive decision that Olivia wins?" Everyone agreed; folding your boss's stiff boxers, regardless of how good they apparently smelled afterward, should win you more than twenty dollars.

Cate took the piece of napkin in her hand and looked down at her chicken scratch handwriting. This was her life. These were the things she spent her days doing. It was her two-year anniversary as Matt's assistant, and the day went on just like any other. Cate wasn't expecting a cake with her face on it or anything. But some kind of acknowledgment would have been appreciated. Something that said *couldn't do it without you* or *I hope these two years have been worth it* or, at least, a simple *thank you*.

What did Cate learn about the publishing industry from booking Matt's vacations? What did she learn by organizing the papers on his desk in alphabetical order? What did she learn from spending a week every November opening up his cabin in Vermont for the season? She *did* learn that he spent $600 every year on a new Canada Goose coat; that the couch in their basement was incredibly uncomfortable to sleep on; and that his wife kept a dildo in the bottom drawer of her nightstand (but what did Matt expect, sending his poorly-paid assistant to his rich vacation house?).

And what had happened while she'd been 340 miles north, spraying salt all over the cabin's front walkway? Spencer filled in on Matt's desk and was asked to "sit in on" three author meetings and one board meeting. She'd met only one author in two years, and the closest she came to board meetings was delivering coffee with strict instructions not to speak. Did anyone tell Spencer to "look presentable"?

For the last two years, Cate had only focused on what was at stake: money, access to stamps for mailing rent checks, free food after author meetings, a foot in the door for her dream job. But it was starting to feel...*fine*. Uninspiring. Empty. What was she working toward?

Cate took one last look at the napkin before dipping the bottom right corner into the tea light's flame. She held it between her fingers, watching Matt Larcey's name burn in her hand as the text slowly turned to ashes and fell onto the wooden table.

After she swept the ashes to the floor, Cate held up her margarita. "Here's to the day when we can make money without doing something degrading."

Their glasses met in the middle, and Cate looked at her friends, the assistants busting their asses, making the rules from behind the scenes. What if they all got together? What if they called bullshit?

What if they all said no?

Lauren rushed down Mercer Street toward Pete's favorite coffee shop, fumbling to take out the twenty dollars he had given her while balancing her phone between her shoulder and ear as she waited for Cate to answer. Why was it that people only asked for coffee five minutes before they needed it? They never left enough time for her to actually get the order. Especially the frilly stuff that writers drank, which begged another question: Why couldn't rich people ever get a regular coffee? Were their palates too sophisticated for pour-overs?

Lauren told herself she would never get that way. She was a regular coffee girl for life, just like her boss, Pete. As the head writer of a workplace comedy where the cast was too hot to be believable, Pete had a big job, which meant she had a big job as his assistant—mostly because it was a direct line to becoming a writer herself. Plenty of writers she knew had been given an episode to write as an assistant—a test run, basically, to give them a credit without having to pay them a proper writers' salary. If the episode was good, then they'd get promoted. From the outside, it was a clear ladder to exactly where she'd been trying to get since she decided to take on $85,000 in student loans to study screenwriting at NYU.

At least, that was what Lauren had thought when she took the job three years ago. Now she realized the ladder was a trick. Apparently, that "direct line" was longer for some than for others.

As her call to Cate went to voice mail, her phone started vibrating against her cheek. Her mom's name coupled with a few kissy-face emojis appeared on the screen, so she clicked the green answer button.

"Hey, Mom—"

"Háblame. I'm going to the train."

Lauren let out a disgruntled huff. Her mom always called when she was bored and walking the ten minutes from her apartment to the subway. As if Lauren could just drop everything to chat in the middle of the day. "Mom, I can't talk right now. I'm at work—"

"What's wrong, cariño? You sound stressed."

She took a deep breath and counted to ten. It was not her mother's fault that she was frustrated with Pete. Her mother was not the right person to vent to right now. "Sorry, I'm fine. Just have a lot going on today." She almost laughed at the irony in her own excuse. That getting coffee was a lot going on.

Her mom paused, skeptical. "I'll let you go, then, since you're so busy you can't even keep me company for a few minutes."

"Dinner this weekend?" Lauren asked.

She could perfectly picture her mother walking quickly down Broadway in Morningside Heights, twisting a finger in her dark hair and smiling at the success of her guilt trip. It had been at least two months since she saw her mom last, which was admittedly too long considering they lived one crosstown bus and three short subway stops away.

"What a great idea," her mother quipped. "Unless you're vegetarian again, then don't bother."

"That was one month, like, five years ago, Mom." Lauren shook her head, laughing. "I'll talk to you later."

"Okay, baby."

As Lauren hung up, she started picturing her mom walking to the train alone, then working the hotel check-in desk alone, then going home alone, and the guilt started building. She should bring her mom flowers this weekend. She'd like flowers. She deserved flowers.

Lauren's phone was vibrating again, this time, with Cate's name. "Hey, what's up?" Lauren answered.

There was silence on the other end. "*You* called *me*."

"Oh, right." As Lauren joined the end of the line outside the coffee shop's ordering window, she remembered why she had vent-called Cate. "Pete asked me to get everyone coffee, again. I feel like he has no idea what I do for him." It was a thought she had often, but rarely vocalized. Her job operated entirely under the radar, and she was only acknowledged if something went wrong. If she did everything right—which, of course, she *always* did—then Pete's life continued swimmingly, all his meetings on time, his coffee hot, his lunch vegan-certified, no questions asked.

"He obviously does," Cate said. "And at least you're not soaking wet this time."

"Okay, yes," Lauren admitted. "But I'm swamped. With actual work. Like fact-checking and setting up the office for next season. And I don't know how I'll ever be able to talk to him about giving me an episode if, after three years, he still only sees me as his coffee-getting assistant."

Cate sighed. "He knows, Lauren," she said. "You just need to talk to him and stop avoiding the conversation."

"Hold on a second." Lauren approached the coffee shop

window and gave her order to the hot tanned guy whose name tag read, of course, *Krew*. "Can I pay for all of these with this—" she handed over her company card "—and pay for one of the iced coffees with this." She slipped Pete's twenty dollars onto the counter.

"Why are you paying for one separately?" Cate asked.

Lauren accepted her card back and tucked all the change in her pocket—knowing that when she tried to give it back, Pete would call it her delivery fee and let her keep it—and backed up to the curb to wait for her order. "I'm not eligible to expense my own coffee without asking the studio first, so Pete usually pays for mine." Expecting the studio in LA to answer emails during traditionally accepted NYC coffee times was as unrealistic as expecting Pete to answer emails during his fantasy football draft.

There was a beat of silence on the other end. "Seriously?" Cate finally said. "This is why you never win The Shit List. He *gets* you coffee, too. I could tell you how many individual grains of sugar Matt likes in his, but he probably doesn't even realize I drink the stuff."

"Lauren Barrero," the barista yelled. Lauren couldn't help but cringe at the way her last name sounded with hard *R*s. She collected the coffee trays, balancing her phone between her ear and shoulder again while Cate continued to rant about Matt.

As she walked back toward set, Lauren spotted the back of someone familiar—a man walking ten feet in front of her. Her heart stopped. The dark spot at the nape of his neck, a bump of spine that jutted out just below it. The tag peeking out of the collar of his white T-shirt. Then his ears: long, thin, wider at the top. The mop of blond hair.

Lauren could almost see his pores.

Her hands went numb, and forty-five dollars' worth of coffee crashed onto the ground with the power of a nuclear blast, spilling all over the sidewalk, her sneakers, her pants, her phone, just as the man stopped on the curb and looked in her direction, quickly glancing for cars before jogging across the street.

Seeing his face, she realized it wasn't James.

Lauren stood still for a beat to catch her breath. She looked down at the coffee on the ground. One cappuccino, two soy lattes, two iced coffees, one matcha tea, one espresso, one latte with almond milk. All blended into a brown nothingness, seeping slowly into the concrete.

It wasn't him, she repeated to herself.

Once she could breathe normally again, she picked up her phone—Cate had already hung up—and then slowly collected the cups scattered on the sidewalk. She threw them in the garbage can on the corner and walked back to the coffee shop, still in a daze. She ordered everything again and paid with her personal credit card—the studio would never let her submit two identical receipts with a five-minute time stamp difference—and told herself she'd worry about how to pay for them later.

It wasn't him, she thought again. But she was always waiting for the day it would be. A city of more than eight million, Manhattan had a keen way of making sure you eventually ran into people you didn't want to see.

FIFTY BLOCKS NORTH in Midtown, Max was also in line for coffee, this time at Starbucks because Sheena liked the presumed hustle and bustle associated with holding a Venti cup and clamoring on her headset. "Rough day, huh?" a stage manager would comment to Max, cautiously watching Sheena nearly spill the contents of the cup while yelling at some network executive about her airtime compared to Richard's. Max would nod and agree, because a rough day for Sheena meant a rough day for her, too.

After grabbing the order and returning to the Broadcast Center, Max could hear Sheena calling for her as she made a left out of the lobby into *The Good Morning Show*'s entry hall.

She stopped to gather herself, wiping the sweat off her forehead and then rubbing her hands on her jeans. Max looked at the posters of Sheena and Richard lining the hallway walls, one for each of the eight years they'd worked as anchors on the show together. As she pushed through the heavy glass door into the broadcast's newsroom, Max could feel Richard's gaze on her ass even from the posters.

The studio was set up with the anchor desk in the center of the room in front of large windows where people could view the broadcast from the street. Around the perimeter of the room were a few desks and printers where the assistants sat during the broadcast. Whenever the camera was on a single shot of Richard, viewers could see the back of Max's head on live television.

"Coffee," Sheena yelled from her seat behind the anchor desk as she stared down at her phone. She was the kind of naturally gorgeous that made Max wonder how they could even be from the same planet. Her brown skin glowed without one acne scar, her long dark locks could hold a curl for days, and she basically lived at Barry's Bootcamp every afternoon. She even kept ten-pound weights under her chair to sneak in some bicep curls during commercial breaks whenever she wore a sleeveless dress on air.

"I have it here," Max said, quickly walking to the desk. Out of her phone case she pulled a worn paint swatch offering five shades of brown—saddle, log cabin, autumn breeze, coppertone, caramel corn—and lightly placed it on the desk beside the coffee. The strip of paper was wrinkled and bent, some of the colors cracking the same way they would on a wall. Sheena glanced up from Twitter for just long enough to point to autumn breeze. Max poured the side of almond milk into the Venti cup oh so slowly, bit by bit, stopping every few seconds to stir, waiting for the milk to fully integrate before comparing its color to the paint swatch. She continued that routine until the color matched autumn breeze: what Sheena deemed to be the perfect shade of coffee for the day. Max secured the lid and backed away, letting out a deep breath as Sheena took a satisfied sip.

When Max had started at *The Good Morning Show*, the first thing Sheena ever said to her was, "I don't have time to say please or thank you, so assume it's assumed. You understand?"

Max had nodded, but she decidedly did *not* understand and spent the next ten minutes crying in the basement bathroom, knowing she wanted the job but wondering what exactly she'd gotten herself into. Just the time it took Sheena to say that sentence could have been a few weeks' worth of pleases and thank yous. The sentence had remained true since.

Max soon learned a lot of things were assumed with Sheena, as well as the show's other coanchor, Richard. He was in his fifties, with slightly graying hair, a set of kind blue eyes, and a smile that made people believe everything he said—all useful traits for a news anchor. That was how he moved up quickly at CBS, until he got the coveted *Good Morning Show* anchor spot ten years ago and became America's dad, welcoming everyone into their morning with a perfect smile. He was lovely until the cameras shut off. Max had always thought Sheena was such an asshole because she never got the kind of fame that Richard did. She'd been coanchoring with him for eight years and she played the part: she wore the skintight solid-color dresses, got a blowout and full makeup done, paid for manicures and pedicures and full-body laser hair removal. But she was always just "the other CBS anchor."

Sheena had once said to Max, "Two years, that's the perfect amount of time to be an assistant." *Well*, Max thought as she sat down at her desk, *it's been three years and three weeks and no one, including me, has mentioned I'm past my deadline.* She'd been itching for a promotion to associate producer, but there was one unavoidable problem: she was a woman. And Richard's assistant, Charlie, was a man. He was going to get promoted first. That was how it worked around here.

"Max!" Sheena stared down at her coffee, holding the lid in her hand. "What the fuck is this?"

Aware everyone in the room was looking at her, Max scampered to the desk like a mouse running toward a trap. "I'm sorry?" Max peeked into the cup. Based on Sheena's reaction, she expected a fly or a finger to be floating on the autumn breeze surface, but instead there was nothing. Not even a stray hair.

"There's too much sugar," Sheena said, as if Max should have gleaned that from looking at the liquid.

Max glanced from Sheena to the coffee, then back to Sheena again. "There's no sugar. It's just black with almond milk."

"There's too much sugar. I can feel it on my teeth." Her tongue made a lapping sound as she ran it over her pearly whites. She pushed the cup away and Max managed to grab it mere seconds before it could tip over and drench all the scripts she'd painstakingly color-coded the night before.

"Do you want me to get you a new one?"

"Obviously," Sheena said. "I can't drink this. Less sugar, more caffeine."

This is fine, this is fine, this is fine, Max repeated to herself as she took Sheena's coffee off the stage, past the crew's wide-eyed stares, through the newsroom, up the hallway flanked with pictures of her bosses, out one door, through another, down a carpeted hallway, and into the moldy basement bathroom, which used to attach to a company gym that didn't exist anymore. While it was mostly now used to store cots and old tapes of interviews and broadcasts, this bathroom was also the perfect soundproof sanctuary for all emotionally and physically exhausted assistants. Max carefully placed Sheena's coffee cup on the floor and let out three long, therapeutic screams. She then picked the disgraced coffee cup off the floor and straightened her blouse before exiting the room.

As she walked down the basement hallway, she spotted two pages in their uniform of black pants and white button-downs, CBS badges hanging on lanyards around their necks. "I can't believe we're here, in this building," one particularly young-looking page whispered. "We could work here one day."

"We officially have our foot in the door," the other page answered enthusiastically.

As she passed them, Max thought back to when she first met Cate, Olivia, and Lauren four years ago as part of the page program right after college. She remembered every wide-eyed, excited conversation in the beginning: too blinded by the dream to see the reality, more than willing to work hard and get paid almost nothing in exchange for "experience" and a paragraph on their résumés. The four of them had grown close quickly because they all knew exactly what they wanted to do, which was rare for twenty-two-year-olds. They had wanted so badly to work in the industries they now found themselves complaining about at a weekly margarita night. Outside looking in, things were fancy and fun—having crazy hours and attending fun parties and meeting celebrities—but once you were inside, you started to see the darkness. Then three years later you were somehow a part of that darkness, perpetuating it, letting others blindly enter and figure things out for themselves the same way you had to.

She could have told the pages all the secrets: the bathrooms on the east wing of the fifth floor were best for pooping; the croutons in the cafeteria were always stale; befriend the security guards because they knew everything. Do not work for Richard Bradley.

But the pages were already up the stairs and out of sight. And Max kept her mouth shut. As everyone did. As everyone *always* did.

3

Cate hadn't thought about her revelation during The Shit List since they left the bar that night. The idea had quickly moved into a drawer in the cobwebby part of her head filled with all the other things it was probably better to forget. She was an assistant. She had no leverage. She had nothing to say *no* to.

Surprisingly, it took only one week for Lauren to allow Cate full access to her closet again. That black midiskirt was hers. Paired with a simple white T-shirt and sneakers, she could wear it all day at work and then easily to her date later. Her New Year's resolution was to date more, and she had quickly come to understand that one shouldn't knock the online dating game until one tried it. The best part? Ghosting. It was so easy to bail last minute when Matt inevitably asked for something ridiculous. Once when she was walking to a sushi place to meet someone, Matt had called asking where his favorite Polo shirt was, and she had to hail a cab to his laundromat to get it for him. On her way to meet a date at his Midtown apartment for beers on his fire escape, Matt needed her to run to Restoration Hardware to take pictures of a couch his wife was considering for their living room. Seconds after planning a date night with another guy, Matt needed her to go up to his Vermont house that weekend and deal with a frozen pipe. None of the dates were rescheduled, none of the conversations continued. She Irish exited out of their lives as quickly as she'd entered. If Matt wasn't so technologically challenged, she'd assume he had her phone bugged with an alarm that alerted him any time she was thinking, in any capacity, about any man other than him.

So it was a miracle Cate made it all the way to the bar for her date with a new guy named Theo. She stood in the tiny vestibule and handed her ID to a very large man sitting on a very small stool. When she pushed through the heavy wooden door into the dimly lit bar, there were only three people inside, two of whom looked like they'd been sipping Guinnesses in those exact spots for approximately eighty years. The third guy, and the only one who could possibly own a smartphone with a dating app on it, was sitting by himself, reading David Sedaris. She'd read *all* of David Sedaris.

"A bow tie announces to the world that you can no longer get an erection," Cate quipped as she took the stool next to him, motioning toward the book.

Smiling, he dog-eared the page and closed it. "Even if this date is terrible, that will forever be the best opening line I've ever heard. Studies will be done on its perfection."

"I'm so glad you read that Sedaris book too, or else that would have been *very* embarrassing."

He laughed. "Well, at least I'm wearing a tie."

As Cate settled onto the flimsy wooden stool next to Theo, the older of the two gentlemen at the bar turned slightly and gave her a look that expressed both *who are you* and *why are you here* with the mere raise of a bushy gray eyebrow. Then she noticed the bow tie hanging gingerly below his neck, and she nearly fell backward off the stool.

"It's just a joke," Theo said to him loudly, offering her a stabilizing hand. "You know, just two joking kids here."

When the man finally turned back around, mumbling something surely obscene under his breath, Cate and Theo stared at each other, unsuccessfully trying to stifle their laughter.

The waiter dropped off the menu, which was a laminated piece of loose-leaf handwritten with their selection of beer, further cementing the vibe they were going for there.

"How the hell did you find this place?" Cate asked, once she calmed herself down. "It definitely wasn't on Yelp."

"I read the obituaries." Theo smiled. He had a quick wit. She liked that.

Considering Matt could interrupt at any moment, Cate wasted no time. Two drinks later, after learning Theo was a journalist, originally from New Hampshire, and had two brothers and a master's degree in political science from Columbia, she asked him to get out of there.

One cab ride later, she was taking off his tie, wrapping the silk around her own neck as they made out in the elevator on the way to his eighth-floor studio. *Oh, to have an elevator,* she found herself thinking on the way up. She shook her head and focused on the kissing. He was hot and well-read; she should not be thinking about building amenities.

Theo unlocked his door, and the first thing she noticed was the wall of factory windows, tinting the whole room silver in the moonlight. Actual moonlight in Manhattan. She followed him around expensive-looking furniture and a bookshelf filled with unorganized paperbacks, dropping her clothes with each step until they reached the bed in the darkest corner of the apartment.

She kissed him as they fell back onto the bed, her hands roving over his chest and back, memorizing muscles so sculpted it was as if Michelangelo himself had chiseled them. He turned her over and started kissing her neck and then—her phone rang.

"What?" Theo asked as she froze.

"My phone." She charged headfirst for her purse, flying off the bed and halfway across the room, desperate to answer before it went to voice mail. Matt hated voice mail. It meant she wasn't available. If she didn't find the damn phone, she'd be finding her replacement by morning.

She managed to answer on the last ring, completely out of breath. "Hello?"

"I need cupcakes," Matt responded. "For Henry's last day of school tomorrow."

Fuck you, she thought. *The cupcakes I reminded you about every day this week? The cupcakes that, when I asked about them this morning you said you "had it handled." Those cupcakes, by chance?*

"Right..." She couldn't find a pen in her purse. She was an aspiring editor. She always had a pen. Usually seven or eight, in fact, pooled next to a surplus of tampons at the bottom of every bag she owned.

"Here," Theo whispered, throwing a pen in her direction.

"Vegan, gluten-free, sugar-free, nut-free," Matt rattled off. "But still something eight-year-olds will want to eat..." Cate scribbled everything on her thigh, the only place she could reach on her body that was large enough for all the bullshit. "They need to be there by nine fifteen tomorrow morning," he continued. "Don't be late or you'll miss the party. You remember where his school is."

"I think so. Fourteenth and—"

He hung up before she finished. That wasn't a question, it was a statement. *I told you once so you must still remember.*

She threw her phone into her purse. It never got less weird to talk to her boss while she was naked. Especially because he had ample time for this conversation at work. During the day. Fully clothed.

"I think I need to go," she said, gathering her clothes around the room.

"Now? Really?"

"That was my boss," she said, trying not to whine. Trying not to seem like she was *complaining*. As much as she hated it, she thrived on it. The on-calls, late-night meetings, and overnight preps kept her going while simultaneously taking years off her life. Living in the city glorified that kind of thing, and Cate was nothing if not a wannabe New Yorker. The second she moved there from Illinois, it was clear: if you weren't working all the time, you were doing something wrong.

"It really can't wait?" Theo asked. "Can you do it in the morning?"

Cate sighed. "Nothing can ever wait with Matt Larcey."

"Not even twenty minutes?" He winked.

It was very hard to ignore the wink. Especially one done right. Theo did it right.

"I'm really sorry," she said, feeling genuinely bad.

"It's all right." He sat up in bed, sheets draped over his lap. "This isn't exactly how I imagined the night ending," he said with a half smile.

"Yeah, me neither," she responded, which was only a partial lie. It may not have been what she imagined, but, based on prior experience, it was what she should have expected.

"Good luck with the cupcakes."

"Thanks. Good luck with..." She looked down at the sheets. "That."

Theo laughed. "I'll be fine. I've got some practice."

So do I, she thought. *So do I.*

SEVEN HOURS LATER at 8:00 a.m., Cate was standing outside Vegan Lovelies Bakery exactly as it opened. She ordered the cupcakes and expensed them under Matt Personal. No one ever questioned the Matt Personal expenses, even though they were objectively things that should absolutely not be covered: his drunken cabs home from wifey date nights; his "coffee" that was actually a $61 full breakfast; the $2,000 bike repairs he blamed on "getting to work wear-and-tear." Rich people didn't pay for anything. That was how they stayed that way, apparently. But the one time Cate put a personal Uber on her company card by accident, she got an email from Finance two hours later asking her to write the company a check for $18.18.

She felt her phone buzzing in her bag and picked up on the second ring.

"Where are you?" Matt asked quickly, the sound of squealing children echoing in the background.

"I'm getting the cupcakes—"

"You're only getting them *now?* You're supposed to be here."

It was 8:10 a.m. "What do you mean?" she asked, trying to fold her pants up her leg to double-check her thigh notes.

"I said to be here by eight fifteen."

"You said nine fifteen."

"I said eight fifteen," he calmly screamed. His voice didn't rise when he was angry, but he talked quickly, every syllable coming out like a bullet. "Why would I say nine fifteen if I needed them at eight fifteen? Am I a fucking moron?"

Yes.

She finally gave up and pulled her pants down. Good thing she was wearing the extra holey underwear she should have thrown out in college. *Sorry everyone. Sorry soul, dignity, women everywhere.*

"What the hell are you doing?" the cashier asked.

She held the phone in one hand and gave him the *one min-*

ute finger while lifting her leg to try to read the blurred notes on her thigh.

G free.

Cupcake.

Sug free.

9:15 nut fr.

Vegan.

14 st.

Matt had said nine fifteen. She knew he'd fucking said nine fifteen. She would have had everything by eight fifteen if he had said eight fifteen. She put her leg down and pulled her pants up. *I'm not a moron either*, she thought. *I haven't worked two years and one week only to be fired over cupcakes.*

"Well, great," Matt huffed. "Now the kids won't have any dessert. Thank you. Appreciate the help."

"I'm sorry," she said instinctively. It was something about his tone, guilt mixed with rage. The kind of tone that immediately made her apologize without thinking. "I'm so sorry."

She felt like she was letting down every feminist who came before her. Every woman who chose not to move out of a man's way on the sidewalk, who protested when a man got credit for her idea, who lady-spread on the subway to make a point. Every woman consciously working to say sorry *less*.

She wanted to say, *I'm not sorry. You're wrong. You made a mistake. You refused to listen when I asked you six times if you had the cupcakes. You are a moron.*

Instead, she said, "I'll be there as fast as I can."

Silence.

He had hung up before the second sorry.

Cate grabbed the cupcakes and ran out of the store just as three empty cabs bolted down the street. She thought about chasing them, but knew she had no chance. And between morning Midtown traffic and incessant subway delays, she had one option. So, in her black pants and red tank top and Steve Madden heels she got for Christmas last year, she ran. Sprinted. Flew. Expertly maneuvered between tourists and businessmen. All while carrying two bags of motherfucking cupcakes.

Thirty blocks later, she was sweating through her bra and standing outside the massive, hulking mahogany door to the most expensive grade school in Manhattan. A huge brass lion knocker sat in its center, staring at her mockingly as if to say, *I'm worth more money than you have to your name.* Which wasn't wrong. Saving money was hard when she only made $500 more than her rent each month. And when her promised "bonus" last year turned out to be a $30 gift card to TGI Friday's.

"The Wright School," the receptionist said over an invisible intercom.

Cate found the button hidden on the side of the wooden door and pressed. "Delivery for Matt Larcey. Class 2-2."

"You can leave it there," she said quickly. "You're Cate, right? Mr. Larcey actually left a message for you."

"Should I come in and get it?" Cate asked.

"He said not to let you in."

Of course he did. Simply yelling at her about cupcakes was not humiliating enough. He needed to add this, too.

"I'll just read it," the receptionist said apologetically. *Don't shoot the messenger,* Cate reminded herself. If there was one thing she had learned as an assistant, it was that the messenger probably deserved better compensation and a massage, not to be shot. "He said, 'please leave the cupcakes there. The party is over. The children no longer need them. I'm writing all this down so I have a record of what was said. Details are clearly an issue for you. Please schedule a car to pick me up at eight fifty-five to go home, wait there, and bring me to the office at eleven thirty—" She paused for a beat, and Cate wondered if the situation was as awkward for the receptionist as it was for her. "Um... Can I just come out and give this note to you?"

Cate backed up from the mahogany and waited until a glass door disguised as a window slowly opened and the receptionist appeared, a tall, blonde twentysomething with legs for days.

"That's just for show," she said, nodding at the thick wooden door. "It's way too heavy to open." She handed Cate a ripped piece of purple craft paper. Matt's all-caps handwriting matched that on the Post-it notes of tasks he often threw onto Cate's keyboard as he left for the day. "I'm sorry about this." She offered a pitying smile.

Don't apologize for Matthew J. Larcey III. He's not worth it.

"Yeah," was all Cate could actually muster.

The receptionist leaned closer, slightly turning her back to the rich people chattering inside. "I'm sorry your boss is an asshole," she whispered. "Mine is too. This morning she basically told me that if I wanted to wear white pants, I should lose some weight first. 'White pants aren't flattering on thunder thighs,' were her actual words. Guess I'll go throw up now."

Well, at least Matt had never called her fat. "I'm Cate." She put her hand out.

"Lindsay."

It wasn't until that moment, as she shook hands with a no-longer-stranger on the side of a bustling Fourteenth Street, with cupcakes melting at her feet and the sun glaring in her eyes, that Cate remembered her Shit List revelation. What if they all said no?

Who would order their bosses' lunches and consolidate their receipts and set up their car service? Who would tell them what it meant when someone put a googly-eyed emoji in an email, or help them type out the long response to said email since they still used the pecking method? Who would roll their calls and book their flights and send birthday presents to everyone in their lives because assistants were the only ones who remembered the dates?

What kind of damage could they do?

SITTING NEXT TO Pete on the fake leather couch in his trailer, Lauren slid her phone into her purse on the floor. It was too early to deal with Cate's frantic texts, rambling on some nonsense about cupcakes and back muscles.

"I don't understand why he wants to keep it," Pete said, standing up and moving toward the strangest example of "movie magic" she'd ever seen: a fake head on a stick lying on the counter in front of them.

Pete was the epitome of a TV writer: haphazardly bearded with straggly brown hair, often found in a beanie and sneakers using the word "dude" too often. He'd be played by Seth Rogan in any rom-com: a little extra weight in the middle, with a revolving door of stunning girlfriends. Funny really did get you laid.

"I guess it'll be a conversation starter when people come to his office."

"A pretty gnarly one." He picked at the head's chalky gray hair, meticulously sprinkled with fake debris. In last season's finale, a character spent thousands of dollars on an exact replica of his head, for the sole purpose of a thirty-second prank on his coworker where he pretended he was decapitated by the office printer. To prep, the Hair and Makeup department had to mold a replica of the actor's head—down to his upper lip mole and stray eyebrow hairs. Now, that head was staring at her.

"It definitely wouldn't be my choice of desk decor," Lauren said. She didn't even like having it in the trailer. It had been an unwelcome lunch companion for a week since Lauren got an email from their network executive's assistant, asking for the head to be mailed to him as a souvenir to keep in his office. She had been storing it in the trailer for safekeeping until she could figure out how to ship it across the country. Did UPS have a box to check for "fake severed head"? Was it considered dangerous materials?

A knock on the open trailer door made her jump, and Pete waved the man inside. He was athletically built, with broad shoulders, a slim frame, and wiry yet muscled arms. When he smiled at her, maintaining eye contact in a way no man had in too long for her to admit, Lauren nearly had the wind knocked out of her.

"You found us," Pete said, shaking the man's hand. "This is my assistant, Lauren." He nodded in her direction. "Lauren, this is Owen."

Lauren seemed to be watching her own hand shake his. She wasn't making it do that. Her mind was completely empty.

"How'd the call go?" Pete asked. They exchanged a few back-and-forths, but Lauren wasn't listening, too busy staring at Owen's muscled arms and wondering what he looked like naked.

A few minutes later, she was alone again with Pete, not entirely convinced that wasn't a strange out-of-body sex daydream.

"You okay?" Pete asked, slowly sitting back down next to her.

She couldn't seem to form sentences in her brain. "Who was that?" Lauren finally managed.

Pete looked down at his phone. "That was Owen, the new writer I hired last week."

Lauren stared at him, but he wouldn't meet her eyes. Guilt was written all over his face. He wasn't just telling her that they had a new writer; he was telling her that that writer had taken her spot. Without saying anything else, he was telling her she was not going to write an episode this season. That she was going to be an assistant for another year. That she would continue to be a piece of furniture in the writers' room, only acknowledged when someone was wondering if an idea they pitched was racist. Because as the only non-white non-man in the room, she naturally represented all non-white non-men in the universe. Now she would get to do it for a whole other season. Great.

"I'm going to get some more coffee," she whispered, barely getting the words out before walking toward the door, tears threatening to boil over.

"I talked to the studio," he said quickly. She stopped in the doorway. "About getting you more money for this season."

She blinked back the tears and took a deep breath. She didn't want more money. Yes, it was helpful. Yes, she could pay off more of her student loans. But it was a temporary solution. What she needed was an episode, a writing credit. That would give her entry into the Writers Guild of America. Proper insurance. Access to managers and agents. *That* was what she needed. Not a raise born from guilt.

Lauren turned to face him. "Thanks, that's very nice of you." Her voice was emotionless, and she knew he could tell. She walked out of the trailer onto West Fourth Street, holding her breath until she got to the crosswalk at the corner when she'd allow herself to cry. She'd have three blocks to wallow and then she'd snap out of it and move on. But, for some reason, the tears never came. She wasn't upset. She was…disappointed. Like she wasn't valued. Like she was being taken advantage of. She was, again, feeling like she was such a good assistant that he'd never view her as anything else. Like she was being punished for being too good at her job.

She took her phone out of her bag and scrolled through the

day's texts from Cate to try to get her mind off of everything—
I'm going to murder Matt. The kind of murder with the icicle so
there's no evidence. Or maybe I'll copy a murder from this thriller
we just acquired. And then, everyone come over tomorrow night.
We have to talk.

Lauren responded with an emoji she wasn't even sure applied and then continued to the Craft Services table to get
herself, and only herself, some coffee.

The following afternoon, Cate was sure Matt was going to fire her. He took his phone off its hook, which meant he was not to be disturbed. Better than a tie on the doorknob, but not quite as good as simply sticking his head out of his office and saying "Hold my calls" like a normal person. If someone asked Cate a year ago what she thought he was doing in there during this time, she would have guessed napping or watching porn. But now she knew he was talking to HR.

Right on cue, the HR rep's shiny bald head appeared around the corner, reflecting the LED bulbs in the industrial-looking light fixtures above their desks.

"He's expecting me," he muttered once he reached Cate, his forehead shiny with a layer of sweat.

"Okay," she responded, motioning toward the office. The door wasn't even completely shut behind him when Lucy and Spencer appeared next to Cate's desk.

"Who is it this time?" Lucy asked.

Cate shrugged. This time she truly didn't know. She wasn't on that email. She didn't even know that Matt was meeting with HR until she tried to transfer a call from his wife, and it went straight to voice mail. That was a problem. Because the only firing email she could think of that she wouldn't be privy to was her own.

"We know you know," Spencer said. "Just tell me. Is it William? If my boss goes down then I go down, and I can't be unemployed right now. I just bought a couch, Cate. You know how expensive couches are?"

"Please." Lucy rolled her eyes at him. "You and William have nothing to worry about."

"What do you mean? This place is sinking."

"This *place* isn't sinking," Lucy said. "*Women* in this place are."

Spencer shook his head. "That's just a coincidence."

"You can't possibly be that dense."

As Spencer and Lucy continued arguing, Cate thought, again, about The Shit List. And about how one of the reasons Matt even got away with treating her like garbage was because of *this*—because she was so afraid of getting fired that whether he asked her for a manuscript to be read or a suit to be pressed, she would be the best damn reader or ironer on earth. Because the fear of losing her job was the most consistent thing about the job in the first place.

"It's probably me," Cate said, admitting for the first time that she, in fact, was not on the email. She was not in the know. She didn't have that power. "I fucked up the last day of school cupcakes. It seemed very last straw-y."

The whole EAB quieted down, the six other assistants looking at her, Larcey's longest-lasting assistant, their inadvertent leader. When you had the most powerful boss, then you were the most powerful assistant.

"Well, I gave Marjorie regular veggie cream cheese on her bagel instead of fat-free," Lucy said. "It's me."

A few other assistants, Erin and Grace, drifted over.

"I bet it's me," Grace countered softly. She looked down

at her pink polished nails. "I couldn't get my boss the bike he wanted at SoulCycle this morning. I'm screwed."

Erin crossed her arms. "Yesterday, he couldn't remember his credit card number, freaked out when I recited it to him verbatim out of habit, and then asked me to call his bank and get him a new card because he didn't want his identity stolen." She fell back into the semicircular couch in the center of the room. "Does he not realize I know his pins and social security by heart too?"

Then it went silent, everyone looking around cautiously. It was the first time they talked about the bullshit out loud. There were plenty of cross-bullpen nods, knowing glances, deliberate huffs. But in general, they tried to maintain appearances. They were a prideful and ambitious bunch, and nothing ruined a facade like admitting you were really just someone's bitch.

It wasn't until then that Cate realized only the women had said anything. Only women thought they were getting fired.

"What about you?" she asked the COO's assistant, Derrick. He shrunk so low in his desk chair his face was hidden behind the computer screen.

"I don't know." He started typing, but it was obviously fake. You couldn't out-fake-type a room of fake-typers.

"You can't think of one reason why you'd be fired?" Lucy demanded.

Derrick shook his head, searching for anything. "Well, yesterday I forgot to print cover options for an author meeting. But Ben said we didn't really need them, and it was fine."

Lucy and Cate exchanged a look. If Cate forgot to print out so much as a receipt for Matt immediately after he asked for it, he would never let it go.

"Spencer?" Lucy asked.

"I misspelled an author's name in a reader's report last week," Spencer admitted. "But William fixed it before the meeting, so...no harm done."

Cate didn't even need to look around to know that Lucy and the other female assistants were all smiling the exact same smile. The one you exchanged with the girl sitting across from you on the subway who was politely responding to a guy's unwanted questions until her stop. The one you gave your barista after you heard the customer in front of you tell her to smile. The one you spotted on the runner across the street after you were both catcalled from the same car.

"No harm done," Lucy said under her breath. "There's no harm done in *that*? But I get chewed out for ten minutes because of fucking cream cheese?" She stomped back to her desk. "And you think it's a coincidence only women are getting fired?"

The knowledge that they couldn't change anything weighed heavily in the air, and gradually, everyone sat down, started responding to emails and answering calls and ordering lunches. Everything went back to normal.

It was in that normalcy that Cate realized if she wanted to say no, she'd have to create the place to do it.

She made sure Matt's phone was still disconnected and his glass wall still curtained off before shifting her computer slightly to the practiced angle where the glare from the overhead lights hit the screen perfectly, blocking the view of any unwanted eyes. And she created a website.

They needed an outlet, a place to tell their stories. Private journaling and Shit Lists couldn't cut it anymore.

Cate would never claim to be a graphic artist or site designer, but, thanks to remarkable strides in technology and the internet, Squarespace was invented so she could make a website with tabs and a contact email and a subscription option where you would be notified of each new post. She wasn't sure exactly what it was going to be yet—they could figure it out once she had Lauren, Olivia and Max on board—but she *did* know that it was time to speak up.

Seconds before the HR rep scampered out of Matt's office,

and the red light on her phone blinked to life, signaling that Matt was again connected to the outside world, Cate named the site *Twentysomething*. Because that was really what they all had in common. It was not specific to industry, education, or ability. It was age. And the ambition and passion that comes with age was what was taken advantage of; what allowed the fear of being fired and fear of failure to keep them from standing up for themselves.

Shortly after, Matt left for the day and the entire room let out a collective breath as he disappeared into the elevator bank. She had made it another day. She wasn't fired yet.

CATE HAD TEXTED the group five times to come to her and Lauren's apartment that night, and Olivia wanted nothing to do with it. Frankly, she was exhausted. Her boss Nate had come back from LA in a mood she hadn't seen him in since he didn't get the lead in that Marvel movie a few years ago. It went to Ryan Reynolds, so Nate obviously didn't have a chance, which he was completely oblivious to, of course. Olivia would describe Nathanial Brooks as this: the guy who was the lead in one thing, and then a minor character in every other thing. Apparently, that small level of fame made Nate rich enough to own an apartment in Tribeca, where he expected Olivia to work. An entire wall of floor-to-ceiling windows looked out on downtown Manhattan and the Freedom Tower and let in so much light that Olivia had gotten sunburned from sitting in it too long. He had a kitchen island the size of her bed, so many bathrooms he used one purely for storage, and a balcony big enough for foliage and an entire dining set. Olivia was the most inexpensive thing in the entire apartment, and Nate never ceased to remind her of that fact.

But something had been particularly off with him lately. The second he returned from a trip to LA, he started making wild demands. Suddenly it was urgent that Nate's closet get cleaned out and his medicine cabinet organized and his patio scrubbed by hand. She spent the last five mornings walking into work terrified that firing her was on the to-do list, too. Luckily that had yet to make its way onto the docket.

Olivia needed to figure out what happened in LA to fix his mood. Though she could anticipate 99 percent of his needs 99 percent of the time, he was one floundering son of a bitch and his moods were impossible to predict or explain.

She messaged his accountant's assistant—maybe he lost money or something, in which case she should probably know if he couldn't afford to pay her anymore—but he had no insight. She emailed his therapist's assistant to no avail. Then she emailed his publicist's assistant—perhaps he found out he didn't get *People*'s Sexiest Man Alive. Again. But she knew nothing.

The only helpful hint she got came a few days later at an expensive price: taking his manager's assistant out for drinks at Café Cluny. Olivia sat with her at a table in the front and sipped rosé while nibbling on cheese that got more expensive the worse it smelled.

"Any idea what the actual fuck is going on with him?" Olivia asked. It was the kind of calm, overenunciated statement that could send chills down your spine. Olivia was good at that. The drama of it all. It was basically the only thing she was *ever* good at. How else did one get attention growing up with six older sisters?

Petting the new Birkin that sat on her lap like a puppy, the publicist's assistant believed the only commonality in the Venn diagram of their lives was that Nate's agent's assistant just got promoted. "I don't know why that would bother him," she said in an accent Olivia could only describe as hoity-toity. "But that's all I can think of," she finished, making sure not to sip her wine above the purse.

Olivia didn't know why that would bother Nate, either, and

accepted he probably just didn't get a job he expected to. Part of her hoped he'd stop pretending he was relevant, and part of her was afraid of what it would mean for her if he finally did.

But, this was still very helpful information, for her, at least. As soon as they left the restaurant, she was sending a congratulatory email to the newly promoted agent, with the joking parting sentence: "If you need any new clients, I'm here!" Before she pressed Send, she added three emojis to soften the plea. Because she wasn't joking; she was desperate.

Olivia needed an agent to get acting jobs, and she needed jobs to get noticed, and she needed to get noticed to get famous. She emailed her reel—a collection of all her best acting work, from college performances, to student films, to that time as a page she was featured on *The Late Show* in a comedy bit—to Nate every few months, hoping he'd finally come through with his promise to pass it along to his agent. *That* was the whole point of working with him: to help her get representation. Unfortunately, that meant she needed to please Nate. And to please Nate, today, had meant repotting his chrysanthemums on the terrace in the scorching midweek sun.

The last thing Olivia wanted to do was sit in Lauren and Cate's small, overheated living room, listening to someone inevitably vent about something, and drinking wine they surely got in a 2 for $20 sale at the liquor store across the street. She wanted to go home, maybe encourage a booty call, then take some melatonin and go to bed.

But Cate's last text had given her pause.

Please come over. It's important.

ONCE EVERYONE ARRIVED and sat on the couch across from her, Cate turned her computer to face Lauren, Max, and Olivia, displaying the interim, work-in-progress website. She waited, watching them carefully. A full minute went by before anyone said one word.

"I want to write about our jobs," Cate finally said, filling the silence that felt like it could have gone on forever. "Olivia, you shouldn't be doing your boss's laundry, and Max, you shouldn't be forced to worry about Richard staring at your ass all day. Lauren, you shouldn't be a professional coffee-getter. And I shouldn't be fired because of cupcakes. If we want to make a change, we have to call bullshit."

"Fuck yeah," Olivia said, setting down her wineglass. "I shouldn't be spending my days repotting Nate's plants and organizing his CBD oils."

Cate looked to Max, hopeful she'd also be enthusiastic, but Max shook her head. "I've signed way too many NDAs to go blabbing about Richard and Sheena. I can't just write about it. I'd get fired immediately."

She wasn't wrong. Cate, too, had signed multiple NDAs when she started working for Larcey. She imagined all four of them had. Calling out their bosses was important, but it was not worth getting sued for. They needed to find a loophole.

"It could be anonymous," Cate posited, realizing the promise in the words as she said them. "We could be untraceable. Make up nicknames or something to speak up without the consequences. Tell our stories without anyone knowing they're ours."

"Anonymous," Max repeated, thinking. "You're sure no one would find out? Really?"

Cate nodded. "How could they? No violated NDAs there."

"This is a terrible idea," Lauren finally said, shaking her head. "There's a reason we do The Shit List once a week. Why we don't text each other or email it. We write it down and then we *burn the paper*. We've worked hard to eliminate any kind of paper trail. Literally. And now you want to intentionally create one?"

Olivia and Max wavered back and forth like a ship being pulled by two currents. Cate almost started wavering herself, but something in her gut was telling her not to back down. This could be a place, unlike Larcey, where she could give a platform to stories that needed to be told. Stories that deserved recognition. All she needed to do was hand over the mic and turn it on.

"Look," Cate said. "I'm going to do this. You can join me or not."

Lauren rose from the couch. "I don't think it's a good idea. But you can do whatever you want without me." Then she muttered something about having to get some writing done and headed into her room, shutting the door on the conversation.

As they watched Lauren leave, Olivia reached for her phone, which had been buzzing all night. Like usual, she blamed it on Nate instead of admitting what they all suspected: she was seeing someone and keeping it a secret. Nate would never text her that many sexually explicit emojis in a row. At least not intentionally.

"Got plans with Mr. Eggplant?" Max asked, nodding at the phone.

Olivia didn't meet her eyes. "Just a booty call from Tinder." She shoved her phone under her thigh and picked up her wineglass. "Anyway, I think this site is a fantastic idea. Nate's been spectacularly more annoying than usual this week and until I figure out why, I don't think it's going to end. I need an outlet so I don't mistakenly push him off the balcony while trimming his shrubs."

"Mistakenly?" Max questioned.

"Well, that's what I'd expect you to tell the police."

Max snorted, then turned to Cate. "Okay, let's do this. As long as we're anonymous."

"As anonymous as could be."

"Forever," Max pressed. "Seriously."

Cate nodded and smiled reassuringly. "I promise."

5
· · · · · · · ·

"**W**hy are you here?"

Max jolted up, her head colliding with the bottom of her desk so hard she was sure she'd bruise. She squinted to see Charlie in an annoying yellow beanie crouched next to her, laughing. "Did I scare you?" he asked.

"Fuck." She rubbed the top of her head and shooed Charlie away so she could get up. Every one of her joints was sore, and it was possible she'd need a chiropractor to twist her back before she'd be able to fully stand up straight again. No more late night website sessions, she immediately texted the group chat. Or, the *new* group chat. The one they formed without Lauren to talk about the website. A week after Cate's proposal, it still felt weird to be doing something without her.

Max had learned two things from working 4:00 a.m. to 4:00 p.m. on a daily morning news show. First: coffee was never a good idea until 7:00 a.m. Any earlier, you just got jittery and sluggish; any later, you risked falling asleep on your keyboard during the live broadcast. Second: be in bed by 8:00 p.m. No exceptions. Except for weeknight birthday dinners; surprise

Broadway lottery ticket wins; all of Lauren's show's premier parties; and so on. Building a website had become the newest addition to that list.

Over the past week, Max had spent almost every night on Cate and Lauren's couch desperately extracting any fossil of skills left from her Graphic Design 101 course at Yale to fix Cate's tragic attempt at a website on Squarespace. Her first offense: thinking the free trial would even allow readers to find them. If they were going to do it, they needed to do it right, so Max snuck her credit card information onto the website while everyone refilled their wine, and never brought it up again. As far as they knew, it was free. No questions about how she could afford it was necessary. Then, Max designed a logo: a simple pink-and-gray coffee cup.

After filing out of Cate and Lauren's apartment at an exhausting 12:30 a.m., Max was forced to decide whether it was worth taking an Uber back to her Upper West Side apartment only to schedule another one at 3:35 a.m. for work, or just take a car directly to the office and snag a few extra hours of rest. Sleep won. When she arrived at the glass-walled entrance, the security guard let her in before she found her ID badge. "Another sleepover?" he asked, holding open the heavy door. She nodded, too exhausted to explain herself.

Inside, the newsroom was empty and dark, the only light coming from the wall of televisions in the back. Where they normally displayed every news channel you could imagine, at that hour they instead featured a smorgasbord of infomercials, funny home videos, and a series of missing posters on rotation. The lights flicked on as she trudged through the newsroom to her desk in the far corner, each step feeling like her legs were made of lead. She reached into the bottom drawer and pulled out two CBS-branded beach towels and a CBS-branded neck pillow and laid them on the laminate wood flooring in the crawlspace under her desk. Between the silent hums of the muted wall of televisions and the warmth of the CPU purring against her cheek, she fell asleep before the motion-censored fluorescent lights flicked off.

But then Charlie had to ruin it.

Max rubbed the top of her throbbing head. "That really hurt. What's wrong with you?"

Ignoring her, Charlie slid off his backpack and sat down in his swivel chair. Charlie was Richard's assistant in the same way Max was Sheena's. They were technically *co-assistants*, but adding *co* to a job title already as insignificant as *assistant* seemed to trivialize it even more, so three years ago they each claimed an anchor and left it at that. Max had been wondering if she'd made the right decision ever since. Yes, her ass wasn't pinched nearly as often as it would be if she'd chosen Richard, but she could probably withstand sexual harassment if it meant getting a promotion faster. Probably.

As Max sat at her desk, she noticed Charlie smelled like tequila and his eyes were a hint more bloodshot than usual. "Are you drunk?"

He winked as he took off the weather-inappropriate beanie, revealing his obnoxious hair that naturally coiffed into place like a spring. God, she hated him.

"Sorry that I have a life," he said. "You're lucky I woke you up. Imagine how embarrassed Sheena would have been to see you down there."

"She wouldn't have noticed." Max glanced at the clock and was shocked to see it was already close to 4:30 a.m. She'd slept *late*. She quickly scanned the AP and other sources for any headlines she missed—a tsunami warning in Alaska canceled; Kanye West announced a new sneaker line "Sneezy" on Twitter; a new study found that the moon was eighty-five million years older than originally thought—and she wrote up a one-page brief, summarizing anything new that had not been slated for coverage in the first hour of broadcast. Sheena liked to read it during Hair and Makeup for the sole purpose, Max suspected, of strutting out of her dressing room yelling last-minute changes to Alyssa, her executive producer, purely to cement her role as the boss. As if anyone could forget.

Just as Max pressed print, Sheena barreled into the newsroom in her black leggings, hoodie, oversize sunglasses, and undeniable bed head. She waved her hand to no one in particular and made her way upstairs to her office.

Richard arrived seconds later, bellowing, "Charlie! What do you got for me?" Max could almost see Charlie's head spinning, as if the gust of Richard's exclamation had made him acutely aware of his impending hangover.

Charlie eyed the brief on Max's keyboard, so fresh the ink was still drying.

"Don't you dare," Max said. "Don't touch it."

"Sheena didn't ask you for anything. *He's* asking *me*."

Sheena never asked, but she didn't have to. Max was always on top of it. "I guess you should tell him to come to me, then, huh?"

Richard reached the top of the stairs and called Charlie's name again. Charlie looked at Max, then at the brief. "Coming boss," he yelled, snatching the paper off her desk and running.

"What the fuck!" Max yelled uselessly. He was already halfway up the stairs taking them by two.

As he reached the top step, he turned back. "Gotta be faster on your feet, Burke."

Max stood in front of her desk, watching as Charlie disappeared around the corner. *No more late-night website sessions*, she repeated to herself. She couldn't afford to be off her game.

That was when she noticed Alyssa staring at her from the

kitchen under the stairs. As Sheena's executive producer, Alyssa controlled everything Sheena said and did on and off the air. As if that wasn't intimidating enough, she was also the first female EP their show had ever seen. Max badly wanted to be the second.

Had Alyssa just witnessed that pathetic example of Max offering Charlie, on a silver platter, yet another reason to get promoted before her?

Shit. Max turned around and faced her computer to print out another copy of the brief for Sheena. Though Alyssa's expression offered nothing—she was impossible to read—Max couldn't bear the weight of her presumed disappointment. No one could be more disappointed in Max than she was in herself.

LAUREN HAD TOLD THEM to do whatever they wanted for the website without her, but she hadn't thought they'd actually go through with it. Olivia, Max, and Cate had been meeting basically every night over takeout and wine to come up with the bones for what Cate named *Twentysomething.* Lauren had to admit it was catchy. Their first official night of writing, an introduction of sorts, apparently, was scheduled for tonight. And each day leading up to it, Lauren waited for a text that said, *You sure you don't want to join?* She practiced her response in her head on the subway each morning, something to the extent of, *I just don't want anyone getting fired or sued.*

The truth? She didn't want to write because she was afraid she had too much to say—about Pete, about James. No one else knew about what had happened. She was afraid if she started talking, if she said *anything,* she wouldn't stop. And that, she'd learned, could get her nothing but trouble.

"Can I work in here?"

Lauren snapped out of her daze and glanced up to see Owen,

the hot new writer who stole her episode, peeking his head through the trailer door. Backlit by their 6:00 a.m. call time, he was glowing like a tanned-skinned, dark-eyed, dark-haired God straight from toga-laden Ancient Greece.

"Of course," she said, moving to the far side of the couch to make room. A ball of nervous excitement filled her chest. After first meeting Owen, she had looked him up. On top of being a stud, apparently everything he wrote turned to Emmys. He had written on seven shows, was nominated for seven awards, won two, and the kicker—he was only three years older than her. She was impressed, horny, and a little jealous, a tantalizing combination.

"Mind if I put my stuff here?" he asked, motioning toward the counter next to the microwave and below the flat-screen TV hanging on the mirrored wall, which was surely reflecting her blush.

"Of course," she said again, her face burning red. Then, when she realized that was apparently all she was *capable* of saying to him, added, "Do whatever you want," which came out rough, like more of a demand than a suggestion. She wanted to crawl under the couch next to Pete's stash of whiskey and gin and ask for a do-over.

"I will," he said, letting out a *ha* while lobbing his backpack onto the wooden counter. "I'm going to get some coffee from catering. You want anything?"

Lauren instinctively sprang to her feet. "I'll get it. I could use a refill anyway." She'd already had three cups when two was her daily limit. But she'd just get decaf and pretend.

He waved her away and lifted the cup from her hand. "Don't worry, I'll get it. Milk, no sugar?"

"How do you know that?" Pete had paid for her coffee, but no one had physically gotten her coffee in the three years she'd been there, much less knew her order.

Owen shrugged, his shirt tightening around his shoulders. "I'm a writer. I'm very observant. Want any food?"

Oatmeal. She would love some oatmeal. But she wasn't going to tell him that. "Just coffee would be great," she said. After he returned, she'd claim she had to do something for Pete but instead sneak out to get food, gobbling it down on the walk back to the trailer so he'd never know she actually wanted some.

He opened the trailer door and the orange sunrise streaked inside, warming her face and filling the room with a gentle glow. "Your hair looks nice like that," Owen said so quietly, Lauren calculated a 7 percent chance she imagined it.

A few minutes later, Owen came back with two coffees in one hand, two bowls of oatmeal in the other, and Lauren almost started to cry. It was such a simple, thoughtful gesture that made her feel, oddly, important. And in an environment where every task was a reminder that she sat lonely at the bottom of the hierarchical ladder, any way to feel important was a special thing.

They ate on the couch together in silence before Owen asked, "So how long have you and Pete been working together?"

"Just about three years." She was never not thinking about how long it had been—often down to the day—and wishing that she had more to show for it.

"You guys seem to have a really good thing," he said, nodding. "Pete's cool. We've known each other for years."

"Yeah, he's the best boss I've ever had." While Lauren meant it, she'd also never had another one to compare. And she didn't want to ruin the moment, but there was something about the conversation, about the way Owen was only three years older than her but had *known Pete for years*, that made her feel insignificant again. Was she unpromotable? Was she not a good writer? She tried to stifle the feeling of embarrassment that was slowly swelling in her gut.

"So, you want to write?" Owen leaned back onto the couch, his empty paper bowl resting on his lap.

Lauren nodded. It was a dumb question considering the path to which her job was meant to lead; but it was also a question, she realized, no one had ever asked her before. She assumed it was assumed, but could *that* be why she was never promoted? Did Pete just not know what she wanted?

"What kind of stuff?" he pressed.

"Comedies. Something like this show. Maybe a little darker." Lauren stood to throw out her oatmeal bowl, using the excuse to look away from him. She didn't want him to see on her face how disappointed she was that it wasn't happening this season. Then the ever-loyal assistant inside her realized she should have offered to take his bowl, too, so she turned around quickly to grab it and smashed directly into his chest so hard she felt her boobs squish against him. Her embarrassed gasp echoed in her skull.

They stood very close together—so close the smell of his deodorant made her light-headed—and she knew this wasn't okay, she should step away, walk to the other side of the room until her head stopped spinning and her pulse stopped throbbing. But she couldn't move. And he *didn't* move. With each breath, their chests touched just enough to notice. Then she felt his muscled arm hook around her as he took the bowl out of her hand and tossed them both into the garbage, the plastic lining crackling when it landed.

"Would've been embarrassing if you missed that," Lauren said in a raspy whisper. There was a beat of silence long enough for her to panic that he didn't like her joke, until he laughed harder than it probably deserved and patted her shoulder.

"You'll be writing soon," Owen said, lowering back onto the couch. "I can feel it."

"I hope so. But for now, I'll keep ordering everyone's lunch."

He offered a half smile that said *I've been there, I get it* even though Lauren knew (thanks to Google) that he had not. "I can't promise I have time right now, but if you wanted to send me something to read, I'd be happy to take a look."

She sat up. "You would? Really?" The promise of a read kept her eyes locked on his until she remembered she had nothing to send him. She had three half-finished pilots. Things she was so excited to start until she got busy with lunch and schedules and commuting that the scripts would sit on her desktop, unfinished, a constant reminder of failure.

"Definitely," he said. "Isn't that why you're here? To get your stuff read?"

Lauren let out a deep breath and looked at him. "Thank you."

"I'm sure my notes won't be as good as Pete's—"

"They'll be great," she interrupted. "Pete's never read anything of mine, anyway." She immediately wished she could take it back. They had *just* talked about how great Pete was, and now she sounded ungrateful. What she said wasn't entirely true, either. She'd written a few lines of dialogue and punched up some jokes that he'd added to the final shooting script. So, technically, he had read stuff of hers. It was just credited to other people, and then quickly forgotten about entirely.

Owen smiled, revealing a slight dimple on his right cheek. "Well, I'd be happy to."

Their eyes met as morning light filled the trailer and then

left, like their moment, with the slam of the door as Tyler, one of the other writers, walked in.

"Dude, did you see the review in *The New Yorker?*" Tyler slapped a copy onto Owen's lap. As he opened to the earmarked page, Lauren read over his shoulder. The article praised a monologue from last season as *one of the most intrinsically complex and darkly hilarious admissions in the season's entire twenty-two episodes.*

A monologue that she had written. That no one knew she wrote. And no one would ever know she wrote.

Because it was credited to James Raymond.

"No wonder Pete's bringing all the writers from last season back," Tyler said. "They fucking loved us."

Lauren froze. "*All* the writers?"

"Yeah." He grabbed the magazine from Owen and looked down at the words so proudly you'd think it listed all the notches on his bedpost. "Dream team's coming back for season three."

No way, she thought. *There was no way Pete would do that.* Lauren sat up straight, steeled herself from descending into panic. Because Pete wouldn't do that to her. Tyler must mean all of the writers were coming back, *except* James. He had been fired last season. She never had to see him again. That was part of the deal.

Pete would never bring James back, especially without telling her first. Never.

As LAUREN TRUDGED UP the narrow staircase of her building, holding a box with two cheesy slices of pizza from the place two doors down, she thought about the rolled-up copy of *The New Yorker* in her purse. She couldn't stop thinking about it. For a moment, she considered framing the article, putting it over her desk in her bedroom as a reminder that even though she'd been ordering and plating people's lunch every day for three years, eventually it would be over. Even though Pete may never see her as more than an assistant, *The New Yorker* agreed that she was a good writer. She also considered throwing it out. James Raymond's name didn't deserve to take up space on her wall.

After Tyler continued gushing about the article to every single person who walked into the trailer, Lauren finally had to excuse herself. She couldn't bear to hear them talk about how great James and his perspective was. She had walked aimlessly around Greenwich Village, twisting down the narrow one-way streets lined with brownstones, thinking about James and, then, *Twentysomething*. Pete had made it clear by hiring Owen that she was not getting promoted this season, but maybe she could use the article to prove to Pete that she should be promoted *next* season. She could show him the emails between her and James about the monologue, connect all the dots for him so he'd have no choice but to admit she was good. She just had to wait it out. Which she could do. She was used to waiting her turn while watching white men get what she wanted.

But waiting it out required keeping her job. And with the mere existence of *Twentysomething* in her apartment, that became increasingly difficult. Unfortunately, she knew what that meant: she had to ensure nothing could be traced back to 2B. As the only writer in their group, she could help Cate, Olivia, and Max write *their* stories, vetting each one for any details that could reveal their identities. She'd take the onus off them—which they'd appreciate—and control everything. They couldn't mess up if she was in charge.

When she finally sat before them on the floor of the living room, it came out just like she practiced.

"I can be the head writer of the blog," she said, peeling a piece of pepperoni off the last slice and popping it into her mouth. "I'll break story, edit your stuff, and make sure everything runs smoothly. I'll write, just without the credit." She was used to that.

"So, you're in?" Cate asked cautiously, trying to hide how happy she was.

"If you'll have me," Lauren said. "And as long as we're *super fucking anonymous*. No one can get fired over this." And they wouldn't. She'd make sure of it.

"We were thinking about using nicknames," Max offered. "To further ensure no one knows who we are." She suggested that they all pick stereotypes of women as a theme. "I'm The Emotional One," she continued. "Because men don't have emotions, only women do. Men are just passionate."

Cate pretended to gag, then said, "I'll be The Bossy One. For obvious reasons."

"And I'm The Aggressive One," Olivia said. "If I were a man, I'd just be getting shit done."

"What am I?" Lauren asked. "Or do I not get one?"

Cate shrugged. "You can be whatever you want. You're the head writer, after all."

Lauren liked being called the head writer. It made her feel important, like she was contributing something meaningful to the world.

"I think I'll be The Bitchy One," Lauren said. "A woman is a bitch. A man is just opinionated."

If her well-being wasn't a high priority on Pete's list, then maybe Pete should be demoted from the number one spot on hers, too. She could think of three people who could easily take his place. She was looking at them.

A FEW HOURS LATER, Cate hesitated before pressing Publish on their first post. Something she was so overtly confident about just a week ago suddenly put a little knot in her throat.

She liked the anonymity of it, of course; the safety that came with telling her story without consequences. It wasn't Cate writing; it was The Bossy One. It wasn't Matt she was going to write about, it was The Boss—the vague, all-encompassing title they decided to use for everyone's boss, so each reader would have a chance to see themselves in their stories.

But something was making her hesitate as they squished on the couch and stared in complete silence at the post Lauren had just finished writing.

"So, we're doing this?" Max said.

Cate wanted this to go viral. She wanted the reblogs and retweets. She wanted a following so big they'd incite real institutional and structural change. This movement she was trying to start was much bigger than just the four of them—every assistant had a story.

"We're doing this," Cate agreed, her eyes focused on the end of their letter.

She pushed aside her unease and, finally, pressed Publish.

Dear Twentysomething readers,

It took us thirty minutes to press publish on the first entry of Twentysomething. Everything we ever learned about how to be professionals told us it was a bad idea. The nicknames won't conceal anything. People will know it's us. We'll all be fired. Or worse, sued for violating nondisclosure agreements.

We've signed roughly one hundred NDAs between the four of us, and we each signed nice thick ones when we started our current jobs: don't share information about the company; don't share information about the clients; don't share information about The Bosses. .

The last was always the most important: their personal lives. Don't tell anyone they have a drug dealer named

"Marcus" who shows up to the office every other Tuesday disguised as a deli delivery man, carrying a brown bag of molly, weed, and occasionally ecstasy. Don't tell anyone that their recurring Friday meeting labeled "lunch with client" was really couple's therapy under threat of divorce. Don't tell anyone if they're wearing their fancy clothes—that pressed blue button-down, that silver tie, those expensive black heels—they have a date with someone other than their significant others.

We know everything. That's the danger of assistant life. It's our job to know everything but pretend to know nothing.

At first, we were afraid of being fired. Of being sued. NDAs are legally binding, after all. A thick book that only calls you by your name once and then forever refers to you by your function—EMPLOYEE. It's oddly parallel to the life of an assistant: your personality matters for the interview, but once you get the job, no one gives a shit about your brain or ambition, so long as you can answer the phone, type fast, smile and look pretty.

But then we realized: if getting fired was the worst thing to come from speaking up, bring it on.

Because this, our friends, is the problem:

We went to great colleges. We had impressive internships. We busted our asses to make sure our bosses have everything.

Yet, we can't speak up. Instead, we're told to be invisible but look presentable. To blend in but wear more makeup. To shroud our faces but put on tighter pants. To be grateful to have a job but barely make minimum wage.

So this is our response. It's what we say in our heads when you tell us a man is overqualified, but we aren't. When you advise we get a thick skin. When you stare at our chests before our eyes.

We're coming for you.

You better start looking over your shoulder.

A woman with an opinion and nothing to lose is a powerful thing.

Enjoy.

The Bossy One

The Bitchy One

The Aggressive One

The Emotional One

6
·······

They decided to start out by publishing one story a week every Sunday. Olivia had been assigned the first post, and a draft was due to Lauren that night. Nate had continued to be more needy and demanding than usual, presenting Olivia with far too many options to choose from. On Tuesday, she had to accompany him to an NYU Tisch acting panel, where he was speaking about how to break into the industry, sharing heartfelt advice with these students that he'd never once shared with her. On Wednesday, she had to return a box of things to the apartment of Nate's ex-girlfriend, who claimed Olivia's name *didn't ring a bell* and there was no way she worked for Nate because *his assistant was much thinner.* And now, it was Thursday and she was sitting in the living room of Nate's apartment, trying desperately to focus on her laptop instead of looking at Nate's ashy butt. He was lying naked atop a massage table an arm's length from the kitchen island so he could easily grab his green juice. One masseuse focused on his upper thighs, kneading her hands up and down like she was working on stale dough, while the other masseuse oiled up his shoulders.

They'd have to start writing more than once a week. That was the only way *Twentysomething* would become popular enough to get her out of there.

Olivia took a deep breath. Then glanced down at the note on her phone, the tally she'd surely be adding to shortly.

Since she started the job three years ago, Olivia kept a note in her phone with a tally of the number of times she'd seen Nathanial Brooks's penis. And she was not talking on-screen, but his real, actual, uncircumcised penis in the same room as her. She didn't create the tally for herself, at first. She figured it could be useful should the seemingly inevitable day come when someone *else* outed his behavior and she was asked to testify. She'd wear her black Chloe scalloped suede heels and navy Victoria Beckham asymmetrical sleeveless dress, and she'd tell the jury everything while cradling her Oscars— possibly to rub them in Nate's face, depending on how petty she became.

Olivia had no plans to bring out her tally until she was successful. For now, it would stay between her, her phone, and her journal, in which she painfully detailed each occurrence purely for the drama in the inevitable deposition.

Because what would come after a lawsuit and an exposé?

A movie deal.

And sometimes justice.

But one of those things was more important to Olivia than the other.

"Oh, Olivia," Nate said, like he'd just remembered she was there. "I need you to clean the storage bathroom. And after that, print the script I sent you yesterday, then replace all the sponges and run me a bath. Gwyneth just sent some Goop bath bombs I'd like to try while reading."

Olivia choked back a laugh. He had asked Olivia to order those bath bombs online. *Gwyneth* had no idea who he was.

"If there's an extra, you can take one home with you," Nate offered in a gesture that made Olivia stop in her tracks on her way to the storage bathroom. Nate had never given her anything in her life. He didn't even let her keep the change when she paid for a fourteen dollar and ninety-five cent sandwich with fifteen dollars.

"That's very nice of you," she responded cautiously. "But I don't have a bathtub unfortunately."

He rolled onto his back with a huff and she turned, quickly, from the sight of his penis.

"You *must* have a bath in your next apartment. It's as necessary as a refrigerator." He closed his eyes, signaling an end to the conversation.

Wait until you find out I only have a mini fridge, Olivia thought as she left the room, adding a line to the tally on her phone. She hadn't yet had the strength to add them all up. She couldn't bring herself to know what that final number was—how many times she'd put herself through this.

A few hours later as she left for the day, she became, again, acutely aware of how different her life could be if only Nate passed her goddamned reel to his agent. If only she could get one audition.

Strolling through the spotless marble hallway, down the express elevator you needed a key fob to operate, and into the black granite lobby, Olivia was reminded that she didn't belong in a building like this, one so extravagant that it bought the air rights—and therefore the view—of the surrounding area. When Olivia arrived at her building on Pearl Street twenty minutes later, a dog with no owner in sight was chewing on the rug in the lobby, and her stairwell smelled like someone had gotten too drunk and couldn't make it all the way to their unit before puking. Twisting her key into her studio's lock and two dead bolts, she threw her things onto the floor as soon as the door shut behind her. From this one spot, she could see every single part of her apartment except the toilet, which was just behind the door on her left. Pulling her computer out of her purse and taking a half-full bottle of chardonnay out of the mini fridge to her right, Olivia walked past her queen-size bed, the love seat she found on craigslist, and the bookshelf that held both her clothes and her television (but no books), and opened the window to the only thing that made this apartment worth it: the fire escape that overlooked the back of the South Street Seaport and the Brooklyn Bridge. She climbed out and tried to find the most comfortable position on the lone cushion she referred to as her "outdoor furniture."

Her breath caught as she looked at the bridge's iconic arches. When she moved to New York City, her only reference beforehand had been *Friends*. Since she didn't have a grandma from whom she could inherit a grand two-bedroom, purple-walled apartment, nor did she have the money to rent one herself, climbing through a window to a makeshift balcony was as close as she could get to the idyllic New York City that had been painted for her since middle school.

On cue, her phone started vibrating—her mom, of course, called at this time every day—but she didn't answer. She didn't feel like lying to her mother right now. Olivia pulled the cork out of the wine bottle and took a long sip until her phone silenced. Balancing the bottle in the corner of the fire escape, she leaned against the brick wall and opened up a blank email on her computer.

She wrote down her day: watching Nate get a naked massage from two twenty-three-year-old masseuses, unclogging the toilet in a bathroom exclusively used to store swag he received from shows he never worked on, and, lastly, organizing a bath with candles and scented balms and reading materials for a grown-ass man. She didn't mention the tally or the addition she'd made to it today.

When she was finished, she looked at the email on her computer for a long time. There was no positioning this job in a good light. That light didn't exist. It was pathetic. Her life was pathetic.

She took another long sip of wine just as her mom started calling again. She'd continue until Olivia answered—until she knew she was home safe and sound for the evening. Olivia could never tell her she'd spent her day with a naked fifty-five-year-old man.

This is my life, she thought as she looked at the buzzing phone. *This is what your daughter does for a living. Is this what you imagined for her when you packed the car, wrapped her in a hug, and told her to kick some Yankee ass?*

Olivia sent the story off to Lauren and texted, This fuckery is all yours now. I want nothing to do with this memory anymore.

Then she sent another message, asking her fuckbuddy to come over. She needed to let out all this frustration.

As the cotton candy sunset slowly faded into darkness, she opened a new email and started another story. There were too many to choose from—so many shitty tasks, so many times when she felt degraded and humiliated. With another gulp of wine, nearly draining the bottle, she made the decision to turn her disgrace into hope. These were no longer her stories; they were The Aggressive One's. Nate was no longer Nate; he was The Boss.

He was going to get what he deserved.

She'd make sure of it.

CATE REFRESHED THE *Twentysomething* homepage constantly. Sitting at her desk in the office, she stared at her computer, everything else in the room blurring except for the site's view count: 108. When she had checked an hour after posting their initial letter, the view count had been 4—presumably, the four of them. It slowly increased to 23 and stayed there consistently for the first week, but after Olivia's naked massage story was published yesterday, it jumped to 99. And this morning, much to Cate's delight, they were at 108. Getting to three digits felt like a monumental moment, even if most of the views were probably just the four of them refreshing the page.

Every time the pink-and-gray coffee cup of the *Twentysomething* logo appeared at the top of the screen, her heart rate rose so sharply her Apple Watch recommended she breathe. The uprising was a long time coming. There was no way it could move this slowly forever; things would pick up soon. Right?

Matt pushed out of his office. "Hello?"

Cate quickly closed the *Twentysomething* tab on her computer. Had he seen her desktop? She could feel her nerves building, mouth drying, hands tingling. She looked across the bullpen, toward the bookshelf that wasn't all it turned out to be. Those red spines not as thrilling as they had been in her dad's walk-in closet office.

Fuck you, she thought. *Fuck all of you.*

Then, suddenly, the nerves were gone, replaced by a sudden surge of adrenaline.

"Do you need something?" Cate asked, sitting up taller, placing her feet firmly on the ground.

Everyone's typing slowed almost to a stop, as if the entire room was holding its breath.

Matt's bushy, graying eyebrows flickered subtly. If you didn't know him, you wouldn't have noticed the movement at all. But Cate did.

"Lunch," he said, quickly glancing at her blank computer screen and then back to her.

"I have to get you on that call with our lawyers in ten minutes. Can Spencer run out for you? William's flying today, so he's available."

Matt lowered his face, just enough to make it clear what he was about to say was for her and her alone. "Why don't you go, and Spencer can connect me? He's a little too old to just be getting my lunch. He's past that."

"I'm three months older than him, and I got your lunch yesterday. What's the difference?"

Cate knew the difference. And the tension reverberating between them proved to her that Matt did, too. He took a step back and stared at her impassively, and for a moment she thought he was going to fire her right there in front of everyone.

But without another word, he turned around and walked back into his office.

Unmoving, she stared at her reflection in the black computer screen for a full minute. Had she lost all the color from her face or did it just feel that way? Was he in his office talking to HR about her *now*? She glanced down at her phone. His line was still red, still on, still connected to the world.

When she looked up, Lucy, Spencer, and all the other assistants were gathered in front of her desk, looking like they weren't sure if she'd start crying or screaming, but they were prepared for either.

"You okay?" Lucy asked.

Cate nodded and reached for her wallet in her purse. "Spence, can you get an Italian sub with extra tomatoes from Happy's? Mustard, no mayo." She held out her corporate card until Spencer took it from her hand. "Thank you," she remembered to add as he headed toward the elevator bank.

Lucy leaned in. "Is something happening with you? Are you—"

"I'm fine." Cate motioned toward her phone. "I have a call to get Matt on. Really, I'm fine."

Cate could feel the other assistants' eyes on her as they backed away, but she pretended not to notice. Instead, she picked up the landline and dialed into the conference call, listening as people joined the line with a *ding* and introduced themselves. Matt was always the last to join. If he had to wait for someone else, it was a problem. Her problem.

Her phone buzzed with a text. How did the cupcakes go?

Then, This is Theo, by the way.

The guy with the hot back muscles and the incredible apartment who read David Sedaris was texting her? After she left him with blue balls to go fetch cupcakes for her boss?

"Everyone's on," a woman said over the phone.

"Grabbing Matt," Cate said, pushing her cell out of the way and dialing Matt's extension.

It went straight to voice mail.

She tried again. Voice mail.

She looked at the darkened light next to his line. He'd taken his phone off the hook.

Before she could process this, she heard a familiar, "He's expecting me." She looked up from the phone to see the bald HR rep approaching.

"Unfortunately, Matt's going to need to reschedule," she said into the conference call before hanging up and bringing her forehead down to the cold glass of her desk.

What had she done?

7

Normally Max had no trouble falling asleep in the car service on her way to work, but this morning instead she looked out the window, watching the sparkling New Jersey skyline as they made their way south on the Henry Hudson Parkway. This was the second *Twentysomething* week, and her turn to write according to Lauren's schedule. Technically her story was due to Lauren yesterday, but she passed out early and forgot. She woke up to a slew of unfortunate texts asking, with more question marks as the night went on, where her story was, until Lauren finally gave up and said, Okay, whatever, just get it to me as soon as you can.

Max held her phone in her lap, thinking about what she wanted to write. When she first agreed to this, there seemed to be an infinite number of things she wanted to say. She matched Sheena's coffee to paint swatches, for God's sake. And Richard was the industry's best kept secret—the biggest butt man broadcast news had ever seen. But as she sat in the back seat of the car, listening to the driver hum along to Lady

Gaga, her mind was blank. Well, if nothing else she could always write about Charlie.

Her car pulled up to the brightly lit marquee just as another one made a U-turn and stopped right behind them.

"You're early," Max said to Charlie as he stepped out of the other car, wearing more wrinkled versions of his button-down and jeans from yesterday. He smelled familiar, but not like himself; she couldn't quite place it.

"And you're late." He walked past her and through the door, not bothering to hold it open, even though she wasn't more than a foot behind him. They continued to ignore each other until they were sitting at their adjacent desks in complete silence, just the way Max liked it.

As 4:30 a.m. approached, everyone else started arriving: Alyssa, then Alex—Richard and Sheena's other executive producer—and finally Richard and Sheena themselves. Before Sheena could yell something about coffee, Max slid from her desk to the copy room to print out the daily brief. If Sheena didn't see Max, maybe she wouldn't yell at her.

Alex came into the copy room looking frazzled, his hair standing up in every direction, face bloated, the bags under his eyes darker than usual. He was oddly intimidating for a guy who was shorter than her. Max didn't say anything as he rifled through the office supply cabinets.

"You two having a party in here? I didn't get my invite."

Max looked up and saw Richard in the doorway, clad in jeans and a T-shirt, pre-Hair and Makeup and Wardrobe. He looked almost as bad as Alex. It was amazing how many years a professional makeup artist could take off your face.

Max laughed at his joke because she felt like she had to. She was too unimportant to not fake laugh at a superior's bad joke. She honestly hadn't thought Richard even knew where the copy room was. He had her and Charlie to do that for him.

Alex asked him what he needed. Richard smiled at Max and said, "Nothing, just looking." Like he was shopping for new jeans. He opened up a file cabinet, picked out a Sharpie, and examined it like he'd never seen one in real life before.

"I never come in here," Richard said. "There's some good stuff." He approached the copy machine and stood behind Max, putting one arm over her shoulders. She felt herself sink a little under his weight, and she had a hard time catching her breath. She was wearing a shift dress, she reminded herself. He couldn't see her ass in a shift dress. He was just being friendly. "I haven't used a copier in a while. Want to give me a tutorial?"

Without moving her head, she glanced at Alex who was still on the other side of the machine, his eyes glued to the stack of papers in between them.

Richard continued talking—asking what each button meant, if it could fax things, if people really scan their butts—but all Max could focus on was his hand moving slowly down her back, leaving a trail of hot embarrassment in its path. She turned her head fully to Alex this time. *Please say something. If you don't say anything, then I definitely can't. You're the executive producer. You're supposed to be the boss. You're supposed to stop this.*

Max stood, frozen on the inside, burning on the outside, as Richard's hand landed on her ass, pinching it so violently her eyes started to pool. It was much harder than his usual pinch; she was sure it would hurt for her to sit down that night. Was he frustrated she never reciprocated? That she never fought back? Or did he just think women liked it that way?

"Never mind," Richard said sweetly as he gave her butt one last goodbye tap, making her wince. "I guess I don't need to learn. I have you guys to do this stuff for me." As he walked out, the room was so silent Max could hear people talking in the hallway on the other side of the thick wall.

Fortunately for her, in her three years as Sheena's assistant, this was only the second time she experienced Richard's notorious proclivity for butts firsthand. It had taken all of twenty-two days as Sheena's assistant to get in on the not-so-secret secret. She'd been standing in the kitchen, working over a broken coffee machine, when Richard walked in. Not five seconds later did Stephanie Brady, an associate producer at the time, stand behind Max, offering to help her figure out why all their coffee came out filled with grounds. When Richard walked away, Stephanie backed off. "Leaning over counters while he's around isn't a good idea," she said before getting back to work.

A few days later, Max had been standing at her desk, bending over her computer when she felt it: her first pinch. She was so startled she knocked over the monitor and it crashed facedown onto her keyboard. When she turned around to see Richard walking away, she found herself, at once, thinking *Richard just touched my ass* and *I must have imagined it.*

The whisper network continued—a publicist in the elevator telling her not to wear such tight pants; a wardrobe stylist commenting that the thicker the fabric the less the pinching would hurt. Then, Max passed along the message to her first intern in the same way. But no one ever said anything to *him.* No one ever told him to back off or stop. They just warned each other. And that was part of the problem.

"Richard touched my ass," Max said to Alex, looking up. He nodded a few times mechanically, not meeting her eyes. Then he turned the papers upright, tapping them lightly against the top of the copy machine to straighten everything out.

"You've got a nice butt. What do you expect," he said flatly, like he wanted it to be a joke, but not even he could laugh at it.

"Well, what do I do?"

Alex let out a deep breath, like *he* was the frustrated one.

Like *he* had to buy a whole new wardrobe because someone on their staff couldn't keep his hands to himself. Like *he* couldn't pick up a pen or read over someone's shoulder or lean over a computer or *stand at a fucking copy machine* without worrying about *his* ass being touched by an old man. "Nothing, Max," he said. "You do nothing. You forget about it." She watched him gather the papers and his notebook, holding the entire collection of things under his arm. "Just be flattered," he said, approaching the door. "He dates models. He has good taste."

Nothing about this was flattering.

"It's fucked up," she said. Out loud. She wanted him to hear it. He didn't pause for more than a second before continuing into the hall, letting the door slam shut behind him.

At least she had something else to write about now.

TWO DAYS AFTER basically calling Matt sexist, Cate was somehow still employed and had a date scheduled with Theo. And after sitting uncomfortably on the edge of her seat the past few days, wondering if that was the day she was going to be fired, she had a lot of anxiety to get rid of.

Immediately following her confrontation with Matt and noticing his phone went off the hook for *another* impromptu meeting with HR—further convincing Cate that her time as a Larcey assistant would be coming to an end at any moment—she had mustered what little tenacity she had left to beeline to the bathroom, where she let herself cry for a few minutes, an *I can't believe I just fucking said that* terrified-yet-congratulatory release of built-up energy.

Once it was over and her face was a bit less puffy and more work-appropriate, she remembered that before her "outburst," as it would surely be called, she had received a few texts from Theo.

Got the cupcakes, she responded. Not worth it though.

He answered quickly. Work rarely is. Any chance you want to try again? Hopefully without the interruption?

She was so excited at the thought of having sex with him that she had to consciously stop herself from typing Let's skip dinner. She told herself to calm down.

I'd love the chance to redeem myself.

It was the fastest Cate had ever scheduled a date. As she walked into the Standard Biergarten feeling like a bombshell, she even found a little satisfaction in getting carded by the bouncer. She'd decided on block heels with tastefully ripped jeans. Hair down, curled. Expensive mascara. Red lips. Oval hoops. But she was immediately barraged with body dysmorphia and anxiety the second she walked through the double doors and remembered she hadn't been there since college. The place had gotten younger and hotter, full of twenty-one-year-olds walking around with beer steins larger than their shorts.

Cate found Theo in the corner, two beer glasses in front of him, engrossed in a paperback copy of David Foster Wallace's *Consider the Lobster.* He was just as sexy as she remembered.

"That for me?" Cate asked, pointing at a full stein as she slid onto the stool next to him.

"It's for my other date, sorry." Theo shifted and slipped the book into his back pocket. Cate officially added "books in back pockets" between "muscular arms" and "half smile" on her list of hottest male attributes. "I figured I'd get an order in before something inevitably comes up and you have to leave."

"Challenge accepted." She put her phone facedown on the wooden bar's ledge.

"Oh wow," Theo laughed, eyeing it. "That's a big deal."

"I don't play around with second dates." Her phone buzzed

almost immediately. She had to actively concentrate on not allowing herself to pick it up.

"I'm honored."

"You should be. I don't do that for everyone."

Theo nudged the beer toward her, and their fingers brushed as she picked it up. Maybe the electricity was in her head—they literally couldn't have touched for more than a millisecond—but either way it made her smile. She needed this.

After chatting for a bit, she finally asked him about work, which was usually the first topic of most New York conversations. He set his glass on the coaster and said, "The *Times* is having a golf retreat thing, and my boss just asked me to go with him. I can't stop thinking about it."

"Go with him as a caddy or something?" Cate ignored a flashback to Larcey's humiliating retreat last year. The emails and the underwear. The copious amounts of wine and venting she needed after. Oddly, she found herself a little grateful for the reminder. Maybe that could be next week's *Twenty-something* story.

"I think as his partner in a foursome."

"Wow, that's…not what my boss would bring me along for."

"What do you mean?"

Cate laughed. "I'd be the person who shined his shoes in the clubhouse. Last time we had a company retreat, it was basically just my boss and the other publishers spending fifteen grand on booze and calling it team bonding."

"Did you go?"

"Technically, yes," she said hesitantly. "I *was* invited, I'll give you that." She took a long sip of beer, debating how much to divulge before deciding *fuck it*. "But only because someone needed to coordinate the dry cleaning and laundry with the resort's front desk. And they got everyone's clothes mixed up, so I spent the entire weekend fielding emails from company executives with pictures of their underwear saying *I'm missing a pair that looks like this.*"

"There's no way that's true," Theo said.

"Why would I ever make that up?"

Her words hung in the air, and she watched him search for what to say. Shitting on someone else's boss wasn't typically second date material. Maybe she shouldn't have brought it up. Finally Theo picked up his glass and clanked it with hers. "To never becoming that kind of boss," he said.

Cate drank, and he did too, their eyes locking. She liked looking at him. And she liked the way he looked at her. Her phone buzzed again on the counter, but she dutifully ignored it, until the buzzing became so loud and frequent that her phone almost jumped off the counter.

"You can pick it up, you know," Theo eventually said, eyeing her phone.

"It's facedown for a reason," she said defiantly.

"It's okay, really. What if he needs more cupcakes? I'll check it for you. Don't need your boss mad at *me*, too."

Cate laughed. "He would be. And he'd find you."

"I don't doubt that." Theo picked up her phone and scrolled. "You've missed more than I thought," he said, staring into the void of what she imagined were an onslaught of texts beginning with Matt's classic *helloooooo* and ending with *don't bother coming to work tomorrow.* The beer must have been getting to her head because she wasn't the least bit concerned. What would happen would happen. That was not a mindset she had *ever* had.

"Your boss is—" he scrolled up and down too many times for Cate to keep track "—Matt?"

She nodded, preparing herself for her unemployed destiny. Maybe Theo could recommend her for a job at the *Times*?

"The only thing from Matt is *hello* with—" He paused. "At least eight o's. What does that mean?"

So, Matt still hadn't fired her after all. "He texts me that to test my response time."

Theo stared at her blankly. "Seriously?"

"You mean your boss doesn't make sure you're at his beck and call every minute of every day?"

"I don't even think he has my cell number, honestly."

It was useless to explain. "Just text *hi* back. With a period so he knows I'm serious."

His fingers moved over the keys. "Done. I also told him to fuck off. Hope that's cool."

"Like all men, he responds very positively to hostile behavior from women."

"Well, don't worry, the rest of the messages are from your squad."

"My *squad*?" Cate laughed. "I'm not an asshole. I don't have a squad."

"That's what you called them last time."

"I did not."

"Your squad. Your ladies. Your peeps."

She shook her head. "I'm sure I had one too many desk whiskeys before saying any of that. I'm not responsible for my actions after more than two."

Theo leaned in. He smelled like soap and salt, and she could feel his breath on her ear. "I have one, too. What's your desk whiskey of choice?"

"Writers' Tears." Someone had given it to Matt as a present (read: someone's assistant emailed Cate asking what Matt liked to drink, then sent it with a typed-up note she wrote pretending to be her boss, then Matt threw it out, and Cate claimed it while recycling the seltzer bottles on his desk that night).

Theo laughed. "Appropriate. Mine's Blade and Bow." He

looked back down at her phone. "So who's Back Muscles?" he asked, flexing his shoulders through his button-down.

"I—um, give me the phone."

He stretched his arm behind him, holding it hostage. "I don't know. I feel like I should keep it until I get some answers."

She lunged forward for it, brushing his chest with hers as he touched her knee, slipping his hand into the jeans' rip and onto her bare leg. Her mind went completely blank. Like when you walk into a room and forget why you went there in the first place.

Chuckling, Theo finally handed the phone over, and she shook off the dizziness.

"This is why you don't let boys play with your phone," she said, suppressing a smile.

He winked, and a wave of heat rolled through her body. The next thing she knew they were in a cab to her place, his hand on her leg, slowly moving it up a little farther the closer they got to Eighty-Sixth Street. She kept wondering if she could die from anticipation. It sure felt like it.

Despite herself, Cate's mind kept wandering to the phone in her bag, and the fact that Matt hadn't fired her yet. What was he waiting for? And how much damage could she do before she was gone?

8
·······

A few weeks later, it was the Fourth of July, and besides celebrating the unofficial start of summer and the fact that Cate was getting laid regularly (without interruption) by someone she referred to only as "Back Muscles," the four of them were also congratulating each other on the website's five hundredth view, which happened to land on the same day as the one month anniversary of *Twentysomething*.

Lauren couldn't believe they had gotten that far. Five hundred views was a lot of people. All of whom now knew that Olivia's boss liked naked massages and Max's boss touched her ass and Cate once ran around Manhattan shopping for a day-of birthday gift for her boss's wife off of only "she likes the color green right now."

Correction: The Aggressive One, The Emotional One, and The Bossy One—not Olivia, Max, and Cate. Lauren had to keep reminding herself of that.

As far as she could tell, the nicknames were actually working. Every time she looked up the *Twentysomething* website, she also Googled each of their names, and nothing out of the ordinary came up. Sure, a few of Olivia's old auditions she had no clue were immortalized on the internet surfaced, but that was it. Nothing connecting them to the site or their bosses.

The four of them were invisible and, while Lauren still thought this was a terrible idea—*terrible, awful, very bad*—she was relieved. The anxiety that had been building in her chest was starting to fade, and she was able to relax for the first time since they published that first letter—since she became The Bitchy One, the most invisible of them all. The one who actually still *liked* her job.

Pete had asked her to work a half day on July Fourth to ensure they got a script out on time, and Lauren had gladly accepted because working on a holiday was time-and-a-half pay. Usually she had to fight to be paid for the overtime she worked, but this time Pete promised he'd speak to the studio to guarantee they gave it to her without question. For a moment she was grateful and, again, regretted associating with a blog meant to call out toxic bosses, but then she saw the Owen-induced guilt lingering in Pete's eyes and she shook it off. The irony was, even though she'd fully settled into her nonpromotion, she actually liked having Owen around— another person her age in the room, someone who had no idea who James was. Someone who couldn't see the scarlet letter on her chest.

Owen started bringing her coffee almost every morning, which she reciprocated one afternoon by buying him lunch from a deli instead of the free catering on set. They ate together, sitting on the trailer steps, and it was honestly the closest thing she'd had to a date in months. But it obviously wasn't a date. For many reasons.

Lauren finished working by midafternoon July Fourth, and Pete sent her eight (she counted) beer stein emojis, telling her to enjoy the rest of the day. She had just enough time to shower, spend all her overtime pay on booze, and meet everyone at Olivia's, where they were going to eat and drink an outrageous amount and watch the famous fireworks show from Olivia's fire escape that overlooked the East River.

That was, until Olivia suggested they go up to the roof for a better view and, thus, how they ended up quite tipsy and bloated from cheese, hesitating in front a thick door secured shut with an arrogant fire alarm arm and a tyrannical number of signs.

"Are you sure this is allowed?" Lauren asked as they stared at the six Do Not Enter signs. The four of them were collectively lugging two coolers filled with enough rosé and Coronas to get them all blackout drunk twice over; a half-eaten platter of assorted cheeses and crackers; and four wooden Ikea folding chairs. Fire Alarm Will Sound was the sign that particularly caught Lauren's eye.

"It's fine," Olivia said, with a slight hesitation. "I'm just going to do it." Before Lauren could protest, Olivia's hand was jamming into the metal crash bar. "I knew the alarm was a fake," she said, holding the door wide, the glowing East River skyline opening up in front of them. "This building wouldn't do anything as legit as a real fire alarm."

They made their way outside, placing the four chairs in a semicircle near the roof's edge and popping another bottle of rosé while waiting for dark.

One hour and two bottles later, Cate jolted out of her seat and faced them, swaying a little too much for Lauren's comfort, considering how close she was to the edge. "I've just been thinking. We've tested the waters, made it a month without getting caught. Everything looks good, the nicknames are working. I haven't been fired yet. Maybe we could start spreading the word at work? See if anyone else wants to contribute their stories, too?"

The *boom* of a test firework went off far south, just as Cate finished talking, adding a strong period to the end of her sentence. If Lauren didn't know better, she'd think Cate planned it that way.

Olivia and Max were enthusiastically nodding with slightly glossed-over eyes. "I've been talking to all of Nate's people's assistants lately," Olivia said. "I could figure out how to get them contributing?"

"And I'm sure I could get some of the other Larcey assistants on board," Cate added. "I bet there are a ton of people interested in telling their stories."

"So we're just throwing the anonymity out the window?" Lauren asked. How were they possibly supposed to stay anonymous if everyone started blabbing about the site at their offices? What are they supposed to say? *Oh, hi, don't tell anyone but I started a website breaking my NDA and talking about my boss. Want in?* Were they kidding?

"We wouldn't tell them *we* started it, just that we *heard* about it…" Cate trailed off, as if she was realizing the flaw in her plan as she was saying it out loud.

"So you're going to go up to an assistant at Larcey and say, what, 'Look at this website. I think we should contribute stories about our jobs, too.' You think it's going to take more than thirty seconds of them reading to realize that you're The Bossy One? Just think about it for a second."

Cate slumped down in her chair like Lauren had ruined her day. Why was keeping them employed and out of NDA jail making her feel so shitty? Why did Lauren *always* have to be the bad guy?

Despite being outnumbered on this roof, Lauren was still convinced she was the majority in general. Would people really be willing to jeopardize their jobs, their livelihoods, their paths forward just to call out the way assistants were being treated? Lauren looked at her three friends who were willing to do this: friends whose parents could afford to pay their rent for a month or two if they lost their jobs, friends whose faces and backgrounds meant they didn't have to work as hard as she did to get the job in the first place. Those were the people willing to do this. People with privilege.

It's not worth arguing more about it, Lauren thought to herself in the uneasy silence. She was positive they wouldn't find as many contributors as they anticipated. There were plenty of women, like Lauren, who had been told to be quieter, less obstructive; not to do anything that could take away the opportunity. They wouldn't be writing in anytime soon.

Two more test fireworks went off, this time closer to them, and when Lauren looked up from her empty wineglass, she was shocked to see how quickly the sky had changed from an orange sunset to purple darkness. She reached behind her chair and pulled out the "Summer in a Bottle" rosé that they were saving for when the fireworks started.

"Look," Lauren said as she filled each of their empty glasses. "We're up to five hundred views, so the stories are starting to resonate. I didn't think *Twentysomething* was a good idea, but you guys proved me wrong a little bit. So maybe I'm wrong about this, too. But all I'm saying is you have to really think about it. One wrong move and we're all fucked." She capped the bottle and put it back in the cooler. "Just think first, act second, okay?"

She could immediately tell by Cate's wry smile that she took Lauren's warning as permission. Lauren had known Cate long enough to make educated guesses about her internal monologues. And this one was saying, *she didn't say no.*

Before anyone else could respond, the show started, and their attention turned to the river. The Fourth of July fireworks always made Lauren emotional. They had somehow become her arbitrary deadline for accomplishments. Last year when she and her mom picnicked in a park along the river in Long Island City, she had thought, *this time next Fourth, I'll be a staff writer.* It was silly, but it felt like each firework burst was a candle at which she was blowing all her wishes.

Watching the brilliantly colored explosions light up the night sky, Lauren wasn't sure what to wish for this year. Her last wish hadn't come true. She was still an assistant, and she hadn't taken even *one* step forward. Would next Fourth of July arrive to see her in the same place, making the same wish, hoping for the same things?

Lauren quickly wiped the corner of her eye. Wishing only led to disappointment.

One thing was for sure: she couldn't risk losing her job or getting sued because of a stupid website. *That* was her only wish for the year.

"Let this website go nowhere," she whispered into the fireworks.

OVER THE NEXT few weeks, Olivia was on a mission to recruit contributors. Everyone was. Except for Lauren, of course. Cate had made it clear after the Fourth of July that they were going ahead with spreading the word. "Just don't be obvious about it and your cover won't be blown," was her only advice about how to stay anonymous.

Olivia didn't know exactly how to go about bringing up *Twentysomething* organically in conversation and, after an aborted attempt to mention it to Nate's publicist's assistant— which started with her saying "I heard about this website" and then ended with a panicked, "Google. It's Google. That's the website" before hanging up—she decided she needed to start with someone lower stakes than an assistant she already had a relationship with. Someone she didn't know, who didn't know her. Someone who in no way, shape, or form could identify her as The Aggressive One.

That's when Nate got called about a guest spot on *Law & Order: SVU*. At first, he wasn't going to take it—"I should at *least* be recurring"—but after a quick call from his agent, Peggy, reminding him that he hadn't gotten any other offers in months, Olivia found herself driving Nate to set. She dropped him off and parked the car illegally at a fire hydrant, sitting with her hazards on, oscillating between the feelings of choking and melting to death. Every time she tried to turn on the AC for thirty seconds of breathable air, a very determined parking cop in a bright yellow vest knocked on the window and yelled, "NO IDLING" until she turned the car off.

Olivia played that game with the parking cop for nearly two hours, waiting for Nate to finish his scene inside and give him a ride to the other location. She'd Googled it: the two sets were a ten-minute walk, and a fourteen-minute drive, away from one another. And yet, there she was, suffocating, sweating through her bra, waiting for him. *Do it for the story,* she chanted to herself.

As Olivia answered some emails on her phone to kill the time, a FaceTime call from her mother popped up on the screen. She always had the uncanny ability to find a reason to video chat at the strangest times, not fully understanding Olivia's work schedule. Or even what her job was.

Olivia turned the car on quickly and pressed her face against the AC until she turned from sweaty to glowing. She looked behind her—there was nothing that would give her away and the parking cop had disappeared—and answered the call.

"Hi, Momma," she said. Her Southern drawl came back

whenever she talked to family. It was embarrassing. She had worked very hard to get rid of it.

"Where are you, Peaches, you're so dark!" She could only see her mom's forehead and eyebrows in the phone's frame, but it wasn't worth explaining where the camera was. She'd tried far too many times.

"I'm in a car," Olivia said, choosing her words very carefully. She didn't want to lie, per se; she just needed to twist the right words. "On set."

"Oh yeah? You doing another commercial? We haven't seen your toothpaste one yet, but we've been recording all of *The Blacklist* and skippin' through the show to look for it."

Olivia sighed. "Oh Mom, you don't have to do that." There was no toothpaste commercial. There were no commercials, ever. Because to get a commercial she needed an agent. And that seemed especially far away in this suffocatingly hot car. But her mom didn't know that. If someone asked her mother, Olivia had been in hundreds of commercials. "It must be another New York only one," Olivia said, digging her nails into her palms. *Some lying was okay.*

"That's all right, honey. You keep at it and soon you'll be sellin' toothpaste all over the country!"

It made Olivia sad thinking about how proud her mom was over a fake toothpaste commercial. "Look, Mom, I have to run. They're, um, they're calling me to Hair and Makeup."

"Oh wow. Okay. I love you. Just make sure they accentuate your cheekbones. They're beautiful. You got them from me—"

"Okay, Mom—"

"—but the chin you got from your daddy. See what they can do about—"

"Mom, love you, got to go." She repeated that a few more times as she pulled the phone farther and farther away from her face until she finally had the strength to hang up. Olivia hated lying to her mom, but she just couldn't take her family's disappointment. No one wanted to know that their daughter did *this* for a living—sitting in an unbearably hot car, waiting for her boss whose penis she knew better than her most consistent fuckbuddy's.

Olivia threw her phone on the passenger's seat and got out of the car to breathe for a second—her anxiety piled on top of the stagnant air was stifling—when she saw a young production assistant walking up the block, weighed down by a belt hauling anything anyone could possibly need (pens, highlighters, a knife, a bottle opener, the call sheet, a notebook, gum, floss, mascara, and so forth), carrying two foam containers.

Olivia watched as the PA carefully approached two messy-haired and baggy-eyed assistant directors standing next to a trailer and offered them their lunch.

"Where's my plate?" one of them asked the PA, looking at the containers but not taking them out of her hands.

"I can get you a plate. Sorry, I didn't— It was just being served in these, but it's—"

"No shit it's served in to-go boxes, but you expect me to eat out of this? I'd like to feel like a human for the eight seconds I have to eat my fucking lunch."

"I'm sorry."

"Stop apologizing, just get it. And silverware. I don't want to see any of this plastic shit when you come back."

Holding the lunch containers, the PA watched them walk up the three steps into the trailer. Even from Olivia's spot ten feet away she could hear one of the ADs say, "Is that *really* too much to ask?" as the door slammed in the PA's face.

If Nate wasn't going to help her career so she could stop lying to her parents, maybe *Twentysomething* could. And if

Twentysomething was going to grow, Olivia needed to stop beating around the bush and just do it.

"Hey there," Olivia said, jogging around the car toward the PA. Out of the corner of her eye she could see the traffic officer moseying back down the block, toward the car, so she had only a few minutes. "Hey! I'm Olivia."

"Parker," the PA said. "You're Nathanial Brooks's assistant, right?"

PAs really did know everything.

Olivia nodded. "Sorry they're such assholes." She gestured toward the trailer.

"I've seen worse," Parker said with a shrug.

"Haven't we all." The traffic officer was five cars away now, slowly examining each one as she passed, looking for any kind of violation she could write a ticket for. "So, um, speaking of assholes... I saw this website the other day, *Twentysomething*, I think it's called. Anyway—" the officer was three cars away "—you should submit a story about those two. It's all anonymous." Olivia started backing up toward the curb as the traffic cop approached the car parked behind hers. "They're trying to change the industry, call out shitty people." She hurried to her car and opened the door just as the officer spotted its unoccupancy. "You should check it out," she called to the PA.

Parker stood on the sidewalk, confused. Then she looked at the trailer and then down at the containers in her hand. "*Twentysomething*, you said?"

"That's it," Olivia answered. "If we want change, we have to make it ourselves."

"I'll think about it," Parker said, nodding. "Thanks."

Olivia got back in the car just in time to watch the paparazzi gear up for someone to walk out of the building, only to see it was Nate and disappointedly stand down. They didn't know him from a crew member, and the look on his face—prideful embarrassment—as he slid into the back seat of the car made her entire day worth it.

"Drive," he said as the door shut. She gave one last look at Parker, who was hurrying around the corner, and did just that.

9

To Cate's utter shock, she still hadn't been fired. But the surprise meetings between Matt and the bald HR rep were getting longer and more frequent by the day. It seemed his phone was off the hook more often than it was connected, leading to an incredible number of excuses from Cate when anyone called. "He's in a meeting" and "he's going to need to reschedule" quickly went stale and turned into "he's at his son's Civil War reenactment?" and eventually, letting it go straight to voice mail. Theo offered a few alternative excuse suggestions, but they all involved mentioning Matt's dwindling sex drive, and proved to be useless other than to make Cate laugh.

Cate realized pretty quickly that her own firing didn't warrant the frequency with which Matt was meeting with HR. All he needed to do to fire her was step outside his office and say the words. In fact, her heart stopped a little every time Matt pushed open his glass door, which explained the stress acne on her chin.

Now that *Twentysomething* was hitting its stride, maybe Matt and HR weren't strategizing about firing her as the assistant, but as the company narc.

Since the Fourth of July a month ago, Olivia and Max both had done their due diligence to recruit all kinds of people— PAs on set, Nate's team's assistants, current *Good Morning Show* interns, former pages. Then, all those people told people, and in just four weeks they had received nearly three hundred contributing stories, were publishing multiple times a day, and had hit their ten thousandth view a few days ago.

That was what happened when a whisper network started whispering a little louder.

Cate, however, had managed to recruit no one. Not one person. She was all talk at the Fourth of July—*I'm sure I could get some of the other Larcey assistants on board*—but when she had walked into the office that Monday, July 6, ready to start a Larcey revolution, she had failed.

Cate had texted the four other female assistants to meet her in the bathroom. As she looked at Lucy, Erin, Penelope, and Grace, her throat had become thick with nerves.

"I just wanted to tell you guys about this website I discovered recently," Cate managed to say.

"That's it?" Lucy said. "Seems like that could have been an email. Or a G-Chat."

"The website has anonymous stories from assistants about their bosses," Cate continued, carefully saying exactly what she rehearsed on the subway ride that morning. "The site is looking for contributors, and I sent them something about Matt, and..." She paused. "I thought maybe you guys would also be interested in writing. About your bosses. Or about Matt."

Very quickly, and all at once, they all started talking—

"Are you serious?"

"I don't want to hear this."

"This is a terrible idea."

"Why are you telling us this?" Lucy cut in. "We're going to get in trouble by association alone."

Cate hadn't prepped this part. She'd thought they would all unanimously agree. Especially after their last group conversation, where they had admitted how their fear of getting fired wasn't even based on job-related tasks, but bullshit that shouldn't be the deciding factor in their employment.

Cate pushed herself off the counter and stood up straight. "I've been on edge for the last two months assuming every day that I was going to be the next one fired. I think we all have, to an extent. And writing about Matt for some *random* website—" she might have overemphasized there "—that's trying to expose the poor way assistants are treated, was the first time in a while I felt like maybe there's hope that this job won't be this terrible forever."

Erin stood up, brushing the couch lint off the back of her pants. "You said it yourself, Cate. They're looking for reasons to fire us. You're just handing them yours. On a silver platter. With all the digital accoutrements they'll ever need to make sure you never get a job in this industry again."

They weren't wrong. She had created a website, pulled her three best friends into this digital black hole with her, and now the word was spreading, bringing other people in with it. She needed to stay strong, be their leader, reassure them that this was a good idea, that they were going to make a difference, and this would make all their shitty tasks worth it one day. But that became increasingly difficult to believe when she hadn't been able to convince her work friends to join her.

After they left their undercover bathroom meeting, no one spoke to Cate for the rest of the week. Now a month had gone by, and they still couldn't look her in the eye. An hour ago, Matt's phone was pulled off the hook and HR scampered into his office, and Lucy didn't even look up. Before their bathroom meeting, she would have immediately swiveled over to Cate's desk offering extravagant guesses about who Matt's next victim was. Instead, they all pretended the conversation never happened while simultaneously making it clear that they wanted nothing to do with Cate.

The hardest part was that during the past month—while Olivia and Max had brought in friends of friends of friends—*Twentysomething* had started to become less of an outlet and more of an addiction. Cate checked their view count multiple times a day, read and reread all the stories they published until she could recite them verbatim. She felt an adrenaline rush every time they got a new email, a new contributor, a new person believing in their assistant mutiny. No matter how many doubts she had, she couldn't quit now. She was in too deep. She couldn't afford the withdrawal.

When she got home from work that night after another day of being ignored by her colleagues, Theo was waiting for her on the stoop with a smile, salads from Sweetgreen, and a bottle of wine. He was becoming the best part of her day, which was another thing contributing to her stress acne. It had been so long since she'd had a boyfriend, she was wary of her every move, hyperaware of anything that would scare him away. Did she laugh too much? Did her feet smell when she took her shoes off at his apartment? Did she talk too much? Did she talk about *Matt* too much?

"I came up with a new excuse," Theo said, standing to kiss her as she approached the door. "He's having a colonoscopy?"

Cate laughed. "Finally, one I can actually use." She unlocked the doors and led him inside, down the dimly lit hallway. "I'm glad you've moved away from Matt's use of Viagra."

"I'm sure I have more of those up my sleeve."

She stopped outside her apartment on the second floor and

looked at him. He was about six inches taller than her, so she stood on her tiptoes to match his eyes. "I like you," she said. "A lot. But I *will* break up with you if you continue bringing up erectile dysfunction."

He bent down and kissed her. "I'm not the one who introduced the concept on our first date."

Cate shook off her laugh and unlocked the door. "I'm never going to live that down, am I?"

"Not while I'm around."

She found herself hoping that was for a very long time.

When they walked inside, Lauren was lying on the couch with a goopy green mask on her face and Taylor Swift on the record player. Theo retrieved bowls and wine mugs from the kitchen, and they plopped on the couch next to Lauren as Cate felt her phone vibrate in her pocket. She pulled it out, expecting to draft up a quick response to Matt's classic *Hellooooo*, when she saw it was an email, not a text.

HR Meeting was in the subject line.

The mug of wine dropped from her hands and immediately started soaking the navy blanket on her lap.

"Oh shit," she barely heard Theo say as he rushed into the kitchen for paper towels. Everything started to blur around her. This was it. Everything the other Larcey assistants had warned her about when she pitched them a month ago was coming true. She'd handed Matt everything he needed to fire her. Her finger hovered over opening the email, wanting to live in the last minutes of employment for as long as possible, but knowing she'd never work in this industry again. She finally opened it.

To: Marjorie Higgins
From: Simon MacDonald
CC: Matthew Larcey, Cate Britt
Subj: HR MEETING

Dear Marjorie,
We'd like to meet with you tomorrow, in Matt's office, at 6:30
p.m. Please be prompt.

Best,
Simon
Simon MacDonald
Vice President, Human Resources
Larcey Publishing

"Holy fucking shit," Cate said, reading the email again. And
then again. Marjorie was getting canned, not her. All those
meetings were about Marjorie, the first C-Suite level person
to be fired yet. Matt didn't know about *Twentysomething*. He
hadn't been spending all those days figuring out how to throw
a knife from his office into her back. He was just organizing
the logistics to fire Marjorie.

"What's going on?" Lauren asked.

Cate shook her head. "They're firing Lucy's boss. This is
insane—" Her phone buzzed again. "Oh shit, Marjorie just
responded."

To: Matt Larcey
From: Marjorie Higgins
CC: Simon MacDonald, Cate Britt
Subj: RE: HR MEETING

Matt, just fire me now and save me the embarrassment. My
ten years here should have earned me at least that much.

"She doesn't want to come in tomorrow. She told them to
just fire her now." Cate's phone buzzed again. "For the love
of God, why the *hell* am I still cc'd on this!"

To: Marjorie Higgins
From: Matt Larcey
CC: Simon MacDonald, Cate Britt
Subj: RE: HR MEETING

You're being let go. Please have your office emptied by noon tomorrow.
ML

Another email followed in quick succession.

And take care to let your assistant go as well.

"Fuck," was all Cate could say as she paced back and forth. "What do I do? I have to tell Lucy."

"You can't tell her," Theo said, perched on the edge of the couch like he was anticipating a potential fainting spell and was getting ready to catch her at any moment.

Cate stopped. "What do you mean I can't? I have to."

"He's right," Lauren agreed. "You just need to let this run its course."

"I would want her to tell me," Cate said stubbornly.

"It's not your place," Lauren said as Theo nodded in agreement.

Cate threw her phone onto the other side of the couch and pulled the now wet blanket over her head. In what world was Lucy fired, but *Cate was fine*? The one writing anonymous stories about her terrible boss and his punishing demands?

It just didn't make sense.

THE OFFICE WAS dark and empty when Cate walked into the bullpen the next morning, save for Lucy, who was slouched on the floor next to her desk, fiddling with a Rubik's cube and staring into the void of the empty banker's box at her feet.

The whole thing made Cate feel even worse. Lucy's normally shiny blond hair was in a bun on the top of her head. Her bangs weren't their expected blown out perfection. And she was wearing a white T-shirt and jeans, a far cry from her usual colorful blouse and pencil skirt combos.

Even the most seemingly impenetrable hire—Stephen King's second cousin or whatever—wasn't safe from Matthew J. Larcey III.

"Hi," Cate said, walking toward her, the motion-detected lights following in her path. "You okay?"

"I can't believe it."

"I'm so sorry." Cate sank down next to Lucy, her butt almost immediately going numb against the hardwood floor. "Honestly, you're probably better off. This place—"

"She's taking me with her." Lucy looked at Cate for the first time, her eyes swollen and puffy. But she was smiling. She seemed almost relieved, like she already knew everything was going to be okay. "We're going to Peacock."

No wonder Marjorie had no objections to the firing. "Marjorie was poached," Cate realized.

"Not exactly," Lucy said. "The second she was fired last night, she called Maggie over at Peacock, and the company offered both of us jobs this morning. I'm going to be an assistant editor. And the six months maternity leave thing is real."

"Holy shit, you got promoted. That's fucking great."

"Turns out Marjorie actually likes me." Lucy smiled wryly.

"Who knew?" Marjorie only ever referred to Lucy as "YOU!"—leading everyone to believe for the past year that Marjorie didn't actually know her own assistant's first name.

Dropping the Rubik's Cube into the box, Lucy let out a deep breath. "I can't believe Matt fired us."

"Me neither," Cate said. "Honestly, I thought you of all people would be safe."

Lucy lifted her hand to the desk behind her, sliding off an LP branded mouse pad. She looked at it for a moment and then lowered it into the garbage can beside them.

"I wrote about Matt," she said, looking over at Cate. "Sent a story into that website last night. You were right. It felt really good. I might do another one."

Cate felt the adrenaline rush again, her heart pumping in her chest. "You did?"

"I didn't deserve to be fired," Lucy said. "People should know how shitty he is. Even if they have to guess who I mean when I write The Boss."

Cate couldn't believe it. She'd recruited someone. She did it.

LATER THAT DAY, the door to Matt's office silently creeped open, and Cate could not have exited out of the *Twentysomething* site fast enough. She knew better than to be looking at it on her work computer the day Lucy was fired, but she did it anyway. She was too excited to read Lucy's story. And it was *good*. It was like all Lucy's reservations suddenly disappeared with the nickname she gave herself: The Feisty One.

"Did you see my email?" Matt asked, looming over her desk just seconds after the website disappeared from her screen.

"I haven't," she responded.

"I need you to print what I sent over and deliver it to the house in Vermont by Saturday."

Normally, everyone's typing would get louder and faster, but the bullpen was eerily quiet.

"Vermont?"

"I'm going up for the weekend with Kristin. I told you that."

She pulled up the calendar on her computer, stuffed to the brim with color-coded meetings and reminders. "I don't have it on here, but I'm sure—"

Matt let out an exhausted breath. "Details are an issue for you, as of late," he said, circling her desk like a shark. Did he say that to anyone else, or was it a level of condescension reserved only for her?

"I'm sure I can overnight it."

"Well, we won't arrive until Friday night, so it can't be there before then. I don't want it sitting out. But I want to read it over breakfast on Saturday. That's when I get all my good reading done." He leaned forward. "Is *that* on your calendar?"

Cate looked at him and smiled. *I'm going to take you down,* she thought. *In fact, I'm doing it as we speak. So far down you'll be buried underneath the ladder I'm clinging to the bottom of.* Until then, she would take a deep breath, lift her head, and kill him with motherfucking kindness.

"What time do you expect to be there on Friday?" she asked sweetly.

"I don't know, Cate. Come on. The plane will land when it lands. You know that."

"You got it, boss." A second more of smiling with a clasped jaw and she suddenly wasn't sure who the kindness would kill first: him or her.

He squinted at her, then stood up straight. "Skim it while you're printing if you want," he said. "It's embargoed, so just… don't be stupid."

He turned to face the rest of the bullpen and Cate had the sudden, unexpected but overwhelming urge to take *Twentysomething* down. Maybe he wasn't as much of an asshole as she made him out to be in her head. He was letting her read a manuscript, after all. Did she overanalyze their conversations? Was she inventing condescension where there was none? Maybe he was changing? Maybe she just needed to prove herself—to gain his trust—and he'd treat her like a person instead of a piece of furniture he had found on the side of Sixth Avenue.

"Where the hell is everyone?" he yelled, shattering the silence.

Cate looked up. All the women were gone from their desks, their chairs empty and still.

Where the hell *was* everyone?

"Bathroom, I think," Spencer said, staring at his keyboard.

"Jesus Christ, you'd think we paid you all to pee instead of work." Matt stomped back into his office. Now *that* was the Matt she was used to.

As soon as his door closed, Cate cleared her internet history and stood. "Can you cover my phone for a second?" she asked Spencer. "I have to go to the bathroom, too."

He looked at the empty desks around him. "What? Are you guys all synched up now?"

She pulled a tampon out of the bottom drawer and tucked it into her sleeve until she reached his desk. "It *does* happen," she said. "Here." She placed the tampon gently on top of his keyboard. "For when it's your turn."

"I don't want this," he yelled after her. She threw him a shrug.

When Cate pushed the bathroom door open, she found three deer in headlights, staring at her as if *every other woman on the floor* hadn't been fired and there could possibly be anyone else besides her walking into that room.

"We're in," Grace said. "We're going to submit stories to that website. We want to write about Larcey."

Excitement zinged up Cate's spine. "Really?"

Nodding, Grace stood from the stained couch and wiped her hands on the front of her jeans. "I'm over this place. If they can fire Stephen King's second cousin, then we're all game."

Cate found herself dumbfounded for the second time that

day. She had successfully recruited multiple *Twentysomething* contributors.

"Welcome to the club," she told them.

They walked back to the EAB in a pack, unconcerned about how conspicuous it looked. Especially after Matt made a point to notice and yell about it.

"Take your fucking time, why don't you." Spencer stood from Cate's chair and put her headset on the keyboard. "Why do girls insist on going to the bathroom together, anyway?"

Cate looked at Grace. Then Penelope. Erin. Then at Lucy's bare desk.

She smiled.

Because we're plotting against the patriarchy.

10

. . . .

Lauren sat on the trailer steps, two iced coffees sweating in her hands, waiting for Owen to bring her oatmeal. It had become an almost daily ritual. She never asked for it, but every day he'd show up with two bowls, whether she wanted one or not. She always did, and today she was reciprocating with *really* good coffee from Abraco. She finally found a writer who liked a drip, and she was going to make sure nothing changed that.

While she waited, she focused on everything other than the phone pinging in her lap. She looked into the windows of the exquisitely expensive apartment building across the street, listening to the screams of giddy kids on summer break in Tompkins Square Park nearby. But her eyes eventually always landed on the phone, lighting up with each new *Twentysomething* email they received. Apparently, she needed to stop wishing into the Fourth of July fireworks universe. In fact, it seemed that might be a surefire way to *not* get what she wanted. If the last month was any indication, her attempt to shut *Twentysomething* down via universal intervention did not work. Not even close.

It was when she picked up her phone to start going through the four contributing stories they'd *already* received earlier that she saw him: a tanned fit guy with blond hair and narrow shoulders, walking into the corner deli. This time it actually did look like it could be him, not just her imagination.

It had been a Thursday morning one year ago when Lauren knocked on Pete's door.

"Can I talk to you about something?" she began, her legs bouncing. "It's…about James."

Pete's brow furrowed as he waved her into his office, gesturing to the guest chair opposite his desk. She felt guilty bringing it up—like an inconvenient gnat Pete would swat away—but he waited patiently for her to speak, smiling kindly anytime she looked up. Finally, she took a deep breath and did it: she told him everything. Every uncomfortable detail.

Well, almost everything.

After she finished, they lingered in silence for what could have been full minutes. She couldn't look at him, as if too much eye contact would reveal the shame and embarrassment she so keenly felt.

Finally, Pete leaned onto the desk. "First of all," he began, "you need to know that you can come to me about stuff like this. The most important thing is that everyone feels safe at work."

She nodded, biting the inside of her mouth to keep from crying.

"What did I just say?" he asked. "Repeat it to me so I know you understand."

Lauren took a deep breath so her voice wouldn't crack. "You said that I can come to you about stuff like this."

"Good." Pete tapped his fingers on the edge of his desk, thinking. "I know it's a lot to put on the shoulders of a twenty-five-year-old," he said with a deep breath, "but how would you want to handle this?"

Lauren's first instinct was that she didn't want to cause any trouble. She couldn't forever be known as the girl who cried wolf. Because if she did it once, everyone would assume she'd scream at every single animal she saw, whether it was a creepy wolf or a gentle labradoodle. Even when she knew no one would look at her the same way.

"I'd rather keep going as if nothing happened," she said. "But maybe I just don't have to talk to James alone anymore?"

Pete considered this, leaning back and forth in his chair like he couldn't figure out exactly where he was comfortable. "I don't think that's an option. I think I have an obligation to tell someone." He glanced at the studio contact sheet hanging on the bulletin board above his computer, listing all of the production executives, creative executives, and people in Business Affairs, Finance, and Marketing. No, HR, though. That, they both knew. There was no one tapped to handle this stuff, and Lauren began to wonder if that was systematically intentional. "I honestly don't even know who I'm supposed to tell—"

"Don't," she said quickly, desperately, looking down at her hands, twisted together so hard her knuckles were white. "Don't tell anyone. Please. I don't want to make a big deal about this."

"It is a big deal, though, Lauren."

She wished she hadn't said anything. The thought of having to repeat this again to some studio suit, then having word get around—as it obviously would—made her sick with regret.

When she looked up, Pete was watching her, reading her face. "Okay." He sighed, leaning forward. "*If* we don't tell the studio—that's an *if*—you two need to disengage, and he needs to go." He seemed to be talking out loud to himself, so she stayed quiet. "He's only got a few more weeks on his contract. He can probably fulfill them from home."

"So we're not going to tell?" she confirmed.

"If you really don't want to... I think I can deal with it myself."

She wanted to say thank you, but something stopped her.

After their conversation, as she replayed each word over in her head, she couldn't help but wonder if keeping it between the three of them worked in Pete's favor, too. Without any finite actions taken, he could play both sides, keep both relationships, keep everyone happy. He didn't have to lose a writer or an assistant. He just had to ask James to work the rest of his contract from home.

What she didn't consider was how her admission would taint their relationship moving forward. That Pete would continue to be friendly, but cautious. That he would think twice about greeting or congratulating her with a hug. That he wouldn't want to be in a trailer with her if the door was closed.

Hands pruning from squeezing the coffee cups, the sun beating down on her, Lauren started to feel panic closing her throat. She was staring at the deli's poster-clad door, breathing hard, when she saw the James look-alike reappear, pausing on the corner and taking a huge bite out of his sandwich. Again, it wasn't him. Again, her entire world had stopped spinning at the mere thought.

Lauren stood up, her hands a little shaky, and placed one of the coffees on the top step, scribbling, *Owen, had to run, got you coffee*, on the back of an old receipt. She couldn't sit still anymore. She hated living in this constant anxiety. The perpetual dread of the day she'd have to see James again. Talk to him for the first time in a year.

Pete would have warned me if he's coming back, Lauren told herself. But the thought didn't quell her fear like it used to.

EMOTIONALLY DRAINED, LAUREN climbed the stairs of the Union Square station slowly, unfazed by the line of frustrated commuters growing behind her. The whole day had been a daze, and she couldn't focus on more than one step at a time. She just wanted to lie in her friends' laps and tell them everything. But she wouldn't because no one could know.

Always the first to arrive, Lauren waved to their favorite Sobremesa host and took their usual spot in the back, ordering a pitcher as soon as she sat down. She drank her first glass in three gulps straight from the rim, salt and all. Olivia and Max showed up as she was pouring her second, and when Cate arrived twenty minutes later, she was already starting to feel the tequila.

"Lauren crushed this pitcher," Olivia said, waving over the waitress to order another.

Cate turned to face the tables around them and then scanned the rest of the room. "Do you think we should get two or three more?"

"Did you get a raise or something?" Lauren asked. "Because I can't afford three more pitchers unless I win The Shit List."

"I think the pot will be a little bigger this week," Cate said as Olivia made the executive decision to get three more pitchers.

"Why?" Lauren demanded. She could tell by the apathetic look on Cate's face that something was happening. Something Cate already knew Lauren wasn't going to like. "Why, Cate?"

"We invited some people," Cate said. "Some of the contributors. So maybe we don't mention the whole *founding the blog* thing and focus on the *writing stories for the blog* thing tonight."

Max laughed. "Then we should probably cool it on the liquor."

Lauren sat back on the hard, wooden bench. "Why would you guys do that?" It seemed incredibly irresponsible to bring other people into this tradition when they had so much to lose with one tequila-induced slip of the tongue.

"They have shitty things to complain about too," Olivia said, pulling a few extra chairs to the table. "Everyone does."

"And if everyone meets and sees the friendly faces behind these anonymous stories, maybe they'll be more inclined to pass the blog along. Try to get other friends involved."

"Exactly," Cate said, agreeing with the point Lauren was sure she put in their heads in the first place. "Plus, we're going to talk about Max and Olivia's assistant society thing. Maybe some of them are members and can spread the word there, too."

Lauren faded quietly into the corner as the others continued to plan who would sit where, what they would say, whether everyone would introduce themselves by their contributor name or if they should discourage introductions entirely. This had Cate written all over it. She never planned ahead, just acted on her ideas and dealt with the repercussions later. It was what she had done when she bought a new couch off an Instagram ad only to realize it didn't fit through the front door; when she "invested" in her college boyfriend's start-up without reading the fine print; and when she created *Twentysomething*. It was just another thing that Lauren, Olivia, and Max were going to have to clean up. But Lauren was sick of cleaning.

Lauren didn't say another word for the rest of the night as contributors started filing in and chatting with each other. She quietly poured herself more tequila until the entire room moved in colorful circles, leaving her to observe, smiling graciously at anyone who looked her way. She hadn't written a story. She hadn't recruited anyone. And she wasn't sure she ever would.

AFTER AN AWKWARDLY silent cab ride—in which Lauren was so sober you'd almost forget she'd been drinking, and Cate seemed to get drunker with each green light they sped through—Lauren, again, found herself in charge of another mess. She was Ms. Reliable, always the one calling the cab, paying for the cab, and making sure Cate didn't drunkenly binge too many Wheat Thins before she went to bed. She hated that whenever she and Cate got home together, somehow without saying, Lauren was automatically responsible for unlocking all the doors. Cate never even attempted to look for her keys. She'd just continue talking until Lauren unlocked the front door, then the second front door, then the three locks on 2B.

Cate didn't even have to think. It was all done for her.

Sometimes all Lauren wanted was a second of *not* having to think.

Walking to the kitchen, she filled up two mason jars with water, spilled some Advil into her palm, grabbed a handful of pretzels. She didn't want to take care of Cate. She wanted Cate to have to grow up as quickly as Lauren had to and do things for herself. But, alas, Cate was sprawled out on the couch, screaming along with Flo Rida's "My House" blasting from the windows of their upstairs neighbors.

Lauren was always the reliable one. She had been taking care of herself since she could walk. Her mom didn't exactly have time to spare between her day job waiting tables at La Boqueria in the West Village and her night job at the front desk of Hotel Beacon. It was Lauren's responsibility to do her homework after school in the emergency stairwell behind the check-in desk while waiting for her mom to finish her shift. It was Lauren who shoved the stack of mail that collected on the kitchen counter into her book bag and carried it to the hotel so her mom could pay the bills on time. It was her mom's job to race her the twenty blocks home after her shift—which Lauren later learned was because they couldn't afford a cab and it was too late for the subway—and to make sure Chef Elmondo saved a little bit of vanilla ice cream for her in the hotel restaurant on Saturdays. She was always keeping everyone's life in line, but now she wanted to be the one to spin out and let someone else be in charge for a change.

Lauren put the mason jar of water and Advils on the coffee table in front of Cate's face. "I'm going to bed."

Cate wobbled to sit up. "You're not going to have a dance party with me?"

"I don't want to dance, Cate, I want to sleep." Lauren was sure 3B had done this on purpose. They'd been waiting all night in bated silence for her to come home, and then turned the volume so high it felt like the music was bumping in her chest and bouncing off the walls.

"Come dance with me!" Cate struggled to get to her feet, holding her hands out for balance, then walked to Lauren and wrapped her arms around her neck. "I love you so much. You're the Chrissy to my John Legend. The Tom Hanks to my Rita Wilson—"

Lauren untangled herself from Cate's grip.

"Why are you being a pooper?" Cate asked, sticking out her bottom lip.

"I'm just not in the mood, okay?"

Cate fell back onto the couch and stayed still, sprawling her limbs in every direction. "You're such a wet blanket. You don't want to dance party. You barely want to do the website. I don't get it."

"Well, two months ago you said we weren't telling anyone, and then fifty people showed up to The Shit List tonight for a website I didn't think was a good idea from the beginning."

"I just wanted to—"

"That's your problem," Lauren spat. "You only think about what *you* want. You don't think, for a second, about other people."

That seemed to sober Cate up. "Are you kidding?" She sat

up on the couch. "I'm doing this whole fucking thing *for other people*. I'm doing it so we *all* don't have to pay these bullshit dues anymore."

"I'm fine paying my dues. I just want to keep my head down, work hard, and move up."

"Sure, but look where it's gotten you. Another year as an assistant."

A tidal wave of exhaustion bore down on Lauren's shoulders. "That's the only option I have, Cate. My mom can't pay my rent if I get fired. And you know how many Cuban girls write for TV? Basically none. I'm the only woman and the only nonwhite person in my show's writers' room. Getting a job in this industry, for *me*, was next to impossible. But it's not impossible for people like you. I don't need change." She rubbed her eyes. "I can't do it anymore. I'm out."

Cate looked at her for a long time before grabbing the closest bottle of alcohol—vodka—and walking toward her bedroom. "Fine. Then nothing will change. If you want to be a lifer, you can be a lifer. Good luck."

Cate slammed her door before Lauren could reply, which pissed her off more than anything else. *Lauren* was the angry one. Cate was supposed to be apologetic. Not slamming doors and calling her a lifer, a fear of all of theirs: waking up at fifty and still being an assistant, still getting his lunch, wondering what happened. Wondering what forced them to stop dreaming of more.

Lauren slammed her door louder than Cate had and collapsed into bed.

She was *not* a lifer. She was going to get promoted eventually. Pete was going to recognize her talent and give her the reward she deserved. She just wasn't going to get it by writing about him, by calling him out on all the shit that he'd done. She was going to do it the right way, not through a shortcut disguised as a "revolution."

CATE WAS TOO drunk and too angry to fall asleep. She was mostly angry, or so she told herself as she paced from wall to wall, the room spinning around her, listening to the quick hollow taps of the rain on her air-conditioning. She took a shot straight from the bottle. Nothing about *Twentysomething* was selfish. Yes, she was thinking about herself and The Shit List when the thought first popped into her head, but she wanted it to benefit everyone. Frankly, if it didn't benefit everyone, if others didn't stand up and join her, it wouldn't work.

Just because Lauren was scared didn't mean Cate was doing the wrong thing. Maybe it meant the opposite. Sometimes it was the scariest stuff that forced the biggest change. Lauren wanted a revolution, even if she didn't know it yet. And Cate was going to make it happen. She was going to get everyone on board. She was going to prove to Lauren that what they were doing was important and so much bigger than the four of them. Then Lauren would have no choice but to come around.

Cate took another shot, then froze as an idea flashed in her mind.

They needed to be impossible to ignore. They needed to make a change. They needed more people.

And something that would help greatly was a very attractive low-level journalist with exceptional back muscles writing about it—not about Cate or about any of them *specifically*, but about the site itself. Something like: *Blog Aims to Oust Bad Bosses* or *Website Tackles Toxic Office Environments*. Something like that. She was just spitballing.

In minutes, Cate was dressed and out the door, waiting in the rain for a black Honda to pick her up and drive her to the West Village.

She buzzed Theo's apartment four times before he groggily answered. When she got out of the elevator on the eighth floor, he was standing in the doorway to his apartment, clad in a black T-shirt and boxers, his hair standing up in every direction.

Squinting in the harsh hallway light, he said, "So you *are* here."

She kissed him and walked inside. "You just let me up."

"Yeah, but part of me thought I was dreaming." He closed and deadbolted the door behind him, then walked past her toward his mattress. "I think I'm going back to bed now," he whispered, lifting his shirt off and throwing it on the floor.

Cate paused and leaned against the bookshelf, watching him crawl under the covers and get comfy again, curling into a ball. She smiled. She liked him. A lot.

With his eyes closed, Theo patted the empty side of the mattress, and she took off her clothes, leaving them in a damp pool on the floor, and climbed in. He was so warm, and she nudged herself into him, kissing his neck, wanting to kiss everything else, too. She reached for the band of his boxers, but he pulled her hand up to his chest.

"You're drunk," he mumbled. "And I'm so tired."

"But I don't want to sleep." She sat up, running her fingers up and down his arm, her head swimming from the vodka. Then she remembered why she was there. "Wait," she said quickly. "I have something to tell you."

He pulled her arm. "Can you tell me in five hours?"

"No!" She nudged his shoulder and he opened his eyes, just barely. "I have something for you to write about." She considered exactly how to phrase this; even drunk, she knew she needed to be careful with her words. "I found this website where people write anonymously about their bosses," she began. "It feels like something that could get a feature. It's going pretty viral."

"I don't know if that's really the right fit for the *Times*." Theo was having trouble keeping both eyes open, and the more she watched him struggle, the heavier her own eyes became. She wasn't sure he noticed he'd been running his finger up and down her calf, but that motion soothed her further into sleepiness. "I'm not sure my boss will be into it, but I can pitch him. If you really feel like it's going viral."

"Basically everyone I know is talking about it," she said, which wasn't a total lie.

"Then sure, yeah, I'll check it out." He yawned and rolled over, pulling her into him, willing her to shut up.

"I mean, it could be a great lead for you." She didn't want to sound too enthusiastic, too eager. She didn't want to give herself up. She'd only *heard* of this website, after all. She was invested in his career, like a good—dare she say?—girlfriend.

If *Twentysomething* could get media coverage, then more people could contribute and more stories could be showcased. And Lauren could see exactly how unselfish this actually was.

11

Throughout the entire Shit List evening with the swarm of new contributors, Olivia had been receiving an absurd amount of cartoon sexts from her nonfriend with benefits. First, the peach emoji and the hand waving emoji. Then the tongue and taco. Eggplant and squirt. Mostly, she loathed him. But the smallest part of her didn't, which was why she always responded. She loved giving and receiving booty calls. No strings attached. Just good, sometimes experimental, fun. Monogamy was an unnatural expectation on humans. That was why there was so much divorce and so many unhappy marriages. Two of her sisters married their high school sweethearts and could, Olivia was positive, do *so* much better. But instead, they were in their early thirties with more children combined than she could count on one hand and had never left their home state of Georgia.

On top of that, nothing was more satisfying than when her mom slipped questions like, *Any boys in your life?* into her daily calls, and Olivia's response was, *Yes, many*, and her mother would sigh and tell her to reread Corinthians 6:16, which said, "Or do you not know that he who is joined to a prostitute becomes one body with her. For, as it is written, 'the two will become one flesh.'" Olivia didn't know if her mother was calling her a prostitute, or denying she'd ever had sex and warning her about what would happen if she did before marriage. Either way, Olivia loved the game.

After making sure Cate and Lauren got into a cab, Olivia called an Uber to Cobble Hill. She arrived at his Brooklyn apartment a bit early, so she sat on the stoop of the brownstone next door and waited to kill time. She couldn't seem needy, or like she rushed to get there. Which she definitely had not.

A bearded man smoking a cigarette walked past, and she asked to bum one. She wasn't a smoker, but she liked the smell. And smelling like cigarettes when she showed up would leave him wondering where she'd been, and with whom.

When she was ready, Olivia stubbed out the cigarette and walked through the always-unlocked front door and down the first-floor hallway to his apartment in the back. She knocked twice, taking a deep, smoky breath.

Charlie appeared in a white Bangerz tour T-shirt—Miley Cyrus's tongue sticking out at Olivia—and blue boxers. His body filled the doorway as he looked from her dark hair to her Celine peep-toes and gave an approving nod. It should have pissed her off—misogyny and all that—but she'd admit she thrived under his appreciative gaze. He moved to the side and she brushed past him, reveling in the knowledge that he was watching her walk away.

His apartment was gorgeous—granite countertops, floor-to-ceiling windows, a meticulously curated record collection—which, once you forgot that his parents rented it for him, made her feel like she was having a mysterious affair with a handsome, rich James Bond character. He pulled a Brooklyn Lager from the fridge and handed it to her, leading her through the kitchen onto the back patio, a private yard that was more square feet than his indoor space, decorated with a wooden dining table, a grill, a firepit, and an outdoor TV.

They sat under a blanket in front of the firepit and drank relatively silently. Theirs was a relationship based in convenience. They had met at one of *The Good Morning Show*'s Christmas parties two years ago, when Max had brought Olivia as a plus-one but ditched her very quickly in favor of networking, leaving Olivia to enjoy the open bar by herself. Charlie sidled up to her, and they got just drunk enough to go home together and have mind-blowing sex without thinking anything through. Two years later, they were still sleeping together (the whole no commitment thing made the epic sex last), and Max still didn't know. Which was why this had to be the last time. No more secrets.

By the second beer, they were making out, his hand under her shirt, hers in his pants. He wanted to go inside but she stopped him, pulled up her skirt, and moved on top of his lap. The blanket over her shoulders was the only thing separating what they were doing from the eyes of the four units above his. There was something incredibly hot about potentially being watched.

She called an Uber home at 3:32 a.m. They never slept over. But sometimes she got tired and rested her eyes. He was all the way in Cobble Hill, for God's sake. She needed a power nap before making her way over any bridges. Plus, she never slept in Ubers or any hired car. That was one of the three pieces of advice her dad had given her when she first moved to New York City: *don't sleep in taxis, don't sleep with your windows open, and don't sleep with boys.* She'd broken one of the three, but that was the last time she'd break the rule with Charlie. She was going to stop. She had to. He didn't know it, but that was goodbye sex. She'd memorized it for future reference, and as of tomorrow, she had a clean slate. She was fuckbuddyless.

It took less than twenty-four hours for Olivia's resolve to fray—she wasn't exactly known for her self-restraint—and a week later, she'd started working out excuses to see him. With every new emoji compilation she received, increasingly graphic, the more she ignored him and the hornier he became, she found herself thinking that maybe one more time wouldn't hurt. Right? A proper goodbye?

Olivia turned this around in her head as she waited for Max on the corner of Fifty-Fifth Street and Sixth Avenue, since they had agreed to walk to The Society meeting together. She finally spotted Max scurrying toward her across the street, carrying too many tote bags full of bullshit, and they headed over to the unnamed speakeasy, found only by following discreetly placed typewriter keys embedded in the sidewalk every two or three feet down the small back alley past dumpsters and marred chairs surrounded by cigarette butts to the secret entrance. They knocked twice on a barred black door with a small eye-level opening.

Four times a year, there was a networking event for assistants with big-time bosses that had become the closest thing underpaid twentysomethings had to a secret society. Potential members were vetted through word of mouth, unaware until you received a shady email from an ubiquitous address with a date, time, and location for your first meeting. Olivia and Max were the only invited members, which drove Cate and Lauren crazy. It was funny how bosses could act so important when in reality, they weren't even significant enough to get their assistants into a stupid club.

Olivia hated these meetings and hadn't attended one in over a year. It was just a bunch of low-level people puffing their chests out and lying about their job titles. The last one she went to, the word *assistant* was not uttered once.

But this time they were there on a mission, along with twelve people who came to The Shit List last week. They were there to spread the word about *Twentysomething*, see if anyone had heard of it and inform them if they hadn't.

Two eyes appeared in the door slit. Max and Olivia held up their phones, flashed the e-vite like FBI badges, and the door clicked open. Surprisingly, the theme of the speakeasy wasn't writing or reading. In fact, it was impossible to decipher. Moroccan poufs were scattered on the floor on top of overlapping Persian rugs. One wall was full of disorganized shelves lined with old books—probably the decorative kind, a leather-bound and gold-spined *Don Quixote* that was really, underneath, just *The Fault in Our Stars*. The room was full of people their age, assistants to some of the most powerful executives in New York, which would be intimidating to most, but not Olivia. Rather, she found the whole thing self-aggrandizing.

They walked up to the bar in the back where they ordered vodka sodas that were delivered to them in ridiculous decorative teacups. It was easy to guess based on appearances where everyone worked. The tall man in a dashing gray suit sipping what was likely an old-fashioned probably assisted someone in corporate NBC. The woman who looked like a mini JLo was, undoubtedly, working for the real JLo. And the model taking the smallest bites of a bacon-wrapped melon and drinking a Bloody Mary was definitely one of Gwyneth Paltrow's assistants. Olivia made a mental note to mention how much Nate loved the "complimentary" bath bombs.

"Do you see anyone from last week?" Max asked.

Olivia scanned the room, looking for any faces that were familiar. It was strange to know the contributors only by nicknames. The Hysterical One was sitting at the bar with two men in baseball caps. The Ambitious One was walking in front of the bookshelf, following two women in long, tulle skirts. The Dependable One was talking to a woman with a color-blocked frock that reminded her of Beetlejuice. The Easy One was at the bottom of the spiral staircase leading to the loft, talking to—

Charlie.

Shit.

"I see a couple people I remember from The Shit List," Max said. "Maybe we should walk by casually and see if they're talking about *Twentysomething*? Eavesdrop a little?"

Olivia broke out into a cold sweat as Charlie excused himself from the conversation and began heading their way.

"Ugh, you're not even listening. What are you looking at?" Olivia immediately looked elsewhere as Max followed her gaze.

Of course Charlie was a member. If Max was a member, then Charlie would be, too. Why didn't Olivia think about that?

"Seriously, what are you looking at?" Max asked.

Olivia downed the rest of her drink, letting it go straight from the cup down the back of her throat before turning to face the bar. "I need another. You?"

Max looked down at her completely full cup. "I'm good."

Frantically, Olivia imagined the perfect excuse to bolt. She could fake food poisoning? She could get a call from Nate? She could say someone died—

"Hey, Max." Panic ran up her spine at the sound of Charlie's voice behind her. "Who's your friend?" he asked, aloof, as if he didn't *love* this.

"This is Olivia," Max said flatly, nudging her to join their conversation. Olivia slowly turned around, until she was stand-

ing in her actual worst nightmare, between Max and Charlie—
her best friend and her secret fuckbuddy who hated each other.

Charlie reached his hand out to Olivia, offering a polite
smile. "Nice to meet you."

Olivia took it, ignoring flashbacks of just what those hands
were capable of.

"I didn't realize you were a member," Charlie said to Max.

"Why wouldn't I be?" Max said, taking a hard pull of her
drink.

Charlie cocked his head, feigning confusion. "I didn't think
Sheena qualified."

Max sneered as Charlie took a satisfied sip of his cock-
tail. Olivia stayed quiet. He knew the power he had in this
conversation, and he fucking *loved* it, holding the secret over
them, leaving Olivia in suspense, waiting for him to spill at
any moment.

"You do look familiar, Olivia," Charlie said, looking her
up and down. "Have we met before?"

"You don't know *everyone*," Max spat. She sounded like she
was fourteen around him.

"Possibly," Olivia managed. *Don't you dare say anything else.*
He smiled with a wink so imperceptible, she might have imagined it. In that moment, she hated him.

But she also couldn't wait to get him naked. *Damn it.*

"That's probably right." He paused. "I would remember
someone like you." His eyes lingered on hers a little too long,
and Olivia turned to keep from blushing. She wasn't a blusher.
Maybe that one time she bumped into Chris Hemsworth at a
movie premiere, but Charlie was no Chris Hemsworth.

"We have some networking to do." Max took Olivia's arm,
pulling them from the bar toward the much more crowded
sitting area.

"Good luck. If anyone's unsure who Sheena is, send them to talk to me," he offered as they walked away.

"He's such a douche," Max said when they reached the pristine leather couches and mahogany side tables on the opposite side of the room. "Honestly, if your boss sexually harasses young women, you shouldn't be qualified to join. Seems like that should be in the fine print."

Watching Charlie sidle up to two pretty brunettes and offer to buy them a drink at the open bar, Olivia was shocked he'd let her get away without more torture. Their entire relationship was a game. Usually that was how she liked it, but not when her friends were involved. She knew she'd have to tell Max eventually, but at the same time, she had vowed to not have sex with Charlie again, so maybe Max never needed to know?

"A total douche," Olivia agreed, glancing around the room, again desperate to change the subject. That was when she heard it.

Twentysomething.

"There it is." Olivia grabbed Max's hand.

"What?" Max asked.

"Just wait." They stared into the room—the dim lights and dark books—and listened.

Have you read it? It's fucking amazing.

That was yours about Jude? I knew it! That was such a good one. I wish I could tweet it or something.

Olivia could hear the whispers growing, the whispers of all the overtired, overworked twentysomethings with small wallets and huge ambitions.

I never realized so many men were so utterly fucked up.

You wrote a story? Ugh, okay I'm going to submit something this weekend. Twist my arm.

It was happening. The word was spreading. Cate was going

to lose her damn mind when they reported back. And so was Lauren, though she'd put enough distance between herself and the website that maybe they didn't have to tell her. At least, not right now.

Max spun around to face Olivia, knocking over an empty glass on the side table. "Charlie." She tried to pick up the glass, but her hands were shaking. "Charlie cannot find out about this. He'll know it's me writing about Richard."

Olivia looked around. "Honestly, if he's in this room he's probably going to hear about it." She could see Max's rising panic before she quickly added, "But he'll never figure it out. Your stories are *very* well hidden and there are so many he'd have to go through, the chances he sees it are minuscule." Then she had the most comforting thought of all. "He probably doesn't even know about Richard's ass fetish, anyway. It's not like he's had to experience it."

Max took a deep, calming breath. "You're probably right," she said, though still unconvinced. "Now I have to nervous pee," she added, pushing toward the bathroom.

Just as Max turned the corner, Charlie appeared in front of Olivia with an arrogant smile. "Boo."

She wasn't shaken by him this time, instead riding a *Twentysomething* high.

"What do you want?" she asked coolly.

He leaned onto the couch beside her. Drinking from a tiny teacup, Charlie looked unreasonably large. "Just wanted to see how all that networking was going."

"It's going great, thanks."

He nodded. "Good, good. I'm here to help if you need any advice, have any questions. You know, whatever I can do."

"I don't need any tips on how to fail upward. You're a great example."

Charlie pretended to look hurt. "At least I'm moving up."

"Is that what kissing your boss's ass is called nowadays? Interesting."

"I know you'd rather I kiss your ass. Don't worry, there's enough of me to go around." Charlie gave her a lazy smile. "Speaking of bosses, I was over there talking to that smoke show—" he motioned toward a woman in a tight black dress with long dirty blond hair braided to the side "—and she was talking about some website she heard of. You should check it out. Seems right up your petty alley."

Of course he already knew. She needed to distract him before he thought too hard about it. "Want to get out of here?" she asked, mustering whatever sexy smile she could bear.

He stood up a little taller and raised his eyebrows. "Should we just find a coat closet?"

She sighed. He'd never change.

Though that would be hot.

"We could…but I have a bed. So maybe we stick to that?" Olivia spotted Max approaching, waving her hands to dry. "I'll meet you outside in five," she said quickly, but it was too late.

"You again," Max said, locking eyes with Charlie. "What do you want now?"

"Nothing." He smiled and side-eyed Olivia in the most obvious way possible. *"Twentysomething,"* he said, remembering, as if he were merely continuing their conversation from before the sex talk. "That's the website. You guys heard of it?"

Olivia shook her head and watched Max lose all the color from her face.

"Seems like something you should look into. You know, since you're both assistants."

You are too, Olivia wanted to say. He always managed to forget it.

Charlie turned and waved to them as he made his way downstairs to wait for Olivia outside. If someone had asked two minutes ago, she would have said her original plan was to leave him out there—The Society had a no reentrance policy—and she'd sneak out the back door with Max later. But now she had no choice but to sleep with him. Even if it weren't for the onslaught of erotic emojis, she reasoned, she couldn't possibly let him look into *Twentysomething* himself. She had to keep tabs on what he knew. Her determination to be fuckbuddyless could wait a few days. Or weeks.

12

It had been just over one week since Lauren had talked to Cate in any capacity other than, "Are you finished in the shower?" and, "Have you seen the can opener?" *Lauren* was supposed to be the angry one. Cate had called her a lifer, basically saying Lauren wouldn't amount to anything more than getting coffee for Pete forever. But the morning after the fight, an extremely hungover Cate came home at noon in sunglasses and a messy bun, and beelined to her bedroom without even a nod hello. Lauren didn't think their fight was *that* bad, but if Cate was going to treat her like that, then Lauren was going to reciprocate. The silent treatment could go both ways, if that was how Cate wanted to play it.

Since Cate was *Twentysomething*'s leader and that was all she, Max, and Olivia talked about, Lauren had inadvertently ostracized herself from everyone in her life except Pete and Owen, who she could argue were the reasons she was in this position in the first place. If she didn't like them so much—and need her job, and the money that came with it—she'd write all about everything that had happened, and she never would have had to bow out.

A day after the fight was Lauren's first weekend without friends, so she visited her mom's apartment in Morningside Heights under the guise of needing some R&R. A weekend was two nights too long for a visit when sharing a bed with your mother.

Lauren didn't tell her what was going on—her mom was never great at the whole advice thing. *A lo hecho, pecho* was generally her response to anything. *What's done is done.* Only nineteen years apart, Lauren watched her mom grow up with her. Even as a kid she found their life frustrating: moving every few years as their rent hiked; watching her mom shuffle from job to job; seeing guys sneak out of their apartment before sunrise. It wasn't until she was an adult that Lauren realized how hard her mother worked.

Now that they were both older and a little more stable, they could have fun together. They walked Riverside Drive, ate BO's Bagels, people-watched on Columbia's campus, and got drunk on Salty Dogs at Ellington in the Park. They did face masks and watched an *I Love Lucy* marathon while her mom swooned over Desi Arnaz and called him proudly by his full Cuban name, Desiderio Alberto Arnaz y de Acha III. "If you were a boy, I was going to name you that," her mom always joked.

Now in her second weekend without friends, Lauren decided to do something self-exploratory and go to a bar alone. She was sick of drinking wine on the couch until she heard the shuffling of Cate's keys entering the lock in their door, when she'd swiftly grab her things, turn off the TV, and hide in her room to avoid any more awkward interactions with Cate and Back Muscles. Gathering her resolve, Lauren decided on the bar in the lobby of the Ace Hotel. She'd only been once, but she figured an upscale hotel bar would be a place where she wasn't the only one drinking alone. She put on going-out makeup for the first time in weeks, surprised she had the muscle memory for a solid smoky eye, and wore a dress that showed off the hips she somehow gained in *Twentysomething*-related stress eating.

Once she entered the lobby, she immediately regretted her decision for three reasons. First, it was packed, and it took a few awkward minutes to find a seat at the very edge of the bar. Second, it felt like this was the kind of place where everyone carried Moleskine notebooks and thought they were writing the next great American novel, which brought the pretentiousness to a new level. Third, a glass of wine was twenty-two dollars. She could get two bottles for less than that at the liquor store across the street from her apartment. She didn't realize she should have pregamed her casual evening of classy drinks.

When Lauren finally got the attention of the bartender, she leaned in. "Can I have a glass of your, uh, cheapest red?"

"It's called the house red." The bartender turned to pour the drink, but not before Lauren saw him roll his eyes.

It was difficult to nurse a glass of wine when she needed, so badly, to loosen up. The first one went down like water, and suddenly she had spent forty-four dollars and wasn't even drunk yet. She decided she did not like drinking in public alone. Instead of feeling freeing or restorative or confidence-boosting, it felt embarrassing and lonely. She wished she was with her friends. They were all probably drinking cheap beers while planning more posts for *Twentysomething*, before deciding to find a bar to go out and dance. She didn't like the idea of them dancing without her.

"You look like you need another drink," someone said close to her ear.

Lauren braced herself for some creep, but turned around to see Owen, smiling, hands to himself, standing a respectful distance away. The dim overhead industrial bulbs and string lights accentuated his broad shoulders. He was wearing glasses, thick black square rims framing his eyes, spotlighting them in a way his contacts never did at work. And his hair looked like he'd been running his fingers through it.

Oh, how Lauren wanted to do that.

"What are you drinking?" Owen asked.

She lifted her nearly empty glass. "House red. It's the cheapest wine, but if you call it that the bartender will ignore you for at least fifteen minutes."

Laughing, Owen leaned onto the dark wooden counter and waved to the bartender, who came over right away. "Two of your cheapest red, please."

The bartender smirked at Lauren, and she pushed Owen with her shoulder, nearly falling off the stool in the process. He had to grab her arm to stabilize her again. She'd had only two glasses of wine; she had to pull it together. She was with someone from work. A colleague. A hot colleague. A colleague she really wanted to see naked— *No. Stop.*

"What are you doing here?" she asked after the bartender presented their drinks. "Do you frequent hotel bars?"

"I do. Holiday Inns are my favorite, but I figured I'd try something new tonight." He smiled.

"And?"

"Not bad. Though, the lack of fluorescent lighting and generic landscape artwork is doing them a disadvantage."

She laughed. "Where *do* hotels get their art? It's all the same."

"It's all Bob Ross wannabes."

"We don't make mistakes, just happy accidents," she said in her best impersonation.

Owen chuckled and looked around her. "Are you here alone?"

She nodded toward the woman on the stool next to her, who was sipping a White Russian and rubbing her hands all over her date, a man wearing a thin-collared shirt unbuttoned just enough to see his dark, graying chest hair. "I'm with my best friend… Roxy. And her boyfriend, Bruce."

Owen shook his head, grinning. "Of course. Roxy and Bruce. You've mentioned them before. Let me introduce myself."

As he moved toward them, she laughed and grabbed his wrist without thinking, pulling him back to her. Then she immediately let go. Too much touching. *Colleague. Colleague. Hot colleague.*

Owen met her gaze. "So, Roxy's here with Bruce… How about you? Where's your boyfriend?"

It wasn't creepy when *he* asked. Probably because he was thirty, not forty. And they were at a bar, not at catering during lunch on set. And she didn't feel like he'd use his producing writer title to punish her if she didn't answer.

"I don't have one at the moment," she said. It felt like the right way to phrase it. Vague and to the point without revealing she hadn't had one for a while.

He nodded a few times, and they were both smiling, unable to look away from each other.

"Interesting," he said, holding his glass toward her. "Cheers to that."

LYING IN BED facing the ceiling later that night, Lauren thought back to the girl in Pete's trailer a few months ago who had watched Owen enter like an angel sent to earth to make her horny, and she couldn't help but grin. She had done it. She slept with him. And it had been fucking fantastic.

"What are you smiling about?" Owen asked, his face pressed on her pillow as he looked at her.

"Nothing," she said instead of admitting she'd been thinking about him. "Can I ask you a question?" She wasn't sure what time it was, but by the color out the window it seemed to be that sweet spot in late summer just before dawn, when the sky started to brighten but the streetlights were still on. She didn't know what she wanted to ask, she wanted to know everything about him. "What's the best advice you've ever been given?" she finally said, the first thing to come to mind.

"Writing advice or otherwise?"

"Let's go with writing."

He let out a deep breath and thought about it. "'Write something important,'" he finally said. "Actually, it was Pete who told me that, when I was first starting out."

"Really?" Pete had never given her any advice like that. Probably because they never talked about writing.

Owen stretched his arms above his head. "Sorry," he said. "Didn't mean to bring Pete into your bed."

She nudged his leg with her foot. "Yeah, I don't like that. I don't like that at all."

"Regretted it the second it came out. Weird for both of us." He paused, like he was genuinely bothered by the mention of their boss's name. Like it pulled him back into reality, reminded him who he was with.

"I haven't felt particularly inspired in a while," Lauren said before admitting she couldn't send him anything to read because she didn't have anything good written.

"I have an exercise for that," he offered, sitting up and motioning for her to do the same. She rummaged under the covers until she found his gray T-shirt and slipped it on. "I've already seen you naked," he laughed.

"Yeah, but not while sitting. Very different."

He tugged at the collar of her shirt. "Right, of course, just doing some other things."

She swatted his hand away. "What's this game of yours?"

"It's not a game, it's an *exercise*." He lined his face up with hers. "Close your eyes."

"Okay?"

"Think of something you're unhappy with."

My love life. My job.

"Something specific," he added, as if he were in her head.

I've never kissed anyone I loved. I'm afraid that, no matter how hard I work, I'm not good enough to be a writer. I'm afraid that I'll never write anything important.

I'm still an assistant.

I'm fighting with all my friends.

That came a lot easier than expected.

"Got something?" he asked.

"A few things." She hadn't realized how unhappy she was. It was easy to make excuses for things that made her unhappy when they were one-offs. But once they piled up, ignoring them became a lot harder.

"Well, pick one or two."

My friends hate me. I'm still an assistant. Those seemed like the most immediate problems.

"I don't want to say it out loud," she whispered.

"I wasn't going to ask," he said softly. "Now, you just have to write about a character trying to change that thing."

"If I knew how to change it, I'd do that in real life, too." If Lauren knew how to not be an assistant anymore, she wouldn't be an assistant. She needed to write an episode of television, but even knowing the solution to her problem, it was impossible to fix. Because people like Owen showed up and Pete threw opportunities at him, keeping her firmly as his assistant. That was easier for him than promoting her, where he'd then have to find someone new.

"Everyone knows how to change," Owen said. "They're just too afraid to realize it."

She thought for a moment. There were too many questions in this exercise, she decided. Too many things for her to reflect on when she had a hot half-naked colleague in her bed. If she let herself think too deeply, her anxiety about Pete would come up and then, inevitably, James, which would force her to think about the repercussions of sleeping with Owen. She'd had a perfectly good time blocking them from her mind since Owen came up to her at the bar. She didn't want to think about any of it. She just wanted tonight to be tonight and nothing more.

She didn't want to anticipate consequences before they happened. For the first time in her goddamn life, she wanted to enjoy her own mess and deal with it later.

BY MORNING, Owen was gone.

It was the first time she hadn't heard a man leave in the middle of the night. Typically, she woke up just enough to watch his routine without him noticing, feeling around for clothes, shoes, wallet. Ordering an Uber, hoping his phone had enough battery life to get him home. Searching for that one sock, undershirt, hat, debating whether it was worth the struggle or if he should just give up and leave it there, unknowingly immortalizing himself in the Box of Left Things under her bed.

Her mom had a box like that, too. Whenever Lauren had found herself home alone after school, she'd sneak under her mom's bed and go through it. To eight-year-old Lauren who had never known her father, it was a choose-your-own-dad box. Any of those left things could belong to him—the brown glasses, the name tag that said MIKE, the alligator money clip that had eight singles in it. The box contained whatever version of her dad she needed in that moment. The possibilities were endless.

All Owen left was a CVS points card on the floor. She picked it up and put it on her dresser. It was the first time she wanted to return it instead of adding it to her collection. What did that mean?

She heard some movement in the hallway—floor creaking, Cate's squeaky bedroom door opening, her air conditioner wheezing in the window.

"You still coming over tonight?" Back Muscles said.

As the front door unlocked, Cate told him, "That's the plan." Then there was an unnecessarily loud kiss, and the door shut again.

Lauren imagined Cate standing in the doorway smiling like it was her first kiss. She was always giddy around Back Muscles. More bantery than usual. And funnier. Like she was in love.

Not unlike how Lauren acted around Owen, she thought, before shoving that thought to the back of her mind.

Lauren inched her bedroom door open, ensuring Cate had enough warning to run away or put in headphones or do one of the many other things she'd done to avoid conversation. Instead, Cate was sitting on the couch with a cup of coffee, reading Emma Donoghue's *Room* for what must be the tenth time. Cate looked up when Lauren appeared in the hallway and hesitated before saying hello.

"Hi," Lauren responded. She shuffled between her feet, unsure what to talk about next. It made her sad to walk on eggshells around her best friend. "How's Back Muscles?"

"He's fine." After an awkward pause, Cate closed the book and picked up her mug. "I have to get ready for something, so… See you later." Quickly, she slipped around the coffee table, past Lauren and into her bedroom. "There's more coffee left in the French press if you want some," she said right before the door closed.

Their conversations had become increasingly awkward the longer they ignored their fight. Lauren was always the first to apologize, which came with always being Mrs. Reliable, the bigger person. And she fought that instinct every day. But she missed her friends.

I slept with a writer, by the way, Lauren wanted to tell her. *I slept with the guy who took my episode. Want to help me navigate that?*

13

Dear Twentysomething,

I look forward to reading your posts every week. I hardly have the Sunday Scaries anymore. Now, I go to bed knowing my Mondays are just as bad as someone else's. I don't know who you are, but I feel like we are sisters in suffering, so I wanted to share one experience of my own. Both to contribute to your cause, and to make sure everyone knows that women can be assholes, too.

I used to assist an important person in fashion.

I stepped away from my desk to use the bathroom. I was midpee when the door opened, and I heard a very familiar click-clacking that stopped right outside my stall. Pink Louboutins with a yellow heel.

"You missed a call," she said.

I squeezed to hold my stream and apologized.

"It's incredibly irresponsible for you to leave your desk when the phone is ringing."

I tried to tell her it wasn't ringing when I left, which was, in fact, the reason I left. But it was no use.

"Please take a message for me," she said while I sat on the toilet, as if I could just pull out a pen and paper, no problem. She relayed the message—something about a Gucci jacket we needed—and click-clacked away.

When I got back to my desk, I wrote the message that she had recited to me on a Post-it in case she asked me for it. Thirty minutes later, she did.

I walked to her desk and placed the Post-it on her keyboard.

"It should really be more detailed in the future," she said, crumpling the Post-it and throwing it in the garbage.

I don't work there anymore, and I haven't had to take someone's messages in a few years, but I'll never forget that day. Thanks for starting this conversation. It's been simmering under the surface for far too long.

Best,
The Sassy One

In the dark back seat of the car service on her way to work, Max squinted at her phone's bright screen, the small text of the email making her eyes spotty. Cate had texted her The Sassy One's story the night before, asking her to publish it in the morning. Since Lauren pulled out of everything website related, Max had found herself named the new head writer, confirming anonymity, spell-checking, and making sure everything was grammatically correct. Of everyone, she seemed the least qualified for this job, but it was very typical of Cate to delegate so meticulously she somehow ended up with the least—and usually most fun—work.

On top of that, their contributors had *tripled* in the days following The Society meeting. Max was reading at least ten stories and publishing two or three of them a day. For a few days they even added a comments section to each story on the site, until Max realized it was only being used to guess who the boss was, and they removed it. There were entire subreddits dedicated to this kind of investigating, and she was fine if that lived only in the seedy underbelly of the internet where not many people knew to look. Lauren would have discovered these things right away, but it took Max a whole week. Not having Lauren around really was a disservice to the blog. It was only a matter of time until they didn't catch something that Lauren would have, and the whole site came tumbling down on top of them. And Max missed her, plain and simple.

The only thing Max could try to control was Charlie, and even there, she had a limited capability. When they were making this plan at The Shit List, she did not even think about him being there, did not think, *Hmm, maybe I shouldn't make my coworker aware of a website on which I wrote unflattering stories about our bosses.* It wasn't until she saw him at the event that panic had set in. No matter how safe or anonymous Olivia was convinced Max's stories were (it was true he was a man and never experienced the infamous butt pinch), there was no fooling Charlie. He wanted to be an investigative journalist, after all. He was hungry for a story that could put him on the map.

Max could not let him figure this out.

The day after The Society meeting, Max got to work forty-five minutes early. As always, the bright lights of the wall of flashing TV screens in the darkness had made her squint until the motion-censored fluorescents recognized her existence and popped on. She sat at her desk in the peaceful hum of the empty newsroom and turned on her computer, waiting for the two friendly beeps that welcomed her to the show's internal server. Then she glanced at the station directly to her right: Charlie's seat.

He had Post-its scattered around the desk and stuck onto the lip of his computer monitor. She slid to his spot and typed his password (FrankTheTank, the name of his family's chocolate lab) into the computer. They'd shared passwords a few months after he started when she was simultaneously on a coffee run *and* had a document on her desktop they needed printed immediately. She clicked on Internet Explorer, then Search History. She looked at the list of websites he'd visited and didn't let out a full breath until she reached the bottom and confirmed *Twentysomething* was not on it. Sure, he could have looked it up on his phone at home, but if he thought there was a story there—something he could pitch to the producers for Richard to cover—he would have definitely researched it at work.

Nothing here, she texted Olivia.

Every few days she repeated this process, and as her search continued to solicit nothing, she gained solace knowing he would remain clueless for the time being.

Today, instead of checking Charlie's computer, she spent the morning publishing The Sassy One's story. Max started going through the other stories on her to-do list as well. The three of them would read stories as they came into the inbox and mark them with a little red flag if they were solid enough to publish. Then Max would go through them, format everything, make sure all names and otherwise identifying characteristics were removed, and post them online. It was so incredibly simple that it made her angry how long it took her to do. It had started to feel like a second job.

"MAX!" Sheena screamed. Max spun around to see Sheena gliding up the stairs in her morning leggings and black hoodie look. "COME. NOW."

She glanced back at the *Twentysomething* logo brazenly glowing at the top of her screen. How long had Sheena been there? How much did she see? Max grabbed her notebook and a pen, slipped her heels back on, and ran after her.

"Good morning, Sheena," Max said breathlessly as she reached the threshold of her Hair and Makeup room. The room was always such a bright contrast to the newsroom in the mornings that Max's eyes needed to adjust. Twelve bulbs ran along the perimeter of a large mirror, bright enough to show every acne scar and chin hair you've ever had. Sprawled along the table in front of Sheena were thousands of dollars' worth of makeup in every shade of brown Sheena would ever need. The thing that always caught Max's eye was the clear box filled with fake eyelashes that looked like a caterpillar farm.

Sheena sat facing the mirror with her back to Max and her head in a copy of *People*. Through the reflection, Max could see Richard's glib face on the cover before Sheena slammed it down on the table, rattling some of the makeup containers.

"Take all of this away," she said, motioning to everything around her.

Max cautioned toward her. "I'm sorry?"

"Take it away," she repeated, as if that would clarify anything. She spun around in her chair so quickly it nearly skidded to a stop as she slammed her sneakered foot down. "The dresses. I won't be wearing them anymore."

Max glanced around at the four clothing racks flanking the walls on which close to three hundred custom-tailored dresses were organized by season, then color. "Do you want me to find you a specific one?" Max asked.

"You're not listening to me!" Sheena snapped.

"You want me to remove the dress racks," Max said, reaching toward one. Luckily, they were all on wheels. "Where would you like me to move them?"

Sheena jumped up from her seat. "Move them, throw them out, burn them, I don't care. I'm never wearing dresses on this show again. Only pantsuits."

"Does Stacey know that?" Max asked, referring to Sheena's

personal stylist, the woman who picked out and tailored the three hundred aforementioned dresses that Sheena apparently wanted Max to burn.

"I don't know what Stacey knows. I can't read her mind," Sheena said, walking out and shutting the door behind her, leaving Max alone, surrounded by clothes.

She sat down in Sheena's seat and texted Stacey to fill her in on what had apparently just been decided. Then she spun to face the mirror to get a closer look at how bad Sheena and Richard were for her skin. Picking up a bottle of under-eye cream, Max applied it generously since it cost more than she made in a day. Then she spotted Richard's face on Sheena's magazine and read the headline spanning across his suited chest: "Morning's Leading Man Richard Bradley Talks Wake-up Calls, Must-have Juices, and Ten Years at *The Good Morning Show*."

Max was surprised she hadn't remembered Richard's ten-year anniversary at the show was coming up next month, right after Labor Day. They'd been loosely planning events for it all year: some magazine exclusives the month before, a trip on the late-night circuit that week, cake and champagne on the broadcast the Friday morning of the actual anniversary, a network party at the Ophelia Lounge to celebrate that night.

Without thinking about it, she threw the magazine into the garbage, Richard's face now smiling at the rotting pear that Sheena took two bites of this morning and threw out. No one needed to read his version of his ten years here. Not when it was a stark contrast to the way everyone else felt. Not when it was practically a lie.

AFTER WORK, MAX walked across the park to East Sixty-Third Street, where Lauren was supposed to be shooting. Max had tried texting her over the last two weeks, but their conversations were oddly formal and short. She couldn't tell if that was because Lauren was annoyed they were going through with the blog without her approval, or if she assumed they were all as angry at her as Cate was. Max was not, for the record. And she wanted to make sure Lauren knew that.

When she spotted the big white trailers lining Fifth Avenue, she knew she was in the right place, and it only took asking three people before she found out Lauren would be in the trailer labeled WRITERS. She knocked with no idea who was on the other side and felt a surge of relief when Lauren answered.

"Hi, I'm the paparazzi for Ms. Barrero," Max said, flashing her phone's light in Lauren's face as she opened the door.

"They don't usually announce themselves." Lauren laughed, which was a relief to Max. "What are you doing here?" she asked, leading her to the couch to sit.

"I just wanted to see you, and you mentioned you'd be shooting around here, so...sorry if it's weird that I showed up."

"No, no, it's not. I'm glad you're here."

They were quiet for a second, and Max watched as Lauren played with the stray hairs falling around her temples from her ponytail. Seeing this upset Max; it must be lonely to work here all day and then go home to a roommate who won't talk to you.

"How's everyone doing?" Lauren finally asked quietly, barely making eye contact.

"I mean, fine. We all miss you."

Lauren nodded to herself, looking down at her lap. "Everything's going okay with the site?"

"So far, so good. There are so many stories we're publishing three times a day."

Lauren gave a small smile. "Spreading the word is working, I take it."

"Seems like it, for now. Who knows how long that'll last." Though Max didn't see them slowing down anytime soon, she also didn't want to scare Lauren off any more than she already was. "But what's new with you? How's work and stuff?"

They didn't feel like Max and Lauren. They felt like strangers, even though it had been only two weeks. But two weeks could feel significant when you were used to seeing each other every other day.

"It's fine, you know..." Lauren trailed off, but Max was skeptical. She was wearing a dress and wedges. Too nice for your average writer.

"You're hiding something," Max said, leaning closer. "What is it?"

Lauren sighed. But she must have been dying to talk because the reveal didn't take any more convincing. "I had sex with Owen."

"Oh shit. Wait, when? Where? How was it? Oh my God, I have so many questions."

"Last week."

"Last *week*? And you haven't said something?"

"I'm not really talking to anyone right now."

"Yeah, but you break weird friend fights for sex news. That's like the number one rule of fighting with your friends."

Lauren snorted. "I'll make a note for next time."

Max let out a laugh, relieved. This was good. She was revealing something. They were starting to feel more normal.

"So are you, like, seeing him? Have you been on a date—"

The trailer door burst open, and Max turned to see a very tall, attractive man in the doorway, who seemed startled to see the two of them there.

Lauren bolted to her feet. "Owen, this is Max but she's leaving, bye," she said in one breath, pulling Max off the couch and shuffling her around Owen before pushing her onto the sidewalk and slamming the door behind them.

"Um, he is so hot," Max said once she regained her balance. "Good job."

"I've been avoiding him for a few days. I'm trying to figure out what to say."

"How to ask him out?"

"No, how to tell him we have to pretend it never happened."

"Oh." That was not what Max expected. Lauren wasn't a one-night stand kind of girl. In fact, Max wasn't sure if Lauren had ever indulged in a one-night stand, *especially* with a coworker. "You should just ask him out. Fuck it. You'd be cute together."

She looked toward the trailer behind her. "I can't."

"Come on. He's clearly interested."

"It shouldn't have happened." Lauren started back up the metal stairs. "I should get back in there. Thanks for coming by, though."

Max wasn't sure exactly what was happening, what Lauren was avoiding saying, but she didn't want to push her. It seemed like she was already teetering on the edge.

"It was really good to see you," Max said.

Lauren opened the door and stood still there for a moment. Max could see her shoulders tense and relax. "You too," she said, before continuing inside.

Max felt her phone buzz in her purse. Publish the one about the girl from Indiana. The Crazy One, I think, Cate texted. Call me when you're doing it. I have one edit.

Max took a deep breath. She didn't want to be the head writer anymore. They needed Lauren back. One conversation at a time.

WHEN LAUREN RETURNED to the trailer, Owen was sitting on the couch with the same confused face Max had on hers outside. Perplexed, wondering if he did something wrong. Ever since they slept together and he left, she had added Owen to the list of people she was avoiding for reasons she couldn't talk about, which was getting longer and more complicated with every new person she met.

"Where have you been hiding out?" Owen asked, two iced coffees in his hands. He held one out, and she hesitated. Was this a peace offering, or something you did after you saw someone naked and felt guilty for leaving?

Lauren took the coffee, making sure their hands didn't touch. Now she knew how nice his skin felt against hers. Soft and warm. But it was a bad idea. All of this was a bad idea.

"Sorry," she said, standing awkwardly before him, not entirely sure what she was apologizing for.

"I miss my oatmeal buddy."

"Me too," she admitted, falling onto the couch next to him. She tried to come up with a reason why she had to immediately leave—print out something for Pete, feminine issues, family emergency. Instead, she let out a long breath. "I've been avoiding you."

His lips curled upward. "I figured that. I was too, at first. But maybe we just cut the balls off the elephant and talk about it."

"The poor elephant."

He let out a laugh and his body relaxed onto the couch. "You know what I mean."

She moved to the very edge of the cushion. According to her mother, there were only two reasons why someone ditched in the middle of the night: because you were definitely never going to see that person again, or because sleeping next to that person was too intimate. Considering she and Owen saw each other five days a week, she could only assume it was the latter. It was one thing to have sex with someone but another thing entirely to hold them while they slept.

Lauren was certain he wanted to make sure they were on the same page. Then she realized she didn't care what his intentions were when, in the dark, he had packed up everything but his CVS card and left. All she cared about was that she couldn't be the assistant who reported one writer for sexual harassment and then started sleeping—very willingly and age appropriately for both parties—with another. That wouldn't just be a scarlet letter. It would be the whole damn alphabet.

"I think we should forget that night happened," she said quickly.

Owen let out a deep breath. "Really?"

"Can we keep it between us?" she asked. "All of it?"

He nodded a few times, processing. She started thinking about the six-pack she now had confirmation lived under that gray T-shirt. And how it felt when she put her fingers on his chest, her lips on his neck. *Stop.*

"I think that's the smart thing to do," he said. "That's a good idea."

"Great." Their eyes met, and she was afraid she was blushing. Could he tell she was thinking about him naked? Was he thinking about her?

I can't let myself slip like that, she thought. *I can't mix work and my personal life.*

The rest of the writers started trickling in—including Bobby and Blaze, two writers from last season who officially returned yesterday—for this meeting Pete had emailed about last night. All he said was, Can everyone come by at 6pm? While posed as a question, it was really a demand. Their first day of writing season three was Monday, and she imagined he just wanted to debrief a little before starting strong next week.

Whenever there were writers around, Lauren had to forfeit her spot on the couch for one on the floor. As everyone but Pete made their way into the room, Owen slid onto the floor next to her, their legs touching. She moved hers so quickly it was as if she'd been electrocuted. Panic set in. She didn't want him to think she didn't want to touch him. She did. She just shouldn't.

"You send Lauren for coffee and don't get anything for us?" Tristan, another writer, asked Owen as he looked at the matching coffees in their hands. That cemented Lauren in her place for the day—his assumption that *she* got the coffee. In the end, she wasn't good enough for Owen. She was just an assistant. That was probably why he agreed to keep it between them. She was below him, and that was all it felt like she'd ever be.

Lauren could tell by Owen's stare that he didn't know what to say. If he admitted it was his treat, how would that look? That would be admitting to the thing they just agreed they'd forget ever happened. Luckily, Tristan was easily distracted and had already moved on to another conversation before Owen could respond.

Pete walked in last and quickly scanned the room. When his eyes found hers, he stopped. She smiled hello, but instead of reciprocating, he cocked his head and bit his bottom lip. It looked like an apology.

It hit Lauren like a bullet. Because there was only one thing he could be apologizing for. And it was something she'd been denying for months.

"Look who's back," one of the writers yelled. Everyone started cheering and clapping, and then he appeared in the doorway of the trailer.

James Raymond.

James and his roving eyes and wandering hands. His blank stare and eerie smile that made her want to sink into the floor.

He was back. Pete had hired him back.

He went around the room, greeting everyone with high-fives and fist pumps.

When he made his way back to the front of the trailer, James's eyes finally met hers, and she couldn't feel her face anymore. She couldn't breathe. She could smell bleach and urine. She had to concentrate on not throwing up.

"Lauren," he said, smiling without teeth. "Good to see you again."

She wanted to look away, but she couldn't stop staring until Pete walked between them, and she was finally able to break free of his gaze.

"Okay everyone, as you can see, good ole reliable is back for season three," Pete announced.

As the guys congratulated him on his return, James stood there, smiling.

Quietly, while everyone's attention remained on James's long-anticipated arrival, Lauren slipped out—just as unnoticed as she, again, felt—and walked across the street to Pete's trailer. The second she locked the trailer door behind her, she could breathe again. She didn't even bother finding the light switch before dropping to the floor in the dark. She thought about James looking at her, amused as if nothing had happened. As if everything had been a figment of her imagination.

If she hadn't said anything, this wouldn't be a problem. Yes, she would have been uncomfortable, would have had to ward off unwanted comments about her body, avoid answering James's questions about her sexuality. But she could have suffered in silence, dealt with it on her own. She had deluded herself into thinking that telling Pete would have given her control over the situation.

It was clear now: Lauren didn't have control over anything.

James was a writer and a producer, and she was just an assistant. It was obvious who was in control.

The only power she'd thought she had was in reporting it. And look where that had gotten her.

Without thinking, she dialed Cate, who was always her first call. It was just habit.

She answered on the first ring. "Hello?"

Lauren geared herself up to tell Cate everything—the strange remarks, inappropriate questions, hot yoga, subway bathroom—but the words wouldn't come.

What if Cate didn't believe her, either?

"Lauren?" Cate asked. "Are you there?"

Lauren remembered they were fighting. They were angry at each other; even though she needed her best friend, they hadn't talked in two weeks.

"Butt dial," Lauren said quickly, hanging up before Cate could say anything more; before she could tell Lauren was crying.

She closed her eyes, fighting to push away a memory that flashed into her mind.

"They're definitely fucking," James had said a little too close to her ear as he sat down on the folding chair next to hers. "Don't you think?" They'd been at lunch on set, held that day in the basement of an old church in Park Slope. Lauren remembered the lighting was so dim it was hard to see the labels on the salad dressings at the buffet. She had felt the coldness of the metal-sided folding chairs on her forearms.

James nodded toward that episode's director—a tall, slightly overweight bald guy—and his assistant—a young woman with huge blue eyes and untamed dark hair.

"They're definitely not," Lauren had responded, sliding a few inches over in the chair until she couldn't get any farther away from him without standing. And then he filled the gap, leaning closer.

"They are. Or at least they were. That's why he keeps her around. He lured her in with his Oscars, they fucked, and now she has something on him so he can't fire her."

"I don't think that's true at all. She's just good at her job." Lauren started collecting the dirty napkins everyone else had left on the table, putting them on top of the rest of the salad on her paper plate.

"That's cute you think that," he said quietly. "It's just what happens in these boss–assistant relationships." He lingered on that a little too long. Before he could continue, she stood and walked to the garbage. *Boss-assistant relationships like mine?* she remembered thinking.

When Lauren opened her eyes in the trailer, they were puffy and red. She'd allowed herself too much time to cry. Amateur mistake. Ten minutes at most. Very few people in life deserve more than ten minutes of tears. Certainly no one from work did. Especially James.

Lauren stood and dabbed some concealer under her eyes and globbed on another layer of mascara. She was still puffy and red but at least *less*. A woman would be able to look at her and immediately tell she'd been crying.

Good thing she didn't work with any of those.

14

It wasn't until Cate was standing in the center of Sobremesa, surrounded by at least one hundred women drinking margaritas, that she realized perhaps things might have gotten a little out of control.

It had been two weeks since the Shit List—last week Max, Olivia, and the other qualifying contributors attended the stupid Society meeting Cate wasn't invited to. She didn't realize inviting a few contributors to one night meant they'd tell friends who would tell friends and suddenly their simple tradition would turn into *this*. She wasn't sure the restaurant could handle any more people; she wasn't sure *she* could either.

She was not one to admit failure, but it was the first time she found herself thinking about a term she learned in the one business class she took in college: rapid growth. She had been skeptical of the idea when she first heard it—how could one possibly not know their business was growing until it was already grown—but that was exactly what happened with *Twentysomething*. It was their small indie revolution until, one day—today, The Shit List—it wasn't. Now it was popular. Or, at least, suddenly Cate realized it was.

The popularity wasn't the part that made Cate question everything. That was her goal all along, after all. She'd wanted to start a revolution, and a revolution wouldn't happen without heaps of supporters. What made her hesitate was the question she heard being whispered among all the *Twentysomething* contributors gathered in that restaurant on that unassuming Thursday night.

Who started this thing?

Everyone seemed to be wondering it: Who were their leaders? Who was the person meant to be pumping her fists and banging her hand against the pulpit? Who were The Bossy One, The Bitchy One, The Aggressive One, and The Emotional One, who signed the first letter and wrote the first stories, setting this all in motion?

Those were questions Cate did not know how to answer.

For two months now the four of them (Lauren only included because she was on the first letter; she never wrote anything, after all) were contributors. Or at least that was what they had told the other assistants from the beginning. They took on additional fake names, writing under pseudonyms for their pseudonyms. They had just "heard of" this blog from a friend or colleague or another assistant. They were not in charge of it. Sometimes Cate was afraid they tried to make that fact so clear, it was almost suspicious. Like how someone could tell you were lying if you protested too much.

Max sidled up to Cate at the bar. "This is kind of insane," she said admiringly, leaning over to sip her margarita. "We're going to have to Shit List at a new restaurant if we ever want it to just be the four of us again."

"I have a feeling *Twentysomething* is the new Shit List," Cate said, still distracted by that fact.

"You might be right," Max agreed. There was a brief pause. "I saw Lauren today," she said, like she had been deciding whether or not to bring it up.

"I see her every day," Cate responded. They hadn't talked much, if at all, since their fight. When Cate had woken up in Theo's bed the next morning, with no memory of how she got there or anything in between, she felt sick. And it wasn't just the hangover or blackout-induced anxiety. She was upset Lauren bailed, and upset at how quickly Lauren could belittle their entire movement.

She thought about Lauren's butt dial that evening, and wondered if it happened before or after she saw Max today. Had she been calling to apologize? Admit she was wrong? Try to come back to *Twentysomething*?

"How is she?" Cate asked. "When you saw her. Did she seem okay?"

"Tired, and more stressed than usual. But she seems to have a lot going on right now."

"More than we do?" Cate motioned to their room full of followers. There was no way Lauren was dealing with more stress than a hundred women seeking your identity.

"Just a lot. Maybe you should try to talk to her—"

"I'm not apologizing," Cate argued. Then she took a deep breath and counted to ten before continuing. "She said this was selfish." And there it was, the part of the fight that hurt her the most. Was Cate selfish for wanting a change? It didn't feel like it. She just wanted to be recognized for her actual skill. She wanted to be seen by her boss in the way she saw herself. And she wanted to stop being treated like garbage. But was it possible putting her career and the career of others on the line for this purpose had a little hint of selfishness attached?

Max put her drink down on the bar and turned to face Cate

completely. "Lauren still gets the notifications, you know. She checks the site and reads the stories. She'll come around."

Cate looked down at the melted ice in her cup, then up at the room, fuller than any Shit List they ever could have imagined. Perhaps Cate's reasoning started out selfish—wanting to get Matt back after the cupcake fiasco—but *this*, the room of people whose stories were finally being told—was important. And she wanted her best friend to be a part of it, too.

LAUREN HAD SPENT the rest of her day in a daze. She was forced to sit on the floor in the writers' trailer and listen to Pete's season three pep talk—he even brought up the *New Yorker* review and how he couldn't wait to see what else James could come up with—but the whole time her mind was completely blank, like someone slowly waking up from a coma. Even though she'd had Tyler's vague warning from two months ago, there was nothing that could have prepared her for being in the same room as James again. Especially now that it was also the same room as Owen.

When the meeting was over, Tyler suggested they all get a celebratory drink. Though Lauren wasn't even sure she was invited, she claimed she had plans. Pete followed the rest of the writers out without saying goodbye. Owen lingered.

"You sure you don't want to come?" he asked.

He was so sweet, she wished she could hug him. Just rest her head against his chest and let his arms curl around her like a weighted blanket. She'd forgotten that part of the reason she liked Owen was because he didn't know her before. She was just Lauren. Not Lauren covered in scarlet letters.

She thanked him. "I have a thing with friends. But have fun."

"We're good?" he asked.

"We're good," she agreed. "I'm expecting some oatmeal tomorrow."

He laughed as he walked out, and she appreciated the moment of kindness and reveled in it while she packed up her things and walked to the subway. She pushed James to the back of her mind and thought of Owen as she sat on the train, then got off at Union Station and walked the four blocks to—

"Oh shit," she said aloud once she realized where she was.

Last week she had been so aware they were fighting, so acutely conscious of her newly lonesome existence that when Thursday came and The Shit List crossed her mind, she purposefully ordered Thai food and sat in her bed with a bottle of wine to brush the memory away and skip the event completely. But today, in her daze after everything at work, her muscle memory had taken over.

It was just habit on Thursdays to come to Sobremesa. Her mouth was even watering for salty lime like some Pavlovian conditioning. She had taken the subway across town, in the opposite direction of her apartment, without even realizing it, and now she was standing outside the restaurant, looking through the tall windows into The Shit List she wasn't sure she was even invited to anymore.

Lauren leaned into the window, cupping her hands around her eyes to reduce the glare. Glancing toward their table in the back, Lauren saw that they had replaced her with what seemed like one hundred other people who were all ready and willing to join Cate's revolution. Assistants who weren't afraid of their anonymity slipping, of getting fired, sued, or ruining their boss's life.

At first, she couldn't spot Cate, Max, or Olivia, and a faint gleam of hope rose in her chest that maybe they weren't there—maybe they had canceled The Shit List all together and all these people inside were innocent strangers. But then she saw them appear out of the yellow hallway that led to the bathroom and walk confidently through the crowd to order drinks at the bar. Olivia said something that made Cate's and Max's heads fall back with laughter. Lauren wondered what the joke was. Were they talking about her?

Unbidden, she remembered the image of James in that room, looking at her and saying it was good to see her again. Her throat felt like it was about to close up.

She stepped back from the window. The neon lights above her head had gone blurry through her rising tears, tinting everything pink and green. She just wanted to talk to her friends. She wanted to hug them, and tell them what happened, hear them call Pete an asshole and James a creep.

Should she write about everything? Was that the only way she could get her life back in order? Regain control over *something*?

Lauren turned away from Sobremesa, from The Shit List, from her friends, and started walking north. She needed to clear her mind. Perhaps she'd walk all the way home.

As the Uber pulled up to her apartment, Cate could see Theo sitting on the stoop, two small pizza boxes in his lap.

"You are my favorite person in the entire world right now," Cate said as she fell out of the car, just barely catching herself before she could face-plant on the ground. "Seriously. I think I love you," she gasped. "For bringing this," she added quickly. She didn't mean that yet.

He laughed and kissed her forehead. "You're drunk."

"I am," she admitted, grabbing at one of the boxes. He held them farther away than her reach and slipped his hand into the outside pocket of her purse to pull out her keys.

The apartment was dark when they got inside, and she immediately looked for light underneath Lauren's door. There was nothing. She was either asleep, pretending to be asleep, or not home yet. Maybe Cate should check on her?

Before she could, Theo took her arm and led her into her bedroom. He put the boxes on top of the stack of books on her nightstand as he threw off his shoes and collapsed into the bed.

"Let's eat out there," she said, picking up the boxes and opening the window in one swift move that she only accomplished because she was drunk. Theo took a towel off the back of her door and laid it on the fire escape's rusty slats. They sat down and leaned against the old brick of her prewar building, opening the boxes to reveal the most perfect, flawless slices she'd ever seen, the smell of cheese and sauce and oregano wafting into her face. She ate the first slice in five bites, leaving barely enough room in her mouth to chew.

"Mmmm," Theo mumbled suddenly. "I meant to tell you, I pitched Kelley about the website—*Twentysomething*—a few weeks ago. But he emailed me today to pass. They don't write about anonymous things often, and apparently they've got something else in the works with a couple of anonymous sources. So, it won't work."

Oh shit. Cate almost choked on a bite of bready crust as flashes of the night of her fight with Lauren came back to her—calling a cab to Theo's, getting wet from the rain, lying in his bed, and, finally, telling him to pitch a website she heard about… She was never drinking again.

Cate spit the half-chewed crust back into the pizza box, needing to take a sip of Theo's water before she could speak, both to soothe her throat and buy herself time. She couldn't admit she didn't remember this. Being so sloppy you forget an entire conversation wasn't cute.

But at least she had nothing to worry about. Her misguided drunken plan after an emotional fight with her best friend didn't end in anything. Thank God his boss didn't want it. How could she possibly have explained *that* to Lauren?

"I got the okay to send the pitch to a few other places, though," he continued. "So I'm waiting to hear back. They're mostly smaller news sites, all online. I don't know if they'd be interested either. But, you know, can't hurt to try."

Cate slowly took another, much smaller, bite, an excuse to not respond. Maybe smaller sites were fine. Smaller sites probably wouldn't do much damage. No one would see smaller sites. Lauren especially wouldn't see them. Right?

She tried to ignore the unease that coiled up in her chest.

15
....

Ever since standing outside of The Shit List last week, Lauren checked the *Twentysomething* email constantly. On the subway. Getting coffee. Putting makeup on. She checked while pretending to listen to Pete, who still wouldn't make eye contact with her, and while trying to ignore James, who wouldn't seem to *stop* trying to make eye contact with her. It was supposed to get easier, seeing him around, but it hadn't. It made her second-guess everything. Maybe what he did wasn't that bad? Maybe it had been her fault? Maybe she misinterpreted him and, by talking to Pete about it, she never gave him the chance to explain himself?

Maybe it had all been in her head.

She had a ball of anxiety sitting on her chest that hadn't gone away in months, and it was only getting bigger every time she saw his mop of blond hair and long neck and knew, without a doubt, that it was him.

Lauren opened one of the thousands of emails in the *Twentysomething* inbox.

Any time I express any kind of emotion that's not smiling and agreeing, my boss asks if I'm PMSing. I get upset with an associate over the phone—are you PMSing? I stub my toe and cry out—are you PMSing? He calls me an idiot for forgetting to add someone to a meeting invite—are you PMSing? He has absolutely no idea what it means.

Closing the email, Lauren marked it as unread. No one could know she was snooping. She couldn't give Cate the satisfaction. Part of her had hoped that the blog would somehow fall into oblivion without her. That—despite not writing any stories—her role was important. She wanted to think she was needed. But she wasn't. She had to understand why her three best friends were so invested in it, and how they'd managed to convince hundreds of people to follow their lead and submit stories about their bosses too.

She opened another email.

After a frustrating call with a client, my boss came into our office kitchen, opened a drawer, took out all the plastic bags accumulated from years of takeout lunches, and threw them on the floor one-by-one. Then she looked at me and said, "Why is this kitchen always such a fucking mess," and walked out.

Mark as unread.
Open.

My boss was designing herself a ten-year-wedding-anniversary ring, and I spent three full workdays driving her around Manhattan so she could test out varying gemstones in different lights. She tested a total of $250,000 worth of gems. Meanwhile, I made $9.50 an hour.

Mark as unread.
Open.

I once texted my boss, "No worries," to which he responded, "Never text that to me again. I'm not worried. Are you worried? Why bring a negative into a positive situation?"

Mark as unread.
Open.

My boss's fiancé told me I could have her "fat clothes" once she lost 15 pounds for her wedding.

Mark as unread.

"Morning, sailor," someone said, almost jolting the phone out of her hand. She looked up to see Owen standing outside the trailer, offering her a bowl. "For you."

They'd been oatmeal buddies again for a week, and it was honestly the best part of her day. Being just friends with Owen after seeing him naked (and dreaming about it basically every night since), was surprisingly easy. The key was to save the naked thoughts for home, when she could do something about them.

Owen opened the trailer door and she climbed inside. They sat down on the couch and leaned back at the same exact time. It seemed absurd how often it was just the two of them in the writers' trailer. Maybe they somehow subconsciously made that happen.

As he crossed his legs, she tried not to stare. His pants were the perfect tightness. It wasn't distracting at all, she had to tell herself.

"I've been meaning to ask you, how's the writing going? Has my advice helped at all?"

"It's…going, I guess. You know how it is."

He looked down at his hands, and she noticed the finger-nails on his left were bitten more than his right. "Maybe we could talk about it more over dinner?" he asked.

"Do we have a writers' dinner tonight?" She immediately opened up the calendar on her phone. She was not dressed to go out to drinks with all her male coworkers. She got weird looks at bars whenever they did that. Why was this short girl surrounded by all these fratty-looking men? Plus, her luck combined with Pete's apparent oblivion, she'd end up stuck sitting next to James pretending everything was fine, as if she wasn't afraid of his every movement.

"No, we don't have a work dinner. I was thinking…more of a two-of-us dinner. A…*date* dinner?"

Lauren was sure she stopped breathing, repeating *a date dinner* in her head in his charming but careful tone. It was cute that he was nervous. That *she* was making him nervous. She had a split-second flashback—remembering him in her bed, kissing him, laughing when he couldn't get the condom wrapper open—but she quickly came back to reality.

If she said yes to Owen, it would be held against her. She'd be *that girl* forever. But if she said no to him, would it be James all over again? She had tried to say no to him: *no, I don't want to talk about this; no I don't want to go to hot yoga with you; no, I don't want to show you my Hinge profile.* If she said no to Owen, would he hold *that* against her?

"You don't have to answer now," he said quickly. "Just something to think about."

Saying yes to him seemed far worse. Agreeing to something she shouldn't.

Maybe she should just quit. Then she wouldn't have to worry about James or Owen or Pete. She wouldn't have to put all her waking energy into avoiding James on set, staying as far away from him as she possibly could. She'd just have rent and health insurance and groceries to stress about. She genuinely did not know which was worse.

"I don't… I don't know if that's a good idea."

Owen stiffened. "I'm sorry," he said, standing. "I didn't mean—" He let out a deep breath. "I think you're fun. And I'd like to spend more time with you. But it's okay if you don't feel the same way. I totally get it."

She'd never seen him like that before. He was Owen. Writer/Producer Owen. Emmy Winner Owen. Hot Abs and Brilliant Kisser Owen.

"I think you're fun too," she said. "I, um—I just shouldn't date someone at work, I don't think. That's all."

"Oh." He lowered himself onto the edge of the couch. "I mean, I don't think Pete would care. I can ask him first, if you want. There are no studio rules against it. I checked after—"

"It's not that," she said, only letting herself linger, for a mere second, on the fact that he checked the studio's relationship guidelines after they had sex, which could be the most romantic thing anyone had ever done for her.

Pete had basically—unofficially, of course; this entire thing was painfully unofficial—sworn her to silence about the James situation. After she reported him, it was an unwritten rule that the three of them were to be the only ones who knew about it. No one told the studio. No one told the network. No one told anyone who could have prevented James from getting rehired for season three. Looking back, she had shot herself in the foot proposing that one. She hadn't wanted to cause a scene. Maybe she should have. A scene would have given her the opportunity to protest or quit or *something*, not that she would have taken it. But Pete should have warned her about James's return. Pete should have sucked up the awkwardness and had a conversation like a boss. Or, even more basically, like an adult.

But, Lauren realized, Pete had broken another unofficial agreement: that he would fix it. And if he could pick and choose which rules to follow, why couldn't she?

"I reported someone," she blurted out. "For sexual harassment. On staff. So I don't think dating someone at work is a good idea for me right now."

Owen stared at her as he slowly leaned back. "Who?"

I shouldn't break all the rules, she thought. "I don't want to talk about it."

He nodded, not taking his eyes off hers, clearly ticking down the list of writers: Who was the most obvious choice? The second? She wondered if James would even be on that list. He was very charming, after all. And charming hid a lot of ugly shit.

"Are you okay?"

The question hit her harder than expected. Pete had never asked her that. Not once. She wasn't okay. This whole thing wasn't okay.

"I'm…fine," she said. "But that's the real reason. As much as I like you—and I do—it just, um…it wouldn't look good. If that makes sense."

Owen sat up again, his face a few inches from hers. Lauren couldn't seem to look him in the eye. She didn't want to see any pity there. And she didn't want him to not believe her, either.

"That's really shitty," he finally said. "I'm so sorry. It's shitty that happened to you, and it's extra shitty that what you said makes perfect sense."

Lauren let out a deep breath and allowed herself to look at him. His eyes were warm and kind and sympathetic. She bit her bottom lip to stop from crying. The concern in his eyes was real, she realized. That was what it was supposed to look like. She didn't have to imagine it, like she had with Pete.

OLIVIA WALKED BRISKLY around Tribeca, trying to find the restaurant Nate wanted for lunch, going off only his description, *the place with the good kale.* She knew that no matter what salad she returned with, he'd claim it wasn't right, but he'd generously offer to "make it work." Though she was sure he was timing her, the walk was a welcome reprieve from his apartment. Despite its tall windows, gorgeous views, and endless natural light, the apartment seemed to be getting smaller with each story she wrote about Nate. Almost as if his walls and furniture were ganging up on her, trying to push her out before she could say too much. She looked forward to going home not because it meant she had a break from Nate, but because she felt like she could breathe again there.

Olivia made her way to the Hudson River, walking out on Pier 25 until the hot metal railings at the very edge pressed against her ribs. She stared at the skyline of New Jersey straight ahead and downtown Manhattan to her right. The river was calm and peaceful except for a lone ferry. A few runners passed behind her, some suited men and women ate lunch along the wooden steps. Teenagers in tiny bikinis sunbathed on the grass.

She pulled out her phone and went into her email messages, searching until she found the one she'd sent to congratulate Nate's agent's old assistant. If you need any new clients, I'm here! the end of the email read. She had never received a response. Not even a *thanks* or *I'll keep that in mind* or something friendly enough to maintain the relationship, in case one day they were both successful and wanted to try to work together.

Without giving it too much thought, she pressed Reply to the email. Just wanted to follow up on this, Olivia wrote. I'd

love to send you my reel, if you're interested. And she sent it.
Just like that. She didn't even spell-check. Or ask Cate, Max,
and Lauren for their approval. She just sent it. If *Twentysomething* had taught her anything, change didn't come unless she
sought it out. So that was what she was finally going to do.

With the same verve, she texted Charlie that she was coming over later tonight. She was still keeping tabs on him—but
that was all she was doing. He wasn't so much a fuckbuddy
anymore as an enemy-with-benefits. Meaning, he could turn
into a potential enemy at any moment so it was better to be
active than reactive, right? It was pure coincidence that the
trade for watching him was mind-blowing sex.

Olivia was in a state of nervous excitement for the rest of
the day—so much so that she didn't even hear Nate's list of
reasons why she brought him the wrong kale. Every time her
phone buzzed she checked her email with hopeful anticipation. And every time it was just a Madewell sale or appoint-
ment reminder for Nate.

The regret didn't take over until she was on the subway to
Cate and Lauren's. Why had she sent that message? She was
way out of bounds. She needed to wait to get referred. Who
did she think she was, being so bold? She was probably blacklisted at the agency already.

As Olivia buzzed up to their apartment, she spent five whole
minutes waiting, surrounded by these doubts, before Cate finally let her in.

Knocking on their apartment door, Olivia was greeted by
Cate standing in the threshold, screaming, "*Holy shit*, you're
never going to believe this!"

"What's happening?" Olivia asked.

"Did you see the email?"

"We get thousands a day. You'll have to be a little more

specific," Olivia said, walking past Cate and taking her shoes off in the hallway.

"She hasn't seen it!" Cate called, presumably to Max, as if the apartment wasn't basically just one large room.

"We have your food." Max was sitting cross-legged on the couch, a heap of veggie dumplings on a plate in her lap.

Olivia followed Cate to Max's computer on the coffee table. "I haven't seen what?"

"Look at this." Cate opened the laptop to a *Twentysomething* contributor email. "Just read it. Here."

It was a short email from a clearly random address, only about ten sentences, the most impactful of which was the opening line: I am an Emmy-nominated actress, and I was harassed by my costar and no one did anything about it. Olivia read it three times to make sure she understood and, when she was finished, she placed the computer on the table gently, like any sudden movement could delete the story from existence.

"So, that's a pretty big deal," she managed to say.

"Yeah," Cate said. "She even said she wanted the 'Emmy-nominated' kept in. She wants him to know she's talking about him."

"*Who*, though?" Olivia asked.

Cate shrugged. "It doesn't say."

"Let's publish it," Olivia said. This was the biggest, most high-profile anonymous story they'd received yet. They needed to use it before whoever wrote this could change her mind.

Cate pulled her knees to her chest and swayed back and forth. "Now?"

"I already published four stories today," Max said.

"Who cares?" Olivia pointed to the email. "This story could put us on the map, move *Twentysomething* past asking for change and starting to *demand* it. If people weren't already paying attention, they would be now."

"Maybe we're moving a little too quickly," Cate mumbled.

Olivia threw her hands up in exasperation. "Isn't this what you wanted? This is all for nothing if we get to the point of making real change and then stop."

Cate hesitated as if genuinely torn, before resolve hardened in her eyes. "You're right," she said. "Fuck it. Let's publish it."

"Again, I've already pushed—"

"We can do five today, Max!" Cate said. "It doesn't matter. They're our own rules. We can break them if we want."

Max placed the dumpling plate on the table and picked up the computer. "Fine. But now if people start asking for five a day, someone else is in charge. I don't know how I got stuck with this job." She took a few minutes to edit the story, making sure to leave the Emmy-nominated part in, just like the contributor asked. Thousands of actors have been nominated for Emmys, so it wasn't an entirely obvious identifier.

They sat on the couch, Max in the middle with the computer on her lap, and looked at the story in the body of the site's neat text box, as Max typed in the headline: The Promiscuous One.

"This could also do nothing," Max said. "Maybe it's too vague for anyone to care, you know?"

Olivia didn't reply, but she had a feeling in her gut about this one. There was an energy coming off the page, something telling her that this was exactly what they needed.

So they pressed Publish.

Then they stared at the view counter in the top right corner and waited.

ON THE SUBWAY HOME, in an effort to push Owen asking her on a *date dinner* out of her mind, Lauren continued checking the *Twentysomething* email.

Every time she read a new submission, she was further convinced that assistants really were the most powerful people in the world. They had inside knowledge of the most important executives, were wildly ambitious, and knew how to be present while also having the uncanny ability of making their future career intentions known. Whether or not their bosses helped, these assistants who were emailing in their stories knew how to get what they wanted and were willing to endure anything to make it happen.

She also realized that there were *a lot* of negative stereotypes to describe women.

The Feisty One. The Ambitious One. The Stubborn One. The Shrill One. The High-Strung One. The Intense One. The Mannish One. The Dramatic One. The Nagging One. The Feminist One. The Slutty One. The Prudish One. The Loose One. The Easy One. The Snobby One. The Modest One. The Moody One. The Dependable One. The Distracting One. The Desperate One. The Sensitive One. The Tomboyish One. The Lucky One.

She got a notification on her phone when the train stopped at Grand Central.

Twentysomething: The Promiscuous One.

They'd published a *fifth* story today?

Lauren hurried to click the link and open the story as the doors closed and the train started moving. All she managed to read was one line before she lost internet connection: I am an Emmy-nominated actress, and I was harassed by my costar and no one did anything about it. That was a big story. How had she missed it?

The rest of the ride home could not have felt longer. Even after she filed out of the Eighty-Sixth Street train station, the site still wouldn't load. She pressed the Refresh button the entire walk to the apartment and still got nothing as she walked up the narrow staircase to her door. That was when she heard the commotion. Frantic movement. Unexplained banging. Everyone stomping around. *They're there?* she thought. Max and Olivia had not been to the apartment, at least not to Lauren's knowledge, since her fight with Cate.

She took a nervous breath and opened the door.

What she saw was utter chaos.

Surrounded by at least two hundred pieces of paper that all looked like they'd been involved in a jam, Max was on the floor, her long, long legs outstretched, yelling into her Bluetooth headphones, "I tried that, yes. Okay, fine, I'll hold…"

"I did that," Cate said, marching back and forth in the kitchen at what could very well have been an eight-minute-mile pace. Her phone was tucked between her cheek and her shoulder while she uneasily balanced her computer in one hand. "I don't think it's just a turn it on and off situation, *sir.*" She faced Olivia. "How have I had to explain that to two people?"

From the couch, Olivia shrugged and clicked something on the computer next to her. "Site's still down," she said flatly.

"Sir," Cate began, "I'm sorry but you have to explain this to me like I'm a child."

Cate stomped into the hallway from the kitchen, stopping short when she saw Lauren, who was still standing in the doorway, so entranced by the commotion she'd forgotten to even shut the apartment door behind her. Lauren had lived there for three years, but for some reason she felt in that moment like she needed an invitation to come all the way in.

"Hi," Lauren said slowly.

Olivia sat up a little straighter, and Max contorted her body around to face them.

Lauren loved seeing them there. She hated coming home to a quiet apartment. All she had wanted for weeks was to tell them about James and Owen and all the unwritten rules she'd broken, but the thoughts had been stuck in her own head where they were doing more harm than good.

"What's happening?" Lauren asked, slipping out of her sneakers.

Cate gave her a half smile and held up a one-minute finger. Lauren could hear the mumbles of the person on the other side of the line. "Yes, sorry, sir, what was that?" She ran back into the kitchen and leaned over her computer, which was now balancing on top of the garbage can. "Yes, I can do that—"

Olivia slowly stood and inched toward Lauren. "Site's down," she explained. "Things have gone a little crazy." She handed Lauren the scotch glass.

It was not water. It was straight tequila. Lauren barely got it down.

"I've missed you," Olivia said, wrapping her arms around Lauren's neck when she was done choking.

"Me too," Lauren whispered, and hugged her back just as Cate slammed her hands against the marble countertop and started jumping in place.

"This fucking sucks." Putting the phone down, Cate marched into the living room and paced, arms crossed. "They said it can't be fixed for a few hours."

"Calm down. Let's just take a deep breath for a second," Max said. "This will fix itself. I know it."

"How is it down, though?" Lauren asked. "I just got a notification on the train that you guys published another story."

Olivia tilted her head at Lauren. "You're still subscribed to notifications?"

Lauren bit her lip. Damn, she forgot they didn't know how much snooping she'd done. Before she could respond, Max cut in. "The site crashed because of that story. Apparently it couldn't handle the traffic."

"Well, it's a massive scoop," Lauren admitted. "An Emmy-nominated actor. Do you guys know who it is?"

Max showed Lauren a Reddit thread on her phone. "No, but people are already guessing."

Cate dropped onto the floor, exhausted. "What if everything we've built dies, just because no one can access it anymore?"

The room was quiet for the first time since Lauren walked in. She could hear a siren outside. Looking at the three of them so distraught over the website being down, Lauren knew that even if this all blew up in their faces, Lauren would much rather go down with her friends than survive alone. Her pseudonym was on that first letter, after all.

"I'm sorry," Cate said softly, breaking the silence. "I've been thinking a lot about what you said—that things are harder for you. And you're right. They are. I'm sorry that it took you telling me that to realize it."

"Sometimes I just feel like you guys forget that there's more at stake for me." Lauren sighed and looked at her best friends. "We all need our jobs, obviously, but you guys have back-ups. I don't. I make more money than my mom. That's why I can't fall back on her—I'm the one *she* falls back on. I'm the one always cleaning up everyone else's mess and *Twentysomething* just felt like another mess that would somehow end up on my shoulders."

Cate fiddled with her hands on her lap, moving her fingers in and out of the hole in her jeans. "I know that my mess has been your mess more times than I can count, and I'm sorry for that. That's not right. But your mess is also ours. And you can let us clean things up for a change. We're all in this."

"We will clean this up," Olivia added. "*Twentysomething* would not fall on you."

Lauren slid her scotch glass across the coffee table until it was in front of Cate. "I'm sorry too."

Cate took the glass between her hands. "There's something else going on with you."

Lauren felt herself sink into the couch a little deeper.

"You've been different for a few weeks," she continued. "And I'm sorry I didn't ask about it when I noticed it. I was mad and you were mad and I just didn't feel like I could. But are you okay? What's really going on?"

Lauren didn't know how much she was ready to talk about. But she also knew that Cate wouldn't relent until she had an answer. Cate knew her too well. "I slept with a writer," Lauren admitted. "Which has been...a lot." She filled them in on her last few weeks: running into Owen at the bar, sleeping with him, the ensuing awkwardness.

"Why does it have to be a one-time thing, though?" Olivia asked. "He sounds hot."

Max nodded. "He is, I saw him. I can confirm."

"I'm not looking for a relationship," Lauren said, a classic excuse. She didn't have to look at Cate to know she wasn't buying this. She'd been silent for the whole story, no doubt reading into her every word for the real reason.

Finally, Cate leaned forward. "That's not it. What's *really* going on?"

There had never been a time after reporting James when Lauren felt good about it. She was constantly oscillating between guilt that she overreacted, embarrassment that Pete didn't want to be in a room alone with her anymore, and shame that she let any of it happen in the first place.

Until Owen asked if she was okay. Until someone finally acknowledged that it was bad. He didn't even have to know what happened or with whom. Just knowing *something* happened was enough. She had been trained to think that no

one would believe her, but here they were publishing four—
five—stories a day, believing women. Why did she think her
friends, of all people, wouldn't take her side?

"One of the writers—James—got fired last year. Kind of.
He was asked to work from home for the rest of the season.
Which is not the same thing, I'm realizing." They looked at
Lauren intently. She took a deep, shaky breath. "Well, it was
because, um—because I reported him for sexual harassment."

There it was. She had said it out loud, told someone. And
they were still sitting there with her, wanting to hear more.

"What did that fucker do?" Cate said. "Seriously. We will
fight him."

"We'll do more than fight him," Olivia added, moving her
hand horizontally across her neck. *I'll kill him.*

Lauren smiled. And then she told them everything.

16

James was the epitome of a frat boy who never grew up. He had the sad college beer belly, the moppy hair that he thought made him look younger, and the invincible attitude that they all had in college when doing keg stands until 5:00 a.m. and then showing up to a final exam at 7:00 a.m. Frat boys who never grew up were always believed, no matter how many times they proved otherwise.

The situation with James was complicated. There was no evidence. There was no proof. There were no texts or emails, no voice messages. He knew how to play the game to make sure he never got caught. Her word against his. And it all started with the classic "Where are you from?" on her first day.

"The Upper West Side," Lauren had responded, knowing full well what was coming next and resisting the urge to roll her eyes.

"No, where are you *from* from?" He laughed as if she'd misunderstood the question.

"The Upper West Side," she repeated sternly. He stared at her, smiling, waiting. "My mom was born in Cuba." She finally succumbed, just to get him to stop looking at her.

Their relationship went even further downhill from there.

"You fascinate me," he had said when they sat together at lunch on set last year. He always maintained the kind of eye contact that made her want to look anywhere but at him. Like he was staring at her for a purpose she couldn't quite identify, rather than just listening to her talk.

"I do?" At first, she was suspicious—what a weird thing for someone to say—but then she realized, *maybe I am fascinating.*

"You never talk about yourself. It's so interesting." He put his coffee on the table and leaned in. "You are very good at diverting attention."

"I feel like I talk about myself all the time."

"Well," he said, propping back in his flimsy folding chair. She remembered hoping it would break underneath him. "You talk about your work and your mom and your friends. But you don't talk about *you*."

"What do you want to know?" she asked skeptically.

James crossed his legs, resting his right ankle on his left knee, and spread his arms onto the backs of the chairs next to him. "We're buddies, right? Friends?"

She nodded. She wanted it to be true—a writer was asking to be *her* friend. Hell yes, if that meant he'd read her scripts.

"If so, then you should want to tell me about your life. I'm not going to beg for information about my *friend…*"

But there were boundaries to work friendships that did not exist in others. There was only so much she wanted to share with a forty-one-year-old man she worked with. There was only so much he should want to hear.

A few days later, they sat in the trailer, both an hour early for work. He smelled like pine, and when he got too close—as he very often did—there was also a hint of sweat. She felt a tad uneasy in the room alone with him, but she didn't know why.

"Do you date?" he asked, finishing off a Coke.

It was an odd question, but she felt like she had to answer. "Yes."

"Men or women?"

"Men…" He slid off the couch and onto the floor next to her—surprisingly limber for someone his age. It was all the hot yoga, she'd later learn. He crushed the soda bottle between his palms and showed it to her like a party trick. Like he was in high school.

"Do you date online or in person?"

She shifted over so their hips weren't touching.

"Both, I guess. I mean, online dating leads to in-person dating, so…"

"Do you like it?"

His bent knee tapped hers, like he was encouraging her to speak—*don't worry, this is a safe space*—but she immediately straightened her legs to the floor. Then he did too. And then their hips touched again. She couldn't move fast enough to stop him from touching her. But he was doing it in such slick ways she already started to feel like she was overreacting with all her fidgeting.

"It's fine, I guess."

He turned his head toward her, and his face was maybe two inches away. She could see his pores. The spot on his jawline that was shaved a little less evenly than the rest. She was sure he shaved with a blade. He seemed like the type. One misstep and he could bleed out.

"You don't seem to like it." His eyes almost glowed they were so blue, and she realized she'd never been that close to the face of someone she wasn't about to kiss. And she had a feeling he knew that. And he was enjoying that power. "Do you not like it because you're busy?" Then, in a whisper that made her cringe, he added, "Or maybe because you should be dating women?"

What was she possibly supposed to say to that? Who cared whether she dated men or women? Did he expect her to have the sudden realization that she was gay? As if, without his suggestion, she never would have figured it out. *Wow, you know me better than I know myself,* she imagined saying. *I'm so grateful. My whole life is forever changed. You are a hero to women everywhere. They'd all love to hear your insights on their sexualities as well.*

She had no response other than, "I'm just busy." He looked at her with one blond eyebrow raised, like he didn't believe her, like he knew better than she did. "I like men," she said again. Then she got mad at herself for feeling the need to convince him. She didn't owe him anything but, for some reason, she couldn't push away the feeling that she did.

"What do you like about them?" he asked.

"I don't know..."

"I mean, do you like their bodies? Their personalities?" He paused. "Do you like having sex with them?"

She'd only ever slept with a handful of people at that point in her life. She was a late bloomer, as some might say. But the experiences she did have were nice. And they were nothing she wanted to talk to him about.

"I think I'd rather not talk about this," she finally admitted.

"But we're friends. Don't you and your friends talk about sex?"

"We do..."

"So why won't you talk about it with me?"

He moved his khaki-clad leg to rub against hers, and she bolted off the floor to her feet. She didn't want to be talking to him, and she didn't want to be touching him. The whole thing made her vomit a little in her mouth. She could feel herself turning red. Embarrassed, *not* flirty. That distinction would be important later.

Lauren hated that he was using the word *friends* against her.

He knew that, as an assistant, building a relationship with someone who could help you down the line was the most important part of the job. And what better relationship than friendship, right?

"I'm going to get some coffee," she mumbled, walking toward the door.

"You're not going to offer to get me anything? That's a little rude. Are you trying to be rude to me?"

She stopped, her back still turned to him, and took a deep breath; an attempt to calm herself down. What did he want from her?

"Yes," she said, rolling her eyes. "I'm being rude to you on purpose. I'm notoriously a very rude person." He breathed out of his nose loudly. "Can I get you something?" she said, relenting. What choice did she have? She was the assistant, after all.

James thought for a second, and she couldn't tell if he was messing with her. This whole entire thing was messing with her. Everything he said and did fucked with her head.

"That's okay, I don't drink coffee." *Of course.* She opened the door—she couldn't get out of there fast enough—and as she walked out, he added, "You shouldn't either. It's not good for you."

He was always telling her what was good for her and what was bad for her. *Eat a hard-boiled egg every morning. That's good for you. Don't eat bananas. They're bad for you. Drink water every hour. Don't eat so much avocado. You must try celery juice. You shouldn't eat your lunch standing up.*

Though normally unsolicited advice was incredibly off-putting, in his case it felt genuine, at least at first. Like he actually did the research and cared enough to share it. But after everything that transpired between them, she realized it was just another manipulation technique. It was another way to prove his superiority.

"Let's go to yoga this weekend," he said a few weeks later, standing over her desk, bouncing from foot to foot in a way that was anxiety-inducing.

"Together?"

"Yeah, I booked you a spot. Sunday evening. It's called a weekend cooldown."

Again, she found herself unsure of what to say. Even if she didn't realize in the moment, something subconsciously filled her in: he didn't ask because it wasn't a question. He was telling her what she was doing Sunday night. He'd already confirmed and paid for it.

"Come on, it'll be good for you." Then he waved his hand in her face, dismissing any more of her protests. "We'll get dinner after."

"I don't know—"

"I was impressed with that monologue," he interrupted. "I think you could make it in this industry, you know. You're good. We should talk about it more. And whatever else you're writing."

And there it was. The kicker. Most creative assistants would do almost anything to talk about their work. Especially since her actual boss, Pete, never asked. Talking about writing was the only way she'd grow. She knew in her gut that James didn't care—if he did, he would have told Pete that she, in fact, wrote that monologue and that she should somehow get credit for it—but, alternatively, he was the first person to even offer to talk about writing at all. And what if that *was* his intention? On the small chance he did care...what choice did she have than to say yes?

"It starts at eight," he added as he left. "Be there fifteen minutes early so you have time to get used to the heat."

That Sunday evening, it took her twenty minutes to figure out what to wear—not because of the ninety-one-degree heat she found out the class used when she looked it up online, but because she never wore tight clothes to work. She was surrounded by men, and sometimes the best way to do the job was to never remind anyone that she was a woman. To work out, she'd normally wear shorts, but she didn't want to expose her legs. She would have worn a tank top, but she didn't want her boobs showing. Finally, she settled on ankle-length leggings and a loose black crew-neck T-shirt that fell just below her butt. Everything covered. Nothing to see.

"You can't wear that," James told her the second she walked into the lobby. He had on shorts that hit midthigh and no shirt. The first thing she noticed was that he had so much blond chest hair it almost looked white. Something she never needed to know about him.

"You're going to sweat to death," he continued as she followed him down a bright white hallway. She held her yoga mat under one arm, a thick towel under the other, and the large lemon water he bought her (*It'll be good for you*) in her hand.

In the studio, he laid down his mat in the center, then took hers and repeated the process, resting her mat directly next to his. There was, truly, a few inches between them.

"I'm worried you're going to overheat," he said again.

"It's not your job to worry about me. I'll be fine." Though she was already feeling uncomfortably hot in the stuffy air, and her clothes were starting to stick to her skin.

"Of course it's my job. I'm your friend."

They both laid down on their mats, facing the ceiling. He told her to close her eyes and focus on her breathing. But she couldn't focus on anything. She wished she hadn't come. She regretted being there, was embarrassed at the thought of everyone finding out they went to yoga together. She hated that she felt like he made her do this; she hated how much power he had over her.

A few minutes before class started, she felt a tap on her rib cage. It was James telling her to sit up. The room was almost full, each person two inches from the next.

"Most people don't wear shirts in this class," he whispered to her, sitting cross-legged in the center of his mat.

He wasn't wrong. Every man was shirtless, every woman in only a bra. She almost looked silly covered from shoulders to ankles, revealing herself immediately as an inexperienced yogi. She felt claustrophobic, like her clothes were getting too sticky, too tight, pressing on her skin so hard she couldn't breathe.

Lauren took her shirt off and placed it at the top of her mat.

"Good idea," James said, just before the gong tolled and it was time to start.

After the class ended, she took a quick cold shower in the locker room, put a baseball cap over her still wet hair, and pulled a black sweater over her sports bra. James was the one who suggested they shower after, to get ready for dinner, but she felt weird thinking of him waiting in the lobby for her. Another unwritten rule was to never keep writers and producers waiting. She rushed to shower and was still sweating as she sat on a wooden bench in the lobby, lacing up her sneakers, drinking lemon water, and trying to ignore her gut feeling that she should make up an excuse to get out of there.

"You weren't breathing enough," James said when he spotted her in the lobby.

"What?"

"You didn't have a steady breath. I was watching you."

She started to get light-headed thinking of his eyes on her sweaty bare skin for the fifty-minute class, watching closely enough to know her breathing patterns. "I'm the one breathing. I'd know."

They argued about it for the three-block walk to the salad place he insisted they go to after. His favorite. He opened the

door for her, and she reluctantly ducked under his arm to enter
first. He greeted the hostess by name, who immediately offered them a two-top in the corner.

"You did improv, right? Before TV?" she began once they
sat down. "Do you think that's helpful?"

He waved her off before she could finish. "We'll talk shop
later. First, you need to work on your breathing for next time.
Your chest wasn't moving at all. In when they say, out when
they say."

Lauren knew there wouldn't be a next time. But she didn't
feel like arguing anymore. Every minute they were together
felt like an hour. She hated that she was still there. But, again,
what choice did she have?

"Okay," she said, determined to brush it off and guide them
back to a professional conversation. "I don't want to act, but
some people say improv on your résumé will help you get
staffed. Do you think so?"

He didn't even acknowledge the question or look up from
his menu. "Also, your hips weren't aligned, and you hold too
much of your weight in your pinkies. When you're on the
floor, your weight should be evenly distributed throughout
your fingers."

It was then she realized they wouldn't be talking about writing
at all. He wouldn't even try. She felt like an idiot. Of course that
was how this was going to go. She never should have assumed—
or hoped—otherwise. And it was the first time she remembered
feeling a little afraid. That he was paying too much attention—to
her hips and chest and fingers. She didn't like knowing he was
watching her that closely. It felt like a violation, but she didn't
know of what, exactly.

As they were leaving, he offered to walk her to the subway. She said no, but he said he was still afraid she was going
to overheat, and he didn't want that happening on his watch.

She didn't realize she was someone even *on his watch*. She insisted she was fine. He insisted she wasn't.

"Can I see your dating profile?" he asked, letting her walk in front of him on the sidewalk as they passed a couple holding hands.

"I don't think so." Lauren gripped her phone in her pocket. She knew he wasn't going to reach for it, but she felt comfort in knowing it was there. She had control.

"Why not?" He nudged her in a way that, until that moment, she would have considered flirty. Now, she only saw it as manipulative. Every move he made methodically chosen to impart the most psychological effects. The most discomfort. The most power. "I'm curious what you say about yourself."

"I'd rather not share it, I think."

Lauren tried to speed up to get to the subway faster, make the conversation end. But he kept his own pace, one foot slowly in front of the other, and she felt forced to match it. Slowly. So *fucking* slowly.

"You still haven't taken my advice about the women, huh?" He had his hands in the pockets of his long beige jacket. "I saw you looking at the instructor."

"For…instruction?" She meant to end that with a period—*for instruction, obviously*—but it came out more like question, diluting her argument.

"She was pretty," he said, shrugging in a *whatever you tell yourself* kind of way. "I just think you'd like dating more if you—"

"I don't like dating because I'm busy and online dating is sometimes annoying," she blurted out. She was talking and walking fast and finally *he* was tasked with keeping up. "I like men. I just don't like men who send unsolicited pictures of their dicks, and that happens all too often."

At the time, she had no idea what made her bring up penises.

This would also prove to be important later. It wasn't until she was home, running the conversation back through her head that she realized it was pure desperation. She was so fiercely trying to get out of the conversation—to *divert attention*—that she would have said anything. And bringing up penises seemed like a safe way to spin everything, to turn the conversation around on him, make *him* uncomfortable, make *him* want to change the subject. Because there were only so many times she could try to before she had to give up.

"That's so disturbing to me," he said, controlling the walk again. She could see the subway. It was just down the block and across the street. "I don't understand what people think is attractive about a penis. If you sent pictures of *your* body, I'd get that. A woman's body is beautiful and curvy and artful. But a penis is all function. There's nothing attractive about it."

She remembered feeling like she was going inward, like she was trapped in this conversation. All she could do was stare at the subway sign, willing herself closer to it. She was fucked, she remembered thinking. He had somehow made her agree to this entire day; he had convinced her to take her shirt off then watched her do yoga; he paid for the avocado salad that kept trying to come up the back of her throat; he didn't leave when she brought up penises. He had dangled mentorship and writing advice over her head to get her to show up, without any intention of following through. She had let it go too far. And there was no turning back.

It was then that she looked up at him and felt a chill run down her spine. He was watching her and smiling at her in a way that made her immediately recoil and speed up her gait. She needed to get out of there. She needed to get away from him.

And this was the part she had never told anyone, not even Pete when she had reported the harassment. It was too embarrassing to say out loud. But it had been sitting on her chest for a year now, and if she let it live there for much longer, she might never take a deep breath again.

When they passed under the entrance to the subway, she pulled her wallet out of her purse with shaking hands and focused on finding her MetroCard. It was like she'd lost all control of her body. Once she pulled the thin laminated card out, she was so concentrated on reaching the turnstile and slipping the card into its slit, that when it was rejected, she bounced off the metal arm and into James standing behind her. He laughed in her ear, joked, "Traffic jam," but continued moving forward, pressing himself into her back like a knife, pushing her stomach into the turnstile's unmoving arm, trapping her between him and it, with nowhere to go, and no one to help her.

She lurched forward and threw up.

It wasn't until later that she realized the following decisions weren't choices at all, but purely fight-or-flight. Careening over the turnstile's arm. Dropping the MetroCard with eighty-two dollars left on it. Sprinting down the platform. Throwing open the single bathroom door. Pulling it closed. Locking it. Sliding down to the floor. Sticking her head between her knees. Bracing when the banging started, as James yelled "Are you okay? You must have heat exhaustion" while attempting to turn the knob with such force her entire body vibrated against the door. "Let me in. You're sick."

Lauren would never forget the smell—bleach and urine—or the way her body shook once the banging finally stopped. She just wanted it to stop. His fists exploded against the door one last time before he mumbled, "I guess you're going to be a fucking bitch about it..." Then he was finally gone.

The next day, she knocked on Pete's door to tell him everything. Almost everything. *Disengage*, he had said. *I'll take care of it*. Because she should feel safe at work. Everyone should feel safe at work.

BY THE TIME she finished telling the three of them everything, they were sitting in complete darkness. Olivia had moved only to refill their wineglasses—though Lauren's remained untouched on the coffee table. They hadn't interrupted her once. Every few minutes they'd just put their hand on her shoulder or her knee, or rub her arm.

"And then, a couple weeks ago, Pete hired him back for this season," Lauren finished, rubbing her swollen eyes. She knew that if she wrote about it, she wouldn't stop, and that was exactly what happened when she talked about it, too.

"That fucking asshole," Cate said. "I'm so sorry that happened to you."

"And Pete didn't give you a warning or anything?" Olivia asked.

Lauren shook her head. "Nothing. And we've barely spoken since. Only about work stuff." She'd started to rationalize it by saying, in the end, he needed to do what was best for the show. And for some reason, Pete thought James was best.

"No," Olivia corrected. "Pete has to be a good fucking human. In the end, he has to be a good person."

"He's a good person most of the time," Lauren said. It was like she had been programmed to defend Pete the second anyone started disparaging him. Why did she feel like she had to do that? Did bantering over silly things and buying her coffee make up for everything else?

"Why are you defending him?" Max asked. "He clearly doesn't defend you."

Pete was her mentor. And, when he was in the mood, he was a great one. But maybe the red flags should have started going up when she realized he wasn't always in the mood. Only when it was convenient for him, when it didn't require much work. He didn't do much when she needed him.

"I don't know," she finally said.

"Why didn't you say anything?" Cate asked. "We've been going on and on about creating a revolution and changing the system, but you…you didn't want any part of it. Why?"

"It wasn't that bad—"

"Don't say that," Cate cut in. "James was weird and creepy, and it was not your fault."

"No, I know," Lauren said. "I just mean… I know I'm supposed to *believe* it wasn't my fault and that I did nothing wrong, but that's hard." So much of Lauren's brainpower went into turning things around in her head. Maybe it had been her fault. Maybe she should have said no, or been more aggressive, or given him a chance to explain himself. Maybe it wasn't actually a big deal. She could feel herself rambling, but she was grateful that they just let her go on. It was hard to explain how she felt, probably because she wasn't entirely sure herself. "I'm afraid that if I think about it too much, I'll realize this whole thing was actually my fault. That telling Pete was an overreaction and that I got James fired for no reason. That maybe I misinterpreted something. And that maybe this is the reason I wasn't promoted this season. I've caused too much trouble."

"You did nothing wrong," Cate said, leaning toward her.

Lauren would be the first to tell another woman it wasn't her fault, but it was hard to believe it about herself. Picking up her glass, she swirled the wine around, the sweet smell wafting into her face. "I know that. But Pete didn't believe me. He hired James back. He clearly thinks I'm just a little girl overreacting or something. Maybe I am. Maybe it was all in my head."

"Pete's fucking trash," Olivia blurted. "He's using you. And he knows it. That's why he's so nice. That's why he hardly ever asks you to do personal stuff for him. Because he knows you should have been promoted already, but he thinks you need him more than he needs you. So he can keep you there because you're not going anywhere. In fact, he thinks you need him so much that not even hiring Creeper James back could get you to leave him."

"He's right, though," Lauren said, realizing the truth in her words as she said them. "I don't have any other options. Finding a job is a game of who knows who, and Pete's basically my only connection in this industry. If he's not going to promote me on his own show after working with him for three years, why the hell would anyone else? I don't have any other options."

Olivia downed the rest of her drink. "Pete is trash and James is a fucking creep. No offense, but you probably weren't the first person to report him and, unfortunately, you probably won't be the last. Not when guys like Pete cover shit up."

"Yeah," Cate said. "If we've learned anything from *Twenty-something*, it's that everything that's happened to us has happened to someone else."

"He's a creep," Olivia said. "Repeat after me. *He's a creep.*"

"He's a creep," Lauren said. But maybe he was only a creep because she let him be one. He saw an opportunity and took it. Because she was so desperate to be a writer—to *feel like* a writer, to *be respected* as a writer—maybe she gave him the impression she wanted to sleep with him.

"Nope," Max said. "Louder. *He's a creep.*"

"I don't want to do this. It's fine. I get it." She didn't feel like talking about it anymore.

"HE'S A FUCKING CREEP!" Olivia screamed so loudly it seemed to bounce off their walls.

Max grinned and echoed, "HE'S A FUCKING CREEP!"

"Lauren, say it," Olivia said. "Or else we'll keep yelling."

"What will the neighbors think? These walls are *very* thin..."

Her best friends looked at Lauren eagerly—eyes wide, chins

up. Smiling. So much love pouring out from them that Lauren felt better. Powerful even.

Finally, Lauren yelled, "HE'S A FUCKING CREEP!" It scraped the back of her throat as it came out. As if all the times she held it in—when she said nothing and kept her mouth shut and was made to feel insignificant and unimportant—it was all just waiting to come out. "HE'S A FUCKING CREEP!" God, she hated him. She hadn't done anything wrong. Nothing. *"He's a fucking creep."*

She paused and tried to catch her breath. In. Out. In. Out. She hadn't gotten him fired. He got himself fired. He had pressed and pressed and wouldn't take a hint. He was supposed to be the adult. He was supposed to know the boundary and respect it.

This was James's fault. And Pete's for bringing him back. She didn't need him. She didn't need anyone but the three people sitting on this small navy couch.

She didn't even realize she was crying again until her friends pulled her into a hug. She had done nothing wrong. This was James's fault. And it was time she started acting like it.

17

In the days following Lauren's confession and the site crashing, Olivia started having anxiety dreams. From what? A now-working website with over five hundred thousand views? An Emmy-nominated actress contributing? Writing about her boss? Sleeping with her best friend's work nemesis? Take your pick.

In one of the more disturbing dreams, Charlie and Nate were running naked on his Peloton treadmill together. Pasty flesh bouncing up and down. They both smiled at her from across the room—Nate's perfect white veneers next to Charlie's uneven coffee-stained teeth—and started whispering her name. "Olivia, Olivia, Olivia," they chanted as they inched closer to her, bending slightly at the waist and walking in sync, getting louder and louder until finally they were right in front of her, screaming, *"OLIVIA, OLIVIA, OLIVIA."*

She woke up in a cold sweat, breathing fast. She could almost smell their breath in her face. It was like they were hunting her down. Taunting her with her own name. A name she never thought twice about until *Twentysomething* started; until she was actively trying to bury it.

She rolled over and was surprised to see Charlie's jet-black hair covering her pillow. He never slept over. That wasn't part of their agreement.

There was something about seeing him sleeping that was—how should she say this—kind of pathetic. She didn't need to see his Eugene Levy eyebrows twitching slightly in a dream. Or his 4-pack (6-pack after a few sit-ups) moving up and down gently as he breathed. In fact, the only thing worse than seeing limp, wide-spread legs on someone you just had sex with, was what Charlie was currently doing: lying on his side, clutching her gray duvet between his arms and legs, like a baby and his blankie.

Olivia shook his back. "Get out."

He didn't move.

She rolled out of bed and dropped her underwear and T-shirt on the floor. She was so sweaty from the dream, she needed to take a cold shower before she tried to go back to sleep. "I'm showering," she said loudly, tossing a throw pillow into his face. "Be gone by the time I get back."

The water was lukewarm, and she thought about Charlie. Sleeping over went against the fundamental pact of being two single people who had sex with each other. There were no strings attached. They weren't seeing each other or dating. They were just having sex. Really great sex. They were welcome to sleep with other people and, if she had time, she would. But who wanted to start the whole "learn how to fuck each other" thing from scratch, after putting two solid years into teaching someone *everything* he needed to do?

They had never officially decided to keep this from Max—it had somehow materialized as an unspoken agreement from day one—but recently the guilt she felt whenever she texted with Charlie when Max was around had disappeared. The guilt of having him sleep over wasn't even as prevalent as it would have been a few weeks ago.

In that moment, the hot water raining down on her face, she reminded herself that this *wasn't* just sex anymore. She was keeping an eye on him, ready with fake answers if he asked her about *Twentysomething* again. This was strictly business. Now, if Max found out, Olivia would have an excuse. So maybe sleepovers were permissible with these new rules?

Olivia turned the shower off and dried herself before standing in front of the hazy mirror. *I'm a spy*, she thought. *A sexy-ass James Bond.*

"You can stay if you want," Olivia said as she opened the bathroom door.

Except the room was empty. Charlie was gone.

In the few days since Lauren had recounted everything to Cate, Max, and Olivia, she was finally sleeping again. She wasn't waking up in the middle of the night with panic attacks, having to soothe herself back to sleep with crossword puzzles and breathing exercises. She was no longer nervous about how James would affect her career. She felt more at peace than she had since this whole thing started over a year ago.

When Lauren woke up after yet another peaceful sleep, Cate was already awake, sitting at the kitchen table with coffee. Lauren still felt a little jump of excitement in her chest when she saw Cate in their apartment *not* avoiding her. They had gone back to normal so effortlessly, Lauren started to forget why they were even fighting in the first place. Nothing was worth being that alone for. Nothing.

"I've come to some decisions," Cate said when Lauren emerged from her bedroom.

"Can I pee first?" Lauren asked.

"No, come here. Sit." Cate pushed a dining chair out from the table and Lauren obediently sat down as Cate passed her a mug.

"What decisions are you making now?"

Lauren expected Cate to talk about Back Muscles, her job, or *Twentysomething*, but instead she said, "I've decided you need to talk to Pete."

"What do you mean?" Lauren asked, surprised.

"You need to tell him how you feel. And ask him for advice on how to navigate the James situation. He needs to know that you're looking to him to be your leader, and that he's not fulfilling that."

Lauren shook her head. "He seems to operate better when problems are specifically *not* talked about." Pete was so conflict adverse he'd rather pretend a sexual harassment report never happened than address it head-on in any fashion.

"But didn't he tell you to come to him with stuff like this? He made you repeat it back to him like a fucking parrot." As Cate spoke, Lauren wrapped her hands around the hot mug, keeping them there until she couldn't take the heat on her palms any longer. "You don't want to write about Pete because you think he's a good person. I get that. I do. But if the way he's handling this is a one-time fuck up, you need to give him the chance to redeem himself. Otherwise, you should put pen to paper on him. He's not worth protecting if he's not protecting you, too."

Lauren repeated that last part in her head on the subway ride to set. Should she test him like that? Was it fair to hold his words back up to him and say, *Remember when you told me I should feel safe at work? Do you still agree with that now?*

When she arrived on set, Lauren found Pete in the producer's tent, sitting in his director's chair, going over some emails. The video camera assistants were working around him—setting up the monitors, rolling out cords, hooking up Wi-Fi—and every few seconds he'd look up and thank them for their work. She waited outside the tent until he was alone, then approached him.

"Hey kid," Pete said when he saw her.

Mouth going dry, Lauren had to take a few deep breaths before she had the courage to spit it out. Rip off the Band-Aid. She didn't know why she was so nervous—it was just Pete, who she talked to every single day. Who she knew more about than any of her own friends or family. She knew how he took his coffee and his steak. She knew his favorite items of clothing and how he liked them washed. She knew what cologne he wore for fancy nights out and what bars he frequented and at which coffee shops he got his best writing done.

Lauren knew everything about him. Except for how he'd respond to this. And that was what scared her.

"Can I talk to you about something?"

Pete gave her a little *what's this about* side-eye, but he must have known. The only other time she'd ever said that to him was when she reported James the first time.

"Anytime Lo Mein." She smiled whenever he called her that. It made her feel like she had a more special relationship with him than anyone else did. A very small leg up that she didn't know how to utilize. "What's up?"

She bit the inside of her cheek. "So, obviously, James is back…"

He let out a long sigh and shut his computer on his lap. "Yes," he said, his expression hardening.

Shit. She shouldn't have said anything. But it was too late. She had to keep going. "Well, the last instructions I had from you were to disengage. And I've been trying really hard to distance myself from him since he's been back. Frankly, I've been totally avoiding him. But that's getting harder to do, and I guess I'm wondering how you'd recommend I navigate this situation now that I can't disengage anymore. Because he's back, and I'm still here, too."

Pete looked at her for a long time. She searched his eyes for concern and, while she did find some, it was overshadowed by annoyance.

"Look, Lauren," he finally said. "We're all here to work. I'm not a camp counselor. It's not my job to deal with interpersonal relationships. Sometimes you have to work with people you don't like. That's just part of growing up."

Lauren could feel her heart beating in her ears as his words echoed in her skull. She was biting the inside of her cheek so hard blood dripped down the back of her throat.

Pete fiddled with his hands, pulling at a cuticle on his thumb, then let out a breath. When he looked up, the annoyance was gone. "The studio wanted him back. He wrote the monologue that got all that attention. What was I supposed to do? My hands were tied."

"I wrote the monologue." The words were out before she could stop herself. "James didn't write it, I did."

There was a heavy pause before Pete sighed wearily. "That might be true. But his name was on it."

She nodded, because that was just a part of the job. Most episodes of television had many more writers than were officially credited. "I should have told the studio," she said, so softly it was nearly to herself. She had fought against it—to keep this just between the three of them, not make a big deal so it wouldn't affect her career—but all that did was bite her in the ass.

"We probably should have." That was the first time he'd ever used the word *we* in conversation about what happened. The first time he tied them together as a team, wanting the same thing. "But we didn't. And we have to live with that.

I can't talk about this anymore, okay? Not with you and not with him. It just needs to be over."

"Over. Of course. Yeah, that, um—that makes sense."

It did not make sense. Nothing made sense anymore.

"Good." He stood up. "I'm going to go for a walk," he added before leaving the tent.

IN A DAZE, LAUREN sat in the writers' trailer on the couch, staring at the crooked TV hanging on the wall. The only thing she'd been able to think about since her conversation with Pete was the email. An email she was never supposed to have read. And Pete's reply he still didn't know she'd seen a year ago.

A week after she'd reported James, Pete had asked her to charge his cell phone. She brought it to the trailer, plugged it in and waited. No one else had been around. Of course Lauren knew his passcode. She knew his social security and TSA precheck numbers. Hell, she even knew his PIN. Even if he hadn't told her what it was, it wouldn't have been difficult for her to guess. She knew all the major dates in his life.

Without thinking, Lauren had entered the passcode and typed her name into the search bar. She hadn't known what she was expecting to see, but in her wildest dreams she hoped something positive—maybe a note to his agent recommending her, or one about an impending promotion.

The first things that had come up were two old emails from her—she didn't understand what the phone's algorithm was—but the third email was from James. No subject line, dated a week before. The day she had told Pete everything. The day Pete told her it was important she feel safe. The day Pete fired him.

Lauren remembered only fractions of the very long email. She wished she had written it down and kept a better record, but she hadn't thought she needed to. She'd thought it had been taken care of.

What she did remember about James's email to Pete was branded forever into her brain:

Pete,

There are two sides to every story, and I'd like the opportunity to give you mine...

If my wife heard Lauren's crazy claims, I'm sure she'd leave me. I have kids. I was a lacrosse coach, for god's sake...

She'd been acting rudely toward me for weeks. In fact, at one point I asked her if she was being intentionally rude and she said yes, she was. I told her she'd get more flies with honey, but, as usual, she did not heed any of my advice... There were often times I'd notice her blushing as we talked, and I figured she had a little crush. If nothing else, she at least wanted a friendship with me. She made boundaries very difficult to maintain...

Knowing she's a runner, I offered to set her up with my yoga studio, which is a great complement to running. She was the one who suggested we go together. Then, before the class started, she removed her shirt...

And, in terms of the conversation about "dick picks" she conveniently left out that she was the one who initiated that line of thought. I removed myself immediately...

I'd never want to turn this into a he said/she said type of situation, but I feel like I need to make sure you know the truth—

"I didn't realize anyone was in here."

Startled from the memory, Lauren looked up and saw James standing in the open trailer door. He closed it and walked in, and her first instinct was to move from the couch to the floor—give the higher-up person the better seat. Her brain and her body were at odds on whether to leave or stay. *He said, she said. Crazy claims. I hadn't wanted to take my shirt off.*

She stayed on the couch. James could complain to Pete about her insubordination, but he wouldn't. Pete wouldn't want to hear it anyway. After all, he wasn't a babysitter.

Lauren watched his back as James gently put his computer, charger, and water bottle on the counter without a sound. He stood still for a beat, staring down at something. She looked at the back of his neck. It didn't scare her anymore. At least, not in the same way.

"I feel like we should talk," James said, turning to face her. "I noticed you've been avoiding me. We need to at least be able to work together."

She nodded. *You shouldn't be working here in the first place.*

He studied her for a long time. Normally, she'd turn away, look at literally anything else. But this time, she stared right back.

"You know, last year, you should have said something to me before talking to Pete," he said. "You steamrolled me."

"I didn't trust that you'd listen."

"You still should have talked to me. You at least owed me a conversation."

"I didn't *owe you* anything," she said without thinking. "You owed *me* a safe work environment. You owed *me* a place I could feel creative and not targeted. You owed *me* boundaries. I didn't owe you shit."

James took a step back and leaned against the counter. "I was just concerned about you," he said. "You didn't seem to have a life outside of work. You still don't. I wanted to make sure you were okay. That you had friends. That you had relationships—"

"My sex life is none of your business." She could tell he was gearing up to say something, but she charged ahead. "I didn't *ask* for this, by the way. For any of this. You made me—"

"You have free will. I didn't make you do—"

"I'm not finished."

His head jerked back like she just spit in his face.

"You did *not* give me a choice," Lauren continued. "I didn't want any of this. I didn't *want* to go to yoga with you. But you made me feel like I had to, then you dangled a conversation about my writing over my head." She could feel herself getting worked up, breathing faster, hands shaking. "I did not *want* to be friends with you. Or anything more than friends with you. *You* made boundaries hard to maintain. And then, you took my words and actions and twisted them to save your own ass." She stood up and grabbed her bag off the couch. "There are *not* two sides to this story. There's only one. And you lied."

Lauren took a deep breath, filling her lungs for the first time in months, and reached for the trailer door. Before she could push it open, James grabbed the lever and pulled it closed. He stood behind her and she could feel his breath on her hair. Head spinning, she stared at the black plastic lock—with its small surface dots and sharp seam and white double-sided arrow—and focused on breathing. In. Out. In. Out.

"You are a privileged, spoiled little girl, you know that," he said quietly, pressing himself into her. Heart hammering, she tried to push the door open, but he had too tight a grip on it. She was back, then, in the subway, trapped between him and the turnstile. She could smell the bleach and urine. She could feel the cold, wet bathroom tiles pressing against her legs. "You can disengage all you want, but if you ever pull bullshit like that again, I can guarantee you won't be on this show anymore. I'm a producer now. You're an assistant. No one will believe you. Because it never happened."

She stood still, not breathing. His body was hot against hers. She could feel her coffee coming up the back of her throat.

"Have a great day," he finally said, swinging the door open and letting her out.

Without hesitation, she ran, not knowing where she was going, not thinking at all. The only image she had in her head was the trailer door lock. Black. Plastic. A white arrow on top.

Have a great day.

Lauren barreled into Owen at the end of the block. "Are you okay?" he asked, holding her by the elbows.

She wrapped her arms around Owen's waist, and he let her, eventually resting his hands on her back, rubbing up and down, absorbing all her weight. Neither of them said anything. They just stood in the middle of the street like that until she could breathe again. Until her head stopped spinning.

Lauren pulled away, but their faces stayed close. He looked at her cautiously.

"I'm fine. I'm just—" She cut off, then took a deep breath.

"Did something happen?" he asked quickly. "Are you okay?"

Finally she caught her breath and was getting enough oxygen to her brain to think. This was not the time to talk to Owen. This was not the time to be standing *this close* to Owen. "I can't talk about it right now. I'll see you later." She quickly walked past him before he could express any more concern. She couldn't handle that right now. Not from him.

It's all good, man. That was what Pete's response had been to James's email accusing her of being the instigator. With that one line, Pete had chosen to believe James over her. This was what made her last conversation with Pete confusing. This was why she couldn't stop replaying the memory in her head. If Pete really did think they were a team and that they should have told the studio, then why did Pete tell James *it's all good* and seemingly accept his lies? Was it to brush him off? Keep him quiet? Make sure James kept it between the three of them? Was Pete looking out for her, or was he trying to be neutral and look out for himself?

The only thing Lauren did know: James Raymond was a fucking creep. And it was about time she wrote about it. All of it. And this time, everyone was going to fucking believe her.

When Lauren got home, she grabbed a bottle of wine—no glass—and headed straight for her desk, not standing up until she finished writing.

She never thought it was possible to write all night. It was how writing was portrayed in any movie ever: the writer always got some breakthrough idea and finished a polished draft by sunrise. But that night did it: she wrote until four thirty in the morning and published it immediately. Before she could take it back. Before she could make a pro/con list. James was trash and Pete was hurtful and she was done protecting them. Cate was right. They didn't deserve it.

If *Twentysomething* was about showing people that they were not alone, that no experience happened in a vacuum, then it was time Lauren spoke out. Lauren's experience was a perfect complement to the story about the Emmy-nominated actress. The one that was so immediately popular it crashed the entire site. The one that maybe, in the back of her mind, gave her the courage to tell everyone her story in the first place. As long as she kept her mouth shut, the cycle would continue.

Lauren scrolled to the bottom of the post and proudly added, *Love, The Bitchy One.* Finally utilizing the pseudonym she'd been given all those months ago.

And then she pressed Publish.

Congrats, it's live! the screen read above a smiley face emoji. Though she could add this story to the growing list of other things she wrote that didn't carry her name, this was the only one that felt like hers. *This* she would frame, not the *New Yorker* article. Even though no one else would know it was her, it seemed appropriate that this post was her introduction to the writing world.

Finally, she had written something important.

18

Cate arrived at work the next morning a few hours early. She walked through the peaceful marble lobby, swiped her ID card to access the third elevator bank on the right, then pressed the button for the forty-ninth floor and watched the small television tell her it was going to be a hot and humid late-August day. When the elevator opened, she swiped her ID card again at the glass-doored entrance to the office, the serif red LP almost glowing above the empty receptionist's desk.

She moseyed down the hall, past the bathroom where she held her first secret *Twentysomething* meeting, past the hulking bookshelf that held almost no excitement for her anymore. She ran her hand on top of Lucy's desk, which was still empty, then on the back of the velvet couches as she made her way across the EAB to her space.

Even after the thrill of a secret bathroom meeting, and the excitement of calling Matt a sexist in front of the entire office, things at Larcey Publishing had, surprisingly, remained largely unchanged. Everyone had slowly sunk back into their routines—she was still Matt's bitch, he was still having un-announced HR meetings, she was still afraid of getting fired every single day. Cate would really appreciate if this revolution happened a little faster.

Like every other morning for the past two years, she sat down and exchanged her Converse for the nude heels she kept in the bottom drawer of her desk as she waited for her computer to warm up. Then, like every other morning for the past three months, she logged in and checked the view count on the backend of the *Twentysomething* website.

Her jaw dropped the second she saw the number:

1,002,784.

One million views. *One. Million. Views.*

Cate wasn't exactly sure what to do next. What *could* she do? They had over one million people reading. And even as she sat there staring, the number was growing, adding a set of eyes every time.

Before she had even composed a full thought, they had another thousand views.

There was no way this was real.

In the stillness of the empty office, Cate nearly fell out of her chair when her cell phone rang.

"Hello?" she answered, realizing she hadn't even looked to see who was calling.

"Hey babe, I have some exciting news," Theo said.

IN THEIR MORNING rundown meeting, Max watched as Alyssa, Sheena's executive producer, stood at the head of the conference table, tapping her foot on the wood floor while staring at Alex, Richard's producer, with a look that fell somewhere between murderous and smoldering. Alyssa was ageless in a way that she could sometimes look like a twenty-one-year-old if she wore ripped jeans and a yacht rock band shirt, or like a forty-five-year-old in a blouse and black pants. It entirely depended on the day and her outfit. Today, in her dark jeans, white T-shirt, and black blazer, she was a solid thirty-five.

As the uncomfortable silence stretched, Max glanced at her phone on the conference table and saw the notification from *Twentysomething* that The Bitchy One had published a story. Max snatched her phone from the table before Charlie, sitting next to her, could spot it.

A text from Cate popped up. Um... Lauren??

Wrote a thing and feel great, Lauren responded immediately. Ready to fuck shit up!

Max could imagine how she felt. It was freeing to let something like this off your chest, even if it was under a pseudonym.

"Are you ready?" Alyssa asked Alex, waiting for him to stop typing on his phone.

Alex looked up and dropped it into his lap. "Is *Sheena* ready?"

"I'm here, idiots." Her voice screeched through the speakerphone in the center of the table. "Richard there?" Sheena typically took rundown meetings from her Hair and Makeup room. Her daily routine took an hour longer than Richard's, so everyone understood that she didn't want to prolong that by taking a thirty-minute break to discuss the upcoming segments. Richard refused to attend these meetings. Instead, he sat in his office, door closed, probably getting in a preshow snooze. *If you tell me to say it, I'll say it* was his motto. He didn't see the point in knowing *what* he was going to say before it appeared in the prompter in front of him.

"He's in the bathroom," Alex said, sitting up. In Max's three years there—plus a few more of interning before that—no one had ever told Sheena that Richard wasn't sitting in the conference room with everyone else and Max dreaded the day she would find out.

"If no one else is going to start, I will," Sheena yelled. "Max and Charlie, come see me after the pretape later, and make sure to come together. I have an assignment for both of you."

"Copy that," Charlie said, faster and louder than Max.

"Alyssa, I don't see a story about that *Times* article I sent you this morning," Sheena continued. "Where are we putting that?"

Alex leaned into the table. "Well, I think we should actually hold—"

"I didn't ask you, I—hold on—*now?*—okay, they're going to blow out my hair. I'll call back in a few. I want that story *today*." She hung up a second after the blow-dryer started.

"Which *Times* article?" Charlie asked, scanning his email as if he would have been included on the thread.

"We're not covering it today, so we'll talk about it later," Alex said. "Let's move on."

As Alyssa continued the rest of the meeting, listing the stories they planned to cover, and anything that broke overnight, Max started to get a heavy feeling in her chest. *Why did Sheena want to see her after the show? And what did it have to do with Charlie?*

WHEN OLIVIA WOKE UP that morning to an ominous email from Nate, she knew she was fucked. Normally, his emails looked something like this:

Subj: can you… Body: print this.

Subj: what time… Body: is lunch coming.

Subj: get regina… Body: on phone now.

But this email began with, "Olivia," and ended with, "Thanks, Nathanial." In between his formalities, was an eerily vague, "We must talk." All of this was a bad sign.

What made everything somehow worse was immediately after reading that email, a notification from *Twentysomething* popped up on her phone: a story from The Bitchy One. Lauren had done it. Lauren had actually done it. But why did it give Olivia a pit in her stomach?

As soon as she clicked open the heavy door to Nate's apartment, he was calling her name. She turned the corner to the expansive living room and was immediately struck by Nate, mid-downward dog. Completely naked.

Olivia averted her eyes, remembering, as always, the advice his last assistant had given her on her first day. *Look at his forehead*, she'd said. *You'll understand*. No matter how many times she repeated *forehead, forehead, forehead*, it was still impossible not to follow the vein that seemed to travel from said forehead all the way down to his balls.

One more notch in her ever-growing tally.

Was she sexually harassing herself by constantly thinking about how his nakedness was sexually harassing her? Or was Olivia inadvertently sexually harassing him because she was constantly thinking—and now anxiety dreaming—about his penis? Or was none of this considered harassment since she was the one who signed up to be his assistant? At what point did it just become too much? At what point was she going to publish the tally and let it speak for itself?

Nate slowly moved from Warrior 1 to Warrior 2, possibly the most dangly of all the penis poses. His bald head was reflecting the midmorning sun. "I have a task for you," he said. "Open my computer. It's on the table."

Forehead. Forehead. Forehead.

Olivia typed his password—leather4hire, which she questioned every single time—and told him the computer was open. He was transitioning through vinyasa flow, so she'd have to wait for him to be ready to speak. Nate never waited for anything, but he *loved* making her wait. She looked at the screen and, instead of what she had been expecting—kinky leather porn or a nudist colony submission form—she was greeted by something much more terrifying.

Twentysomething. Open, on his desktop, weeks-deep into their story archives.

"I need you to research this website," he said, touching his toes.

"What website?" she asked nervously.

"Olivia," he said, exasperated. "I can't think of it right now. It's on the computer. That's why I had you open it."

She let out a deep breath, but even that couldn't keep her hands from shaking. *"Twentysomething?"*

"Yes, that's it. What do you know about it?"

"Nothing," she said too quickly to be convincing. "I've never heard of it."

Nate sighed. "Olivia, you really should read the news. You're too old to be uninformed." *What the fuck does that mean?* she thought, looking up at him just in time to see him prep for Mayurasana. Even in her panicked state she could determine *that* was actually the most dangly pose. "I'd like to be on the website," he added. "It's been generating a lot of buzz. You can read about it and figure out why for yourself, I won't bother explaining. But I would like you to figure out how to write for it. And then we will find some things about me for you to write about."

There were so many thoughts spinning in her head, she felt like she might pass out. *He knows about the site. He wants to be on the site. Stare at his forehead. Generating buzz. Read the news. Forehead.*

"What...exactly do you want me to write about?" she managed to ask.

"I will think about it. And I'll come up with a few scenarios we can discuss later. They'll need to be anonymous, obviously, but have just enough detail so eventually people come to realize that I'm the boss you're writing about."

She had to be in a waking nightmare. "You *want* people to know it's you? Things on this site—from what I've read in just the past minute, of course, I've never seen this before—but things don't seem necessarily...positive."

"We won't do anything so terrible. My publicist said my IMDb score is lower this month than it was last. Generating some interest around my name would be good, especially with that potential Scorsese film in the pipeline. I'd like them to speculate it's me, but we'll never confirm." He stood and walked into the bedroom, leaving his sweaty yoga mat on the floor for her to sanitize and roll up. "I'll obviously need to read them before they're published," he added. "For accuracy, and, you know, you're not exactly a writer."

Ten years ago, Nate wrote *one* movie. It got completely rewritten, but his name was still attached with the "story by" credit, and it was nominated for an Independent Spirit Award that he didn't even win. Yet that small half-accomplishment gave him just enough of an ego boost to forever refer to himself as an actor-writer-producer. Too many hats for a man who was always naked.

"Also—" Nate popped his head out from the bedroom door "—I haven't had time to show Peggy your reel yet but the summer's slow. Come September, she'll be open to seeing some new talent."

He knew exactly what to say, what to hold over her head, to make her do anything. And that promise still pulled her in, even knowing it was empty after three years. As long as he held her reel and representation hostage, she was his. She'd do whatever he asked.

Closing the computer, running this new task through her head, Olivia was still hung up on one thing Nate had said.

What had he meant by telling her *she needed to pay more attention to the news*?

As Lauren sat alone in the writers' trailer in the late morning, she thought about how anonymity was a strange thing. After writing and publishing her story, she couldn't sleep. At sunrise she ran around the Reservoir in Central Park, then went to a coffee shop and treated herself to a sit-down breakfast. She even ordered a mimosa. The pit in her gut was gone. She was at ease for the first time in months. On her way to work, she could feel the bounce in her step. Anonymity was as freeing as it was limiting; only so much of a personal story could be told and believed without a name attached. Part of her wished she could sign The Bitchy One's post as Lauren Barrero. Claim it as hers and make sure everyone knew it. Lauren wanted people to read her story and believe her.

It didn't take long before the emails reacting to Lauren's story started pouring in. As Lauren sat in the trailer, scrolling through the two hundred new submissions they received just that morning, she realized people were craving an outlet to be believed themselves.

Tyler and Owen opened the trailer door with a bang, pulling her out of her thoughts.

"Someone gave this to me and told me to give it to you." Tyler plopped a paper bag on the floor in front of Lauren.

"Where's it from?" She peeked inside to see a cold brew, fruit and yogurt bowls, avocado toast fixings.

"Couldn't tell you," Tyler said, walking into the trailer's tiny airplane-like bathroom. She heard him turn the faucet on, an unsuccessful attempt to cover up the sound of him peeing.

"I think it's from the studio. Breakfast or something?" Owen sat on the couch next to her. "Anyway, how are you?"

Lauren ached to touch him. To hug him like she had on the street yesterday. Without realizing it, she slipped her hand under his. It was warm, and her entire body was washed over with what she could only describe as calmness. She wanted to memorize that feeling, let it soak into her skin.

"Thank you," was all she said. *For the hug. For noticing. For caring.*

He squeezed her hand. They looked at each other, their faces so close she could have leaned in to kiss him, but then Tyler guffawed from inside the bathroom, breaking the moment.

"Owen, look at what my girlfriend just sent me," he yelled, throwing open the door of the bathroom. Lauren pulled her hand away from Owen's before Tyler could notice, busying herself with unpacking the studio's breakfast "gift."

"What is it?" Owen asked.

"This is fucking crazy." Tyler pulled out his phone and flashed an article at them that read "Anonymous Blog Takes Aim at Bad Bosses."

Lauren almost spit out her coffee.

"It's a blog where you can anonymously tell everyone how shit your boss is," Tyler said. "It's kind of cool. I wonder if anyone we know is on it? There are a lot of assholes in this town."

"What's the blog called?" Lauren asked slowly, calmly. She knew the answer. There was only one. She just needed to hear it aloud.

"*Twentysomething,* I think."

Someone wrote an article about the website, Lauren thought, trying to understand exactly what was going on. Someone found the blog and decided it was worthy of news coverage?

And now people were reading the article and going to the blog, including Tyler, and…

Holy shit, Pete was on it. She just put Pete on it.

AFTER THE BROADCAST, Max waited around the corner from Sheena's office for Charlie. She'd been wondering all morning what this could be about. Ten minutes later, she spotted Charlie turning the corner, walking slowly, not at all bothered by the fact that Max had been waiting. He walked right past Max toward the office, forcing her to jog to catch up, and he still walked in three seconds before she did.

"This a good time?" Charlie asked, pausing in the doorway.

Sheena was at her desk, the phone balancing between her ear and shoulder. She waved toward her guest chairs. "I completely agree," she said into the phone. It was her network voice: higher pitched, her bitterness more subtle. "Anyway, I have to go. Let me know what they say."

Charlie and Max sat down across from her and watched her hang up. Max could hear Richard typing on the other side of the wall of bookshelves to their right. Sheena's office was adjacent to his, and the wall between the two was so thin, they practically shared the space.

"Are you coming?" Sheena yelled through the wall.

The typing stopped. "I thought we were meeting in here," Richard replied. "I've been waiting."

Sheena squished her red lips between her teeth. "Yes, Richard. Everyone's sitting in *my* office because we're meeting in *your* office."

"Mine is roomier…" Max could hear him stand up with a grunt. A moment later, he shuffled into the room in the oversize Ugg slip-ons he wore around the building.

"Take a seat," she said, pointing to the chair between Max and Charlie.

"I'm fine, thank you." Richard walked behind Sheena and rested his back on the windowsill, looming like an overbearing shadow. Sheena looked at him, her eyebrows raised. When he didn't move, she squeezed the bridge of her nose and let out a deep breath.

"Okay then," she said, slipping her glasses back onto her face. "There's an associate producer job opening up. Both of you—for the most part—deserve it."

"You do…" Richard agreed slowly. He seemed like he didn't know where this conversation was going.

"I have a task." Sheena slid a few pieces of paper across her desk, and Charlie nabbed them before Max could lift her hand off the armrest. "I need you to do some research into—"

"I-can-do-that," Charlie said so quickly his words seemed to mush together into one long word. "I-got-this-not-a-problem."

"Great, Charlie can handle it." Richard leaned forward and put both hands on the edge of Sheena's desk. "Let him take the lead."

Richard's face was two inches to Sheena's left but she ignored him, keeping her eyes on Max.

"I can handle it too," Max finally said, meeting Sheena's gaze. "I've got it." She grabbed the paper from between Charlie's knees. He jumped like she was about to hit him in the balls, which was tempting.

Max unfolded the paper, feeling Sheena's eyes on her as she read the headline of the *New York Times* article in her hands: Anonymous Blog Takes Aim at Bad Bosses by Theo Delaney.

"Whichever one of you finds out who's behind the blog first gets the AP job," Sheena said. "If you can get us an interview or anything better, we'll negotiate your promotion salary appropriately."

Max broke out into an instant sweat, hands growing clammy,

shirt sticking to her lower back. Underneath the papers on her lap, she could feel her phone buzz. She glanced at Cate's group text on the screen and felt her stomach drop.

We have to talk.

Max looked up to see Richard staring at her. Was it possible he knew he was on the website? That she'd written about him? Would Charlie figure it out? Would he think to talk to some assistants from The Society? Could he follow the trail of *Twentysomething* bread crumbs from all their contributors back to her?

Richard was quiet. He moved from one foot to the other and finally settled back against the windowsill again. Max couldn't seem to stop looking at him. What had started as fear about how much Richard knew turned into curiosity. Did she sense a little nervousness in his stance? Or was he too obtuse? If they were being told to uncover the truth about the blog, was everyone in that room really so delusional to assume Richard wouldn't be included?

Open secrets only stayed secret for so long.

19

Lauren poured herself a glass of rosé in her apartment's hot living room and waited for Max, Olivia, and Cate to arrive. The rest of her day at work had been a blur of anxiety. Even just remembering the site's view count number made her nauseous. How many of those people had read about Pete or James without *knowing* they were reading about Pete or James? Did any of them know? Briefly she thought about taking her story down, pulling it off the site before any permanent damage had been done. But something stopped her. As the other writers arrived for the day, she listened to Tyler and Owen and the rest of them read the shorter posts—stories that were only one or two paragraphs—and speculate who was who. As they listed the most famous assholes—the ones who have monthly write-ups in Page Six about yelling at waitresses or pushing paparazzi—Lauren was sure James would never cross any of their minds.

So, she left her story up. She was done hiding.

Finally, Max and Olivia arrived in quick succession. Olivia threw her things on the floor in the hallway, grabbed the wine bottle out of Lauren's hand, and took a swig before Lauren could even say hello. Cate showed up not a minute afterward and collapsed onto the couch.

"What the fuck happened today?" Olivia shook her head disbelievingly.

"Shit hit the fan," Lauren said.

"Shit hit the motherfucking fan," Max agreed.

"How did this happen?" Lauren asked. "We *literally* became a viral sensation overnight. I didn't think that happened in real life. Where did the *New York Times* article come from?"

"Guys, I fucked up," Cate mumbled, pulling her knees to her chest. "I mentioned the website to Theo a while back— just that I'd *heard* of it and it could be something for him to write about—"

"Oh shit." Lauren knew where this was going.

"He pitched it to his editor, who said no," Cate continued. "Then, after the story from the anonymous actress blew up, his editor wanted the article again. I didn't know about it until this morning, though. I promise I didn't know about it until today."

"Why would you even bring it up to him?" Max asked at the same time Lauren snapped, "You told a *journalist* it existed. A *journalist!*"

"I was really drunk. And it was right after our fight and I was mad—"

"The girl promising we'd be *super fucking anonymous* turns around and nearly blows her load for a guy," Olivia yelled, perched on the edge of the couch like a lion ready to pounce.

Cate hung her head helplessly. "Yeah, I know. It's bad. I fucked up. I'm sorry."

Lauren stepped in the center of everyone. It wasn't worth their now very limited energy to be angry, to yell at each other. They couldn't change anything now. "A lo hecho, pecho," she said, recognizing this as the first time she'd ever used her mom's favorite phrase. "What's done is done. Let's focus on what's next."

They sat in silence for a moment, everyone still laboring over Cate's drunken decisions, until Lauren stood and walked to the kitchen. If they were going to be plotting all night, she needed food. And all they had was frozen chili, so frozen chili would do.

"Chili? It's at least ninety-two degrees in here," Cate said when the microwave went off and the apartment smelled like oniony tomato bliss. Lauren pulled out four bowls and spoons, always the mom, making sure everyone was fed.

"I think I know what we need to do," Max said, taking the bowl from Lauren and setting it on the coffee table. "We need to use Richard."

Over chili and rosé—a combination Lauren was not sure she'd ever recommend—Max explained the task she was given this afternoon, and laid out the plan to buy themselves some time.

"It's almost his ten-year anniversary of starting on the show. There are all these big parties planned, and he's doing so many interviews, the last thing he'll want is bad press, right? People sniffing around the weird shit he does to women in the office? What if I hint that he's on the site—say something that's not incriminating of me, but makes it clear he should shut his mouth, and shut down this stupid assignment Sheena gave us."

"That's really risky," Cate said. "What if he thinks you're bluffing? Or what if he just doesn't care?"

That was also true. All the stories had been anonymous thus far, including anything Max wrote about Richard. Just the mention of the website, now that everyone knew what it was, could get Max fired.

"He'll care," Max continued. "He's not as dense as you'd think. He knows he's on there. Plus, I also happen to know he's renegotiating his contract. Even if he doesn't care about the press, he'll care about how it affects his money. He'll bury the coverage. And he'll stop Charlie from looking into it. That's at least *something*."

Lauren thought back to their Shit Lists from BT—Before *Twentysomething*—where they got all their frustration out by simply writing down a work horror story and burning it in a tea light. They had all been miserable, yet so desperate to advance in their jobs—for their bosses to mentor them, listen to them, promote them—that they let themselves stay in those situations for too long. If only they'd done this earlier, if they'd spoken up for themselves earlier, they wouldn't have wasted so much time being unhappy.

Now, they were buckled into a roller coaster that, already, had caused Lauren to confront James and become disillusioned with Pete; inspired Cate to set up an assistant mutiny at Larcey; pushed Olivia to the edge of her breaking point; and, now, forced Max to decide between exposing herself as a *Twentysomething* founder and the promotion for which she'd been yearning for the past three years.

They needed to buy themselves time. Plan Richard seemed to be their most viable option.

MAX LEFT LAUREN'S apartment at 3:00 a.m. and went straight to the twenty-four-hour Old Navy on Fifty-Seventh Street, whose hours always seemed excessive until this very moment. She bought a change of clothes, checked out, and ran to the Broadcast Center. She accepted the fact that she would live at work now. As long as *Twentysomething* was the story, they needed to know everything that everyone was talking about. Sleeping at home was a luxury she could no longer afford.

She stood under the metal marquee that lit up the entire block with the network's neon name and scanned her keycard.

As she turned the corner onto *The Good Morning Show*'s narrow entry hall, she felt dwarfed by the giant posters of Sheena and Richard that surrounded her on both sides. They were standing in different power poses for each season. Sheena's arms always crossed. Richard's eyes always emotionless, despite the pearly white smile on his face.

The next time Max saw him, she'd be executing Plan Richard. She stared at the poster from three seasons ago, right into Richard's 2D face, with such bold verve she half expected it to spontaneously combust.

She took the rest of the walk to her desk slowly, like she was both memorizing and eulogizing it. The risk she was about to take was very well going to get her fired, so she tried to collect all her memories. Waiting for that elevator, Katie Couric had once asked her where the exit was. Down that hallway, Mindy Kaling had complimented her skirt. Max stopped outside the glass entrance to *The Good Morning Show*'s newsroom. Outside these doors over three years ago, Max had stood in her page uniform and realized she wanted to work in news. She wanted to expose the bad and highlight the good. She wanted to make a difference. She'd never imagined how difficult that would be.

Max sat down at her desk and changed clothes in the darkness. She didn't think she could sleep. She was too hyped on adrenaline, the nerves building in her chest. But her eyes were heavy, and her mind was getting foggy, and the room was so still. *I'm going to confront Richard today*, she thought. *I have to. I have no choice…*

She woke with a start when Charlie yelled, "Got a tag on your shirt!" from the other side of the dark room. She picked her head off the keyboard and rubbed her numb cheek, feeling the indent of some keys on her jawline. "You come in for the website thing?"

"No," she said instinctively, then, "Wait, what?"

Charlie picked a remote off a desk and pointed to the wall of televisions. The local news volume powered onto the speakers.

"A website popped up recently named *Twentysomething*, calling for people to submit stories about inappropriate workplace behavior. Run by four unidentified assistants known to their readers only as The Bossy One, The Bitchy One, The Aggressive One, and The Emotional One, the site has garnered millions of views and currently hosts over five thousand anonymous stories about everything from flying across the country to pick up a suit to doing your boss's dirty laundry.

"What seems to have started as a place to complain about non-work-related tasks that often fall on assistants, the site has evolved into reports about workplace harassment and abuse. Now with countless stories, mostly from anonymous women, including a self-identified Emmy-nominated actress, detailing incredibly crude behavior—from being told to wear shorter skirts to impress board members, to being physically touched by a superior—the site is garnering attention as people start to wonder, who are the bosses featured? Are they someone we know? Could they be you?

"We were unable to reach *Twentysomething* for a comment at the time of broadcast. For now, back to you, Carrie—"

"I guess we're not the only ones trying to get an exclusive with the founders, huh?" Charlie sat down and sent a few texts. "All I have to say to you is this, Max." He turned to face her and brought his chair so close their knees were almost touching. "I want this promotion. And I'm going to get it. No one ever stays anonymous for long."

He extended his hand, and without hesitating she shook it. "Game on," she said.

Max logged into her computer and wrote up a page brief for Sheena, summarizing everything that was public knowledge about *Twentysomething*, which was, essentially, nothing. *Twentysomething* had not commented. None of The Bosses on *Twentysomething* had been confirmed. Everything on *Twentysomething* was anonymous, and The Bossy One, The Bitchy One, The Aggressive One, and The Emotional one had not yet been identified.

As she pressed Print, Richard arrived. Charlie jumped to follow him up the stairs toward his office. On his desktop, open and on display like it was taunting her, was the homepage of *Twentysomething*.

And so it begins, she thought.

20

While Max was gearing up to execute Plan Richard, Olivia was just waking up to the text she'd been dreading since the day she started working with Nate.

I need you to find my light gray, striped couch and bring it to the apartment, his text read. Keys are in the lockbox. 2820. Then, a few minutes later: This can be your first story for that website. The following text was an address in the Bronx.

On top of all of Nate's other lovely and admirable traits, he was also a low-key hoarder. You'd never know it from his clean, minimalistic, light-filled apartment, but he rented a dark warehouse in the Bronx where he stored 10,000 square feet worth of bullshit. In the three years Olivia had been working for him, she'd never needed to go up to the warehouse. When Olivia asked about it during her first week, Nate's former assistant shuddered and said, "Just pray you never need to do the things I've done."

And now, thanks to *Twentysomething*, it was finally time for Olivia to see the warehouse for herself.

At 9:30 a.m.—while fielding frantic group texts from Max

about making a game plan to deal with Charlie—an Uber dropped her off outside a brick building on the outskirts of the Bronx, in a deserted neighborhood made up of vacant warehouses, scrap metal yards, dumps, storage facilities, and wastewater treatment plants. In her jeans, black blouse, and favorite Madewell oversize plaid blazer, Olivia stood out in the otherwise deserted street.

"You sure this is it?" the Uber driver asked after she told him *right here's fine.*

"I hope so," she said, only half-joking. She had spotty service on her phone, and Max's frantic messages were coming in two or three at a time.

After figuring out which key fit into the warehouse's heavy metal gate's padlock, she managed to lift it and open the two exceptionally heavy doors within. Once she was inside the cavernous space, she felt around until she found a light switch. In front of her was a maze of thirty-foot-high shelving stuffed with every piece of furniture one could imagine: sleeper sectionals, midcentury credenzas, enough folding chairs for an entire high school cafeteria, a pink bathtub, plush leather swivel chairs, large wooden hand-carved desks, a refrigerator, two 1960s stoves, a forklift, a stack of round plastic garbage cans at least ten feet high, a collection of 1990s computer monitors, and so much more it was impossible to fully describe. She somehow had to find a striped, light gray needle in a 10,000-square-foot haystack.

Olivia walked up and down the aisles for an hour, sending pictures of anything that could qualify, until she reached the back corner, which could have been an ad for The Container Store. Stacks of clear plastic bins lined shelf after shelf, meticulously labeled with things like tablecloths, tissue paper, lampshades, watches, white sheets, burlap, paint swatches, old notebooks, and about seventy-five boxes labeled, simply, taxes. Olivia couldn't imagine owning the amount of stuff that Nate stored in this warehouse. The fact that there were *at least* eight gray couches that could have been what he was looking for—but weren't—blew her mind. She owned *one* love seat, not even a full couch.

Olivia blew out a frustrated breath. The air was thick with dust and clearly hadn't been ventilated in months, if not years. She was sweating through her shirt but was afraid to take her jacket off and leave it somewhere she couldn't find later. She was running out of patience, and the ability to hold in her bladder…and also, she realized in that moment, Cate's chili.

After wandering around, Olivia saw that this particular warehouse had only one bathroom with three urinals and two stalls, but no running water. The stench was almost visible, like heat waves off the blacktop on a summer's day in Georgia.

No running water meant no flushing. No flushing meant she could probably collect DNA samples from every single one of Nate's previous assistants in that bathroom.

She did not want to add her own to the mix.

Olivia was able to plow through another hour or so, running around the barren neighborhood to find no other bathroom options—not even a gas station—while her phone buzzed with Max's step-by-step text updates about how nervous she was about Plan Richard.

I don't think I can do this, Max texted.

You have no choice! Cate said.

Maybe I can do it tomorrow?

No!

I'm backing out. This isn't a good plan.

Max Eileen Burke it is our only plan. You must do it!

He left for the day. I'll do it tomorrow.

Olivia sent a picture of two more couches—one that seemed like more of a bluish-gray, and one that was just an extra-wide chair—but Nate told her those weren't right, either. She started to think the couch was imaginary, or he kept it in a second storage unit he forgot he also owned. If every item wasn't so meticulously cataloged by some poor assistant from years past, she could redecorate her entire studio, and Nate would never know.

Olivia was walking through the curtain section—of both the shower and window variety—when she officially hit her breaking point. Without thinking, she picked the closest plastic container off its shelf and dumped all the decorative ribbon out. She held it to her chest like a life jacket as she called Nate, squirming while telling him she couldn't find the couch. Beads of sweat rolled down her temples like she'd just accelerated at spin class, chills sending goose bumps up and down her arms.

"I need to come back," she said in short breaths. "I can look again tomorrow."

"Olivia, you have one task. Just get the couch."

"I don't think it's here."

He sighed directly into the receiver. "I wouldn't have sent you there for nothing."

You absolutely would, she thought.

"While you're at it," he added, "why don't you take a few minutes and write up your story about this for that site. It's better to do it up there. More authentic, while the memories are fresh."

Olivia nearly threw the phone across the room at the thought that she was being sent on a fucking hunt through a massive warehouse for a nonexistent couch all to submit something to a website she created where *she had already been writing about him FOR MONTHS.*

"I can do that later tonight," she said calmly. She'd spanned the entire length of the warehouse during this conversation, her hips moving like a professional speed-walker as she snaked through stacks of furniture, squeezing the empty bin, thinking about anything other than the fact that she was wearing a thong.

"It'll be more genuine if you write from there."

"You realize there are no bathrooms here, right?"

She could imagine his shrug, practically see his classic wide-eyed, *what do you want me to do about it* expression. "You'll make do, I'm sure. You're a capable woman."

He hung up before she could ask how he'd recommend she *make do*, leaving her wondering how many labor laws Nate was breaking. Though, it didn't matter because she'd never tell anyone about this anyway. Her stomach bubbled again, and Olivia knew she didn't have time to call an Uber to the closest bathroom. She wouldn't make it.

That left her with only one option.

Olivia dragged a twin mattress into a corner of the warehouse and leaned it on a wooden desk, blocking her from the view of any potential security camera that could witness the most humiliating thing she'd ever had to do in her life.

Olivia put the small plastic container on the floor, pulled her jeans down, underwear around her ankles, squatted, and, well…

She shit in a bucket.

She shit in a fucking bucket.

With as much dignity as she could muster, Olivia cleaned herself up with dried-up makeup wipes from her purse and threw those into the plastic container so she didn't have to look at what she'd just done. She cleaned her hands with sanitizer, also from her purse, then closed the bucket, and did a lap of the warehouse.

"I'm still a woman," she said out loud. "I'm still strong and independent. Pooping in a bucket in a warehouse in the Bronx hasn't changed that."

236 | AMANDA PELLEGRINO

While walking she picked up an old grocery bag and returned to the scene of the crime, putting the container inside
the bag and tying it up. Searching for the right place to dis-
pose of it, Olivia eventually stopped outside the cursed bathroom, knowing what she had to do. She held her blazer to
her face, took a deep breath, moved five steps closer to the
entrance, and chucked her bucket of shit into the bathroom
as hard as she could.

She backed away until she hit a shrink-wrapped couch and
lowered herself onto it in a daze. Staring at the bathroom, she
wiped the sweat off her forehead and rubbed her eyes. The
last ten minutes could not have been real.

I chose to do that, she realized. Olivia was told not to come
back to that apartment without a couch, so she needed to find
a motherfucking couch. She did it because Nate, her boss,
someone who was meant to look out for her and her career,
gave her no other option. He was the first priority in her life,
but she was the last priority in his.

She was just disappointed that it took shitting in a bucket
for her to understand that, when it was evident in pretty much
everything he had put her through for the last three years.

She didn't need this. She didn't need him coming up with
wild tasks and crazy assignments so she could get him featured
on a bad boss blog that *she* had created. That he was already on.

Her phone buzzed.

Never mind, Nate's text read. It's in the storage basement
here. You can come back. And pick up a vegan veggie salad from
that place with the balsamic dressing I like.

She was still for a very long time before finally calling him.

Olivia always imagined her resignation would be triggered
by asking her boss to put clothes on, but instead it began with
her taking a shit in a bucket in a warehouse.

He picked up on the sixth ring.

"Nathanial," she began, professional yet stern. "Thank you for the opportunity, but I'm going to quit now."

"Excuse me?" He sounded genuinely shocked.

"I quit. As of today. I'm done."

For a moment it was so silent she thought he had hung up. She was almost relieved, but then he spoke. "Is this because of the couch?" he asked flatly. "You need to be less sensitive."

Olivia reminded herself to stay nice and pleasant. To keep her tone high and energy up and not curse him out. She didn't want him to have anything negative about her to spread around the industry. But he was always making that very difficult.

She told him she was grateful for the last three years, but that she had learned everything she could, and it was time for her to explore other avenues. As politically correct and inoffensive as she could be, when what she wanted to say was, *I hate you, motherfucker. You did so little for my career I may as well have been working at the Gap.*

There was a beat of tense silence. He was leaving room for her to apologize, but she was decidedly *not* sorry, so why the fuck would she say it?

"Your job is to make my life easier. Do you understand that?" She stopped herself from instinctively nodding. "This is, in fact, making my life more difficult. What purpose do you serve me if you're doing the opposite of your job? I understand that spending a day in a warehouse isn't ideal, but it was something I needed you to do. It's not been easy since I came back from LA, I realize that. I didn't—I didn't get a job I was expecting to. But there is no need to quit."

It wasn't immediately clear whether anyone had ever quit on him, or if he even understood the concept. Olivia was shocked that he would actually *admit* to not getting a role. He must want her to stay, which made sense since she had done everything he asked for three years without ever questioning it to his face. She did a fucking great job. She was still the best assistant he'd ever had.

"I think it's time for me to go," she said, ignoring his rant. "I'll leave your keys and the rest of my petty cash with Ron at the door."

"There's no turning back from this, Olivia. I'll never show your reel around if you quit. You'll never be an actor. I'll make sure of it."

She laughed, which caught her by surprise. It was the moment she realized how pathetic he was. Nathanial Brooks needed her around—a young, naive assistant—to make himself feel better that his career wasn't going anywhere near where he wanted it to. Keeping her down ensured he was always higher, better, more important. She was no longer going to let him do that.

"It's been three years," she said smoothly. "If you were able to help me break into the industry, it would have happened by now." She paused to let that sink in. "You've given me a lot to write about. I'm hanging up."

The second she did, she knew what needed to happen.

First, she had to get the fuck out of there. She grabbed her purse, left the warehouse, and ten minutes later got in her Uber home.

Second, she needed to get everyone to her apartment. Everyone come over now. I have a brilliant idea. Everything's changing. Also, I just quit.

Third, she needed to write it all down. She took out her computer in the back seat of the black SUV. She tuned out the driver's loud music, the honks on the Bruckner Expressway, and the skyline of uptown Manhattan as they crossed the Third Avenue Bridge. By the time she got home, she had the whole blog post written.

OLIVIA WAS DRUNK when Cate, Lauren, and Max filed into her tiny apartment that night. She didn't even offer them a drink before explaining her day—in unfortunate detail for everyone—and making them swear on their sex lives never to tell a soul that she shit in a bucket.

"And then you *quit?*" Lauren repeated, as if she didn't understand the word.

Olivia nodded and took a swig of tequila. "I'm done. And it was more than just the bucket incident. He never even *considered* that I'd already been writing about all the horrible things he made me do."

Cate shook her head. "He's so out of touch."

"Aren't they all, though?" Lauren agreed. "I mean, it's been twenty-four hours since the blog went viral and none of our bosses have seemed worried about being implicated."

She wasn't wrong. Matt had ignored Cate, as usual. Pete hadn't said one word to Lauren. Max's bosses yelled at her per their routine. And Nate was as oblivious as they came.

"I think there's one more thing we have to do before Max talks to Richard tomorrow." Olivia had rehearsed her speech in the car on the way back from the warehouse. "I think it's time I tell you about the tally."

She took out her phone and displayed it in front of them, detailing the times she saw his penis that she could remember: doing yoga, blending a smoothie, getting a massage, tending a garden—

"I'm sorry, *what?*" Cate's eyes bugged out. "Nate's just naked? All the time? What the fuck?"

Olivia shrugged. "It didn't seem like that big of a deal,

when I first started. It was weird, sure, but it's not like he was ever hard."

"It's still a big deal!" Lauren exclaimed.

Cate and Max nodded furiously in agreement, their shocked expressions unchanging as Olivia continued to explain that if they wanted Richard to really take them off the air, use his power to actively suppress the news, he needed to be scared. And the thing that would really scare him: not being anonymous anymore. Having someone come out with their real name, encouraging other contributors to do the same, would scare him more than a story hidden behind a pseudonym. He needed to think that this was entirely possible for him too, that any one of the women whose butts he'd pinched or slapped could come forward. They needed to put the pressure on high. And she could do that now. Use her first name.

After a beat of stunned silence, to Olivia's surprise, everyone slowly started nodding. Even Lauren, who was full of surprises lately, seemed to agree that they needed to turn the heat on Richard to make this work.

"What if Charlie figures it out?" Max asked nervously. "You guys met, remember? He knows we're friends."

"Let's not worry about him," Olivia said quickly. Charlie was the unknown part of her equation. Now that *Twentysomething* was on *The Good Morning Show*'s radar, she was taking a risk in potentially connecting the dots for him. But there were a million Olivias in the world, and she wouldn't identify Nate outright. There was a chance no one would even discover it was her, including Charlie. There might even be other Olivias with a similar tale. How easy could it be to connect her full identity to this post?

"That's a big deal," Cate said. "Are you sure you want to do this?"

Olivia thought about the warehouse. And the tally. And the

fact that Nate never once passed along her reel to his agent, and the agent's promoted assistant never responded to what was essentially her begging for representation. She was done. She wanted Nathanial Brooks to burn.

Dear Twentysomething,
My name is Olivia. That's a very important thing for me to tell you.

My name is Olivia, and I quit my dream job. Or, at least, the job that would, eventually, lead me to my real dream job. It took me a while, but I finally realized that if you have to make concessions for your safety and sanity at work, it's probably not your dream job. And that's exactly what I'd been doing.

In the last three years, I've seen my boss's penis on 124 separate occasions. I wrote it down. Every time he was cooking lunch naked, or doing yoga naked, or sending emails naked, I added one number to the tally I kept on my phone.

At first, I kept track for someone else; to support whomever in the future had the balls to say something; to come forward with what I didn't say. But now I realize I was always doing it for me.

I'm very grateful for this website and the comradery I've felt from the thousands of women whose stories are like mine. I'd be a very different person if I weren't able to read your powerful essays about the discrimination, injustice, and inappropriate behavior you've encountered in the workplace. In case no one's told you lately, you're brave.

I feel like I have an obligation to your experiences, and my own, to suggest a change—not just a website change, but a real-life change. A change to the jobs and terms that we readily accepted as working women. If we continue to allow this treatment, it will continue to happen. Through Twentysomething, we've been able to stand up and call bullshit, but I think we need to take it one step further.

The only option to change the way things are done is to do something that's, frankly, quite terrifying: take the anonymity out of our essays. I never viewed the clever Twentysomething nicknames as covers, but more as offering the privilege to tell our stories without consequence. They allowed us to be honest and unabridged without the worry of being fired, sued, or unable to get another job.

But our time has come.

We need to hold people accountable for their actions. We've spent our entire careers behind the curtain. That's where we're supposed to be as assistants, as women—always a few steps behind, but a few thoughts ahead. It's time we open the curtain and expose the dirty secrets of our industry outright.

Because of you, and because of this site, I know I'm not alone—women have been going through this for years and will continue to unless we stand up and speak out.

We're brave behind the curtain, and now we need to be brave in front of it. This is our opportunity to force a change that's been a long time coming.

Sometimes it only takes one voice to start a revolution, and I'm telling you this may be it. Now it's your turn to decide if you want to join me.

Olivia

It took eight minutes for them to get their first nonanonymous contributor email. After twenty minutes, they had nineteen. As they stared at the screen, watching the number of unread messages rise every few minutes, they were silent. Head spinning, Olivia poured herself more tequila, keenly aware that this post might have been a mistake. This was reversing everything they'd done to stay nameless and faceless, to keep their jobs. But Olivia didn't have one anymore. It took quitting to realize maybe a job that made you this miserable wasn't one worth hiding for.

An hour after the story published, Olivia's phone buzzed with a text. It was from Charlie.

We have to talk. I'm on my way over.

Shit. She'd underestimated him.

Wasting no time, Olivia kicked Max, Cate, and Lauren out of her apartment like a boy out of her childhood bedroom when her parents got home early. It couldn't have been more than two minutes after they were gone that Charlie rang the apartment buzzer. She thought about letting him up, but she hesitated. What if there was evidence up here? What if he could use something in her room—her half-assed journal, her weed, her phone—against her?

"I'm coming down," she said into the speaker, then rubbed her temples. She needed to sober up.

When she got outside, Charlie was standing on the steps of her building.

"Um, hi," he said, grabbing her arm.

Olivia shoved his hand off her. "What are you doing here?"

"You're Olivia from *Twentysomething*, right?" Charlie demanded, looking her straight in the eye. When she couldn't find a response, she became acutely aware of how drunk she was. "I need this promotion, Olivia. I'm sure Max has told you all about it. But you have to help me. That story was you, wasn't it." Her mind went completely blank. "I'm not stupid. How did you get it published? Did you have any contact with anyone in charge? I mean, how did they possibly let you become the first one to not be anonymous. Do you *know* who founded this thing?"

That was when she remembered: to everyone on the outside, *Olivia* was only a contributor. She'd submitted her essay just like any of the other thousands of women. He had no idea that she was one of the founders he was looking for. That he'd seen one of the founders naked. That he worked with another one. That he was essentially surrounded by them.

She shook her head, slowly, forcing off the dizziness. "Nope, I just emailed the address on the site, like everyone else. Then it went online."

"You never got any kind of confirmation or anything?"

"Nothing."

"Really? Nothing? Or are you just telling me that because you want to help Max instead?"

"I'd definitely help Max before I'd help you, but I have nothing to say. Believe me, she's already asked."

Olivia was actively impressed with her own drunk lying. Just enough detail to make it true without seeming overdone.

He blew out a loud, frustrated breath. "Well, fuck me," he said, slumping down onto the steps of her stoop. His legs were so long he had to sit on the top step and put his feet on the sidewalk.

She sat down next to him. Moving to the ground made her a bit dizzy, and she rested her shoulder against his to get her equilibrium back. She suddenly felt much more drunk. The streetlights were brighter and blurrier.

"I need this promotion, Olivia," he repeated. "I've been working so hard."

"So has Max."

"Yeah, but, no offense, she doesn't really have hard work

to do. She just gets coffee and schedules their travel. I'm doing actual editorial stuff."

Olivia scoffed. "That's because it's easier to be a man at your show than a woman."

He turned to face her. "What does that mean?"

"It's easy to do the hard stuff when there's no one pinching your ass or trying to touch your boobs every few weeks."

"Who's doing—" Charlie stopped and leaped to his feet as if she had just flipped a light switch on in his head. "Oh my God."

"What?" She couldn't remember what she'd said. Did she mention Max? Did she just give them up after all that?

He jumped down the steps. "I have to go."

"What?" She stood up faster than she should have and grabbed his arm, holding on to him so tight she could feel her nails digging into his skin.

This time *he* shook *her* off. "Max has contributed too, hasn't she?"

Olivia stared at him, concentrating very hard to control her face, make sure she wasn't revealing anything. "I don't know."

He started backing away. "Thanks for the help."

"Where're you going?"

He winked. "I'm getting this promotion." Then, as he turned and jogged down the street he added, "Call me when you're horny!"

Fuck, she thought as she watched him run toward Fulton Street.

She took out her phone to call Max—who *thank God* had taken a car back to work or else she'd probably be waiting at the Fulton Street stop when Charlie got there—but then she stopped herself. What could she say? *Charlie knows you might have written about Richard's butt pinching and if he reveals you, then you'll be fired and he'll get the promotion? Charlie is digging deeper than anyone thought he had the capacity to, and it was working?*

But how would she explain why Charlie was asking her about *Twentysomething*? Why would Charlie be talking to Olivia at all?

You have to talk to Richard first thing tomorrow, she texted Max. This can't wait any longer.

21

By seven the next morning, Olivia had received so many SOS texts she didn't know which to answer first. Almost every single person she'd ever interacted with in any capacity in the industry was asking if she was *Twentysomething* Olivia. Nate's financial adviser's assistant. Nate's accountant's assistant. Nate's therapist's assistant. His publicist's assistant. A PA from *Law & Order: SVU.* The showrunner's assistant from the series Nate pseudoproduced a year ago. In less than twelve hours, five strangers got her email from The Society's apparently not-so-secure database, three people wrote her on LinkedIn, and she received six Instagram messages and two Facebook notifications. Charlie wasn't the only one digging. The most important message, however, came from Nate's former assistant, the one who tipped her off to the forehead trick: *I'm going to submit my story, too.*

Apparently it was *very* easy to connect Olivia's ambiguous story to her name. And if strangers and friends could find it and figure it out, it was only a matter of time before Nate did.

Olivia would be the first to admit that she didn't generally think more than, say, two steps ahead. She believed that if something was right in the moment, it was right in the long run.

Well, ousting her manipulative boss on an up-and-coming blog the day after she quit, for instance, fell into that category. It felt right while she was shitting in a bucket and it felt right while he was threatening her career, but she could honestly say it didn't feel right the next morning, when her best friends' jobs were on the line and strangers were emailing to ask about her identity.

What was most surprising was that she felt like she betrayed Nate's trust, as if she owed him some level of loyalty for giving her three years at a job in the industry of her dreams. It shocked her how difficult that was to shake off, especially considering her reel was still in his inbox, never opened or shared, just held over her head to get what he wanted.

Olivia started to think that maybe Nate *could* impact her career. He was a dumbass, but male dumbasses often failed upward. If writing about Nate was going to be the kind of publicity he wanted and cause his IMDb score to skyrocket, then she was fucked. He'd be on all the talk shows, and his whistleblower assistant wouldn't be able to work ever again. *She was a nightmare,* he'd say to Kelly Ripa. *The worst assistant I've ever had. Sometimes I even caught her* looking *at my penis. She clearly didn't mind it that much if she was always staring. And she stayed for three years!* Then he, Kelly, and Ryan Seacrest would have a great laugh and she'd listen to it all on the radio driving to Georgia where she would move back in with her parents, start selling makeup for some multilevel marketing scheme, and attend so many family functions she'd get her accent back.

This felt like the right thing in the moment, she thought as she sank under her covers. She really hoped it was.

It wasn't until after 8:00 a.m. that Olivia checked her phone and saw three missed calls from Nate. She didn't want to call him back—he wasn't her boss anymore and she owed him nothing—but, unfortunately, it didn't feel that simple. She dressed in her favorite outfit when she needed to feel good about herself—Gap jeans and a white Madewell T-shirt, classic and cheap—and when Nate called again, she was going to pick up.

"This is Olivia," she said, answering the phone the way she did when she didn't recognize the number. She obviously hadn't deleted his—and she'd probably remember it by heart for the rest of her life—but it felt weird to just say "hi" normally. There was nothing normal about the situation.

The line was quiet for a moment—she knew he was doing this on purpose—so she fought the desire to fill the silence with small talk. She was not going to let him win. Instead, she stared at the illustrated map of Georgia on her living room wall, imagining which route she'd be taking home after Nate sued her.

Finally, Nate said, "What do you think you're doing?" His voice was low, each word coming out like the anticipatory tick of a bomb.

For a second she debated playing dumb, pretending she had no clue what he was talking about, but quickly decided *fuck it.* "I got you on the website, didn't I? That's what you wanted." She'd never spoken to him like that before, so confidently, defiantly.

"This was not what I meant. It needs to come down immediately."

"It's my story. I don't need your approval to write it."

"You do when it's about me."

"I didn't use your name, so there's no proof—"

"Oh, don't worry, Olivia. My lawyers are on it. Unless this comes down now."

She pulled all the nerve she could find out of her forty-eight-dollar power outfit and steeled herself. Yesterday she shit in a fucking bucket for God's sake. "If you want to sue me for this, be my guest." She could hear him start to laugh, but she ignored it. "Everyone who's read this hates you. Do you realize that? But they don't know they hate *you*. They hate The Boss. Because I didn't say your name. And I won't. But don't assume I'm the only one of your former assistants writing in. So go ahead and sue me. Really. Do it." She paused for dramatic effect just like her thesis acting professor taught her to. "But if you sue me, you'll have to sue all of us. And then you better believe everyone will know that the man who exposed himself to his assistants every day for years was Nathanial Brooks. I'll whisper it to one woman. She tells a few more who tell a few more. I won't do it publicly, and you'll never be able to prove it. But *you'll* never get a job in this industry again. *We'll all* make sure of it." She let out a deep breath. "Let me know what you decide," she finished. "Good luck."

She hung up the phone and could feel herself smiling as she imagined the very satisfying state Nate was in on the other side: holding the phone, mouth agape, in complete shock, with a very limp dick.

With Nate handled, there was only one more loose end for Olivia to tie up.

She had to tell the truth. But now, with *Twentysomething*, the truth wasn't pathetic; she was a part of a movement.

Olivia dialed from memory—it was probably the only phone number she'd never forget—and on the third ring her favorite Southern drawl answered, sounding echoey through their landline.

"Hi, Mom," Olivia said, her own accent distorted as her voice cracked and tears spilled down her face. Then she told her everything.

MAX HAD READ Olivia's text at least eighteen times that morning. You have to talk to Richard first thing tomorrow. This can't wait any longer. There was an urgency in it that Max didn't expect from Olivia. Her go-with-the-flow personality tended to subvert urgency with *whatever happens, happens*. But this felt different. It felt desperate. And that worried Max more than anything else.

Work had been two days of nearly constant *Twentysomething* coverage, which got even heavier after Olivia's admission last night. When Max left Olivia's and came straight to the office, she was shocked to see the newsroom wasn't dark and silent. The wall of TVs wasn't full of infomercials. There were people running, moving, printing. Phones were ringing, coffee was brewing. Alyssa didn't look up from her computer for at least three hours. Every time Max approached to see if she needed anything all she got was a hand wave without eye contact. Even Sheena and Richard were there, spending most of the time in their respective producers' offices with the doors closed. It was when Charlie showed up that Max's anxiety level spiked.

"Morning!" he exclaimed. "Busy here, huh?"

Now he was making small talk? Energetic small talk? "Yeah," was all she could respond.

"Lots going on with that website stuff."

She nodded and watched him log onto his computer, then open his email and check the *Twentysomething* website as if that was the newest addition to his morning routine. Before today, she wouldn't have guessed he even *had* a morning routine.

Max perked up as she heard Alyssa stomping through the bullpen's commotion, followed closely by Richard's slippered shuffle.

"Anything I can do?" Max said as quickly as she could to catch Alyssa as she zoomed past.

"All good, thank you," she responded before slipping down the hall toward the copy room.

Richard appeared a few seconds later and stopped when he reached her and Charlie's desks. "How's it going here?" he asked, leaning onto the back of Max's chair, making it feel like she was going to tilt over.

"Fine," she said, scooching to the front of the chair to balance the weight rather than stand up. She was not putting her ass that close to his hands if she could help it. She'd rather fall backward in her chair and get a concussion.

Charlie looked at Richard and nodded. "All good, boss." Then he looked at Max, who was sitting like she had a ruler taped to her back. He had an expression on his face that she couldn't read. "I have an update on that website, if you want it now?"

"Website…" Richard repeated, as if he needed a reminder of the biggest story on air.

"*Twentysomething,*" Charlie said as Max glared at him. Just hearing it come out of his mouth made her anxiety flare up. She reminded herself to lower her shoulders, but that was difficult when she could feel the man she wrote about literally breathing down her neck. "For the promotion," Charlie added.

To Max's relief, Richard stood up straight. "Of course," he said, walking toward the studio. It seemed like even Charlie didn't know how to dissect that dismissal, so he quickly gathered his things and followed.

"I think I have a lead on the newest story…" she heard Charlie say as he trailed after him.

Max reread Olivia's text from last night. She had to confront Richard, say something to scare him into burying the story. Hopefully, it would buy them time, make their promotion task irrelevant, and get Charlie off the hunt. But what the hell was she supposed to say?

She repeated that question in her head throughout the entire broadcast, as she sat at her desk off camera in the studio, and watched Sheena and Richard report on the new *Twentysomething* updates.

"In our continuing *Twentysomething* coverage," Sheena began, "late last night the first nonanonymous story went up on the site's contributor page. Citing herself as only Olivia, a woman claimed to have kept a tally of the number of times her boss exposed himself in her presence. 'We need to hold people accountable for their actions,' her letter said, encouraging other women to come out with their names. As always, this is a developing story and we will continue to update you as things change."

When they went to commercial, Max texted Olivia, Well, you're officially a topic of this morning's news. And Charlie thinks he has a lead. I hate all of this.

Just after she pressed Send, everyone's computers started to ping. Everyone went silent reading the same AP report that had popped up on Max's screen: *Emmy-nominated actress Claire McKenna accuses costar of sexual harassment.*

Max's jaw dropped. The actress from the blog had come forward with her name.

Alyssa and Alex bolted through the glass greenroom doors into the studio, out of breath, and ran to the anchor desk.

"Move the Washington stuff to G block," Alyssa yelled.

"Richard, you intro it," Alex said. "Ad lib for, I don't know, five, ten seconds. We'll give you a cue when the prompter is ready and there's something for Sheena to say about—" He turned to Charlie. "What's the fucking story?"

Before Max could open her mouth, Charlie jumped in, faster, louder, stronger. "Claire McKenna, Emmy-nominated actress, came out via an Instagram post as the contributor behind a *Twentysomething* story alleging inappropriate behavior—"

"What was the behavior?" Sheena cut in. "We've got fifteen fucking seconds until we're back. Get to the goddamn point."

"I'm sorry—the—I—" Charlie stuttered.

The problem with never getting yelled at was that when you inevitably did, you didn't know how to handle it.

Max cleared her throat. "McKenna claimed long-time co-star Lawrence O'Connell intentionally walked in on her during fittings, encouraged writers to include more scenes with her in a towel, asked her out, and after she said no, talked to the producers to get her downgraded from a series regular to recurring—"

"We're live in five," Alyssa yelled, running behind Max's desk and crouching to the floor to hide just as the stage manager pointed to the camera and gave Richard *three, two, one*.

"In a breaking story," Richard began, and everyone took a collective deep breath. That was why she wanted to work in news, Max thought. For moments like those. And if she wanted any more of them, she had a pervert to confront.

Max looked down at Alyssa, who was still hiding from the camera's view.

"Good job," Alyssa whispered. "But be louder than Charlie from the get-go next time."

After they wrapped the broadcast, Max stood, readying herself to clear off the anchor desk. When they'd first started, Charlie dealt with Richard's half of the desk, and Max did Sheena's. They each had very specific, and opposite, ways they liked their scripts—Sheena's pages were all over the place, spread out with notes and scribbles, and couldn't be thrown out until they wrapped; Richard's stayed in a nice, neat stack to his right, and he liked old scripts shredded during each commercial break. Then one day, about a year into the job, Richard told Max she was "better" at cleaning off the desk than Charlie. After that, it suddenly became only Max's job.

But if she was going to stand up for herself with Richard, she should start with Charlie, too.

"You can do Richard's half of the desk today," she told him.

Charlie slouched in his chair. "But you do them both now."

"Not today," she said, walking to Sheena's side of the anchor desk, and her side only.

Sheena ignored her as Max picked up the scripts, organizing them into three piles: to throw out, to review, and to keep.

"I can't believe his assistant gave him up," Richard said into the phone, leaning back in his chair, his right ankle over his left knee. "Yeah I just saw the embargoed press release. That's fucked up." Max carefully bounced the papers up and down, lining them up so she wouldn't get any paper cuts. "Don't they sign agreements about this shit?" he continued. "It's pretty pathetic to have your entire career hanging by a thread because of a fucking blog, probably started by some bored teenagers." He let out a condescending laugh.

Just do it, she thought. *Can't turn back now.*

"Don't be so sure you're not on there, too," Max whispered so softly that for a moment she wasn't positive the words actually came out.

But then Richard looked up at her, the phone loosening in his hand. "What did you just say?"

She stared at him as a flush ran through her body and she suddenly felt cold from the inside out. And he stared at her. And neither of them dared to even blink as the producers and grips and PAs ran around them, cleaning up.

Finally, she flashed a flat, closed-mouth smile. "Nothing," she said, before walking back to her desk, holding her breath and feeling his eyes on her back as she sat down.

When she turned toward the anchor desk to get one more satisfying look, a flood of terror washed over her. It wasn't because Richard was still looking at her, the wheels ever so slowly turning, thinking about the times he pinched her ass or got too close, thinking about exactly *what* she could say. And it wasn't because Charlie was next to him, cleaning up his papers and pitching him a Claire McKenna follow-up because he *knows someone.*

It was because when she turned to get a good look at Richard, Sheena was holding her glasses on the tip of her nose and staring at her. Even when Sheena slid her glasses back up and finally looked away to her phone, Max couldn't move. What had Sheena heard? And what would she do about it?

22

Max had Sheena's face stuck in her head as she tried to sleep on a couch in the back of the pages' locker room that night. Instead of ignoring her for the rest of the day the way she had in real life, Max kept dreaming about Sheena staring at her above her glasses. After hours of tossing and turning, Max finally gave up on sleep about an hour before her alarm was going to go off, brushed her teeth, slapped on some deodorant and dry shampoo, and slipped out of the page locker room. She pushed through the glass doors of *The Good Morning Show*'s newsroom to see Charlie already sitting at his desk, watching her.

"What?" she asked from across the room. As she reached her desk, she could see Charlie closing a bunch of tabs on his computer too quickly for her to read.

"Hiding something over there?" she asked, looking at his now-blank screen.

Charlie shrugged. "I should ask you the same thing." He looked at her for a minute longer than she was comfortable with, like he could see right through her, and she had to turn away to face her computer. Anxiety built in her chest. He knew they had been talking about *Twentysomething* at The Society meeting, and he apparently thought he had a lead about Olivia, but what other connections had he made that she didn't know about?

Her line of thought was shattered as Alyssa yelled into the bullpen, "Get to the conference room, now." She wasn't typically a yeller. Something had happened.

Max quickly grabbed her notebook and followed everyone else into the conference room, where Alyssa and Alex were silently staring at each other. Max tried to peer at the scrunched-up rundown on the table in front of Alyssa, but couldn't see anything besides today's date.

"Richard there?" Sheena asked over speakerphone.

Alex shifted in his seat. "He's just getting some water."

"Is he now?"

"Man's gotta hydrate," was Alex's response. It was unbelievable to Max that they were still playing this game—pretending Richard was there, that he cared. Sheena wasn't stupid.

"I'd like to pitch something," Charlie said, standing.

"What is it?" Sheena asked impatiently.

"The girl from the website, Olivia—the first one to break her anonymity—works for this actor, Nathanial Brooks. We could do a feature on her, on this tally she's been keeping—"

"Okay, fuck this. Richard's not there. I'm not doing this anymore," Sheena said before the phone clicked off.

Charlie stood there looking like an idiot. An idiot who tried to *pitch Max's best friend as a news story*. Without talking to Max first. Without even a heads-up. But Olivia's blog post had been vague; how could he possibly put those pieces together? He didn't know her well enough. And if he thought Olivia was the *Twentysomething* Olivia, did he think that Max was involved too? Did he know she was The Emotional One?

"You still there, Sheena?" Alex waited, then slammed his hand on the table. "Control your fucking anchor, Alyssa."

"Charlie, thank you," Alyssa said with purposeful calm. "Alex, care to explain why we're not going to use his pitch?"

Charlie visibly slouched, and Max felt a wave of relief and, then, confusion. Why *weren't* they using the pitch?

"Let's just start the meeting," Alex said, lowering back into his chair. "Sit the fuck down, Charlie. Thank you. But, not now."

"I'm not running the meeting today," Alyssa said, taking the most defiant sip of coffee Max had ever seen. That was a *mood*.

"You're not," Alex said flatly, like this was yet another thing he didn't feel like dealing with today.

Alyssa shrugged. "You moved my *Twentysomething* coverage from A-block to O-block. You turned my two-minute debrief into an eighteen-second summary. So I guess this meeting is your job now, since you're moving things around the rundown without telling me."

Max glanced at Alyssa's rundown again. *Twentysomething* had been at the top of the broadcast since they started reporting on it a few days ago. That was where all the important news went: the first twenty-two minutes of the show, then the next eight minutes between the first and second commercial breaks. O-block was for videos of animals playing with babies and stories of soldiers coming home. O-block wasn't for breaking news.

Oh shit. Plan Richard had worked.

And, even more, it had stopped them from listening to Charlie's pitch on Olivia. It was like Max had defused two bombs with one snip of a wire. Max had scared him. She'd scared Richard into burying the coverage. She wasn't fired. She wasn't blacklisted. She wasn't getting sued. *It had worked.*

"It came from the network's lawyers—" Alex started.

"Did it?" Alyssa picked up her phone and started dramatically scrolling, then shook her head with an accusatory frown. "I didn't get that email. Strange that legal would only go to one of the show's executive producers and not both of us."

"Run the fucking meeting, Alyssa."

"Put *Twentysomething* in A," she countered.

The entire room was looking between them across the long table like a tennis match. It made Max wonder, briefly, why Alyssa was fighting so hard to report on *Twentysomething*. Did even *she* not realize the possibility that there were essays about Richard, essays that would bring this show down?

"No," Alex said, resting his hands behind his head. "It's not moving. There's nothing left to cover."

"Charlie just pitched a lead."

"Alyssa, we've beaten this story to the bone. That's it."

She let out one singular, disbelieving *ha*. "Okay," Alyssa said, standing. "If you think that's true, you're in for a very rude awakening." She picked up her things and walked out without another word.

In that moment, Max understood: it wasn't that Alyssa didn't realize Richard's behavior was inevitably on the site— she *knew* it was. And she wanted it to come out. Plan Richard was shutting *Twentysomething* down, buying the four of them some more time; but by doing that Max was working against Alyssa, her boss. She was now putting both their jobs at risk.

After the broadcast, somehow (because of Alex, obviously) the network got word of Alyssa's "outburst," as they called it, and asked her to get on the phone with them. When she called them back, Max listened from her desk six feet away.

"I think we need to keep doing some original reporting here," Max heard Alyssa say. "Some of the assistants are looking into the founders, but in the meantime, maybe we can take a story from the site that no one's uncovered and see how far we can—" She stopped, her eyes rolling. "I understand that, but we're missing—" She paused and sprung up straight. "You *what*? You want *Richard* to take over the sexual harassment stories? Do you think that's the best idea?" As Alyssa listened, Max could guess well enough what the network was telling her. "Fine," Alyssa finally said. "But I don't want my name anywhere near that. Alex will produce it. I'm out." She slammed the phone down and rubbed her face until her glasses fell onto her keyboard. "Fucking idiots," she mumbled.

This was not the move Max had expected the network to make when she scared Richard into burying the story. Did they think watching *him* talk about women who reported their bosses instead of Sheena would redeem him? Or did he just want control of the messaging?

The next morning, Alyssa was angrier than ever. She stood in the back of the studio, behind the cameras, arms crossed, watching Richard cover the harassment stories in the O-block. When Sheena threw the *Twentysomething* segment to Richard, she had such disdain in her eyes that, to hide it, Alex made them switch to a single of Richard instead of the normal two-shot where both anchors were in frame.

Richard looked into the prompter and smiled. "Oscar-winning producer Jeffrey Moore is being accused of verbal abuse by two women on the *Twentysomething* website. His films currently in production have been suspended barring an investigation into the claims, which his representation anticipates will surface nothing. Financier Richard Cohen is also dealing with another accusation this morning. A third woman has come forward with an alleged claim of sexual harassment…"

Watching Richard smile and talk about this made Max feel hot and panicky. It was like she could feel her ass rebruising where he had pinched it. As she adjusted herself in her seat, the echoes of Richard's story bouncing around the studio, she looked at Alyssa, who was staring forward. When Max followed her gaze, landing on Sheena who was staring right back at Alyssa, Max knew.

There was nothing revealing about it—their eyes were dead, uninterested, bored—but it was the fact that they were looking at each other, not moving, not blinking, that was important. They both knew Richard's time was running out—a constant ticking in the background every time he was on air, every time someone said there was a *Twentysomething* update. They both knew eventually the bomb would go off and destroy everything.

And they, like Max, were trying to figure out what to do about it.

SINCE THE BLOG had become a viral sensation, Cate had spent the majority of her days at work strutting into the EAB each morning feeling like a damn queen. She would soak in the image of her fellow assistants and contributors sitting in front of the glass-walled offices where their bosses lived in peaceful oblivion, Matt especially. But Cate's job had not slowed down whatsoever. She was running errands for Matt to prep for the Kenyan safari he was taking with his wife in a month; scheduling his kids' doctor's appointments before the start of school; designing and printing invitations to his wife's fortieth birthday bash; and also organizing and planning said birthday bash. She was on the move constantly and didn't even care that most of it was personal, both because she could write about it, and it meant her mind was busy too. If she gave herself too much quiet time, too much time to reflect on all the problems the popularity of *Twentysomething* presented, she was afraid her anxiety would start spiraling.

To keep her mind busy after work, she spent every moment she wasn't at the office either working through contributor stories in the *Twentysomething* inbox, or at Theo's. Though they never officially made it official, one night a month ago they were watching Netflix in bed and out of nowhere he pulled a new toothbrush from his nightstand and tossed it into her lap. She'd been adding to her supply of overnight stuff ever since, which seemed pretty official to her.

Standing in the bathroom doorway using said toothbrush, Cate watched Theo. He rested his book—*Alphabetical Africa* by Walter Abish—on his lap and rolled to the edge of the bed. She liked watching him, thinking about him. Purely existing in silence in the same room was, at once, thrilling and calming to her. She liked when he was around and missed him when he wasn't. Was that love? Because it felt like it.

When she came back into the bedroom, he was staring forward into the factory windows like there was something more exciting out there than the brick building across the street.

Cate slipped under the covers, finding Theo's phone and handing it to him, a blitz of messages popping onto the screen.

"All good?" she asked.

Theo put the phone on his lap. "Yeah, just work."

"You need to get cupcakes?"

He rolled over, phone in hand, and smirked at her. "You're lucky you're cute," he said, kissing her softly.

"Who's emailing you at 11:00 p.m.?" She closed her eyes and nestled her face into his neck as he reached around her and pulled her closer.

He looked down at his phone for a long while, which confused Cate—it wasn't a difficult question—and when Theo looked up, his smile had faded. "Well, actually, people have been asking me for a *Twentysomething* follow-up, trying to see how much I know and I, um—" He pinched the bridge of his nose and then slid a little farther down the bed, until their faces were aligned. "I've been reading a lot of their submissions and some of the stories, well, really just one person's stories from early in the archives…seem kind of familiar to me."

Speechless, Cate pulled back to look him in the eyes, and saw the truth. He was telling her he had figured it out. He knew she was The Bossy One. And he was a journalist being begged for follow-ups. Follow-ups about her.

"You don't have to say anything," he said softly. "I'm not asking for answers, and I realize where I work makes all of this…complicated." He put his hand on her arm, and she let him, soaking in his warmth as he caressed her skin. "But this—you and me—it's pretty great. And I just want you to know you can talk to me. I don't write about *everything*."

Cate pulled the covers to her shoulders and curled into him. She hated lying to him, sending him on this fruitless search for answers he'd never get. And the way she felt in his arms, curled up, warm, cared for…she didn't want to lie anymore.

"How'd you figure it out?" she mumbled into his chest.

"I think I know enough about Matt at this point to write my own submission about him." She let out a little laugh, which allowed them both to relax. "It's the four of you, right?"

"When we started, it was supposed to be an outlet for our frustrations, but it's grown so fast and gotten kind of out of control, and now everyone's wondering who we are, and we're just doing whatever we can to keep that a secret." She let out a deep breath. She'd never said this out loud to anyone before, and damn, it felt good to talk about.

"Thanks for telling me," he said, kissing her forehead. "You guys are doing a good thing. These people need to be exposed for the total assholes they are."

She laughed into his skin. "Yeah, but now we're getting a little freaked with all the publicity. We even had Max mention to her boss that she wrote about him. He's the news anchor. And he bumped their coverage—"

"Richard Bradley?" Theo asked quickly. Cate nodded. "She tipped him off? When did she do that?"

"A few days ago, I don't know. Why?" she asked, feeling him tense up underneath her.

"It's nothing," he said, tapping his fingers on the back of the phone nervously.

"Why?" she pressed. Why did he know Max's boss's name so quickly? Had she mentioned it before? She usually just called him the pervy news anchor, without specifying which one she was talking about.

"No reason." He squeezed her closer and reached for the remote.

She watched him turn the TV on, navigating to the next episode of *The Wire* they'd been bingeing together. She wanted to ask again, keep repeating the question until he told her exactly what was going on, but she stopped herself. Cate trusted Theo, and Richard was a famous man. A famous man who people invited into their homes to deliver the news every morning. Finding out someone like that was an asshole could be shocking and disappointing, which Cate often forgot since she'd known for years.

23

From her spot on the couch in the page locker room, Max woke up to the sound of her phone vibrating. All the messages were from Sheena, in their group chat with Richard, asking for—well, *demanding*—coffee. As she freshened up in the bathroom and headed to the Starbucks on the corner, Max thought about the last time she did this. Had it really been a few *weeks* since her last coffee run? Had Sheena and Richard really been that self-sufficient lately? How had that happened?

It wasn't until Max was ordering Sheena's coffee that she realized Richard hadn't asked for anything. She ordered him his usual—black coffee with almond milk on the side, same as Sheena—and texted Charlie: Richard didn't ask for coffee so you may want to make sure he's awake.

As Max fumbled to open the door while balancing the coffee cups, Charlie responded, Get here now.

Max didn't think twice before sprinting down the block, holding Sheena's coffee still as a board—she'd notice if even a smidge were missing—while Richard's spilled down her arm and all over her shirt and jeans. When she walked into the studio, looking for Charlie, the first thing Max noticed was that Sheena was camera-ready, sitting at the anchor desk. Her hair was blown-out into curls, her makeup on, her pink pantsuit pressed and tailored.

The second thing Max noticed as she walked toward Sheena with her coffee was that all the desk chairs were set up in rows, facing the anchor desk. That only happened for all-staff meetings, but no meeting had been announced, and as she poured Sheena's milk into her coffee cup—today matching the color log cabin—she noticed that everyone else who filed into the room seemed equally as surprised by the meeting as she did. Max watched as Charlie found his spot in the center of the first row, in between Alex's and Alyssa's empty chairs, nowhere near where he belonged. Meanwhile, still sticky wet from coffee, Max took her regular seat behind a decorative pole in the back. She learned early on that if she sat closer to the anchor desk and wore a skirt, Richard would spend the entire staff meeting staring at her crotch, no matter how crossed her legs, how closed her knees, or how granny her panties.

Alyssa didn't walk into the room until it was full, every seat taken, every desk and pole leaned on. Behind her was a man in a suit that Max recognized but couldn't quite place. And then Alex followed, in a state Max immediately identified as postcry, and sat in his chair next to Charlie.

Alyssa stood behind Richard's chair at the anchor desk, and Max realized what was happening: Richard wasn't there. And he wasn't coming.

"I'm just going to rip off the Band-Aid," she finally said. "I'm sure everyone's noticed that Richard isn't here today. We got a courtesy call from the *New York Times* last night. They've apparently been researching allegations against Richard's behavior for months and, because of *Twentysomething*, decided it's a good time to come out with it now." A stunned silence before she continued, "They're planning to publish this evening, with claims of sexual harassment and misconduct from at least five former employees of this network."

The *New York Times*? Where the *Twentysomething* article was broken? By Cate's chiseled-back boyfriend? What did she do this time? That was when Max saw Alex slump in his front-row chair, his shoulders bouncing slightly up and down. Max always heard rumors that Alex cried when he found out they hired Richard as the new anchor. Everyone thought it was in celebration of how much the ratings were about to spike. But now, as Alex cried in the front row of the staff meeting, it was clear he was mourning his own career. He must have known from day one that hiring Richard as the anchor was poking a hole in a ship. It was just a matter of time until it started to sink. And, as Richard's producer, Alex knew he'd be going down with it.

Sheena stared down at her phone for most of this conversation. If Max didn't know her, it could have come off as disrespectful. But Max knew it was a coping mechanism. If she looked up, she'd notice how many people were looking at her, leaning on her, needing her to be a pillar of strength and composure in these uncertain times; a representation of the good parts of the show. That was a lot of pressure.

Alyssa made her way in front of the glass desk and leaned on Richard's spot. "We have reason to believe these are not isolated incidents, and that this behavior has been pervasive for years. Until our lawyers do an internal investigation into the *New York Times*'s claims, Richard will be suspended, and Melissa from *Evening News* will temporarily be taking his spot as host in the interim."

Alyssa adjourned the meeting shortly after that and everyone went back to work in the kind of silence that came from a mix of shock and suspicion. Everyone was looking over their shoulders, whispering to trusted colleagues in the kitchen, in the bathroom, in the stairwells—*who talked? What did they say? Was it one of us?*

Max put her things down on her desk and took the no-camera way down a back set of stairs, around a few corners, and finally into the basement bathroom. She shut the door behind her and leaned back, banging her head lightly against the chipping wood. *Richard is gone. Richard is suspended. Richard is being investigated.*

She slid down onto the floor and pulled out her phone. "Richard's out," she announced, when she had all three of them on the line. She told them about the meeting and the *New York Times* article.

"It's a *Times* article?" Cate asked.

"What does Theo know?" Lauren asked. "Did he write this?"

"Alyssa said the investigation's been going on for a while," Max said.

"Fuck," Cate interrupted. "I have to go."

"What did you tell him?" Olivia asked.

"I'll call you later." Cate hung up quickly and left the three of them quiet, processing what that meant.

"Has Charlie said anything?" Olivia asked.

"About what?"

"Just, I don't know, has he told you anything about how close he's getting to finding the founders? Has he tried to pitch me again?"

Max had nearly forgotten all about that. So many things had happened over the last week that Charlie pitching Olivia as a story—or investigating them at all, really—seemed like a very small problem. Now Alyssa might figure them out. Or Sheena. Or the fucking *New York Times* and then the entire world.

"We fucked up, didn't we?" she asked. "If we never tried to use Richard, then he wouldn't have buried the story, the network wouldn't have wanted him to cover it, and the *Times* wouldn't have been so eager to publish this thing. Assuming Theo didn't write it—I just can't handle *that* fight right now—then it's our fault. We did this."

"So what do we do next?" Lauren asked.

"I don't know," Max said. "I mean, I do know, and it's telling everyone that we're *Twentysomething.* Plan Richard stopped Charlie from digging and prevented me from having to report on myself. But I think we might need to stop delaying the inevitable and realize that it might just be here…" She looked down at the watch on her wrist. "Shit, okay, I have to go—"

She hung up before they could protest and ran back to the studio, just in time to hear Sheena screaming her name. The whole room was back to normal, as if nothing had happened. Max approached the anchor desk from one side and noticed Charlie making his way from the other. They reached Sheena at the same time, and she waved her hands, making them get in close. "If a fucking internet blog," she whispered, "can bring down one of the network's most untouchable assholes…" She paused, then suddenly screamed, *"How the FUCK is it possible that we don't know who they are yet!"*

Max and Charlie jumped backward, Max nearly falling off the short pedestal the desk was perched on.

"I'm working on it," Charlie said as Max caught her balance. *You have no idea what you're talking about*, she thought to herself.

"Me too." She tried to be louder like Alyssa told her to be. "I'm really close."

"Not close enough," Sheena spat. "We should be *reporting* these stories, not getting them from the fucking *New York Times.*"

Charlie said, "We'll figure it out," and Max was disappointed at how convincing he sounded. Like maybe he already had.

"You better," Sheena said. "This AP job is only on the table if we get an exclusive. None of this second-act bullshit." They waited for her to continue, but instead she rolled her eyes and waved them off like even *she* couldn't handle how frustrated she was with them.

Max scampered back to her desk, her mind whirling between Back Muscles and Richard and Sheena's task, when she was hit by another thought that scared her the most: if Back Muscles was involved, then Cate was too, and if that was the case...how much does he know? Did she tell him about *them*? Was *that* article coming next?

THE SECOND MATT left for lunch, Cate grabbed her stuff and marched out. She walked across Midtown with such gusto she didn't even notice she was sweating or that she'd forgotten to change from her office heels to her walking Converse and her right foot was bleeding. As if the universe knew it shouldn't get in her way, as she hit each corner, the light switched and she was greeted with the neon white hand, beckoning her toward her final destination: the *New York Times* office.

Cate always thought the building was quite special, the way the curtained exterior unveiled the publication's name, like the entire city should be proud of all the work being done within it. She used to imagine taking a photo of the first *New York Times* bestseller she published with the building in the background, and she'd frame it for the author as a gift. But as she approached around the corner, the building seemed more menacing, looming. Like Big Brother reminding you he was there, watching, writing, ready to report whatever he saw. Ready to report her.

She waited outside for fifteen minutes before she spotted Theo exit one of the side doors with a few friends, laughing as they no doubt headed to lunch.

"Hey," she called out, walking toward him. He did a double take, then was immediately happy to see her, the smile radiating on his face as he excused himself from his colleagues to envelope her in a hug and kiss.

She stayed stiff in his arms, and he squeezed her a bit tighter. "What are you doing here?" he asked.

"We have to talk," she said, untangling herself from his grip.

Theo stepped back, and she watched the confused look on his face closely. She could see his wheels turning, trying to figure out what was going on. If he knew why she was there, this performance of his could be nominated for an Oscar. Cate waited for him to start talking, but he was too skilled a journalist to fill the silence. He knew better.

"Tell me the Richard Bradley story isn't your follow-up," she finally said. "I told you that Max wrote about him in confidence." He rubbed his hand against his mouth and chin. *Shit.* She took a step back. "I can't believe you did that. I haven't told that to *anyone.* I—"

"I didn't know about the article until recently," he said quickly before Cate could continue. "They've been doing the investigation into him for months. After I wrote the *Twenty-something* article, they asked me to contribute to this one."

Cate felt her skin getting hot, like the pressure of the last few months had been building and building and was about to burst. "I don't believe you. *Last night* I mentioned that Max talked to Richard about it. That Max *tipped him off.* Did you bring it up last night because you needed confirmation? That The Emotional One was about him—"

"You can't be mad at me for this," Theo argued, louder than before. "Honestly, I brought it up because I sensed it was you guys and I wanted to know the truth. No *Twentysomething* stories are included. They had no way to know which stories were about him. And even after the confirmation last night, I *didn't* mention Max. Or you."

"You could have at least given me a heads-up—"

"I wasn't thinking about you, Cate. Sorry. But I wasn't. The second you said Max tipped Richard off, I knew we had to publish. All these women came out with their incredibly traumatic experiences and, even anonymous, if Richard sensed he was being ousted, he'd act. He'd start getting lawyers involved, threatening anyone whose ass he's ever slapped. Then our sources could start retracting. We're *this close* to exposing him as someone abusing his professional power to take advantage of women. Isn't that what you want? What your whole mission is...?" He trailed off, his brow furrowing. "This article's not about you, Cate. It's about these women and their experiences. Putting your names in the article could overshadow the entire investigation. You have to trust me."

Cate wanted to. She wanted to so badly. She loved him.

But in this moment, standing outside his office, the place that was about to break everything they built, she wasn't so sure. This was the first time any of their direct bosses was being revealed. It wouldn't take long before they were next. The walls were staring to close in on them. And this article— Theo's job—had just put that on overdrive.

He started backing away, just as his friends rounded the corner with bags of lunch and cups of sweating iced coffee. "I'm sorry that I couldn't warn you. But I'm a journalist. And this is part of my job. This is an important story and I have to protect my sources."

Cate didn't try to call after him or follow him into the building as he walked away. When his friends waved at her as they all shuffled through the tall glass doors, she waved back and smiled like nothing happened. The truth was, she didn't know whether she believed him. But she did know he was right. This was an important story—and a version of what they were trying to achieve when they started the website in the first place. They wanted to take assholes down. And her boyfriend was doing that in a major way.

Theo paused for a second in the building's entrance, glancing back at her through the streaky glass. She loved him. She loved everything about him.

But in that moment, as he disappeared into the building, something in her gut told her it was time to plan for the worst. They were going to be mentioned in this article. He gave them up.

And that broke her heart.

EVERYONE CAME OVER that night and sat around Lauren's computer, waiting. They stared at the clock on the wall, watching the hands tick second by second. When the time hit 7:35 p.m., they refreshed the *New York Times* page, bracing themselves as the article finally popped up, the headline bold at the top of the screen: "Richard Bradley's Decade-Long Sexual Misconduct Uncovered."

It was a pretty damning piece. Even with entirely anonymous sources, the information carried within—patterns of groping female colleagues, offering professional gain for sexual favors—was hard to ignore. The hardest, though, was the sentence calling *Twentysomething* "the accelerant" the world needed to start speaking out. The investigation into Richard had been ongoing for so long, the *Times* had all their sources before *Twentysomething* even existed. It was the creation of the site, and the discussion that followed, that pushed them to publish. It did make Lauren wonder if anyone featured in the article had also written their experiences into *Twentysome-thing*, too.

Then she thought the same about James.

Even after everything, Lauren didn't want Pete to hate her. She didn't want Pete to think that all the good he did—the overwhelming percentage of their relationship in which he was a generous, gracious mentor—was voided because of this one small, though massively hurtful, fuck up. What was bizarre about it all was that her chest hurt with the thought that Pete would feel as betrayed by her writing for *Twentysomething*, as she felt by him hiring James back. She never wanted to make him feel that way, though he did it to her seemingly without thinking twice. Without so much as a warning. Without a promotion. Without offering her any sense of autonomy— anything that would make her feel like she was important, like she could defend her place on the show to James, if it came down to it. Instead, James's presence was a constant reminder to Lauren that she wasn't important, she was an assistant. That was it. That would always be it.

Since her confrontation with Pete and James, since she finally stood up for herself, even in the smallest way, she felt invincible at work. She wasn't afraid of James anymore. She wasn't hiding in the corner every time he walked through the trailer. Part of that was realizing how pathetic he was— how he needed to pressure a young woman to take off her shirt in order to feel something—and part of it was Owen. She would never be a damsel in distress—she was brought up too self-sufficient for that—but it was when Owen was in the room that she felt safe at work. She felt like at least one person would have her back.

Though their new dynamic at work wasn't ideal, it was something she could live with. But, would this article finally direct Pete to *Twentysomething*? Would he read The Bitchy One's submission? And if he did, if he learned the *whole* story with James, would that change everything?

CATE SLOWLY LEANED back onto the couch, her head resting against the scratchy pillow behind her. Admittedly, she had a hard time concentrating on the article. The second she saw the mention of *Twentysomething* without their names attached, without the scoop that every single outlet was desperate for, she felt sick to her stomach. He hadn't included them. He had told her the truth, and she hadn't believed him.

I fucked up, she kept repeating to herself.

Theo was right: including their names could have potentially tainted what had clearly been months and months of thorough investigative work. He was helping to expose one of the news industry's biggest perverts, and that was an incredible feat. And the thought of him, standing over some gray desk, sleeves rolled up, tie askew, as they pressed Publish, was very hot.

Honestly, if the situation were reversed, Cate probably would have done the same thing. She would have put her work over her relationship. She would have chosen these women and their stories over giving her boyfriend a heads-up, which could potentially jeopardize the entire thing. And he probably would have supported her, which made her hate herself even more.

It was selfish of her to think she was the most important news story. Revealing her name would do nothing but cause more of a stir, while ousting Richard was the biggest thing he could be reporting right now. He was making real change. And she loved him for it.

She hoped it wasn't too late to fix it.

AFTER READING THE ARTICLE, Olivia's brain was preoccupied with thoughts of Charlie and Nate. Charlie already knew she was the Oliva behind the first nonanonymous submission. And he hadn't stopped looking into the founders since. Every day the contributors' stories were more widely investigated, picked apart detail by detail, was a day closer to when Charlie would figure them out. Olivia determined the best plan of action was continuing to keep Charlie very, very close to find out exactly what he knew. What was the point of a secret, potentially devastating "relationship" if she couldn't use it to her advantage? She quickly texted him to come over later tonight.

Luckily, with Claire McKenna talking about Lawrence O'Connell and, now, the *New York Times* talking about Richard Bradley, no one cared to uncover the C-List actor who'd exposed himself to his assistant for years. The lack of interest in Nate's identity only firmed her disregard for his threat of blacklisting her from the industry. She'd brushed it off the moment after he said it, and continued to each day he didn't act on it, but every time an email of hers went unanswered or an audition submission was ignored, the threat floated back to her.

You'll never be an actor. I'll make sure of it.

MAX COULDN'T RECOGNIZE any of the article's anonymous sources, but she'd heard versions of all of these before. The touching, the pinching, the "love-tapping"—none of it was new. These stories were all part of the whisper network she'd been looped into just a few days into being Sheena's assistant.

Richard was finally publicly called out. And it was about damn time they stopped having to warn each other, adjust what they wore, how they looked, where they bent down, just to keep his secret. It was time for him to adjust *his* behavior and for everyone to know about it.

"Oh shit," Olivia said, pulling Max out of her spiral. Olivia was looking at her phone, her mouth in a shocked smile. She glanced to Cate on her left then Max on her right. "We've gotten emails from NBC, ABC, *The New Yorker*, the *Times*, the *Post*—oh shit, this one's from *People*—"

"Now you're just naming magazines," Lauren said.

Olivia turned her phone around, the *Twentysomething* email pulled up on the screen. There were at least twenty with some variation of REQUEST FOR INTERVIEW in the subject line.

"What do they want?" Lauren asked.

The room was silent as Olivia pulled the phone back and continued scrolling. They all knew the answer to that question—though no *Twentysomething* stories were included in the article, it credited the website as the spark to this wildfire— but no one wanted to admit it. But maybe it was time.

"They want us."

24

The next morning, it seemed like an odd calm had stunned the entire staff, Max included. Everyone was eerily quiet. There were now four security guards stationed in the lobby—for what, Max wasn't sure. As she made her way to Sheena's office, she realized she hadn't heard from Sheena all night, which was unusual. She didn't double-check her car's pick-up time, she didn't need a script update, or ask for last-minute research. She didn't even send through a coffee order.

Max walked past her office, glancing inside to see Sheena, at her desk, concentrated on writing something. The network did not want her to comment on the situation; to say anything that wasn't approved by the onslaught of lawyers now involved. But Max knew Sheena wouldn't listen. If Max had learned anything from that look she got when Sheena overheard her initiate Plan Richard, it was that Sheena had something to say about this. And now that he was gone, she could speak up.

As they were gearing up to go live, the studio was packed. Crew lined the walls, sat on desks, took up any space that wasn't on camera. Everyone wanted to see for themselves how

Sheena handled the first live broadcast after the article came out. The first broadcast without her coanchor. The first one where he wasn't Richard Bradley the reporter, but Richard Bradley the *alleged* pervert.

Just as the timer started ticking down, the stage manager retreated to her spot, a sudden hush fell over the studio. Sheena looked up and Max followed her gaze toward the glass walls of the greenroom—where the show's guests were normally seated drinking coffee before their segments. Inside was Richard, buttering half a cinnamon bagel, then sauntering toward the newsroom. As if nothing had happened. As if he wasn't under investigation. As if he was *supposed* to be there.

The last time Max had spoken to Richard, she had threatened him with *Twentysomething*. Did he think she was responsible for the *New York Times* exposé?

And if so, what would he do?

Sheena glanced down at the yellow paper, presumably carrying her speech and, as the stage manager began waving her into action, Sheena tucked it under her scripts, looked at the prompter, and began to read. Nothing about Richard was mentioned.

After the broadcast, Max walked back to the newsroom, trying to quell her rising panic as she wondered why the hell Richard was allowed back in the building. He was suspended. He was being investigated.

She stopped when she saw Richard sitting in her chair, talking to Charlie. She almost turned around to wait it out in the basement bathroom until he was gone. But then she decided not to. *You have control*, she told herself as she approached. *You control him now.*

"Can I have my seat back?" she asked, more pleasantly than she would have liked.

Richard glanced up at her, eyebrows raised, smiling in a way that made her blood run cold. "I don't know...*can you?*"

It was a question that pissed her off now as much as it had in grade school.

She peeled her coat off the back of her chair, tugging extra hard to pull it out from under his thick body. "I guess I'll work from your desk, then..."

Richard was quiet for a beat, then turned to Charlie. "Grab me a coffee, would you?"

Charlie hesitated—he wasn't used to being the coffee-getter—but eventually sprang to his feet and hustled off, leaving the two of them alone.

Terror creeping up her spine, Max moved toward the door and said, "I should get Sheena some too—"

Richard stood and took three large steps until he was an inch away from her, close enough she could see the wrinkles on his button-down, the puffy bags under his blue eyes, the dark hairs on his unshaved chin. His perfect facade was cracking. And she was the cause.

"You can't speak to me like that," he whispered menacingly, grabbing her forearm and pulling her closer, his manicured nails digging into her skin. "You have no idea how hard I'll come down on you if you open your goddamned mouth again."

"I don't know what you're talking about." Max jerked her arm away, but his grip only tightened. At that point, they weren't making a scene, but they could. She only needed to scream to get everyone in the studio running toward them, armed, now, with enough anonymous evidence to question his every move. "Don't touch me," she said, just loud enough to make him nervous.

"Hey—" Alyssa entered through the glass doors, nearly stopping in her tracks when she made eye contact with Richard, who dropped Max's arm like it suddenly scorched him. "Max, I need your help," she said, moving past them.

Relieved, Max ran to follow Alyssa into the copy room, rubbing the skin on her arm that he'd twisted into a burn. Without a word, Alyssa lifted up the hood of the copy machine, put a blank piece of paper in the feed, clicked 2-0-0, then *copy*. As the machine cranked into action, she slid onto the floor, her back against its vibrating body.

She patted the ground next to her. "You okay?" she asked, eyeing Max's red skin.

"I'll survive," Max said shakily, joining her. "Why is he here? Isn't he suspended?"

Alyssa let out a long, deep breath, sliding her legs out straight in front of her. "Honestly? He's cocky. Rubbing it in everyone's faces. Their investigation, or whatever you want to call it, isn't going to come back with anything. He wants to make sure everyone knows that he's not going anywhere." The copies finished printing and, without looking, she reached her hand to the keyboard, pressed a few more buttons, and the machine started again. "You know who's running the investigation?" Alyssa asked with a soft laugh. Max shook her head. "A group of men. Ten of them." She stared forward at the bookshelf stuffed with reams of colorful pastel paper. "And they all probably hold stock in the network, so even if they were genuinely looking into it, they're not exactly unbiased."

"They didn't have any kind of third party?"

Alyssa shrugged. "No one asks who does the research, as long as we say the research was done. I'm sure soon they'll come out with an official statement that none of the *Times*'s anonymous sources could be verified. That they can't prove anything." Max was surprised how candid Alyssa was being, like she was talking to a peer, not a subordinate. "They won't let Richard back on the air immediately," she continued. "But soon. Too soon. And then *we*—" she pointed to herself and Max "—will have to do some kind of harassment training and sign a thing that says that if we're ever feeling harassed, we should report it. And then nothing will change, because if people cover up for you the first time, they'll do it again."

Max and Alyssa sat in silence for a few minutes, breathing to the rhythm of the pages printing behind them. When the machine switched off, and the white noise turned to silence, Alyssa stood, taking the blank papers that were printed and returning them to the paper tray.

"I'm around if you need anything," she said. "My copy room escape is your copy room escape."

"Thanks," Max said. She was suddenly tempted to tell her that it was in this exact spot in this exact room that Richard had harassed her. And it was that story that she wrote about as The Emotional One for the first time on the website everyone's obsessed over. But she held her tongue. There was no escaping this kind of behavior. But Max had a feeling Alyssa already knew that.

Alyssa had the door open and one foot out when she turned back to Max. "Did you submit anything to *Twentysomething*?" She must have seen the panic flush Max's face because she quickly added, "It's really okay if you did. I promise."

Max took a deep breath—Alyssa rarely asked questions she didn't already have the answer to—and nodded.

Alyssa smiled. "Good for you." Then she shut the door and left Max on the floor of the copy room, wondering what the fuck she had just done.

OLIVIA SAT ON her bed in underwear with a bottle of tequila on her lap, waiting for Charlie. She took a swig, willing it down like the two other sips before, and looked out the window, watching the people on the sidewalk blissfully move through life without thinking twice about Richard Bradley or *Twentysomething* or her fuckbuddy-turned-fucknemesis. Last night after the article came out, she invited Charlie over, and greeted him by lying naked on her bed and saying, "Let's do anything you want tonight." She'd even been tempted to let him sleep over, but he insisted he needed to go back to the office. All day, she'd texted him. It started with sexy emojis—their preferred method of communication—then moved to sexy voice messages. She would have resorted to full-on nudes if he hadn't said he'd come over tonight, too.

When the apartment buzzer rang, she braced herself, putting the tequila bottle on the singular kitchen counter, and pressed the button next to her front door.

She was a spy. Even if she didn't know exactly what she was looking for.

Charlie knocked twice before Olivia answered, again, in her birthday suit, keeping her body behind the door as he sauntered inside so she didn't flash anyone in the hallway.

"Beer in the fridge, tequila on the counter," she said, plopping down in bed, mimicking last night's approach. He seemed unfazed by her nakedness, which was both liberating and a little disconcerting. Shouldn't he have a more visceral reaction to seeing a woman greet him with her boobs? Maybe she'd overused the technique.

He opened a beer with a *shhk* and leaned back against the bookshelf.

"How's that assignment coming?" Olivia asked, tracing a finger up her thigh.

His eyes followed her touch. "Are you asking as my girlfriend or Max's inside man?"

"Neither," she said quickly. She was more offended by the girlfriend part than the insinuation that she was spying on him, even though she absolutely was doing the latter. "Don't call me that."

"An inside man?"

"Your girlfriend."

Charlie laughed into his beer and perched on the edge of the bed. "I figured that was a more politically correct way of saying fuckbuddy. It implies more wining and dining—" he lifted his drink "—which happens on occasion."

"Wining and dining is just the societally mandated prerequisite to sex in order to not be considered a slut."

"Is that why you're so bad at it?"

She opened her legs ever so slightly, and then closed them right before he could get too much of a peek. "Hmm..." She rolled onto her stomach and crawled toward him, stopping short when her face was about a foot away from his crotch. "What am I bad at exactly?"

He swallowed hard as she moved her hands to his belt buckle, playing around with the latch instead of unbuttoning it. "Nothing..." He cleared his throat and his body relaxed back onto the bed, watching her. There was some movement under her hands. *That* was the reaction she had been looking for.

"But really..." Slowly, she pushed the tongue through a punch hole and pulled the brown leather through the buckle to the very tip. "How's it going?" she murmured. "Have you figured out who's in charge of *Twentysomething*? I'm sure they're riding your asses now that all the Richard stuff is on the news."

"That, um...that probably won't last," he said, his voice getting lower the more she played with his belt. He shifted, moving an inch away from her and looking up from his pants to her face. "I have an angle into it I'm working on." He held her gaze for a moment too long, which seemed to turn his sentence into more of a threat. *I'm getting close to you.*

Olivia couldn't seem to shake that for the rest of the night, while they were drinking, while they were having sex, while they were lying in bed after. There was something in his tone, a confidence that made her think he already knew. He knew everything. He just didn't know how to use it yet.

Charlie actually slept over, though Olivia drew the line at cuddling, and at an ungodly hour, Charlie's phone alarm started going off. She pretended to be asleep as he patted around the bed for the noise until he found it and turned it off. He rolled over for a second, taking a little too much blanket for her liking, before letting out the loudest sigh imaginable, standing, and walking to the bathroom. She heard the shower turn on and, a few seconds later, just as her eyes were heavy enough to go back to sleep, his phone started buzzing again. The fucking idiot snoozed it.

"Ughhhhh," she whined, loud enough so hopefully he'd hear it through the shower, as she rolled over and picked up his phone.

After she turned the alarm off, a series of text messages from someone named Alex Humphry flashed on the screen.

1:05: I think you're right. Don't tell anyone else.

1:08: Come to my office as soon as you get in.

2:24: I've held a minute in the A-Block.

3:09: Just reread it. I was definitely there for this story.

Then, with the phone in her hand, one more message came:

3:10: Max is The Emotional One.

Olivia shot up and threw the phone to the end of the bed. "Fuck," she whispered. "Fuck, fuck, fuck, fuck..." She found her phone and immediately dialed Max. It rang four times before she hung up, redialed, and tried again. "Come on, come on, come on," she repeated to herself, hoping Charlie never got out of the shower. Hoping, for the first time, that he'd never leave.

"Olivia?" Max answered. "It's so early—"

"Charlie knows," Olivia blurted out. "Do whatever you need to do, but Charlie knows you're The Emotional One, and probably that we're the others, that I'm not just a contributor. And he told someone named Alex and they held time in the A-block, whatever that means."

There was a beat of silence on the other end. It was so quiet she could hear the pigeons outside, tapping against the fire escape's railing. "How do you know that?" Max finally asked.

"I saw some messages on his phone. Max, you have to—"

"Why do you have his phone?"

"I don't have his phone, he's here. I mean, he's not here, he's in the shower. But he's—"

"Oh my *God*, Olivia," Max screeched. "*Charlie* is your secret boyfriend?"

"Secret boyfriend? What are you talking about?"

"We all knew you'd been seeing someone, but—*Charlie*. Really?"

"He's not my boy—wait, this is *not* the point. We can talk about it later. He knows you're The Emotional One, what are you going to—" Olivia looked up and saw Charlie, staring at her, a towel wrapped around his waist.

"What are you doing?" he asked.

"FUCK," she heard Max scream. "I can hear him!"

Olivia hung up, quickly tucking the phone under the covers. "Nothing."

"Who were you talking to?" He spotted his phone on the bed and walked toward it.

"No one."

"No one?" When he picked it up and saw the messages, all the color drained from his face. "Fuck." He looked up at her. "Max is—" His eyes darted around the room, like suddenly everything was falling into place, every interaction he'd had with them over the last few months was making sense. "It's the four of you, isn't it?" She didn't say anything. "Holy shit. That's—"

"I don't know what you're talking about."

He dropped the towel and started collecting his things, putting on clothes as he walked around to find the rest. "I can't believe you didn't say anything. I'm busting my ass trying to figure this out, trying to get a promotion I deserve more than anyone, and you tell me you don't know what I'm talking about? That you're only a contributor. That you have no answers." He stood up straight, his pants on without a belt, holding his shirt in his hand. "You're so fucking selfish, Olivia. I get that you don't have to work for anything, but some of us do. Some of us—" He stopped suddenly. "Who were you on the phone with?"

Olivia silently looked at him. *You know who*, she wanted to say.

"Did you tell her?" He looked like he could have started crying.

"Obviously," she said as Charlie snatched his backpack off the floor. But she realized he didn't really have a right to feel angry. "Why do you think this is your story to tell?" she asked him as he fumbled to unlock the door. "It's not, for the record. It's hers and mine and ours. If you've never had your ass pinched at work or had to rethink your wardrobe to evade a man who couldn't keep his hands to himself, then this isn't yours."

He stood in the doorway, glaring at her. "Fuck you," he said. "This is over." Then he slammed it closed behind him.

25

The way Max was running down the hallway you'd think the president had been assassinated and she was the sole person responsible for breaking the news to the country—navigating through the hallways that seemed longer and narrower than ever, swerving past assistants and talent alike.

"Do you have a second?" Max gasped as she skidded to a stop outside Alyssa's open door, holding on to the frame and bending forward to catch her breath.

Alyssa looked up from her desk, bewildered, and waved her in. Her office was small and looked even smaller because of the stacks of papers and tapes and books scattered on every surface. "You okay?"

Still breathless, Max nodded and moved a stack of papers off a guest chair and collapsed into it.

Richard, she thought. *Plan Richard Part Two.*

"I have a question," Max said, wondering if Alyssa could hear her wildly beating heart. "If what you said is true—that they're not doing Richard's investigation right—could someone else do it?"

"What do you mean?"

"What if *Twentysomething* did an investigation into Richard? Like what the *Times* did, but better?"

Alyssa lifted an eyebrow. "You think bloggers can do it better than top-tier journalists?"

Max sank in her seat a little. "I mean, a crime blogger basically found the Golden State Killer. And plus, *Twentysomething* has something the *Times* doesn't." Alyssa waited and Max took a deep breath. She was going to say it. She was going to admit everything. "A woman on the inside."

After a moment, Alyssa closed her laptop with a satisfying click. "How do you know that?"

Max looked up at the three clocks hanging on the wall above Alyssa's head: New York, Los Angeles, London. She didn't have time to beat around the bush. If she didn't say it now, Charlie would. And it was her story to tell, not his.

"I'm *Twentysomething*," she said. "Well, more specifically, I'm The Emotional One. I started the site."

Alyssa scoffed like she had never heard anything more ridiculous in her entire life. *"You?"* She shifted in her chair. "I don't believe you."

"Alex and Charlie know. I don't know how they found out, Charlie's sneaky and—that's beside the point. That hold in the A-block?" Max pointed to the sheet of paper on Alyssa's desk. "That's where they're going to talk about it."

Alyssa sat back, looking Max over like she was deciding exactly what to do. Like Max was a pig, and Alyssa was judging if she was fat enough for the slaughter. "Why didn't you say anything sooner?"

"I was afraid of getting fired."

"Yeah, you can definitely be fired for this," Alyssa admitted. Max didn't have the brainpower to unpack that. Or panic over it.

"Look," Max said instead, "I know this is probably it for me here. But Alex can't go out with this today. My friends and I—we have to tie up some loose ends before we're uncovered as the people behind this thing. And I want to buy myself that time by looking into Richard." She paused for a second, making sure Alyssa heard every word of what she was about to say. "If I'm going to be fired, I'd rather go down making sure Richard can't work here ever again."

Alyssa was quiet for a long time, and Max could feel her mouth dry with anxiety.

"I'll take care of Alex and Charlie," Alyssa finally said. "Push their story. But if they can figure it out, anyone can. They're fucking idiots." She tapped her finger a few times on the top of her desk. "You have three days."

"What?"

"I can hold them off for three days. Get me a story by end of day Thursday. Then we'll publish it right before we go on air Friday. We'll be the first ones to break it at seven."

"That's not—"

"That's all I can give you, Max. This only works if we break the story—both about you, and about Richard. Otherwise it's moot."

She was right. If anyone else got the scoop earlier, figured them out, she'd be fired, and they'd have no more leverage. There would be nothing for her to do but accept it. And she didn't want to accept her fate, she wanted to define it. She became a journalist for a reason. For *this* reason. If you were lucky, the opportunity to write an article like this came *maybe* once in a career. This was her shot. This would put her on the map as a journalist and also save them. If they had any chance at not getting fired, at coming out of this as the good kind of whistleblowers, they needed to attach themselves to taking down Richard. They needed to fight. They needed to win.

"Okay." Max nodded and stood.

"Okay," Alyssa agreed. "Let's fucking take him down."

CATE WOKE UP with a pit in her stomach. She rolled onto her back and, as the prior two days' events started cycling back into her mind—Richard, the article, Sheena on air—she tried to tell herself everything was going to be fine. But the anxiety didn't ease, and it wasn't until she picked her phone off the nightstand and was disappointed to not see any messages from Theo that she realized *he* was the source of her anxiety, not *Twentysomething*. The fight and her unanswered messages that came after it were sitting heavy on her chest. Every day that passed when their names weren't a *New York Times* exclusive, she realized how much she had fucked up. How much she should have trusted him. How much she needed to clean up this mess she created.

Can we get coffee before work, she texted him, adding another message to all the others she'd sent him in the last twenty-four hours that he hadn't answered. Holding her phone to her chest, she closed her eyes and waited. She didn't care how pathetic the one-sided blue bubbles looked in her messages—she needed to fix this.

When her phone buzzed a few seconds later, her heart leaped. But it was Max.

We have to talk. I have thirty minutes to shower tonight before going back to work. Come over later.

Cate wanted to pull the covers over her head and disappear. It wasn't even seven in the morning. How did Max already have a problem? How was there *already* something they had to deal with? Now, her anxiety was twofold.

Cate spent the day at her desk trying to get work done in

between staring at her phone for an update. At this point, she'd be happy if Theo messaged her on LinkedIn to at least confirm he was alive. She'd take anything. And Max—what? They were just supposed to go through the rest of the day not wondering what the hell she was talking about?

It was the longest day ever, but finally Matt left (surprisingly early to catch the end of his son's camp graduation, whatever that meant). As she left the office and rode the subway, Cate realized she'd never been to Max's apartment, which didn't even seem possible. It was when she arrived outside Max's tall building with a marble entrance and a doorman that she realized why.

"You *live* here?" Cate began as soon as she saw Max, Olivia, and Lauren standing inside the double-doored entrance. She planned to continue with some variation of *what the fuck* but before she could, she realized Max and Olivia were fighting.

"Are you fucking kidding me?" Max yelled.

"Sorry I didn't tell you," Olivia said sheepishly, which was *very* uncharacteristic of her.

"You didn't just *not tell me*. You didn't tell me for two years? Seriously? You've been sneaking around and—"

While Max continued to yell, Cate sidled up to Lauren. "What's happening?" she whispered.

"Olivia's been sleeping with Charlie for years behind Max's back," Lauren said without taking her eyes off the action. "Plus, this is apparently where Max lives."

"—I can't believe you'd betray me like that. You know how much I hate him. You know how awful he is to me. I mean— he's been working to expose us for *weeks*."

"He's really not that bad. I mean, yes, he's an annoying shit. But, I wasn't exactly in it for his personality…"

Max looked like she was going to barf. "That's disgusting. I hate that. I hate that so much."

"Look, I get it, it's weird, and I'll stop, okay? But at least I was able to get a heads-up that he knows about our identities. What did you do after I called this morning? Because I don't know what the A-block is, but I know that I watched your whole damn show waiting for our names, and they didn't come out."

Without another word, Max turned and walked deeper into the lobby. They followed her slowly—admiring the tall ceilings and staring dumbfounded at the signs pointing toward a gym and a theater and a rooftop—into the elevator. Cate was in a state of disbelief. They were supposed to know everything about each other. They were supposed to be the only people who Cate knew better than Matt. But now Olivia had been dating Charlie for *how long*? And there was a fucking luxury-apartment-sized hole in her friendship with Max, too?

When the elevator opened, Max marched straight into the door on the right. For a moment Cate wasn't sure they were allowed inside but then "Wine or tequila?" echoed from Max's vast apartment and the three of them cautiously entered, half afraid of some kind of "you break it you buy it" rule. They made their way into the living room and spotted a bottle of tequila on the coffee table as Max waved them toward the West Elm couch, and the four of them sat, silent.

"So, you live here?" Cate started again, ogling at the marble countertops and view of Central Park West.

Max sighed. "Yes, I live here. Yes, there's a doorman. Yes, there's a gym. My parents own it. I don't pay rent. Yes, I realize I'm extremely privileged." Max stood with her arms crossed and began pacing in front of them. "Now if that covers everything, we have to talk." Max filled them in on her and Olivia's mornings, then continued, "First, we need to game plan this investigation. And second, we have to, you know, *talk to people*." Max looked between Lauren and Cate. "If you want to give your bosses a heads-up that this is coming, then now's your chance."

All the color drained from Lauren's face. It was like Max had just told her someone died.

"Also," Max continued, "we have three days."

"Three days," Olivia repeated. Max nodded without looking her in the eye.

"Three days to take down Richard Bradley," Cate began, processing. "And three days to tell Matt…and three days until everyone knows we're—"

"I don't think I can do it." Lauren buried her head in her hands.

"The train's already in motion," Max said. "They're going to say who we are on national television on Friday no matter what. The only decision we have is whether we control what they say, by writing this article about Richard, or we give ourselves up to… Charlie," she said with an eye roll. "And let him say whatever he wants."

"He won't say whatever he wants," Olivia started. "He'll—"

"You don't know him better than I do," Max snapped. "He'll do whatever he needs for a promotion."

"We need to control it," Cate said.

"I agree," Olivia said. "I think that's the right thing to do."

The three of them looked at Lauren, who'd regained some pink in her cheeks. "What other choice do we have?" she said miserably.

Max took a notebook out of her purse and opened it before resting it in the center of the coffee table. In Max's bubbly handwriting was a series of lists: names of women organized by type of source. She pointed to the first three names. "They've told me directly that they had weird experiences with Richard." She pointed to the group of eight names. "I've never spoken to them about it, but I've heard through the whisper network that they've all had issues." Lastly she pointed to a list of fifteen women. "I have no idea about them, but they're all hot and wore tight skirts that would have attracted Richard's eyes and hands."

Twenty-six names. Twenty-six names in three days.

"This is everyone we have to talk to," Max said, standing.

Olivia scoffed. "What do we even say? Hi, heard you were sexually harassed by this famed news anchor? Please, tell me everything!"

"I think we say…" Max paused. "We tell them we're with *Twentysomething*. They'll trust us then."

They were quiet for a moment, and it was clear everyone was making sure they understood what they were about to do. The herculean effort that was before them. They were taking Richard down, and they could only hope by doing so, they didn't go down with him.

"Okay," Max said, taking a deep breath. "We have three days."

AFTER THEY FINISHED brainstorming, Cate quickly got in a cab—it was easy when you had a doorman to hail them for you with a whistle—and zipped through the post-rush-hour traffic downtown. Out the window she watched the end of the sun set over the New Jersey skyline. It was the sad kind of sunset that came at the end of a good summer—when you first started to notice it was getting darker earlier, that the days were shorter, your time enjoying outdoor drinks were nearly numbered. The cab dropped her off just as it officially got dark, the moment the streetlights became brighter than the sky.

Of course, it wasn't until she buzzed three times and watched her cab pull away that she realized Theo probably wasn't home, and it started to rain. Just a few drops at first, but that quickly turned into a downpour. She tried hiding under his building's small, circular awning, but it was useless. Within seconds she was soaked through to her underwear. Wet, cabless, boyfriendless, and—

"You've really made a habit of surprising me here in the rain, huh?"

She turned around to see Theo standing under a nice, dry umbrella, and remembered the last time she was standing outside his door, frantically buzzing in, under a downpour: when she first told him about *Twentysomething* and started this avalanche in the first place. How appropriate.

"At least it's not the middle of the night this time." She hoped she looked charming and not pathetic. At that point, it was a fine line.

Theo reached the umbrella forward and stepped toward her until they were both covered, standing close, the familiar smell of him making her a little light-headed.

"What are you doing here?" he asked, voice low.

The core of her frustration, she realized, hadn't been with Theo at all. Yes, he knew about the investigation and didn't give her a heads-up—even after she let him in on her big secret. But that was his job—an important job. And she would have done the same thing.

For the first time she could recall, she cared about something other than work, and that freedom was liberating. She was going to make it up to him. She was going to prove to him that she trusted him; by not letting him be surprised.

"We're doing a follow-up article about Richard for *Twentysomething*." She paused. "Nonanonymous. Something that really digs his grave."

The rain came down harder, and they moved closer. "Why are you telling me this?"

"Because I'm sorry, and I do trust you," she said. "And also, I think I might love you."

He smiled, his eyes glowing as he reached past her, his face pausing two inches from hers, and he opened the door with a simple turn of the handle.

"It's broken," he whispered, and her heart skipped like he was saying the sexiest thing she'd ever heard. "Always unlocked." He took a step inside and looked at her. "Want to come up? I might be able to connect you with some sources from the article. If they're interested."

Theo popped the door open and did an *after you* roll of the wrist. Was that his way of accepting her apology? Offering to help them write their article? The one that they claimed they could do even better than his team did? And was he just going to ignore the whole—

"I love you too," he said as he followed her down the hall to the elevators. "Also that."

Cate nearly jumped him right there.

26

M ax sat at the best corner booth in the cafeteria, scanning everyone who walked in for Jenni Mason, the first name on her investigation list. The normal news day was meticulously scheduled: each step carrying a distinct timecode down to the second. Therefore, it was easy to get the hang of each show's—and staff member's—routine, because if your show was timecoded, your life was timecoded. In non-breaking-news scenarios, Max had her first cup of coffee, pressed Print on Sheena's briefs, and got in a fight with Charlie (ugh, just his name made her throw up in her mouth now) at the same time every day. They had their rundown meetings and then the live broadcast at the same time every day. It was pretty sad, if she let herself think about it too much: how little of her life she actually controlled.

It was because of this routine, however, that Max had no doubts that Jenni was about to enter the cafeteria. Any moment now she'd walk in, head straight for the coffee station, and fill up a medium cup after wrapping her overnight shift before heading home.

Her blond hair stood out first—long and slapped into a makeshift bun that sat directly at the top of her head and wobbled with every tired step she took into the room. Max casually stood and approached her.

"Come with me," Max said as she passed, hoping Jenni would follow. Without looking back, she turned out of the cafeteria, walked down the hall and into the women's restroom. When she didn't hear any noise inside, she glanced under the three stalls—all empty—and then leaned on the sink, getting a little nervous until Jenni pushed through the door a few seconds later.

"Do you need a tampon or something?" Jenni asked. "Because I don't get my period anymore with my IUD."

"No, no. I have a question for you, but you have to keep it to yourself."

Jenni glanced at the stalls behind Max and rested all her weight on the back of the door to make it harder to open. "A Richard thing, I'm assuming?"

"How did you know?"

She let out a *ha* louder than Max would have expected. "This investigation is like the biggest thing to happen at this network since Letterman admitted to fucking his intern. And yet everyone thinks they need to start conversations about him with *don't tell anyone, but*—" Jenni pushed forward a few inches as someone tried to barge through the bathroom door. "Out of order," she yelled until the person outside gave up, then looked at Max. "Do you know why he's back? Shouldn't he be wallowing in the Hamptons, watching the sun rise with his multimillion-dollar buyout contract or something?"

Max nodded. "That's exactly what he should be doing. Instead, the network is slowly bringing him back because the lawyers 'couldn't prove' any of the *Times's* anonymous allegations."

"Are you fucking kidding me?" Jenni yelled. "He's a pervert. It's like the biggest open secret in news. They basically teach a class on it at NYU. What do you mean the lawyers can't prove it?"

Max shrugged. "I don't know." She figured they just weren't trying very hard. Like Alyssa said, *no one asks who does the research, as long as we say the research was done.*

"They're clearly not talking to the right people. I have plenty of questionable emails, but no one's come knocking on my door asking for a statement."

And there it was, the perfect lead in, handed to Max on a silver platter. "Well, that's why I wanted to talk to you. I'm..." She paused. *Just rip off the Band-Aid*, she said to herself. *Or else Charlie's going to rip it off for you.* "I'm investigating Richard myself. For that website *Twentysomething.*"

Jenni's eyes widened. "Seriously?"

"Don't look so surprised."

Jenni was quiet for a moment before saying, "What do you need from me?"

"Those emails. On the record."

"Definitely," Jenni said, without hesitation. "Should I just forward everything to you?"

Max had to consciously contain her excitement. "That would be great. Are you okay with going on the record?"

Jenni sprung away from the door and walked into the first stall. "Put my name all over it. I don't give a fuck. He's an asshole. Plus, I work overnight at Ingest now—the guys who work with me in the basement have been here since World War II. They'd fuck up anyone who tried to fire me over this."

She started peeing and Max wasn't sure if this conversation was over or not. But she didn't want to give Jenni too much time to change her mind, and she didn't want to give herself time to mess with this rock-hard journalist facade she'd just perfectly performed. "Great," Max said quickly. "I need everything by tonight." She walked out before Jenni could object, turning into an empty stairwell before allowing herself a skip and a pat on the back to celebrate. She did it. It was happening.

One down. Twenty-five to go.

LAUREN FOUND A quiet spot a few blocks from set and dialed the number that Max had given her last night for an old assistant on *The Good Morning Show.*

"Hello?" the woman answered. Lauren knew exactly what to say—Max had given her a script and she'd practiced it all morning—but it somehow didn't make any of this easier. She was still saying *Twentysomething* out loud to a stranger for the first time. She was still admitting she had a relationship to the website that was bringing down asshole bosses everywhere. And admitting all of those things just brought her closer to the day she'd have to talk to Pete about it all, which she was dreading so much she felt almost numb.

"Hi," she answered. "My name is Lauren Barrero and I'm calling because, um—are you alone?" Lauren spotted Pete across the street, talking on the phone and walking in the direction of his favorite coffee shop. She didn't like when he left set without telling her. It made her feel stupid and like a terrible assistant when someone on the crew would ask where he was and she didn't know.

"Yes?" the woman said, forcing Lauren to shake it off. She'd deal with him later.

"I just mean, can you talk privately for a second?"

"Sorry, what is this about?"

Lauren took a deep breath. *Concentrate,* she told herself. "I'm calling on behalf of *Twentysomething,* in reference to Richard Bradley. We have a source that says his suspension at *The Good*

Morning Show is ending soon—and we're looking for women to go on record about their experiences with him."

"How did you get my number?"

"We have a few women at *The Good Morning Show*, and within other divisions of CBS, who have been talking to us—"

"Who?"

"I can't name them right now." There was silence on the other end. It was so dead Lauren pulled the phone away from her ear, checking the screen to make sure she didn't get hung up on. "Are you still there?"

After another moment the woman said, "I'm here," and then paused again. "Are you sure this will get him fired? The *New York Times* article didn't."

"I mean, we can't guarantee it, no. But—" When Lauren looked up from her feet and the grassy sidewalk crack, she saw Pete, two cups of coffee in his hands, walking slowly and looking into shop windows. She couldn't wait until she was a writer and could just walk away in the middle of the day if she wanted to.

"I don't really feel comfortable talking about this," the woman said after yet another excruciatingly long pause. "I'd rather not get involved—"

"Something like this happened to me too," Lauren said quickly. This wasn't part of the script, but it came out more organically than anything else she'd mentioned thus far. And when the woman didn't hang up, Lauren kept going. "Something similar happened to me. And it took a year, but I finally said something—" she looked up at Pete who was getting closer "—and, you know, all my problems weren't solved, and a bolt of lightning didn't strike him from the heavens…but I spoke up. And I was believed. By friends and strangers. And there's a certain power in that."

Lauren trailed off and lived in the staticky silence for a moment. Just her and this stranger with a similar experience, two versions of the same story. Like most of the *Twentysomething* contributors. They were all in it together.

"I'm sorry," the woman finally said, softly. "I can't. Good luck with your story."

She hung up before Lauren could say anything else. Lauren wasn't sure what she would have said anyway. She debated calling her back, when Pete started waving and calling her name from down the street.

"I got you a coffee," he said proudly, handing her a cup.

"For me?"

"You get it for me all the time, so I wanted to return the favor."

He watched her take a sip and she smiled, surprised. "Milk, no sugar, just the way I like it." She never would have thought he'd know her coffee order.

"I pay attention," he said, smirking as he backed away. "You always doubt me, but I do listen when you speak, you know."

He always does this, Lauren thought as she watched him continue down the block. This was why she didn't want to write about him. This was why she didn't want to do the investigation. This was why she hated the idea of *Twentysomething* from the first time Cate brought it up. She loved her boss. Even when he was an asshole. Even when he was rehiring the guy she reported for sexual harassment and then pretending like nothing happened. She really did love him. And he really did love her, even if he showed it in unconventional ways.

Maybe she shouldn't do this. Maybe her name didn't have to come out and Pete didn't need to know anything. They were in a good place.

By the time Lauren got back to Pete's trailer, she'd decided she was out. She couldn't do this to Pete. James, she didn't care if his name came out. She'd figure out a way to deal with

306 | AMANDA PELLEGRINO

him on set, like she had for the past few months. It would be awkward and awful, but she'd make do. It just wasn't worth dragging Pete's name in the mud, too.

As she reached for her phone to call Max, tell her that they could do this without her, it buzzed with a text from an unknown number.

I'll do it, the text read. I'll tell my story.

Then, a second later, But only to you.

As CATE EXITED the Eighty-Sixth Street subway to her apartment, she was immediately hit with that poststorm kind of humidity, thick and damp. She was sweating through her bra, sporting hair so frizzy and large not even a ponytail was able to contain it. No one looked cute at the end of summer. And, even so, she had a boyfriend who loved her. Even with frizzy hair.

Her phone started ringing and she looked down to see it was Theo, who, she was amused to notice, was still listed as Back Muscles in her contacts.

"I got in touch with one of our sources, the one who backed out," he said, stopping her on the sidewalk. After they had made up (twice) last night, he mentioned that one of the anonymous sources for the *New York Times* article had wanted her name to be public. It wasn't until the very last moment—forty minutes before it went live—that she pulled out and requested anonymity like the others. After spending the day attempting to get people to talk, Cate understood. Out of the six names she'd been assigned, only two had agreed to go on record. A third had been on board, but just moments after they hung up, redacted what she said and threatened to deny everything publicly if her name was ever revealed. Lauren's success level was relatively the same, Olivia wasn't able to connect with anyone, and Max brought on five women.

Cate was astounded how afraid everyone still was of Richard. Shouldn't Richard be the scared one at this point?

By the end of the day, they had nine stories. Nine women willing to go on record about their experiences, all of them journalists themselves, so each of their stories came neatly organized with corroborating evidence, emails, text messages, voice messages, and witnesses. Like Olivia with her penis tally, each woman had also kept a record, detailed and true. They knew one day they'd need it.

"I told her someone from *Twentysomething* was interested in talking to her, on the record," Theo continued. "She was... hesitant. But I think she does regret not giving her name. She said she needed a minute to think about it and that she'd reach out to you guys directly if she wants in."

There had to be some catch, right? They spent the entire day fielding rejection after rejection, but a tenth source was potentially just falling into their lap. "Can you tell me her name?" Cate knew the answer, but she had to ask.

"You know I can't," he said. "But hopefully she tells you herself."

LATER THAT NIGHT, Lauren was lying on the floor of the trailer, three gin and tonics in, thinking about how Pete should really hide his booze stash better.

"What's happening in here?"

When she opened her eyes, Owen was standing above her, smiling through his confusion. She wanted to smooth the wrinkles out of his forehead with her hand.

"You okay?" he asked.

She reached up, and he pulled her to her feet a little faster than she expected. Her knees gave out, and Owen kept his hands on hers, stabilizing her until she backed onto the couch.

"Are we a little drunk?" He picked up the blue Bombay

bottle, surprised by how empty it was, before closing it and slipping it under the couch where she had found it.

"Does everyone know he keeps his alcohol there?" she asked, barely slurring.

Owen sat down on the couch next to her, and she couldn't help but lean in toward him—not so much that they were touching, but enough that they both noticed.

"Of course. That's not even his original bottle. A few of us finished that one off last week when we had those night shoots. Then Tyler went out and got another one so Pete wouldn't notice. It's like stealing booze from your dad in high school."

"Pete would be a good dad."

Owen paused at that. "I think his kids like him. They're old now."

"I didn't know my dad. My mom said she didn't really know him either. Do you have any kids who don't know about you?"

He laughed. "I definitely do not." Owen leaned his head against the back of the couch, his face just a few inches from hers. There was a stray eyelash on his cheekbone, and she reached over and brushed it off, leaving her finger there for a second longer than necessary. "I should probably get you home. Before Pete sees you like this. We're wrapping soon anyway."

"It's okay. I'm going to be fired on Friday, so what's the difference?"

He paused. "Why do you think that?"

She took one last look at him and then faced forward. "I wrote about Pete on that website," she said matter-of-factly. "I wrote about him and I wrote about James and it's all coming out on Friday and I wasn't supposed to tell anyone, let alone the internet. I was just supposed to keep it between us and work with people I don't like. But I got angry, and now I'm going to get fired for it."

Lauren said it like she was telling him her plans for the weekend. It was just what was going to happen, and she was resigned to her fate.

"James is the one you reported?" Owen asked carefully.

She nodded. "I swear I didn't want to go to hot yoga with him. And I didn't want him to keep asking about my sex life. He made me work out in a bra and he made me answer his questions and—" She cut off, not wanting to get further into it. None of it mattered anyway.

"I believe you," Owen said. She could sense his eyes on her for a long time, and it made her feel safe. And seen. "Let me get you a car home."

"Come with me." She was breathing faster just at the thought of him in her bed. It seemed to sober her up, enough to know what she was doing but not enough to regret it yet.

His voice was low as he said, "You're drunk."

She shook her head. "Not that drunk."

Owen put his hand on her waist and Lauren locked their fingers together, and they stayed like that for what could have been an hour, but even drunk Lauren knew it was only a few heartbeats.

"Why did you leave?" she asked. "The night we were together." She'd been wanting an answer since that morning when the only trace left of him was a CVS card, but it had seemed like an impossible question to ask. Now, however, it was the smallest of her concerns.

"Honestly?" He rubbed his eyes. "I panicked. I'm a writer, you're an assistant. There's a power dynamic there that makes things…complicated. And I just got nervous that you felt pressured to sleep together because of it…" His voice got softer, and he slouched a little. "But when I got home I immediately regretted everything. I think you're great. So I wanted to try to do it the right way."

310 | AMANDA PELLEGRINO

"When you asked me out?"

He looked down at his white sneakers. "And then when you mentioned the whole reporting thing, I mean... I didn't know what to do."

"You should have stayed."

He nodded, slowly, but couldn't meet her eyes. Instead, he stood. He put the tonic back in the mini fridge and refilled the ice cube tray she'd let melt on the floor. She watched him move around the trailer silently and thought back to that night. To his arms and chest and every other part. To his advice. He should have stayed.

Moments later, as he put her in the black car, she thanked him, for everything, and he smiled.

Then he shut the door and sent her home alone.

27

The next morning, Max sat in Alyssa's office in a cold sweat. Alyssa read the article the four of them wrote like she was watching a play unfold: eyebrows rising, corners of her mouth twitching, her eyes widening. Max had printed everyone's stories, all the evidence they were able to get. The statements ranged from *he groped my breasts at a holiday party* to *my main task as an intern was to shred carrots for his dog's dinner every night.* While the latter may seem inconsequential compared to the former, it was also important to note. He didn't just start off with sexual harassment; he dipped his toes in the water with other abuses first: running around with cupcakes for a school party, not holding a creep accountable when an assistant came to him for help, making an assistant see him naked. Once someone was able to get away with those things—things that made women feel too small and unimportant to speak up— then he was able to move on to pinching butts and, eventually, what James did to Lauren.

"Okay," Alyssa finally said, resting the papers on her desk and looking up at Max. "Okay, this is good."

"Yeah?" She could barely hide her smile. This was the first real piece of journalism she'd ever written. And her executive producer thought it was *good*.

Alyssa turned her attention to the folder of evidence, a thick manila envelope with Post-its sticking out. Max had color-coded every email, memo, and witness statement for each source; they had at least three supporting documents per claim. Max had done a lot of research for Alyssa in her three years on *The Good Morning Show*, but nothing compared to this. The article was so backed up, so reviewed, so supported, Max had no question that if their lawyers attempted to attack any of the accusations, they'd be able to prove it true beyond a reasonable doubt.

Alyssa fingered the papers, skimming page by page, making comparisons between the folder and the article. The texts stood out the most; they were more damning than long emails where the questionable statements were hidden among actual work.

"This is unbelievable," she finally said. "Great work." She put the folder down and lifted the article again. Her eyes scanned the top page, then the second and third, then she looked at Max. "You guys really did your research here." Max nodded. *That* was an understatement. "Truthfully, I was skeptical about this, but…you're very good. I don't know how the hell you got in touch with the *Times*." She shook her head, and Max listened very carefully. To Max's knowledge, they hadn't reached out to the *Times*. Alyssa continued, "You know, I wanted to put my name to my story in that piece. I really did. But when they told me how many anonymous stories they had, I really thought that would be enough. And I thought maybe we could take him down and I could save myself, so I pulled my name. But I shouldn't have."

Max had to consciously close her shocked mouth. *Alyssa* was part of the *Times* exposé, the source that Cate said Theo talked to? Alyssa had been trying to bring down Richard this whole time?

Stacking the papers on top of the file folder and bouncing the pile on her knees, Alyssa continued, "Okay, there are two things left to do. First, I give you my story, with my name."

"Thank you," was all Max could think to say. For a lot of things.

"And second, we have to talk to Sheena."

"Sheena?" Max never thought Sheena would be part of the equation. Sheena was also on *Twentysomething*; there weren't many stories, but if she looked hard enough, they were easy to identify. And more importantly, wasn't Sheena part of the problem? Wasn't her knowledge of Richard's behavior—because there was no way she didn't know about it—and her lack of response part of the thing they were trying to uncover? And wasn't it equally damning for a woman in power to allow space for this kind of behavior?

"We can't blindside her," Alyssa said. "We have to tell her what we're doing."

"Why?" Max demanded. "There's no way she'd let us publish this. Wouldn't you rather ask forgiveness than permission?"

"I'm not asking for permission," Alyssa corrected. "I have a gut feeling she's more on our side than you think. She wears plenty of tight dresses."

That was true. But did Richard actually have the balls to touch Sheena? She was his peer and had as much clout as he did; she could speak out at any moment. He wouldn't have been stupid enough to get caught that easily. Right?

"Did she know that your story was in that article?" Max asked.

Alyssa looked down at her hands, then at Max. "No. And that was stupid. Because I think she would have encouraged me to keep my name in, and then we could have avoided all of this."

Max followed Alyssa out of her office, through the newsroom, past Charlie at his desk, who watched them with such fury Max could feel it, up the stairs, past Hair and Makeup, and into the glass hallway leading to Sheena's office.

She was sitting behind her desk with curlers in her hair and golden patches under her eyes, crossing something out in the morning scripts and writing in the margins.

Alyssa knocked and walked in before getting a response. Max wasn't sure she'd ever be that important. If she knocked and Sheena didn't answer or wave her in, she'd usually walk away and come back half an hour later to try again. She once spent seven hours coming back and forth simply trying to give Sheena her mail.

"What's up?" Sheena asked, staring at her papers.

"Can we have you for a second?"

From the doorway, Max watched Alyssa sit down in a guest chair, the same one she was in when Sheena called her and Charlie into the office to give them the impossible *Twentysomething* assignment. When Max sat down, slowly and skeptically, Sheena was surprised to see her there, too.

"Is this about the poetry segment? Because it's shit. I have a right to edit things that come out of my mouth."

"It's not about that," Alyssa said, opening her notebook to an already-full page. "But we'll talk more later because if you make changes, I have to edit the graphics." She added a bullet to the seemingly endless list. "We want to talk to you about Richard."

Sheena put her pen down, and Alyssa turned to Max. "Do you want to tell her about the thing, or should I?"

Max wasn't sure she'd be able to say the words aloud, reveal herself as a *Twentysomething* founder after having daily conversations—most involving Sheena screaming—railing at them to find the founders' identities.

"You can do it," Max said. She was biting the inside of her mouth so badly, she could already taste blood.

"You sure?"

"Someone fucking say it," Sheena hissed.

"Max is *Twentysomething*," Alyssa said quickly.

Sheena's eyes were on Alyssa's for a long time before she said, "Excuse me?" It sounded more like a threat than a question.

"Max and three of her friends started the website." Alyssa nodded toward Max. "So that exclusive we've been trying to get…it'd be with her."

Sheena looked at Max for the first time, diamond-sharp daggers coming out of her eyes. "Is that true?"

We're not asking for permission, Max reminded herself. *This is happening. They don't control* Twentysomething, *I do.*

Max nodded, unable to make eye contact with Sheena for more than a second at a time.

"I need to hear you say it," Sheena demanded.

"I'm *Twentysomething*."

Slowly, Sheena took off her reading glasses and placed them gently on top of a stack of books to her right. She folded her arms onto her desk and stared at Max for what could have been one minute or twenty. Time didn't exist anymore.

Then, Sheena bellowed, "ARE YOU FUCKING KID-DING ME?" She stood, towering over them, one golden patch falling off her face from the force of her glare. Max couldn't stop looking at the other patch, which was slowly slipping down her cheek. And clearly Alyssa couldn't either because once the remaining patch fell onto Sheena's desk, Alyssa started laughing. *Laughing.*

"Is that out of your system?" Alyssa asked. "Can we start talking like adults?"

Sheena lowered herself back into her chair and spun around to face the window. The curlers at the nape at her neck were crooked. This conversation was really hurting her hair and makeup routine for the day.

"For the last few days, Max and her friends have been investigating Richard." Alyssa paused, then quickly added, "With my supervision. Because, as you know, the lawyers aren't doing shit, and more than enough proof exists out there to get him fired." She dropped the papers onto Sheena's desk. "They wrote an article. About him."

Sheena turned back to them, looking at the papers on her desk.

"We want him out," Alyssa continued. "And we want everyone who protected him through the years out. So Max is going to publish this article on *Twentysomething* tomorrow. Everyone is willing to go on the record with their names, which is more than the *Times* got. We have multiple sources corroborating every story. We can publish on the site a few minutes before we go live in the morning, then break it on air. And release the names of Max and her friends with the article."

Sheena picked up the paper. Max expected her to try to stop them. This wouldn't make her job easy in the morning. She'd have to talk about Richard on air without knowing how the network would handle these new nonanonymous accusations. Would she even have a news staff once they wrapped the broadcast? Would any of them still have jobs? It could be the end of *The Good Morning Show*.

Or, Max realized, it could also be the beginning of something else.

Sheena read the article carefully, word by word, page by

page, while Max and Alyssa watched, patient as they could pretend to be.

When she put the papers down, she let out a long breath and ran her tongue over her teeth. "This is impressive," she said. "Disgusting, but impressive."

"It was all Max," Alyssa said. "Maybe we should have given her that AP job a while ago."

Sheena looked at Max skeptically. She probably thought Alyssa was making it up. When all you did for three years was match coffee to paint swatches, organize interns, book travel, and make sure her shoes matched her dress, Max couldn't blame Sheena for being surprised she was actually good at the thing she was working hard to become.

"Good work," she said, two words Max never thought she'd hear from Sheena in her life. "I have two conditions."

"Conditions?" Max scooted to the edge of her seat.

"Yes, conditions," Sheena said. "If you want to be a journalist, you've got to know about the politics of getting things published. There are always politics."

"What do you need?" Alyssa asked.

"First, we publish tomorrow at seven, then cover the article in the A-block. Then, in the eight o'clock hour, we get an interview."

"Interview?" Max asked.

"We've been trying to get an exclusive with the founders since this whole thing started." Sheena shrugged. "I still want it."

"You want to interview me and my friends?"

"Yes."

Max was reeling. "What if we get sued?" she asked.

Sheena cocked her head, confused. "What?"

Max sat up in her seat, her mind suddenly swirling with everything that could possibly go wrong, everything they considered in their first post but never imagined could actually come true. "What if our bosses sue us? For violating NDAs or whatever."

Sheena leaned forward. "If that happens, it's a battle they will lose. My legal team and I will handle it."

Max took a deep breath. She believed her. Sheena was a good person to have on your side.

Their plan had been to put their names in the byline of an article and then have that article, and therefore their names, revealed on national television. That was *very* different from physically appearing on that national television and being interviewed themselves. "I have to talk to my friends about the interview," Max said. "That's a level of exposure I'm not sure we're all prepared for."

"It's no less than the exposure that will come when your names get out. It just allows you to control the narrative instead of having everyone Google you and make assumptions about you themselves."

Sheena was right, which Max hadn't considered. This entire time they'd been grasping for control of *Twentysomething* coverage, which always seemed two steps ahead of what they were prepared for. Sheena wanted her to have the control that they all sought. But there was a lot of pressure that came with controlling the narrative; being the name *and face* behind a revolution.

"I can't make any guarantees, but I'll ask."

"We have to know by the end of the day," Alyssa said. "Seriously."

Max nodded. Another deadline. Another clock ticking down their fate.

Alyssa looked at Sheena. "What's your second condition?"

Sheena pulled at a cuticle on her otherwise perfectly manicured thumb. "I'd like to add my story. About Richard. When I joined the show. Then we can publish it."

"You have a story?" Max asked, unable to stop herself. Sheena looked at her with an expression that clearly said, *of course I do, you idiot.* It seemed everyone did. Even the higher-ups. Even the people you'd think were exempt.

With Sheena's story, the article was guaranteed to be taken seriously as a huge deal. Sheena was only speaking to *Twentysomething.* This would be the first time anyone had ever heard her story. She was putting all her trust in Max, Lauren, Cate, and Olivia.

The least they could do was put some trust back in her and do the interview.

MAX WALKED INTO the hallway, leaving Alyssa and Sheena in the office to discuss the logistics. She had this feeling in her gut—a mix of crippling anxiety and overwhelming excitement. The duality of change.

She had pulled her phone out to call Cate when suddenly she found herself being pushed into a dark supply closet, nearly tripping over her own feet. When her eyes adjusted, she saw Charlie standing in front of her.

"In this climate, you really shouldn't go pulling women into closets without their consent," Max said.

"What the fuck, Max?" Charlie spat. "I know everything. I know all about *Twentysomething.* I know that it's the four of you. And I know that you managed to curb my story—my *promotion.* But I still know everything." He stepped toward her, suddenly taller and larger than she ever remembered. "And don't think I'm not going to find a way to use it."

Max was frozen, her back against the cold metal of the storage bins, when anger flared hot up her spine. *He* was out of line. *He* was sleeping with Olivia behind her back. *He* was

willing to just give them up, without warning, without anything. She was sick and tired of being under his foot, of letting him walk all over her while never saying anything about
it. She hated him. And she was about to get fired. She had
nothing to lose.

"What the fuck, right back at you!" she yelled, shoving him
until he was cornered on the other side of the closet. "You
were sleeping with my best friend and didn't tell me? You
were ready to just throw me—and her—under the bus? Did
you even think *once* about anyone but yourself?" She stepped
back, saving her breath. This wasn't even worth it. His story
wasn't coming out. Max's was. She'd already won. She'd stood
up to him when she went straight to Alyssa the morning Olivia called her. And she stood up to him when they started
investigating Richard herself. And she was going to stand up
to him one more time when they went on air for the interview. "We're coming out as the founders tomorrow," Max
said defiantly. "And with it, we're hopefully getting Richard
fired." She ran her fingers through her hair, smoothing the
frizz down, letting her adrenaline fade. "If you want to get
in the way of that, do something stupid, fine. But then *you're*
the reason this pervert still works here. You may have been
willfully oblivious, but I know you were privy to everything
he did. You just kept your mouth shut. You all did. And I'm
not going to do that anymore."

Max turned around and walked into the brightly lit hall
without another word. And she kept walking until she was
back in her basement bathroom. Her heart was racing so fast
you'd think she just ran a marathon. For the first time, she
felt in control. She felt like she had a grasp on what they were
about to do.

Now she just needed to convince her friends.

28

When Lauren got to set, she could immediately sense the vibe was off. Everyone was keeping to themselves and seemed to be tiptoeing around her. That only happened if Pete yelled at a crew member—usually they deserved it for being unprofessional or loud or ruining a take. They'd be momentarily afraid of him, which made them feel bad for Lauren—the assistant who, presumably, had to deal with outbursts like that in private all the time.

The Craft Services breakfast buffet was abuzz as Lauren unenthusiastically picked some fruit off a platter, but the whispers surrounding her weren't about Pete or an outburst, but about a fight. Lauren heard the conversations in snippets as she snaked through the catering tents: "It was wild. He just attacked him."

"They just started punching each other like crazy."

"No one could break it up. It went on for twenty minutes."

"They were both taken to the hospital."

"I heard one had a broken nose."

"It was pretty hot."

Lauren marched straight from breakfast to the line of actors' trailers, looking for production assistants. They were the keepers of every single piece of on-set gossip and information. And when Lauren found a few huddled together, whispering, she knew they could give her the details.

"What happened?" Lauren asked. "Was there a fight?"

They looked at her excitedly. "You don't know?" the redhead asked. "It wasn't just a fight, it was a brawl. Two writers started going at it last night, just before wrap. One just attacked the other one. Came in like he was ready to kill him."

"It was crazy. Fists flying. One definitely broke a rib. They had to call 911—"

"Which writers?" Lauren interrupted, heart sinking. She needed to know, but she wasn't sure she wanted to. *What did she do?*

They looked around. "The blond one and the hot one. What are their names again?" As they debated—*Buddy? Marcus? No, more common*—Lauren spotted Pete storming toward her. She could almost feel his footsteps hitting the ground as he got closer. He was looking at her like an enraged bull, and she was a matador with a big red flag.

He pointed to her, then his trailer door. *Now*, he mouthed before walking inside.

Lauren let out a deep breath and started walking in a daze. "Thanks for the info," she mumbled as she took her time moving toward the trailer. Her phone was buzzing in her pocket over and over, but she ignored it. *Fuck*, she kept repeating to herself. *Fuck, fuck, fuck.* This was it. She was walking the plank. She was about to get fired.

When Lauren reached the door, she stood outside and steeled herself. She didn't want to cry when it happened, though she inevitably would. Mostly, she didn't want to look Pete in the eye. But that was impossible. It was time.

OLIVIA HADN'T GONE on an audition in months. It was rare to find one on a weekend and even rarer that she'd be able to take a day off during the week to do it. She had tried a few times in the past—told Nate she had an audition, asked for an afternoon off—but he would laugh and tell her *why bother, I'm going to give your reel to my agent, she'll get you jobs*, and then Olivia stopped trying, waiting for his promise to come to fruition. She was afraid she'd forgotten the drill: that it had been so long she'd forget to print her headshot or résumé or memorize the lines. But when she found the inconspicuous brick building in Midtown and walked up the steep wrought-iron stairwell, following arrows on neon paper she assumed would lead her to the audition, it was like she'd been doing this every day for the past three years. She felt comforted with how natural this was, like it was truly what she was supposed to be doing.

Olivia exited the stairwell into a narrow hall, approaching the brunette sitting in the corner with a clipboard. She asked for Olivia's name and, after scanning her list, the brunette held out a piece of paper and pointed to a chair across the hall. "Fill this out. Have a seat. When we call you, bring that, your résumé, and headshot in with you," she said flatly.

Taking the paper, Olivia sat down in the row of other women auditioning. They all had their lines out, reading the page and then closing their eyes and repeating it in their heads as their lips moved. Olivia felt an immediate kinship with these women. They were all competing for the same role, yes, but she was happy to be back among peers, people who wanted this as much as she did, people who were also busting their asses for the dream of acting. They all came into it knowing the stats, knowing that they were set up to fail from day one, but they did it anyway. Just like her.

She smiled down at the script on her lap. *This* was what

she was supposed to be doing. Hustling. Grinding. Pushing through the trenches. *This* was what she loved.

They called Olivia's name quicker than she expected. Maybe the embarrassingly long wait time was an aspect of auditions that had changed? As she followed the brunette down the hallway toward the audition room, her phone started ringing. Olivia quickly pulled it out of her pocket and silenced it, throwing it into her purse before entering the room.

It was bare and white with a piano in the corner and a fold-up table near the far wall, behind which two men in their fifties and one woman in her thirties sat. Handing them her paperwork with an excited smile, Olivia moved backward until her feet found the X made of painter's tape on the floor.

"I'm Olivia Medina and I'm auditioning for the role of Party-Goer #3."

After a few seconds, the man in the center of the table leaned forward, resting his weight on his elbows. "Can we ask you something before you start?"

Olivia nodded. That was unusual. Rarely did they ever engage with you. Sometimes you could go an entire audition without anyone making eye contact, let alone asking you a question. She started to feel excited—maybe that was a good sign? Maybe she fit the part so perfectly she didn't even have to audition—

"Why did we get a call this morning from Peggy McCormack telling us not to work with you?"

Peggy McCormack. Nate's agent. The one who had repped him for years. The one he never gave her reel to. The one whose assistant she emailed asking for a chance, which she never got.

Apparently, Nate did still have some power. He wasn't as washed-up and desperate as she'd thought. He had contacts. He could do things like this.

He could make sure she'd never be an actor. Just like he promised.

She carefully chose her words. Their industry was a very small world—everyone knew everyone, especially in New York. "I recently left a job assisting one of her clients."

"It was not an amicable departure, I'm assuming?"

Olivia didn't know what to say. All she could seem to focus on was the sound of her phone vibrating in her bag. Not only had Nate made her last three years a living hell, but now he was going to control the rest of her career. Manipulate everyone around her until she had no choice but to walk away. To stop trying.

"I should probably go," Olivia said, walking toward the door. "Sorry to waste your time."

CATE STOOD BELOW the bookshelf, staring up at it like she did whenever she was being introspective. She stopped on the titles she worked on, the ones she saw (via cc'd emails) go from a Microsoft Word document in an email to First Pass Pages to, finally, a thing with an interior design and a cover and a title in an eye-catching font. The ones whose authors she knew so much about but who knew nothing about her. The ones who had occupied so much of her time, but whose acknowledgments she wasn't even considered for. Only Matthew J. Larcey III.

Her time at Larcey was surely ending and, while there were many things about the last two years she had worked very hard to forget, this bookshelf was not one of them. It had been everything she strived for—an editor who published something that mattered. To find the next great American novel. To be in the acknowledgments.

And she would be. One day. She just realized it wouldn't be at Larcey. And that was okay.

She took mental pictures of the bookshelf for another minute to memorize it, and then she slowly backed into the bullpen, remembering that first bathroom meeting when she had asked everyone to join her in writing about Matt. *We're plotting against the patriarchy*, she remembered thinking. Well, now that plot was in motion.

And now, Cate was waiting for the right moment to quit. Matt had been in his office with the phone off the hook all morning. He hadn't even told her what he wanted for lunch yet, which was occasionally the only thing he'd say to her all day.

Her phone had starting ringing on her desk—it was Max, for the third time—and she was about to answer when Matt called her into his office. She pulled his door open and peeked her head through.

"Come in, shut the door," he said, keeping his eyes on his computer. "Sit," he added once she was a few steps into the room.

It was the first time she'd ever been invited to sit in his office in two years which, as you could imagine, made her nervous to her core. Something was happening. While she waited for him to address her, she searched the room for context clues: HR wasn't there, so it wasn't about layoffs; there was no broken glass or damaged technology so he wasn't mid-outburst. When her eyes scanned his desk, passing his seltzer can and calculator, she stopped short when she saw it: Theo's article about *Twentysomething* on his keyboard, freshly printed.

"I just wanted to check in, see how you're doing," he said, finally looking at her. "So…how *are* you doing?"

She tried not to look at the article, but it was impossible. He'd never asked her that question. Nor did he ever seem to care. Now, with that article on his desk, he suddenly cared about her feelings, her well-being? Not a chance. It was a threat. He was self-aware enough to realize he had a bad behavior streak—or career—and knew that if Richard Bradley was on this website, he likely was as well. He was playing a game with her, as always: *I know what you did, and you're either going to admit it and I'll fire you, or you don't admit it and now I have something to hold over your head forever.*

But, for the first time, this was a game she was ready to play. She knew how this meeting was going to end. She knew she had the upper hand. So why not let him simmer for a minute? It was what he'd done to her every single day the last two years.

"I'm fine," she said carefully. "Thank you for asking."

"Good, that's good." Matt looked at her for a long while, smiling, waiting for her to get on her knees and beg for forgiveness. He really was an idiot.

"Is that all?" she asked, looking from Matt's face—losing its stoic facade with each second—to Theo's article. "Or do you need something else?"

She felt like she was in the most pathetic staring contest of all time, until Matt finally broke it and leaned forward, which gave Cate immense satisfaction. "I need you to pick up some stuff at this address—" he handed her a scrap of paper "—and then deliver it to my wife at home. Also, Henry needs cupcakes. For his first day of school."

It took only the word *cupcake* out of Matt's mouth for all the memories to flood back in waves: her first date with Theo; creating *Twentysomething*; the hundreds of Shit Lists, watching all of Matt's stupid tasks burn in the candle at her fingertips. She wouldn't do it anymore. It was over.

"I quit," she said, the words echoing in her bones. She watched his face turn from surprised to confused to angry. He stared at her for a long while, and she stared at him right back. "I quit," she repeated.

He let out a deep breath and leaned back in his chair, moving both hands to the back of his head, his elbows out. Subconsciously, Cate knew, Matt was making himself bigger, taking up more space, seeming more intimidating. But you only did that when you were compensating for feeling small.

"Goodbye," he said. "Don't bother coming in tomorrow."

"I won't." Cate smiled as she stood and walked toward the door. She wouldn't have to come in. She'd be all over the news. He wouldn't be able to escape her face or her story if he tried. For that, and for everything else, she was thankful for *Twentysomething*.

"Good luck with the cupcakes," she added, before shutting his door for the last time.

OLIVIA SCURRIED OUT of the audition room and down the hallway, hugging her vibrating purse to her chest. She had never been more embarrassed in her entire life. It had been a few weeks since she quit, and this was the first time she truly believed she fucked up. He really could make sure she never worked in this industry again. She'd have to move and change her name and dye her hair in order to even come close to another audition room.

"Olivia," she heard echo in the hallway. When she stopped and turned, she saw the woman from the audition rushing toward her. Putting her purse on her shoulder, Olivia quickly wiped her tears.

When the woman reached her, she stopped, breathless. "You worked with one of Peggy's clients, you said? Which one?"

Olivia bit her lip. "I don't really think I should say." She felt like naming Nate in that moment would just make it all worse for her.

"Was he the guy in your tally?"

"What?"

"You're Olivia, right? The one from *Twentysomething*?" Olivia didn't need to nod or confirm for the woman to know it was true. "Here," she said, pulling a business card out of her pocket belonging to an agent at United Talent Agency, one of the big ones. "This agent is a friend of mine. Always looking for new talent. He'll be expecting your call."

The woman offered a knowing smile, one that Olivia reveled in, before returning to the room. Staring at the business card, Olivia dug for her phone in her pocket to take a picture of it in case she lost it, when she saw Max's fourteen missed calls and a text.

> If we're publishing tomorrow, Sheena wants us to do an interview on air. I'm in if you guys are.

LAUREN AND PETE were silent for a long time. Pete was standing against the counter, arms crossed, while Lauren sat on the edge of the couch, her foot erratically moving up and down.

"Want to tell me why Owen attacked James last night with the most pathetic attempt at a punch I've ever seen?" Pete finally said.

"They weren't hospitalized?"

He let out a wry chuckle. "Where'd you hear that?"

"That's the rumor. There was a brawl. Broken bones. Nine-one-one. Ambulances. The works."

Pete shook his head. "I mean, it was two writers trying to punch each other. It was pathetic. They could have done more damage slapping."

This time Lauren laughed, and Pete's stance relaxed. He sighed and rubbed his face with his hands. "Why did Owen want to punch James?"

Her phone was still buzzing, and she wished it wouldn't be weird for her to reach into her pocket and turn it off. Instead, she looked down at her hands and cracked her knuckles. "I told him that I reported James."

"Why would you do that? I thought we had an understanding."

"I thought we had an understanding, too," she said softly. She could already feel the nervous tears coming and was afraid her voice was going to crack. "You said he was going to be gone. You said we would disengage and that you were going to take care of it and then—"

"I took care of it, Lauren. He was gone. You know how impossible that conversation was? Telling him he couldn't produce his episodes anymore because it was more important for me to have my assistant on set than him?"

"But then you brought him back. And you didn't give me any warning. And then when I went to you for help you said it wasn't your problem—"

"I didn't say that—"

"You said you're not a babysitter and it's not your job to deal with interpersonal relationships."

He leaned back into the counter. "I also said I didn't have a choice. The studio wanted him back."

"You could have at least given me a heads-up. There's more to the story that I didn't tell you."

"What do you mean there's more?" Pete asked slowly.

Lauren could feel her face flush, her breakfast rising in the back of her throat, the smell of bleach and urine. She couldn't tell him. It was all too embarrassing, too disgusting. But he could read it, if he really wanted to know.

"I wrote an essay about him—everything that happened, all of it. And it was published a few months ago anonymously online." Pete looked up, confused, and she continued, "Tomorrow it's going to come out that I wrote it. I didn't say James's name, or yours, but once it starts circulating again you should read it. So you can really get both sides of the story. I'm not a liar," she said, standing. "And if you need to fire me for telling my story, I understand. After all, he's a producer and I'm an assistant. I get who's easier to believe."

Lauren walked out of the trailer without another word. She was done with the conversation—and the whole thing was out of her hands anyway.

Pulling out her phone, Lauren saw ten missed calls from Max and a few texts.

Max: If we're publishing tomorrow, Sheena wants us to do an interview on air. I'm in if you guys are.

Olivia: Yes. 1,000% yes. My parents can finally see me on tv!

Cate: I'm in. Just tell me what to do.

Lauren could feel herself smiling as she walked away from the trailer. She didn't know where she was going—maybe to get more coffee, maybe to the producer's tent on set, maybe to find a video of this pathetic fight that she could rub in Owen's face.

Yes, she responded to the group. Let's do it.

She realized in that moment it didn't matter where she went. All that mattered was that she was finally moving forward.

29

At 6:45 a.m. the next day, Max sat between her best friends in Sheena's office, staring at the computer in front of her. The article was ready to go. Fact-checked, spell-checked, edited and reedited.

"You know what to do?" Sheena asked. Since she and Alyssa had to leave to record affiliate promos before they went live at 7:00 a.m., she was camera-ready in her green dress, green shoes, blown-out hair and perfect makeup, out of place compared to the rest of them, all in T-shirts and jeans to avoid wrinkling their broadcast outfits. They were getting the full *Good Morning Show* hair and makeup treatment, *and you never got dressed before you had your hair and makeup done*—nothing like a blush stain or hairspray goo to ruin your outfit.

"We've done this before," Max responded. "Go. We've got this. I'll text you when it's live."

"Six fifty-five," Alyssa said.

"Six fifty-five," Max repeated. They had strict instructions exactly when they were to press the Publish button. Not too early—they didn't want any other networks picking this up—

but not too late. They wanted a few people to have seen it before they broke it on air.

Alyssa and Sheena headed to the studio. Max didn't have to be there this morning. She didn't have to get Sheena's coffee, print scripts, or deal with Charlie.

When the glass door closed, the four of them sat at Sheena's desk in silence. Max couldn't help thinking back to when all this started. When Cate pitched them on the idea of a blog; a place to vent and commiserate and realize you weren't alone; a place to talk about how your boss treated you like shit, and to question why that behavior was allowed. Why *they* were allowing it to happen to themselves.

They had come far in just a few months. They'd grown together. Encouraged each other to speak up. To stop taking it. Because all four of them deserved better. And sometimes you didn't realize that until your best friends told you so.

At 6:54 a.m. they took one collective deep breath. Max reached for Cate's hand. Cate for Lauren's. Lauren for Olivia's.

"You guys ready for this?" Max asked. For the first time in their *Twentysomething* journey, not one of them hesitated. They all nodded, instinctively, immediately, freely. For the first time, they weren't assistants—they were *founders*. They were in charge. They were the boss.

Cate's hand moved the mouse slowly to the Publish button, hovering over it. And at 6:55 a.m., they clicked the button, and their essay was sent into the universe. They knew their power, and now it was time for everyone else to see it for themselves.

Dear Twentysomething,

On my first day at The Good Morning Show, I was introduced to our whisper network—the unofficial channel through which women on the show communicated. It consisted of just that: whispers—in the bathroom, in the elevator, in the copy room, in the kitchen. Warnings from one woman to another. These networks are lifelines, always created with a purpose.

Ours started and grew because of Richard Bradley, the show's cohost, America's dad, and our boss.

When Bradley, 54, was looking for a new cohost five years ago, he invited Sheena Patel, a rising star at the time, to a friendly dinner at a western-themed hotspot in the West Village.

"I didn't think anything of it," Patel recalled. "He was such a veteran, and I was still shocked I was even being considered for the job." Bradley had been hosting The Good Morning Show accompanied by a slew of guests. Whoever he chose would be the first permanent coanchor in the show's history. "When I got to the restaurant, it was immediately clear he'd been drinking, and within minutes he had his hands on my legs under the table."

That was the first whisper I'd ever heard about him: "Be cautious when you bend over. He likes a good butt and long legs and he's handsy."

Patel, unfortunately, had not been informed. "He invited me back to his apartment to finish the conversation," she continued. "And when I declined, he got visibly upset. He started making a scene, so I finally agreed to quiet him down."

When they got back to his apartment, he excused himself to go to the restroom and appeared, moments later, in a robe. He held out his wife's matching one and asked if she wanted to join him.

"I remember thinking, his reach at the network is unparalleled. Getting that job would change everything about my life. And it was entirely in his hands."

She reported this encounter to network executives and

was told that it wasn't typical behavior, he was just drunk. It wouldn't happen again.

"The next day I got the job, along with 25 percent more money than I asked for and an NDA specifically about Richard and what I should expect from his past and future behavior. And I signed it. Maybe my entire career has been purely network's insurance. But I realized in that moment that no one was on my side—or on the side of women here in general—about this. The entire game has been rigged from the beginning. We were always going to lose."

When Alyssa Curran, Patel's executive producer, was brought on a month later, Bradley tried something similar. "He invited me to his summer home for brunch," she said. "He organized a car service for me and claimed the other producers and executives would be there and that I should get to know everyone. When I got there, it was just the two of us."

When they were finished eating, he insisted on giving her a tour of the home, "spending extra time in all the bedrooms," she recalled. "When he asked me if I wanted to take a dip in the pool, I realized I needed to get myself out of there."

She tried to excuse herself, saying her fiancé was expecting her back, but he got angry, pulling her back by the hair. "He finally did let me leave but he refused to let me take the car service he paid for. I ended up spending over $300 to get myself home."

She, too, reported her experience to the network executives. "I emailed two people at the network on the ride home. I knew I'd want a record of what happened because, frankly, I was upset by it. One called me seconds later and told me to delete the email and that he'd take care of it. I didn't delete the email and he didn't take care of it."

At least eight of the women profiled here, including Patel and Curran, reported Bradley's behavior to network executives, HR representatives, or Bradley's executive producer Alex Humphry. Every claim was received the same way: forget about it, don't worry about it, that's just Richard being Richard. Nothing more than a whisper was ever spoken.

Richard Bradley has sexually harassed at least eight other women on The Good Morning Show.

Hillary Lawrence, a former intern, detailed in an interview her experience of driving him to his summer home weekly. "The first time, he started massaging my shoulder, asking if I liked how it felt. I told him it was distracting while I drove, so the next week he moved to my knee and by the third time his hand was basically in my crotch. I asked the producers if I could not drive him anymore. I never gave them a reason, but I also didn't really have to."

"I was afraid of him," recalled Alexandra Canter, another former intern. "I could handle the occasionally lewd comment, talking about my breasts or imagining out loud how they'd perfectly fit in his hands. But I was scared for the day that escalated and he'd try to actually do it. I was under no impression that he'd ask permission first."

Former associate producer Stephanie Brady recalls he used to rank the interns every year on how excited he got at the thought of sleeping with them. "The ones that could give him erections at work, from just looking at them, would be at the top of the list."

Among the other confirmed accusations are: giving unwanted back massages to Bernadette Maxwell, a producer, in his office, even after she told him she was uncomfortable; showing up, uninvited and drunk, at assistant Jennifer Mc-Govern's apartment asking for oral sex; calling assistant Ashley Samson a "fat whore" and offering to pay for her liposuction if she gave him a blowjob; forcing the costume department head, Angie Stephens, to touch his penis while fitting him for a suit; masturbating in the back seat while intern Shannon Rodriguez was driving; requesting via email a massage from intern Jenni Mason, and insisting she be removed from his team when she refused.

Since the network is not willing to take appropriate action themselves, the current and former women employees of The Good Morning Show must take it upon themselves.

This is us killing the whisper network.

This is us yelling to the world something that we know to be true: Richard Bradley has harassed at least eleven current or former employees of The Good Morning Show. He, and those who knew and covered it up, must be held accountable for their actions.

If the New York Times's recent article wasn't enough to get everyone's attention, this better be.

Sincerely,
The Good Morning Show Women
Reported by:
Cate Britt (The Bossy One)
Lauren Barrero (The Bitchy One)
Olivia Medina (The Aggressive One)
Max Burke (The Emotional One)

Five minutes later, the opening music started, and Sheena faced the camera, sitting in the center of the anchor desk, the place she used to share with the man she just helped bring down. Max, Cate, Olivia, and Lauren stood behind the cameras in a line next to Alyssa, and as the opening tune faded and the stage manager pointed to Sheena, her eyes found Max's, and they shared a smile—one of relief. It was over. And yet, it also felt like something was just beginning.

"Welcome to *The Good Morning Show*," Sheena began, moving her gaze from Max to the cameras. "We have breaking news..."

Max watched as their names popped up in big black letters on the giant screen behind Sheena's desk. Not THE EMOTIONAL ONE, as had been reported thus far, but MAX BURKE.

Her name looked almost alien to her in that moment, carrying more weight than it ever had before. As she stood there, looking past Sheena at the letters on the screen, she realized her name didn't just belong to her. It belonged to this movement. It belonged to her friends and her colleagues, and everyone who fought beside them. There was something remarkable about that; about living for a greater purpose. About not just wanting a change but demanding it. *Creating* it.

Not even ten minutes later, *Entertainment Weekly* published their names and Instagram photos. "The Twentysomethings behind *Twentysomething*" was the headline.

Within fifteen minutes the article had been shared over fifty thousand times.

During the first commercial break, twenty-two minutes into the show, they got word that Richard had been fired. He was gone. The network was coming up with a statement for Sheena to say on air by the end of the broadcast. A statement, Max hoped, that would expand on the original one Richard gave on his social media: "These accusations are absolutely false and cannot be proven. I've never treated any colleagues with anything other than the utmost respect."

"He's such an asshole," Alyssa whispered to Max as the show went live after the commercial break and Sheena announced

Richard's termination. "Sometimes I forget that under all the makeup, Richard's just a flaccid dick in a tight suit."

Max smothered a laugh. She couldn't think of a more apt description for Richard Bradley.

For the next twenty minutes, while the four of them were getting camera-ready in Hair and Makeup, every other news or entertainment outlet imaginable reported on the story, too. *Time* magazine, *Vanity Fair*, and *Rolling Stone* emailed asking to shoot them for next months' cover stories, and the *New York Times Magazine* offered a six-page exclusive with the author of the original article. A dozen other outlets reached out within the hour offering whatever they could to tell the founders' story first.

While she sat in the makeup chair, Max received 12,957 Facebook friend requests and gained over one hundred thousand Instagram followers. In minutes. Her phone was buzzing so much it was like a malfunctioning vibrator.

Alyssa came into the Hair and Makeup room at 8:37 a.m. "You guys excited?" she asked.

"I'd be more excited if I could take a shot of something right about now," Olivia said to herself.

"I think we can have that arranged. Hope you like tequila." Alyssa looked at the makeup assistant. "Can you grab the bottle in my desk? Bottom drawer." Then she said to Max, "Can I borrow you for a second?"

Max followed her out to the hallway and expected her to stop at the door, but they kept walking. "What's going on?" she asked.

"Network HR rep is here. He wants to talk to us. Alex was fired. So was the show's HR. Did you ever meet them?" Max shook her head. "Well, this guy wants to talk to us."

"To us?"

Alyssa nodded. "Also, you see that email from corporate?"

Max hadn't checked her phone in a while. She had been getting so many social media notifications, she had to turn it off. "What email?"

Alyssa stopped outside her office. "Richard's anniversary party next week is officially canceled," she said with a satisfied smile as she opened the door.

That was fast, Max thought. Maybe the network was more prepared for this catastrophe than she assumed.

Inside, a man with a long face and big ears was sitting behind Alyssa's desk. Alyssa and Max took the guest chairs and waited. He was making them cook a little, classic HR, until he finally decided it was time to speak.

"You realize you've put us in a very precarious situation," he said, sitting about a foot taller than them, adding to the intimidation. "Writing about Richard's behavior behind the network's back was inappropriate and, honestly, breaks every NDA you've ever signed here." He crossed his right leg over his left. "A lot of people wanted you two gone, and Sheena, too."

Max glanced at Alyssa. She seemed stoic—sitting straight up, unfazed, unflinching. She'd get a job at another network in a second after all this. Max wouldn't be surprised if she was already getting calls. Alyssa and Sheena had always been the assets that brought in ratings—Alyssa logistically, allowing the show to go on without a hitch, and Sheena as the (gorgeous and well-spoken) face of the broadcast. Women loved them. They were welcomed into kitchens and living rooms around America every morning.

And then it hit Max: she was sitting in that meeting because Max was one of them. *She* brought in the ratings. She could get a job at another network in a second, too.

"But a lot of people didn't want you gone," he continued. "Including me." He put his foot back on the floor and leaned toward them. "I'm sorry you've had to put up with that. Needless to say, this was long overdue. Thank you for some truly powerful reporting."

He stood up and put his hand out. Alyssa shook first. When Max's hand gripped his, he lingered for a moment, putting her hand between both of his. "You're a great reporter," he said. "Don't let anyone tell you otherwise."

WHEN MAX GOT BACK to Hair and Makeup, Cate, Lauren, and Olivia looked camera-ready and like they had taken more than one shot of tequila each.

"This is the closest we'll ever get to a spa day," Cate said, handing Max a shot.

Lauren threw her hands up. "They gave me under-eye patches that were *gold*. Gold!"

There was a knock on the door and before anyone could answer, Charlie popped his head in. Olivia didn't seem to notice, and Max wasn't quite ready to be in a room with the two of them at the same time again, so she hurried toward him and shuffled him outside.

"Yes?" she asked.

"You're on in ten." He shifted from one foot to the other nervously.

"Thanks," she said, expecting him to march off in a huff. When he didn't, she was surprised. He rubbed his face with his hands and swiftly put them in his pockets, like he wasn't exactly sure what to do with them. Against her better instinct, she kind of felt bad for him—being so close to a story this big and not being able to do anything about it. "You didn't tell everyone about us, huh?"

He shrugged, looking tired, more than usual. "It's not my story to tell," he said, probably the first smart and self-aware thing he'd *ever* said. *Was he apologizing?* she asked herself. This seemed like the closest he was going to get, so she decided to take it. He glanced toward the greenroom, then back at Max. "Tell Olivia her ass looks good in those pants," he said as he started to back away.

"I will not do that," Max said, then, knowing she'd regret this, she added, "You should tell her yourself."

When she walked back into the greenroom, while her friends admired their newly poreless skin, Max poured two shots. She held hers up and handed the other to the makeup assistant, who she noticed was wearing a pencil skirt for the first time in years, and they both smiled.

"To the end of Richard Bradley's reign," Max declared. "Over our workplace, our clothing, our dignity...and our asses."

Lauren lifted the shot to her mouth, and when no one was looking, she dumped it into her glass of water. She was so nervous, if she even had a taste of tequila she'd be drunk on national television.

Trying to not let herself check her phone, she silenced it and put it facedown on the floor. She just wanted to revel in the moment, remember it, feel her friends' excitement, appreciate everything they'd done. Lauren looked at Cate, sitting cross-legged on the couch, smiling so hard she was beginning to form new dimples. Then at Max, closing her eyes as she had fake eyelashes applied to her face. Then at Olivia, picking out a song that would immortalize the moment. Someone suggested Beyoncé's "Single Ladies" to fuck with her, and everyone bellied-over laughing.

Lauren pulled her phone out of her pocket and saw some texts pop-up on the small screen.

I'm sorry, Pete's text read. I do believe you. And I'm going to take care of it. With the studio this time. I hope you can forgive me.

Then, a second later, another message: You're a great writer. Good job, Lo Mein.

Lauren blinked hard so the tears welling in her eyes would go away. She'd forgive him, of course. She forgave him even without an apology. Once she gave the experience some time and space, it was clear that Pete was in a difficult position, too. He didn't know how to handle it any more than their entire industry did. But for the first time, surrounded by her friends, Lauren was grateful she spoke up. She was grateful she told her story.

And she was grateful Owen punched James in the fucking face. Even if it was a pathetic writer punch.

OLIVIA'S MOOD CHANGED every few seconds: from nervous before going on camera, to thrilled her hair and makeup were professionally done, to relieved they were going to be able to move on from this—to finally be able to stress about normal, non-change-making things. They were free, and that required a song. And Olivia was very good at picking out songs.

It didn't take thirty seconds until she found the perfect one—"Wannabe" by her childhood loves, The Spice Girls. She put her phone into a glass cup, creating her own speaker, and pressed Play. Everyone's eyes lit up the second they heard the opening "hahaha" and by the chorus they were jumping, arms flailing, messing up their blowouts but no one cared. She certainly didn't at least. She was surrounded by her best friends, wearing fake eyelashes and industry-level shapewear. She was going to get an agent at UTA. She was going to be an actress. She was going to make it. They all were.

They bounced up and down, singing about lovers and friends and all of the random songs—the lyrics were permanently branded into her brain since she was a kid.

They played it twice—the Hair and Makeup woman joining in for the second song—and when Alyssa came in to bring them to the studio, she felt ready. When they were seated around Sheena, facing the bright lights and cameras, she felt confident they had done the right thing. This whole ordeal was the right thing.

Olivia looked to the stage manager, who stood between the two cameras, and pointed three fingers at them, then two, then one.

JUST AS THE RED On Air light started blinking behind Camera A, Sheena tapped the top of Max's hand with hers. "Thank you," she said quickly, just seconds before the camera was on her and the prompter started rolling. The words came out so softly there was no way her mic picked it up. Max would have liked to have recorded evidence of the first time she ever said that to her. And how much Sheena seemed to mean it.

"Welcome back to *The Good Morning Show*," Sheena began. "I'm here with Max Burke, Cate Britt, Lauren Barrero, and Olivia Medina, the women behind *Twentysomething*—"

Max reminded herself to breathe and speak slowly and un-cross her arms and tell the truth. *Just look at Sheena*, she told herself. *Don't worry about anything else. Just have a conversation with Sheena.*

"*Twentysomething* has forced many noteworthy changes in this industry over the last few months, but how does it feel, Max, to be so close to one of them? As an assistant on this very show?"

Max let out a deep breath. *Tell the truth.* "It feels like a massive accomplishment," she started. "Both personally and for the ongoing women's movement. I think this sends a very clear message to others like him, who have yet to see any repercussions for their behavior. Not just us—" Max motioned toward the five women at the desk "—but women as a whole. We aren't going to stop until we bring them all down."

"Did you expect this kind of reaction when you started *Twentysomething?*" Sheena asked. "Did you publish the website with the intention of spearheading a movement?"

Cate smiled at Max, then at Sheena. "Honestly, I think this movement was a long time coming," Cate said. "This behavior isn't new. It's been systematically happening for generations. Entire laws and organizations were built to keep this behavior in the shadows. Women have been fed-up and whispering change for years. They just needed the right outlet…"

Max listened to Cate and, for the first time, looked away from Sheena and toward the cameras. It was just bright lights and prompters until her eyes adjusted and she could see behind the machinery, behind the operators, behind Alyssa and Charlie, standing next to each other.

The studio was full, she realized. Every inch of off-camera space was taken. Rows and rows of women stood next to each other, shoulder to shoulder, watching them. Watching her.

Watching their revolution unfold.

THE FOUR OF THEM laid down on the floor of the creepy, dirty bathroom Max had brought them to, surrounded by makeup wipes and a bottle of the most expensive champagne Cate had ever seen (she looked it up; sixty-seven dollars!) that Alyssa had gifted them once the red On Air light turned off and they went to commercial.

As they were following Max off the stage through the crowd, Cate got a text from Theo. Proud of you was all it said. But that's all it needed to. She was proud of herself, too.

They formed a circle in the center of the floor, bodies splayed out, too tired to even make themselves comfortable. Cate took a sip of the champagne, letting the bubbles tickle her throat, and then passed the bottle to Lauren, who did the same. They hadn't said anything since they went off the air. It was possible no one knew what to say, but it was more probable that everyone was just memorizing the moment—trying to live there for as long as possible before it was over and they had to figure out what was next. What could possibly top *this*?

Cate thought back to her two-year anniversary at Larcey, which felt like ages ago, though it had only been a little over three months. She found herself thinking, again, about that bookshelf in her dad's home office, all the spines emblazoned with red LPs. How that small collection led her to Larcey, to that bookshelf in the EAB she stared at for two years, waiting for the day books she acquired would join that shelf. She never would have guessed the most important stories she'd discover wouldn't have come from Larcey at all, but from *Twentysomething.*

"I have something for you guys," Cate said, sitting up and dragging her purse toward them. She put it on top of the drain cover in the center of their circle: a candle, with the Sobremesa logo on the glass holder.

"Did you steal that?" Lauren asked.

"Borrowed," Cate corrected. She took four pink Post-its out of her pocket.

"You want to do The Shit List now?" Olivia asked.

"Not exactly," she said, handing each of them one specific Post-it. But it wasn't blank this time.

"The Emotional One," Max read off her paper.

"Our anonymous names?" Lauren asked.

Cate pulled a lighter out of her bag. "This I did steal," she said, lighting the candle. "I figured we're out now. Our names are important. We should burn these just like we burned everything else."

They smiled at her, then down at their Post-its, and it was

silent—everyone saying goodbye to these names that had become part of them; names that protected them and freed them at the same time. Names that allowed them to finally stand up, speak out, and be heard.

Lauren went first, rolling The Bitchy One into a ball and putting the whole thing in at once. Then Max, who ripped The Emotional One into pieces and dropped it in one by one. Then Olivia, who set The Aggressive One on fire with one hand while drinking with the other.

Cate looked at her paper, at The Bossy One, at everything that title represented. She thought back to the fateful day she ran around Manhattan with cupcakes only to get scolded through an intercom, moon a bakery employee, and leave the man of her dreams with blue balls on their first date.

Cate slid the corner of the paper into the flame and then pulled it out, watching The Bossy One turn into ashes in her hand.

She was never going to have to do that again. None of them were.

As their papers burned in the candle's flame, they didn't speak, they didn't think. They just watched and smiled and sipped champagne.

And, when the fire sprinklers suddenly activated, drenching them in brown water that smelled like feet, they laughed so hard their stomachs hurt.

★ ★ ★ ★ ★

ACKNOWLEDGMENTS

I could spend an endless amount of time and pages thanking the two biggest champions of this book: my editor, Natalie Hallak, and my agent, Liz Parker. Natalie, thank you for your incredible patience, keen eye, and remarkable vision. You have befriended Cate, Lauren, Olivia, and Max in the same way I have, and I couldn't be more grateful. Liz, thank you for finding me in the slush pile and believing in everything that this book could be. Thank you for pushing me. Working with you has, quite literally, changed my life.

To Brynna Robinson and Dina Robinson: thank you for your very, very, very early reads. To Shivani Doraiswami: thank you for your insightful notes. To Stephanie Viggiano and Maggie Jacobsen: thanks for the introduction. To Claire Fahy and Sheena Samu: thank you for answering all my questions and loaning me your name.

To the Burkes, Rogers, Dovealas, and Robinsons: thanks for the much-needed happy hours on the beach while I was writing. To Brandon and everyone at DTUT on the Upper East Side:

thanks for letting me sit at the bar with coffee for eight hours a day while I was editing. Next round for all of you is on me.

To Ashley Rose Folino, Shannon Smith and Scott Weinstein: I'm so grateful to have been in the trenches with you. When your entire job revolves around telling people where the bathroom is while standing next to a sign that also tells people where the bathroom is, working with you made it bearable.

To Bernadette Poerio: thank you for letting your confidence rub off on me and for never letting me sink into my imposter syndrome. But most important, I need to thank you for hiding onion rings in our room freshman year. Even though we bicker, we'll always have Paris.

To Kristin Spitz and Maggie McCabe: you have listened to me talk about writing a book since we were kids. There's no one I'd rather dance around a tiny room celebrating with.

To Danny, Erin, and William: you are the best people I could have asked to grow up with. I love you. Most of all, to Mom and Dad: I learned to write through the education you gave me, but I loved to write through the years of sitting on your bed typing nonsense into your laptop. Thank you for listening to every long-winded story I've ever wanted to tell, and for believing me when I said I wanted to turn that into a job. All of this is because of you.

SMILE AND
LOOK
PRETTY

AMANDA PELLEGRINO

Reader's Guide

PARK
ROW
BOOKS

1. How would you define Lauren's, Cate's, Max's, and Olivia's relationships with each other? And how do those relationships change as the blog grows in popularity? Which character was your favorite and why?

2. Cate, Lauren, Olivia, and Max are all dealing with bosses who abuse their power in some way. How have our workplace cultures perpetuated this type of behavior? Do you believe their decision to start *Twentysomething* and write about their bosses was justified? Discuss why or why not.

3. The book begins by Cate saying, "The signs were always there," followed by examples of a toxic environment that she'd noticed after two years at Larcey Publishing. Why do you think it took her years to realize these were signs of a harmful workplace? Have you had to deal with a toxic work environment, and if so, what are some other signs that you've experienced?

4. Max experiences terrible behavior at the hands of both her male and female bosses, Richard and Sheena. Why do you think Sheena acts the way that she does even if she herself has been through workplace abuse? What reasons might she have had for not coming forward or standing up for other women in the office sooner?

5. Cate, Lauren, Olivia, and Max all work in creative industries where the boundaries between work and life are often blurred, all for the sake of their "dream job." What negative and positive roles does ambition play in the novel and in the lives of our characters—both in relation to their jobs, their website, and each other? Would you sacrifice your mental health and well-being for your dream job? Is there a point in these women's relationships with their bosses that would have been your breaking point?

6. In the email James writes to Pete after Lauren reports him, he explains his side of the story. What is the problem with he said/she said situations? If you were Pete, who would you believe? What kind of manipulation tactics does James use to get Lauren to do what he wants? How does that manipulation force two very different sides to the story?

7. Matt's, Pete's, Nate's, and Richard's behaviors are all somewhere on the toxicity spectrum. How would you rank them, from best to worst? How much awareness do you think they have of their bad behavior?

8. Throughout the book, Charlie is constantly taking Max's work and claiming it as his own. What part does Max play in this behavior? And how important are Alyssa's recognition and positive affirmation of Max's work to get Max to finally stand up for herself?

9. Discuss the meaning of the title *Smile and Look Pretty*. Have you ever been told a version of that phrase?

10. What will be the thing you remember most from *Smile and Look Pretty*?

At its heart, *Smile and Look Pretty* is about four best friends who come together and risk everything to become whistleblowers at their respective jobs. What was your inspiration for the characters and story?

Smile and Look Pretty *was inspired by my experiences and my friends' experiences and my friends of friends' experiences. Everyone I know has a story like this—about a bad boss or bad coworker. It's such a universal experience for young people in office environments, especially young women, and it felt like a story that hadn't been told yet. A story I'd want to read. I also think that it's in this time in a person's life, when you're working so hard toward your dream job, when you make some fast and fierce friendships. I love Cate, Lauren, Olivia, and Max in the same way I love the friends I met in my first jobs out of college. Being an assistant can be the most stressful and the most fun time of your life, and it all depends on the friends you're in the trenches with.*

What was your toughest challenge writing *Smile and Look Pretty*? Your greatest pleasure?

The toughest challenge writing Smile and Look Pretty *was also the most rewarding: changing it from first person to third person. When my editor, Natalie, proposed the idea when we first talked, I was hesitant, but only because I knew how much work that would mean for me—essentially writing the entire book, and having to learn all four of my characters' voices in a different way, again. But I knew Natalie understood the industry better than I did and wanted what was best for the book, so we went for it. And, of course, she was right! This is exactly how this story was meant to be told.*

I've also loved learning about this industry and about the book-publishing process. Every aspect of it is exciting to me because it's new and truly a lifelong dream come true. From handing in the manuscript to talking cover art to submitting my author photo to being assigned a publicist—each step, no matter how tedious—is thrilling to me.

Can you describe your writing process? Do you write scenes consecutively or jump around? Do you have a schedule or routine? A lucky charm?

I have a lot of writing processes, which vary mostly depending on whether or not I'm working my day job.

When I'm in between TV jobs, I like to write for a few hours in my apartment every morning, then go for a jog, then write for a few more hours in a coffee shop in the afternoon. It's a good way to break up the day so I don't get too stuck. I usually try to get five hundred words in the morning and five hundred words in the afternoon. Or some version of that that brings me to over a thousand words a day. I always write consecutively and like having a loose outline—usually in the form of index cards on a bulletin board in my apartment—but I don't stick to it too closely.

When I'm working on a TV show, the writing turns into small sprints while shooting fourteen-hour days on set. One hundred words in between camera setups, two hundred words at lunch, one hundred and fifty words when I get home at midnight. It's a great way to just get everything down on the page and works surprisingly well for first drafts since there's no time to be too picky. I just need to get it down and worry about making it pretty later.

Do you read other fiction while writing or do you find it distracting? Is there a book or author that inspires you the most?

I always try to read while I'm writing. I notice that my writing gets better—my word choices more particular, my sentences more interesting—when I'm actively reading. It doesn't even need to be a book that's a similar genre or tone to what I'm writing. It can be anything. Reading great fiction is like studying your craft. I'm constantly learning so much from other writers.

I'm a huge fan of Jessica Knoll. In fact, she was writing her second book, The Favorite Sister, *while I was writing* Smile and Look Pretty. *Her honesty about how writing can sometimes be difficult was really inspirational. It's helpful knowing that an author I love also has days of writer's block. It makes the whole thing seem less daunting and more achievable.*

How did you know you wanted to be a writer? Can you describe the journey to publishing your first book?

I wrote my first book when I was ten. It was about a girl in high school who moonlighted as a detective. (I really loved Nancy Drew at the time.) The story is still sitting in a notebook on a bookshelf in my parents' house. I've always wanted to be a writer. It's the only job I ever wanted. I love it so much, I've doubled down: my day job is a TV writer and my night job is a novelist. Smile and Look Pretty is my first published novel, but not my first novel. There have been plenty (including my take on Nancy Drew) that have never, and will never, leave my desktop or the shelves of my parents' house.

I went out to agents with one book prior to this one. It was a mystery and it took me two years to write. It didn't get any bites. No one wanted it. I queried agents with it for about eight months, all while I was brainstorming what my next novel would be. But it was just rejection after rejection.

That's when Smile and Look Pretty came to me. I wrote it in about three months, which, I realize, is ridiculous. When I took it out to find an agent, I was still getting rejections on my mystery book. Liz Parker, my wonderful agent, responded to my query for Smile and Look Pretty the same day and offered me representation three days later. I remember getting her email to "set up a call" and crying in my living room. I had almost a year's worth of rejections in my inbox for my first book, but this novel got me an agent in less than a week. I framed the email.

Liz and I edited the novel together for about a year, really making sure it was in its best possible shape before sending it out to editors. It was a long process, and it's a lot of work to do without knowing if any publishers will even buy it. But it was immensely worth it, because once the novel was finally ready, my editor, Natalie Hallak, bought it in a preempt. And I cried again, this time in my office of the TV show I was working on.

Then Natalie and I edited the novel together for about another year. The biggest hurdle: changing the book from first person to third person. It felt like I was writing the whole thing over again. But it was completely worth it. The Smile and Look Pretty that will be in the world is the best version of this book. I couldn't be prouder that, of all the novels sitting on my desktop or on my parents', shelves, Smile and Look Pretty *is the first one to see the light.*

What do you hope readers will most take away from *Smile and Look Pretty*?

For a really long time, whenever I was in an uncomfortable position or asked by a boss to do something annoying, I'd tell myself, "Just do it for the story; it's worth it for the story." If there's one thing I'd like readers to take away from the book, it's that you don't, in fact, have to "do it for the story." You can say no. You can create boundaries. You can stand up for yourself. And you should. We all should.